Welcome to two siz...
from internationa...

PENNY JORDAN

The path to true love doesn't always run smooth and these two couples are in for a bumpy ride. Especially as they have only met for one reason: a passionate desire for *revenge!* But the worst intentions can lead to the best results – like falling head over heels in love…

SWEET REVENGE

Vengeance with a passion!

Includes:

The Mistress Assignment

and

Lover by Deception

And the passion continues…

Don't miss the *Sweet Seduction* collection
On sale next month, April 2005!

Penny Jordan has been writing for more than twenty years and has an outstanding record: over 150 novels published including the phenomenally successful *A Perfect Family, To Love, Honour & Betray, The Perfect Sinner* and *Power Play* which hit *The Sunday Times* and *Nwe York Times* bestseller lists. Penny Jordan was born in Preston, Lancashire, and now lives in rural Cheshire.

Coming soon:

A brand new novel from Penny Jordan:

Possessed by the Sheikh

On sale next month, April 2005
In Mills & Boon Modern Romance®

And this autumn, look out for
JET SET WIVES

a brand new trilogy from
Penny Jordan!
Only in Mills & Boon Modern Romance®!

PENNY JORDAN

SWEET REVENGE

Vengeance with a passion!

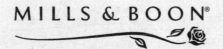

MILLS & BOON®

The collection first published in Great Britain 2005
Harlequin Mills & Boon Limited,
Eton House, 18-24 Paradise Road, Richmond, Surrey, TW9 1SR

SWEET REVENGE © by Harlequin Enterprises II B.V., 2005

The Mistress Assignment and *Lover by Deception*
were first published in Great Britain by Harlequin Mills & Boon Ltd
in separate, single volumes.

The Mistress Assignment © Penny Jordan 1998
Lover by Deception © Penny Jordan 1999

ISBN 0 263 84529 X

062-0305

Printed and bound in Spain
by Litografia Rosés S.A., Barcelona

THE MISTRESS ASSIGNMENT

by

Penny Jordan

CHAPTER ONE

'WELL, here's to Beth; let's hope that this trip to Prague is a success and that it helps her to get over that rat Julian,' Kelly Harris announced, picking up her glass of wine.

'Well, she certainly deserves *some* good luck after all that's happened,' Anna Trewayne, Beth's godmother, sighed, following suit and pausing before drinking her wine to add worriedly, 'I must admit that I feel partly to blame. If I hadn't persuaded the two of you to open your shop here in Rye-on-Averton, Beth would never have met Julian Cox in the first place.'

'There's only *one* person to blame for Beth's unhappiness,' the third member of the trio, Dee Lawson, Beth and Kelly's landlady, announced starkly, 'and that's Julian Cox. The man is a complete and utter...'

She stopped speaking momentarily, lifting her glass to her lips, her eyes darkening painfully as she quickly hid her expression from the others.

'We *all* know what he's done to Beth, how much he's hurt and humiliated her, telling her that he wanted to get engaged, encouraging her to make all those plans for their engagement party and then telling her the night before that he'd met someone else, making out that she'd misunderstood him and imagined that he'd proposed. Personally, I think that instead of bemoaning what's happened what we should be doing is thinking of some way we can punish Julian Cox for what he's done to her and make sure he can never do it again.'

5

'Punish him…?' Kelly enquired doubtfully. She and Beth had been friends from their first days together at university and Kelly had enthusiastically agreed to her friend's suggestion that they set up in business together.

'Rye-on-Averton is the kind of pretty rural English town that artists and tourists dream about, and my godmother was only saying the last time I was there that the town lacked a shop selling good-quality crystal and chinaware.'

'Us…open a shop…?' Kelly had protested a little uncertainly.

'Why not?' Beth had pressed enthusiastically, 'You were saying only last week that you weren't particularly enjoying your job. If we found the right kind of property there's no reason why you shouldn't be able to make your own designs to sell in the shop. With my retail experience I could be responsible for the buying and we could share the work in the shop.'

'It *sounds* wonderful…' Kelly had admitted, adding wryly, '*Too* wonderful… We'd need to find the right kind of premises, and it would only be on the strict understanding that we share the finances of the business equally,' she had warned her friend, knowing that although Beth had no real money of her own her grandparents were rather wealthy and Beth was their adored and adoring only grandchild.

But Beth had swept aside all her objections, and in the end Kelly had been as enthusiastic about their shared project as Beth herself.

Over the last twelve months since the shop had first opened they had gone from strength to strength and then, just over eight months ago, Beth had met Julian Cox.

He had pursued her relentlessly whilst Kelly had stood helplessly to one side and watched as her friend became more and more emotionally dependent on a man whom Kelly had never liked right from the start.

'Don't you think you're letting him rush things a little bit?' she had suggested gently, just after Beth had announced that they were getting engaged. But Beth's face had clouded and they had had their first real quarrel when she had responded uncomfortably, 'Jules said you'd say something like that... He...he thinks that you're...that you're jealous of us, Kelly... I told him that just wasn't possible, of course...'

Jealous of them! With that comment Kelly had been forced to acknowledge that Julian Cox had very skilfully robbed her of the chance to pass on to her friend a piece of information she ought to have given her weeks before. But right now, under the influence of her second glass of the strong Italian wine the three of them had been drinking in the busy Italian wine bar where they had gone for a drink after they had seen Beth off on her buying trip to Prague, the idea of revealing Julian Cox as the unpleasant and untrustworthy character they knew him to be seemed to have taken on the air of something of a crusade, a moral crusade.

'Why should he be allowed to get away with what he's done, to walk away from his guilt in the same manner he walked away from Beth?' Dee had asked the others now.

'Walk away! What he did was even worse than that,' Kelly exploded. 'He practically forced Beth to publicly humiliate herself. I can't believe how many people seem to have fallen for the lies he's been spreading about her, implying that not only did she misunderstand his intentions but that she also actively pursued him, to the point where he was supposedly thinking of taking legal action to stop her. Bunkum! I *know* which one of them was doing the lying and it wasn't Beth. For goodness' sake, I even heard him telling her how much he loved her, how much he couldn't wait for them to be married.'

'That would have been around the time when Beth's grandfather was so seriously ill, I expect?' Dee said grimly.

Kelly looked at her in surprise, but it was Anna who answered her question first, exclaiming, 'Yes, that's right! It was when her grandfather was ill that Julian proposed.'

At thirty-seven Anna was the oldest member of the quartet. As Beth's mother's younger cousin she had just missed out on being a bridesmaid at the wedding through a serious bout of German measles. In compensation Beth's mother had asked her several years later to be one of her new baby's godparents. Only a teenager, Anna had been awed and thrilled to be considered grown-up enough for such a responsibility and it was one she had taken very seriously, her relationship with Beth even more precious to her since she and her husband had not had any children of their own.

'What's the connection between Beth's grandfather's illness and Julian's proposal of marriage?' Kelly asked Dee curiously.

'Can't you guess?' Dee responded. 'Think about it. The girl Julian dropped Beth for is known to have a substantial personal trust fund.'

Kelly made a small *moue* of distaste and looked shocked.

'You mean that Julian proposed to Beth because he thought...'

'That her grandfather would die and Beth would inherit a lot of money,' Dee finished for her. 'Yes. Once he realised that Beth's grandfather was going to recover he must have really panicked, but, of course, he met this other girl, whose inheritance is far more accessible...'

'It sounds like something out of a bad melodrama,' Kelly protested, her forehead puckering as she added, 'Besides, I thought that Julian was wealthy in his own right. He certainly gives that impression.'

'He certainly *likes* to give that impression,' Dee agreed. '*Needs* to, in fact. That's the way he draws the innocent and the naive into his web.'

Kelly's frown deepened as she listened to Dee.

At thirty, Dee was older than Kelly and Beth but younger than Anna, and the two girls had originally met her after their estate agent had suggested that they might want to look at a shop property Dee owned and wanted to let.

They had done so and had both been pleased and impressed with the swift and businesslike way in which Dee had handled the letting of her property to them. She was a woman who, although at first a little reserved and cool, and very choosy about her friends, on later acquaintance revealed a warmth and sense of humour that made her fun to be with.

Anna, who had lived in the town for the last fifteen years following the tragic death of her young husband in a sailing accident off the coast of Cornwall, had known Dee a little before Beth and Kelly had arrived on the scene. After the death of her father Dee had taken over his business affairs as well as his position on several local charities, and so was quite a well-known figure in the town.

Dee's father had been an extremely successful entrepreneur, and others in her family were members of the local farming community, and the more Kelly and Beth had come to know her, the more it had astonished them that such a stunningly attractive woman, and one whose company the male sex quite plainly enjoyed should not have a man in her life.

'Perhaps it's because she's so busy,' Beth had ventured when she and Kelly had discussed it. 'After all, neither of us have partners at the moment...'

This had been in her pre-Julian days, and Kelly had raised her eyebrows a little, reminding Beth wryly, 'We've only been in town a matter of weeks, and besides...I *saw* the look in Dee's eyes the other day when we all went out to dinner and that little girl came trotting up to talk to her—the one from the other table. Do you remember? She made an immediate beeline for Dee and it was as though the pair of them were communicating on some special wavelength that blocked out the rest of us...'

'Mmm... She *does* have a very definite rapport with children,' Beth had agreed, adding helpfully, 'Perhaps she's just not met the right man yet. She strikes me very much as a woman who would only commit herself to a relationship if she was a hundred and fifty per cent sure it was right for her.'

'Mmm...' Kelly had agreed reluctantly. 'Personally I think there must be rather more to it than that.'

'Well, maybe,' Beth had agreed. 'But I wouldn't like to be the one to pry into her past, would you?'

'No,' Kelly had agreed immediately.

Friendly though the four of them had become, and well though they all got on, there was a certain reserve about Dee, a certain sense of distance, an invisible line over which one knew instinctively one would not be encouraged to cross.

'*You* seem to know a lot more about Julian's background than the rest of us,' Kelly told Dee now.

. Dee gave a dismissive shrug.

'He's...he grew up locally, and in my position one...learns things.'

Kelly's frown deepened.

'But surely if you knew his reputation was unsavoury you could have warned Beth?'

'I was away when she originally met him,' Dee reminded her, adding dryly, 'And anyway, I doubt she would have listened...'

'No, you're probably right,' Kelly agreed. 'I never liked him, but Beth was so loyal to him she wouldn't hear a word against him. It's all very well saying that we ought to do something to show him up for the rat he really is, but how can we? He's dumped poor Beth, humiliated her, and he's got clean away with it.

'I'd like to tell this new girlfriend of his just what he's like...' she continued darkly.

'It wouldn't work,' Dee warned her. 'She's as besotted with him as Beth was. No, if we're going to have any chance of getting any kind of restitution for Beth, any kind of public recognition of the way Julian lied about her as well as to her, we're going to have to use his own weakness, his own greed against him.'

'We are? But how...?' Kelly asked her curiously. Beth was such a loving, gentle, kind person, the last thing she had needed was the kind of pain and humiliation Julian had handed out to her, never mind the potential damage it could do to their own just burgeoning business. The whispering campaign Julian had so carefully and cleverly instigated when he had dropped Beth, insinuating that she had been the one pursuing him, obsessed by him, was bound to have its repercussions.

'I do hope that Beth will be all right on her own in Prague,' Anna put in anxiously, joining the conversation.

Fine-boned and very youthful-looking, Anna was, in many ways, so far as Kelly was concerned, the epitome of a slightly old-fashioned type of femininity and womanhood.

Married young and then tragically widowed, in a medieval century she would have been the type of woman who would no doubt have withdrawn to the protective security of a small convent, or perhaps in the Georgian or Victorian age she would have been the doting aunt to her siblings' large broods of noisy children.

As it was, she was apparently content with her single life, her pretty little house and her pets—a large fluffy cat and a smaller but just as fluffy dog. Her home had become for both Kelly and Beth a surrogate home from home since they had moved into the area and, whilst Kelly could never for a minute imagine Anna ever stepping into the role so vigorously occupied by her own energetic and feisty mother, there was still something very comforting and special about the gentle concern Anna showered on them both.

It was a pity she had never remarried, in Kelly's opinion, and she knew that Beth agreed with her.

'She adored Uncle Ralph; they were childhood sweethearts and they had only been married a few months when he died,' Beth had told her.

'Beth will have a wonderful time,' Dee responded robustly now. 'Prague is the most beautiful city.'

'I've heard that it's a very *romantic* city,' Anna agreed a little wistfully, or so it seemed to Kelly. 'I just hope it doesn't make her feel even worse. She's lost so much weight and looks so unhappy.'

'She'll be far too busy going round glass factories to think about anything other than business,' Dee predicted firmly.

'Mmm... It's a godsend that this trip came up when it did,' Kelly agreed. 'And that's all thanks to you, Dee. That was a brilliant idea of yours to suggest to her that we should think about buying some crystal from the Czech Republic. It's been so awful for her.

'You'd think that after what he's done to her and the way he's let her down Julian would at least have the decency to keep a low profile with his new girlfriend, but he actually seems to enjoy flaunting their relationship.'

'Like I said, the man needs teaching a lesson and being given a taste of his own medicine,' Dee reiterated. 'And if you want *my* opinion we're just the ones to do it.'

'Us...? But...' Anna started to protest uneasily.

'Why not?' Dee overruled her. 'After all, you are Beth's godmother, Kelly here is her best friend... If the three of *us* can't be relied upon to do the right thing by her...if she can't depend on *us*...then who can she depend on?' Dee said firmly.

'It sounds a good idea in theory,' Kelly allowed, moved by Dee's obvious emotion. 'But—'

'Have some more wine,' Dee interrupted her. 'There's still over half a bottle left.'

Deftly she refilled both Kelly's glass and Anna's.

'I—' Kelly started to protest but Dee cut her off.

'It's got to be finished and *I* can't have any more; I'm driving.'

It was true. It had been Dee who had taken charge when Beth had virtually collapsed after Julian had callously told her that he no longer wanted her, just as it had been Dee who had come up with the suggestion that Beth travel to Prague on a buying trip that would also hopefully take her mind off Julian and her unhappiness.

And it was Dee who had driven them all to the airport so that they could see Beth off on her journey, and now it seemed that Dee was still taking charge and making plans for them.

'So, now that we've agreed that Julian *has* to be punished and exposed for what he is, what we need to decide is *how* we're going to put our plans into action.'

She paused and then looked at Kelly before saying slowly, 'What I think would be best would be for us to punish him through his greed. You mentioned the other week, Kelly, that almost right from the first time you met him Julian was coming on to you, making overtures to you, trying to encourage you to date him behind Beth's back...'

'Yes. It's true, he was,' Kelly agreed. 'I didn't tell Beth at the time because I didn't want to hurt her and then, when it was too late, I wished I had...' She paused and then added uncertainly, 'Dee, it's all very well to *talk* about us punishing Julian for the way he's hurt her so badly, but realistically what can we do?'

Dee smiled grimly at her before turning to Anna.

'Anna, you've told us how Julian approached you for a loan, claiming that he wanted the money to use as a deposit on a house he was planning to buy for Beth and himself...'

'Yes...' Anna agreed. 'He called round out of the blue one afternoon. He said that all his cash was tied up in various investments, but that Beth had seen this house she was desperate for them to buy and he didn't want to disappoint her. He said he'd only need the money for a few months—'

'Yes, no doubt because he was expecting that by then Beth would have received her share of her grandfather's estate,' Kelly cut in angrily. 'How *could* anyone be so despicable?'

'We aren't talking about anyone,' Dee pointed out acidly. 'We're talking about Julian Cox, and Julian has a long record of very skilfully and deceitfully depriving the innocent and naive of their money—and not just their money,' Dee concluded quietly.

There was a look in her eyes that made Kelly check and study her a little woozily. The wine Kelly had drunk was beginning to make her feel distinctly light-headed, no doubt due to the fact that she hadn't had very much to eat, but she knew she was *not* imagining that unfamiliar combination of vulnerability and haunted pain in Dee's distinctive tortoiseshell-coloured eyes. Even so, there was something she still felt bound to pursue.

'If you knew just what kind of man Julian is, *why* didn't you say something to Beth?' she asked Dee for a second time.

'I told you why—because quite simply, when she first became involved with him, if you remember, I was in Northumberland nursing my aunt. By the time I'd come back and realised what was going on, how deeply she was involved with him, it was too late; she was on the verge of announcing their engagement.'

'Yes, I remember now,' Kelly acknowledged. It was true—Dee *had* been away for several months earlier in the year, looking after an elderly relative who had undergone a serious operation.

'It seems so unfair that Julian should get away with convincing everyone that poor Beth is some kind of compulsive liar as well as breaking her heart,' Anna put in quietly. 'I *know* her and I *know* she would never, could *never* behave in the way he's trying to imply.'

'He's very adept at maintaining a whiter than white

reputation for himself whilst destroying the reputations of those who are unfortunate enough to become innocently involved with him,' Dee informed them bitterly.

Kelly was feeling far too muzzy with wine to take Dee up on what she had said, but she sensed that there was some kind of past history between Julian Cox and Dee, even if she knew that Dee would not welcome any probing into it on her part.

'What we need to do,' Dee was telling them both firmly, 'is to use his own tactics against him and lure him into a position where his true nature can be exposed. It's no secret now to any of *us* that the reason he dropped Beth is because he realised that there wasn't going to be any financial benefit to him in marrying her.'

'Since we do know that, I can't help but agree with Kelly that we ought to do something to warn his new girlfriend and her family just what kind of man he is,' Anna suggested gently.

Dee shook her head. 'We know how blindly in love Beth was, and, although I hate to say this, we could all be done an untold amount of harm if Julian Cox started trying to tar us with the same brush he's used against Beth to such good effect. The *last* thing any of us needs is to be publicly branded as hysterical, over-emotional women, obsessed by some imaginary sense of injustice.'

She was right, Kelly had to acknowledge.

'Besides, if my plan works successfully, and it will, then he'll drop his current victim just as swiftly as he dropped Beth, and for very much the same reason.'

'Your *plan*? *What* plan?' Kelly asked her uneasily.

'This plan. Listen,' Dee commanded. 'We are going to mount a two-pronged attack against Julian where he's most vulnerable.

'I happen to know that one of Julian's clever little

ways of funding his expensive lifestyle is to persuade gullible people to invest in his apparently initially sound financial schemes. By the time they realise that they are anything but sound, it's too late and their money has gone.'

'But surely that's fraud?' Kelly protested. Dee shrugged her shoulders.

— 'Technically, yes, but Julian relies on the fact that his victims feel too embarrassed or are too timid to complain. For that reason he tends to prey on the elderly and the vulnerable, the innocently naive, too trusting and honest themselves to see what he really is until it's too late.'

'The man's a menace,' Kelly complained sharply.

'Yes, he is, and we're going to expose him as he fully deserves to be exposed,' Dee told her. 'You, Kelly, are suddenly going to become an extremely rich young woman. You have a great-uncle, previously unknown and now deceased, who has left you a considerable amount of money. This inheritance isn't something you yourself have made public, of course; in fact you refuse to talk about it—its existence is something you wish to keep a secret—but its existence has subtly filtered through the town's grapevine, at least as far as Julian's ears.

'We already know that he finds you attractive; you've told us both that he made advances to you whilst he was pretending to Beth that he loved her… All you have to do is let him believe that you're prepared to commit yourself, and, more importantly, your future to him. His own ego and greed will do the rest.'

'But I can't pretend that I've inherited money…I can't lie about something like that,' Kelly said. 'What will people think when they know?'

'Only *Julian* will ever know about your supposed inheritance,' Dee assured her. 'Just as only Julian will ever know that you are a wealthy widow and have money to spare for investment,' she told Anna.

Anna looked at her uncertainly.

'He has already tried to borrow money from me, Dee, it's true, as I've just told you both, but I'm certainly not a wealthy woman and...'

'Look, when it comes to convincing Julian that you both have financial assets that we all know simply don't exist, you can leave everything to me. I promise you that Julian is the only person who will be made aware of these imaginary fortunes.'

'But will he believe it? Surely he'll...'

'He'll believe it,' Dee assured Kelly. 'He'll believe it because he'll *want* to believe it. He needs to believe it,' she told them grimly. 'From what I've learned, his own financial position is so perilous at the moment that he'll grasp just about any straw he can to save himself.

'Once he switches his allegiance from his current girlfriend to you, Kelly, and once he tries to draw you, Anna, into one of his financial scams, we'll be able to publicly reveal him for the cheat and liar that he genuinely is...'

'It sounds plausible,' Kelly acknowledged. 'And it would certainly exonerate Beth if we could pull it off.'

'As well as preventing his current girlfriend from suffering a potential broken heart and losing *her* inheritance,' Anna supplied protectively.

'So it's agreed,' Dee slipped in quickly. 'We don't have any option but to go ahead and bring him to book.'

'No, I suppose we don't,' Kelly acknowledged.

She still wasn't totally convinced that she was going to be able to carry off the role Dee had apparently cast for her as a wealthy heiress, but her head felt too muzzy for her to protest properly.

There was one thing she had to say, though.

'How can you be so sure that Julian *will* drop his current girlfriend for me?'

'He wants you, we already know that,' Dee told her forthrightly, 'and besides, you're on your own, unprotected... It's *your* money...yours to do with as you please... His current girlfriend isn't; she's got a brother who stands between Julian and her inheritance. Julian is running out of credit and credibility. He won't be able to resist the bait you're dangling, Kelly. He can't afford to resist it.'

'The bait...' Kelly swallowed shakily. The bait Dee was referring to, as she knew only too well, wasn't just her imagined fortune, it was Kelly herself, and since she personally thought that Julian Cox was the most loathsome, obnoxious, revolting and undesirable man she had ever met...

'But if Kelly's going to pose as a wealthy heiress, then surely Julian won't be interested in my money as well,' Anna protested.

'Don't you believe it,' Dee corrected her. 'Julian is greedy and avaricious; he won't pass up any opportunity to get his hands on some extra cash.'

'But I've already refused to help him once,' Anna pointed out.

'You're a woman; you can change your mind,' Dee told her mock-sweetly. 'Look, you can both leave all the details of putting our plans into action to me. All I want from you is your agreement, your *commitment*, to help Beth, and I *know* I can rely on both of you completely for that... Can't I?'

Kelly and Anna exchanged uncertain looks.

'Beth is very dear to us,' Dee reminded them, looking first at Kelly and then at Anna.

'Yes. Of course…of course you can,' Anna agreed immediately.

'Yes. Of course you can,' Kelly agreed a little less confidently. Something warned her that, foolproof though Dee's plan sounded, things might not fall into place just as easily as she assumed, but her brain felt too clouded by the wine she had drunk for her to be able to formulate any determined assault on Dee's confident arguments and besides, Dee was right about one thing— she *did* feel that Julian deserved to be exposed for what he was…

For the next few minutes they continued their discussion, and as they did so Kelly's doubts as to the feasibility of Dee's plan resurfaced.

'I've got an early start in the morning, so if you don't mind we really ought to make a move,' Dee announced finally, checking her watch.

As she stood up Kelly realised dizzily just how strong the red wine she had been drinking actually was. To her relief Anna seemed equally affected by it. Of the three of them, Dee was the only one who seemed to have a properly clear head, which was just as well since she was the one doing the driving.

As she shepherded her two slightly inebriated charges out into the car park and to her car, Dee acknowledged ruefully that she would thoroughly deserve it if both of them blamed her in the morning for their thick heads— she, after all, had been the one who had kept on refilling their glasses—but she comforted herself with the knowledge that what she was doing was right; she owed it to— Her eyes closed. She must not think of the past, only the future—a future in which Julian Cox would meet the fate he so richly deserved!

She hadn't been able to believe it when she had discovered that Julian was up to his old tricks, but this time he wasn't going to get away with it. This time…this time he was going to discover to his cost just how strong and powerful a woman's desire for justice could be.

With an almost maternal concern she helped her two friends and fellow conspirators into her car. She intended to take very good care of them from now on, very good care… As they settled a little woozily into the rear seat Dee reflected that it was just as well that they couldn't read her mind and that they didn't know the truth. There had been one or two decidedly awkward moments back in the restaurant when Kelly had tried to question her, to dig a little deeper into the past, but fortunately she had managed to sidetrack her.

'Poor Beth…' Anna hiccuped mournfully as Dee started the car engine.

'Poor Beth,' Kelly agreed, blinking as she tried to clear her increasingly blurry vision.

'No, not *poor* Beth,' Dee corrected them sternly. '*Lucky* Beth. Just think how much more unhappy he could have made her if he'd waited until after they were engaged, or, even worse, until after they were married before betraying her,' Dee pointed out to them.

'It's going to be easier for her this way. If she had married him…'

Instinctively she glanced down at her own wedding ring finger. It was slightly thinner than its fellows as if once…? Then determinedly she looked away.

In the rear of the car her two fellow conspirators were succumbing to the effects of the extremely potent red wine she had deliberately fed them, their eyes closing.

She knew she ought to feel guilty about what she was doing—they were both so innocent and unaware, so unsuspicious…

CHAPTER TWO

KELLY woke up with an aching head and a dry mouth. Groaning, she rolled over and looked at the alarm clock on the bedside table.

Ten o'clock. She must have slept right through the alarm. Thank heavens it was Sunday and the shop didn't open until later than usual.

Swinging her legs out of bed, she winced as the ache in her head became a thunderous nausea-induced pounding.

It was all Dee's fault, insisting that they finish that bottle of red wine.

Dee…

Kelly froze in mid-step and then collapsed back onto the bed, groaning. What on earth had she done? She would have to telephone Dee straight away and tell her that she had changed her mind, that there was totally, absolutely, completely and utterly no way she could go through with the ludicrous plan she had agreed to last night.

Tottering towards the phone, still clasping her head, Kelly saw the answering machine light was flashing. Obediently she pressed the reply button.

'Kelly,' she heard. 'This is Dee. I'm just calling to confirm the plans we made last night. I've discovered that Julian and his new girlfriend will be attending a charity bash at Ulston House this evening. I've managed to get you a ticket and an escort—just as a bit of extra insurance. Julian is going to find you even more of an irresistible challenge if he thinks you're with someone else. Remember, all you have to do is egg him on whilst playing just that little bit hard to get. I know how close you and Beth are and I know that you wouldn't dream of reneging on our plan or letting her down.

'Harry, your escort, will call for you at seven-thirty. He's my cousin, by the way, and completely to be trusted, although, of course, he knows nothing of our special plan. He thinks you just need a date for the evening because you're attending the do for business reasons. That could be the truth, incidentally—an awful lot of influential local people will be attending the dinner and the ball afterwards. Bye for now...'

What on earth did Dee think she was doing? Kelly wondered as she stared at the phone like someone in shock. And how on earth had she managed to get two tickets for that ball at such short notice? Kelly knew all about it. Those tickets were like gold dust. Not that she intended for one minute to go. Dee was taking far too much for granted and Kelly intended to tell her so. Where on earth had they put her telephone number?

Kelly winced as pain throbbed through her head. Last night's red wine had an awful lot to answer for—oh, an awful, awful lot!

Dee's number had to be somewhere and she certainly had to speak with her. Ah, there it was; she had missed it the first time in the address book. Breathing out noisily in relief, Kelly punched in Dee's telephone number.

The tell-tale delay before the call was answered warned her what was going to happen even before she heard the familiar sound of Dee's voice on the answering machine message.

'I'm sorry, I shan't be able to take your call today. Please leave your number and I'll call you back tomorrow,' Dee was announcing. Thoroughly exasperated, Kelly hung up.

Perhaps she could drive over to Dee's and persuade her that they ought to change their minds and their plans. What had seemed a reasonable plan last night, this morning seemed more like a totally implausible, not to say highly dangerous thing to do. For one thing, it went totally against all her own principles and, for another, how on earth was she supposed to give Julian Cox the impression that she found him attractive and desirable enough to want to break up his relationship with someone else when the truth was that she found him loathsome, reptilian and repulsive?

Yes, physically he was an attractive enough looking man, if you went for his boyish brand of fair-haired good looks, but looks alone had never been enough to attract Kelly, and there had been something about him, something about his attitude not just towards Beth but towards *her* as well, which had set alarm bells ringing in Kelly's head virtually from the first moment she had seen him. She had made a point of keeping out of the way whenever he was around and when they had had to meet she had kept a very cool and formal distance from him.

So how on earth was she supposed to convince him now that she suddenly found him the epitome of male sexiness?

She couldn't. She wasn't going to try. She had been a fool even to *think* of agreeing to Dee's outrageous plan, but she *had* agreed and something warned her that it wasn't going to be easy to convince Dee that she wanted to change her mind.

And if *she* backed out and Anna didn't, how was it going to look? She was, after all, Beth's best friend and, indeed, perhaps the best way of convincing Dee that her plan wouldn't work would be for her, Kelly, to show her how impossible it was going to be, by going to tonight's ball. She would be safe enough. There was no way that Julian Cox was going to repeat his attempt to come on to her, not after the way she had put him down the first time. And once she had failed to re-attract his notice Dee would surely accept that she had done her best and allow the subject to drop.

Yes, far better to do things that way than to risk offending Dee, who was, after all, only acting out of kindness and affection for Beth.

Where on earth were those wretched headache tablets? She had pulled everything out of their small medicine cabinet without finding them, and she knew she had bought some. And then she remembered she had given them to Beth, after the terrible crying jags she had had after her break-up with Julian had left her with a splitting headache. Glumly Kelly made her way to their small kitchen and filled the kettle.

The flat above the shop was on two floors; on the upper storey were hers and Beth's bedrooms and their shared bathroom, and on the lower floor was their comfortably sized living room, a small dining room and an equally small kitchen.

Outside at the rear of the property was a pretty little garden, and at the bottom of it was the workshop which Kelly had made her own territory. That was where she worked on her new designs and painted the china she had accepted as private commissions. Painting pretty porcelain pieces and enamel boxes was her speciality.

Before joining forces with Beth, Kelly had worked as a freelance from her parents' home in Scotland, supplying her pretty hand-decorated enamel boxes to an exclusive London store.

At three o'clock, with the shop still busy with both browsers and buyers, Kelly acknowledged that she was not going to be able to make time to snatch so much as a quick sandwich lunch, never mind drive over to Dee's.

Ironically this Sunday had been one of their busiest since they had opened the shop, and she had not only sold several of her more expensive pieces, she had also taken orders for seven special commissions from a Japanese visitor who had particularly liked her enamel-ware boxes.

At four o'clock, when she was gently showing the last browser out of the shop so that she could lock up, she was beginning to panic, not just about the fact that it was becoming increasingly obvious that she was going to have to go through with Dee's plans for the evening but, femalely, because she knew that she simply did not have in her wardrobe a dress suitable for such an occasion. She and Beth had ploughed every spare bit of cash they had into their business—both of them had been helped with additional loans from their bank, their parents and Beth's grandfather. Anna, too, had insisted on making them a cash gift, to, as she'd put it, 'cover any extras'. They were beginning to show a small profit, but they certainly weren't making anything like enough to warrant the purchase of expensive evening dresses.

Ordinarily, knowing she was attending such an occasion, Kelly would have done as she had done for her graduation ball and trawled the antiques shops and markets to find something she could adapt, but on this occasion there simply wasn't time, and the smartest thing she had in her wardrobe right now was the elegant dress and coat she had originally bought for her brother's wedding and which, though smart, was hardly the kind of outfit she could wear to a charity ball.

After she'd checked that she had securely locked the shop and that the alarm was switched on she made her way up to the flat. She was still finding it hard to understand what on earth had possessed her to agree to Dee's outrageous scheme last night. She was normally so careful and cautious, so in control of her life. Beth was the gentle, easily manipulated one of the two of them; *she* was far more stubborn and self-assured. Too stubborn, her brother often affectionately told her.

Certainly she knew her own mind; she was, after all, a woman of twenty-four, adult, mature, educated and motivated, a woman who, whilst she would ultimately want to have a loving partner and children, was certainly in no rush to commit herself to a relationship. The man with whom she eventually settled down would have to accept and understand that she would expect to be treated as an equal partner in their relationship, that she would expect in him the same qualities she looked for in a best friend: loyalty, honesty, a good sense of fun, someone who would share her interests and her enthusiasms, someone who would enhance her life and not, as she had seen so often happen in so many other relationships, make the kind of demands on her that would prevent her from living her life as she really wanted to live it.

'But what happens if you fall in love with someone who isn't like that?' Beth had once questioned when they had been discussing men and relationships.

'I won't,' Kelly had responded promptly.

Poor Beth. What was *she* doing right now? How was *she* feeling...? Kelly had never seen her looking so wretched or unhappy... Beth had really believed that Julian Cox loved her.

Since their break-up Kelly had heard rumours that

Beth wasn't the first woman he had treated badly. No, Beth was better off without him, Kelly decided as she went into their kitchen and filled the kettle. She gave a small shudder as she remembered the night she had returned early from a weekend visit to her parents to discover Beth almost unconscious on her bed. Taking too many sleeping tablets had been an accident, an oversight, Beth had assured her, and had pleaded with her not to tell anyone else what she had done as Kelly sat beside her hospital bed. Unwillingly, Kelly had agreed. Luckily she had found Beth in time...luckily...

Remembering that incident, Kelly slowly sipped her hot coffee. Was Dee really asking so much of her? No. She didn't relish the role she was being called upon to play—what modern woman would?—but it was only a means to an entirely justifiable and worthwhile end.

But that still didn't solve the problem of what she was going to wear. She and Beth were approximately the same size although Beth was fair-skinned and blonde, with soft, pretty grey eyes, whereas she was brunette, her skin tone much warmer, her eyes a dark purplish brown, damson—the colour of lilac wine, one besotted admirer had once called them.

The ball had been the subject of a great deal of excitement and speculation in town. It was to be the highlight of the town's social year. The de Varsey family, who owned the elegant Georgian mansion where the event was to be held, had been local landowners for the last three hundred years and, despite their cost, tickets had been snapped up and the event sold out within a week of them going on sale, which made it even more extraordinary that Dee should have been able to produce a pair at such short notice.

Kelly could remember how thrilled and excited Beth

had been when Julian had told her that he had bought tickets for the event.

'I'll have to hire something really special. This isn't just a social event for Julian, it's a very important business opportunity as well,' she had told Kelly breathlessly.

Kelly had never properly discovered just exactly what line of business it was that Julian was in. He had talked very grandly about his own financial acumen and the hugely profitable deals he had pulled off, and he certainly had spent a lot of time talking into the mobile phone he took everywhere with him. He drove a very large and very fast BMW, but lived in a surprisingly small service flat in a new and not particularly attractive apartment block on the outskirts of town.

Kelly hadn't been at all pleased when she had learned that he had suggested to Beth that she allow him to have some of his business mail addressed to their flat, but she had refrained from making too much fuss, not wanting to upset her friend.

Beth had been thrilled at the prospect of attending such a prestigious social event with him—as his fiancée; now another woman would be going there with him in Beth's place.

'Remember she could be just as much a victim of his ruthlessness as Beth was,' Dee had reminded her and Anna last night when Kelly had commented that she didn't know how any woman could date a man who she knew was supposedly committed to someone else.

If that was the case, Julian Cox deserved to be revealed as the unpleasant and untrustworthy creep that he was, for her sake as much as Beth's, Kelly acknowledged, frowning as she heard her doorbell ring.

She wasn't expecting any visitors. Although she and

Beth had made several new acquaintances since moving to the town, as yet they hadn't progressed to the stage of many close friendships. Getting up, she went downstairs to open the door that faced onto the main street.

A man was standing outside, a large box at his feet, a delivery van parked on the roadside behind him.

'Kelly Harris?' he asked her, producing a form for her to sign. 'Just sign here, please...'

'What is it?' Kelly asked him uncertainly, automatically signing the form, but he was already picking up the box and handing it over to her.

Fortunately, despite its awkward shape, the box was very light. Mystified, Kelly carried it up to the flat and then, placing it on the sitting-room floor, sat down beside it to open it.

The outer layer of strong brown paper, once removed, revealed an elegant, glossy white box. There was a letter attached to it. Opening it, Kelly quickly read it.

Dear Kelly, you'll need this to wear this evening. Good hunting! Dee.

Intrigued, Kelly opened the box and then folded back the tissue paper inside it to reveal a dress that made her catch her breath in delight.

Two layers of material, one in conker-brown, the other a toning deep, dark damson, in the sheerest silk chiffon, floated through her fingers. Picking up the dress, she hurried into the bedroom and held it against herself, studying her reflection in the full-length mirror.

In both colour and design it might have been made with her in mind, the toning shades of chiffon so perfect with her colouring that they immediately drew attention to her eyes and made them look even more dramatically pansy-dark than usual. And as for the style—the current vogue for Jane Austen-type high-waisted, floating, revealing evening dresses was one that could, in the wrong hands, look insipid and totally unflattering to anyone over the age of seventeen, but Kelly knew instinctively that this dress was far from insipid, and that its deceptively sensuous cut could never be worn by a woman who was anything less than totally at ease with herself and her sexuality. In other words, Dee couldn't have chosen a dress which would suit her more, and Kelly had no need to look at the immediately recognisable designer label attached to it to know that it must have been horrendously expensive.

Wonderingly she touched the fine chiffon. Although the dress was fully lined, the flesh colour of the lining meant that in a dimly lit room it could easily look as though she was wearing a dress that was virtually transparent.

Dee had even managed to get the size exactly right, Kelly acknowledged ruefully. Placing the dress reverently on her bed, she went back to the sitting room.

Inside the box beneath another layer of tissue paper lay a pretty matching chiffon stole and a pair of high-heeled satin sandals with a matching satin evening bag.

Dee had thought of everything, she admitted as she sat back on her heels.

Fortunately she already had some flesh-coloured underwear she could wear underneath the dress—a birthday present from her sister-in-law—and the pearls which had originally been her grandmother's and which her parents had given her on her twenty-first birthday would be perfect.

It was a dream of a dress, she acknowledged ten minutes later as she carefully hung it on a padded hanger. A dream of a dress for what could well turn out to be a nightmare of an evening.

There was no way that Julian Cox wasn't going to notice her wearing it. Although it was far too elegant and well designed ever to be described as sexy, Kelly knew even before she put it on that those soft layers of chiffon would have instant male appeal and be about as irresistible as home-made apple pie—although to a very different male appetite.

She glanced at her watch. If Dee's cousin was going to pick her up at seven-thirty she ought to think about starting to get ready. Her hair would need washing and styling if she was going to do full justice to that dress. Fortunately its length meant that it was very adaptable and easy to put up. Equally fortunately it possessed enough curl to mean that she could attempt a very similar if somewhat simpler style to that adopted by Jane Austen's heroines.

On the other side of town, someone else was also getting ready for the ball. Like Kelly, Brough Frobisher was attending it under protest. His sister had persuaded him to go, reluctantly wringing his agreement from him.

'Julian especially wants you to be there,' she had pleaded with him anxiously when he had started to refuse, adding slightly breathlessly, 'I think…that is, he's said…there's something he wants to ask you…'

Brough's heart had sunk as he'd listened to her. Initially when she had begged him to go with them to the ball he had assumed it was because her new boyfriend was looking for a backer for the new business venture he had already insisted on discussing with Brough; that had been bad enough, but now that Eve was dropping hints about Julian Cox proposing to her Brough was beginning to feel seriously alarmed.

At twenty-one Eve certainly didn't need either his approval or his authorization to get married, and at thirty-four he was mature enough to recognise that any man who married the sister whom he had been so close to since the death of their parents nearly fifteen years ago was bound, in the initial stage of their relationship, to arouse in him a certain amount of suspicion and resentment. Since their parents' death he had virtually been a surrogate father to Eve, and fathers were notoriously bad at giving up their claims to their little girls' affection in favour of another man; but, given all of that, there was still something about Julian Cox that Brough just didn't like.

The man was too sure of himself, too adroit… too…too smooth and slippery.

Eve had, after all, only known the man a matter of weeks, having initially met him quite soon after they had moved into the town.

Brough had decided that he had had enough of city life, and had sold out of the pensions management partnership he had founded, downsizing both his business and his equally hectic city social life by setting up a much smaller version of the partnership here in Rye-on-Averton.

Being a workaholic, city life—these were both fine at a certain stage in one's life. But lately Brough had begun to reflect almost enviously on the differences between his lifestyle and that enjoyed by those of his peers who had married in their late twenties and who now had wives and families.

'It's a woman who's supposed to feel her biological clock ticking away, not a man,' Eve had teased him, adding more seriously, 'I suppose it's because you virtually brought me up with Nan's help that you miss having someone to take care of.'

Perhaps she was right. Brough couldn't say; all he could say was that the prospect of living in a pretty market town which had its roots firmly secured in history had suddenly been an extremely comforting and alluring one.

As for wanting a wife and family, well, over the years he had certainly had more than his fair share of opportunities to acquire those. He was a formidably attractive man, taller than average, with a physique to match—he had played rugby for his school throughout his time at university and it showed. His close-cropped, thick, dark hair was just beginning to show a sexy hint of grey at his temples, and his almost stern expression was enlivened by the dimple indented into his chin and the laughter that illuminated the direct gaze of his dark blue eyes.

'It's not fair,' Eve had once protested. 'You got *all* our inherited share of charisma... Look at the way women are always running after you.'

'That isn't charisma,' Brough had corrected her dryly. 'That's money...'

In addition to the money both Brough and Eve had inherited from their parents, Brough's own business acumen and foresight now meant that if he had chosen to do so he could quite easily have retired and lived extremely well off his existing financial assets.

Perhaps it was his fault that Eve was as naive and unworldly as she was, he reflected a little grimly. As her brother, stand-in father and protector, he had perhaps shielded her too much from life's realities. Every instinct he possessed told him that Julian Cox simply wasn't to be trusted, but Eve wouldn't hear a word against the man.

'You don't know him like I do,' she had declared passionately when Brough had tried gently to enlighten her. 'Julian is so kind, even when people don't deserve it. When I first met him he was being stalked by this awful woman. It had gone on for months. She kept telling everyone that she was going out with him, calling round at his flat, ringing him up, following him everywhere. She even tried to arrange a fake engagement party, claiming that he'd asked her to marry him...

'But despite all the problems she'd caused him Julian told me that he just couldn't bring himself to report her to the police and that he'd tried to talk to her himself...to reason with her... He'd even taken her out to dinner a couple of times because he felt so sorry for her. But he said that he simply couldn't get through to her or make her understand that he just wasn't interested in her. In the end he said the only way to get her to accept the truth was for her to see him with me. Luckily that seems to have worked.'

When he'd heard the passionate intensity in his sister's voice Brough had known that it wouldn't be a good idea to give her his own opinion of Julian Cox. Certainly the man seemed to be very attractive to the female sex, if the number of women's names he peppered his conversation with were anything to go by.

No, he wasn't looking forward to this evening one little bit, Brough acknowledged grimly—and he owed Nan a visit as well.

Nan, their maternal grandmother, was coming up for eighty but was still fit and active and very much a part of the small Cotswold community where she lived, and thinking of her reminded Brough of something he had to do.

His grandmother had in her glass-fronted corner cabinet a delicate hand painted porcelain teapot, together with all that was left of the original service which went with it. It had been a wedding present passed on to her and Gramps by her own grandparents, and Brough knew that it was one of her long-held wishes that somehow the teaset might be completed. Brough had tried his best over the years, but it was not one of the famous or well-known makes and it had proved impossible to track down any of the missing pieces. The only avenue left to him, according to the famous china manufacturers Hartwell, whom he had visited in Staffordshire, was for him to buy new pieces of a similar style and have them hand-painted to match the antique set.

'The original manufacturers we amalgamated with produce a small range of antique china in the same style, but unfortunately we do not produce either that colour nor the intricate detail of the landscapes painted into the borders,' the sympathetic Hartwell director had told him. 'And whilst we could supply you with the correct shape of china I'm afraid that you would have to find someone else to paint it for you. Our people here have the skill but not, I'm afraid, the time, and I have to tell you that your grandmother's set would be extremely time consuming to reproduce. From what you've shown me I suspect that each of the tea plates probably carried a different allegorical figure from Greek mythology in its borders, so your painter would have to be extremely innovative as well as extremely skilled. Your best bet might be someone who already works on commission— paints and enamels and that kind of thing.'

And he had suggested to Brough that he get in touch

with a particularly gifted student they had had working with them during her university days. No one had been more surprised than Brough when he had tracked down the young woman in question only to find she lived and worked in Rye-on-Averton.

The telephone number and the young woman's name were written down on a piece of paper on his desk. First thing in the morning he intended to get in touch with her. Time was running out; his grandmother's eightieth birthday was not very far away and he desperately wanted to be able to present her with the missing items from the teaset as a surprise gift.

Although his grandmother hadn't been able to take on Eve full time after their parents' death—her husband had been very ill with Parkinson's disease at the time—she had nevertheless always been there for them, always ready to offer a wise heart and all her love whenever Brough had needed someone to turn to for advice. She had a shrewd business brain too, and she had been the one to encourage Brough to set up his first business, backing him not just emotionally but financially as well.

She still took a strong interest in current affairs, and Brough suspected she would be as dismayed by Eve's choice of suitor as he was himself.

And tonight Eve was expecting him to put aside his real feelings and to pretend that he was enjoying Julian Cox's company, and no doubt, for her sake, he would do exactly that.

Eve might be a quiet, shy young woman, but she had a very strong, stubborn streak and an equally strong sense of loyalty, especially to someone who she considered was being treated badly or unfairly. The last thing that Brough wanted to do was to arouse that stubborn female protectiveness on Julian Cox's behalf when what he was hoping was that sooner or later Eve's own intelligence would show her just what kind of man he really was.

He looked at his watch. Eve was already upstairs getting ready. First thing tomorrow he would ring this Miss Harris and make an appointment with her to discuss his grandmother's china. For now, reluctantly he acknowledged that if they weren't going to be late it was time for him to get ready.

Seven miles away from town, in the kitchen of an old house overlooking the valley below and the patchwork of fields that surrounded it, Dee Lawson turned to her cousin Harry and demanded sternly, 'You know exactly what you have to do, don't you, Harry?'

Sighing faintly, he nodded and repeated, 'To drive into town and pick Kelly up at seven-thirty and then escort her to the charity ball. If Julian Cox makes any kind of play for her I'm to act jealous but hold off from doing anything to deter him.'

'Not if, but *when*,' Dee corrected him firmly, and then added, 'And don't forget, no matter what happens or how hard Julian pushes, you must make sure you escort Kelly safely back to the flat.'

'You really ought to do something about those maternal instincts of yours,' Harry told her, and then stopped abruptly, flushing self-consciously as he apologised awkwardly, 'Sorry, Dee, I forgot; I didn't mean...'

'It's all right,' she responded coolly, her face obscured by her long honey-blonde hair.

Seven years his senior, Dee had always been someone Harry was just a little bit in awe of.

Dee's father and his had been brothers, and Dee had been a regular visitor to the family farm when Harry had been growing up. It had surprised him a little that she had chosen to continue her career in such a small, sleepy place as Rye-on-Averton after her father's death. But then Dee had never been predictable or particularly easy to understand. She was a woman who kept her own counsel and was strong-willed and highly intelligent, with the kind of business brain and aptitude for making money that Harry often wished he shared.

There had only been one occasion that Harry could recall when Dee had found herself in a situation over which she did not have full control, a situation where her emotions had overruled her brain, but any kind of reference—no matter how slight—to that particular subject was completely taboo, and Harry would certainly not have dared to refer to it. As well as being in awe of his older cousin, it had to be said that there were times when he was almost, if not afraid of her, then certainly extremely unwilling to arouse her ire.

'Kelly will be expecting you. You'll like her,' Dee informed him, adding almost inconsequentially, 'She'd fit in very well here, and your mother...'

'My mother wants me to marry and produce a clutch of grandchildren—yes, I know,' Harry agreed wryly, before daring to point out, 'You're older than me, Dee, and you still haven't married. Perhaps we're a family who don't...'

'It's hardly the same thing,' Dee reproved him. 'You have the farm to think of. It's been passed down in the family for over four hundred years. Of course you'll marry.'

Of course he would, but when he was ready and, please God, to someone he chose for himself. Although he tried desperately to hide it, considering that such idealism was not proper for a modern farmer, Harry was a romantic, a man who wanted desperately to fall deeply and completely in love. So far, though, he had not met anyone who stirred such deep and intense emotions within him.

CHAPTER THREE

VERY gently Kelly fingered the soft silk of her gown. Once on it suited her even more perfectly than she had expected, the colour of the chiffon doing impossibly glamorous things for her colouring.

As she looked up she saw that Dee's cousin Harry was watching her rather anxiously. She smiled reassuringly at him as they waited in the receiving line to be greeted by their host and hostess. She had known from the moment he arrived to pick her up that she was going to like Harry. He was that kind of man—solid, dependable, reassuring, as comfortable as a familiar solid armchair, with the kind of down-to-earth, healthy good looks that typified a certain type of very English male. Just having him standing there beside her made her feel not merely remarkably better about the scheme which Dee had dreamt up but somehow extraordinarily feminine and protected. It was rather a novel sensation for Kelly, who had never been the type of woman to feel that she needed a man to lean on in any shape or form.

'That colour really suits you,' Harry told her earnestly as he arched his neck a little uncomfortably, as though he longed to be free of the restriction of his formal dinner suit.

'Dee chose it,' Kelly informed him, adding truthfully, 'I feel rather like Cinderella being equipped for the ball by her fairy godmother... Although...' She paused and then stopped. There was no point in discussing with Harry her doubts about what she was doing.

They had reached the line-up of dignitaries now. Kelly smiled mischievously as she caught the discreetly admiring second look the Lord Lieutenant of the county gave her before he shook her hand.

It's all right, it's not me, it's the dress, she wanted to reassure his rather austere-looking wife, but then, remembering her new role as a *femme fatale*, instead she gave him a demure little smile plus a wickedly sultry look from beneath lowered lashes. It worked... His Lordship might be close on sixty, but there was no doubt that he was still a very virile man—at least if the look he was giving her was anything to go by.

Perhaps the evening wasn't going to be so much of a challenge to her thespian talents as she had originally believed, Kelly mused as they passed down the line and then turned to accept a glass of champagne from one of the hovering waiters.

As Kelly already knew, the tickets for the ball had been unbelievably expensive, with only a relatively small number available, but, as she glanced appreciatively at her surroundings, she could well understand why.

Instead of more conventionally attaching a large marquee to the house to accommodate the event, guests were allowed to wander at will through the elegant antique-furnished reception rooms. Her own Regency-inspired dress couldn't have been more felicitously in keeping with the decor, Kelly recognised, her attention caught by a pretty inlaid Chinese lacquered cabinet in one corner of the room, its shelves filled with what she suspected were Sèvres figurines.

Touching Harry's arm, she pointed it out to him.

'I'd like to go over and have a closer look,' she told him. Nodding, Harry gallantly forged ahead to make a pathway through the throng of people now filling the hallway.

Kelly had almost reached her destination when abruptly she stopped dead. There, not a dozen feet away from her, stood Julian Cox. He hadn't seen her as yet. He was busy talking with a pretty fair-haired young woman standing with him. In looks she was very similar to Beth, Kelly recognised, and she looked somehow as though she too possessed the same gentleness of nature that so characterised her best friend.

She doubted very much that that same description could be applied to the man standing on the opposite side of her. Tall, with incredibly powerful shoulders and frowning heavily, he looked extremely formidable and extremely masculine, Kelly recognised as her heart gave a sudden unsteady lurch against her ribs and her breathing quickened idiotically.

As though—impossibly, surely—he was somehow aware of her attention, he turned his head, seemingly focusing fiercely on her.

Kelly's heart gave another and even sharper lurch. He had the most intensely dark blue eyes, and such a penetrating gaze that she felt almost as though he could see right into her soul.

Now she *was* being ridiculous, she told herself stoutly, firmly assuring herself that there was no way that either he or anyone else could have guessed what was going through her mind as she looked at him. And anyway, she reminded herself as she determinedly looked away from him, she was not here to start fantasising about the admittedly very interesting sensual allure of an unknown man; she was here for a very specific purpose, and that did *not* include allowing herself to be side-tracked by anyone or anything—not even her own still very disturbed heartbeat.

Even so, she managed to sneak a second brief glance at him, and she wished she had not done so as she saw the tender and protective way in which he was bending towards the soft-featured blonde girl who was standing close to Julian. Was she, as Kelly had first assumed, the new woman in Julian's life, or was the other man her partner? Had those magnetic blue eyes that had focused on her so directly and so immediately been giving a stern warning that he was *not* available to any other woman, rather than conveying a virile, masculine awareness of her female curiosity?

Well, no doubt before the evening was over she was going to find out, she reminded herself. Julian had not seen her yet, but... She took a deep breath and started to move discreetly into his line of vision.

'Are you okay?' she heard Harry asking her in concern. 'You look a bit flushed. It's pretty crowded in here and hot...'

Rather guiltily Kelly gave him a reassuring smile. Any heat flushing her face had rather more to do with her emotional and physical reaction to the sexily masculine good looks of the man standing with Julian Cox than with the heat of the room.

Irritatingly, Julian had now turned away to talk to someone so that she was out of his line of vision. Boldly she deliberately changed direction, plunging through the crowd in order to bring herself back into it and, in the process, losing Harry, who became separated from her by the busy throng.

Julian might not be aware of her presence, she recognised after a discreet glance in the trio's direction, but *he*, whoever *he* was, most certainly was. Slightly breathlessly she instinctively curled her toes, and a delicious thrill of feminine reaction ran through her as she realised just how intently she was being studied. Sternly she reminded herself of just why she was here and the role she had to play. The temptation to abandon it and to revert to her normal self beckoned treacherously. She had never been a flirt, never been the kind of woman to go all out deliberately to attract a man's attention—she had never needed to and she had certainly never wanted to!

But, almost as though it was fate, just as she was wavering, a direct pathway opened up between her and Julian. Sternly she made herself take it.

'Julian... How lovely to see you...'

Had she got the note of flirtatious invitation in her voice pitched correctly? Anxiously she held her breath as Julian turned his head to look at her, wariness giving way to a look of lustful male appreciation as she continued to smile at him.

'Kelly! What a surprise...'

'A pleasant one, I hope.' Kelly pouted, deliberately stepping closer to him, angling her body so that she was placing herself with her back to the blonde girl standing silently at Julian's side and thereby excluding her from their conversation.

'I thought for a moment that you'd forgotten me...'

'Impossible,' Julian assured her with heavy flirtatiousness, his glance deliberately and meaningfully lingering on her body.

Really, he was a total creep, Kelly decided.

'Here on your own?' Julian quizzed her.

Throwing back her head, Kelly gave a small, sexy laugh.

'Of course not,' she chided him, her voice and the

look she gave him emphasising that *she* was the type of woman who would *never* be without a male escort.

'You're looking very well,' she praised him, adding purringly, 'Very well...'

'Then that makes two of us,' Julian told her smoothly.

'Julian, I think it's time we started to make our way to the table.'

The cool, authoritative male voice intruding on their conversation caused Kelly to turn her head to look at its owner.

Close up he was even more sizzlingly sensual than she had first imagined. It must be the new persona she had assumed that was making her aware of him in such a very intimate and sexual way, she decided dizzily as her glance slid helplessly from the dark watchfulness of his eyes to his very sensual mouth. Certainly she could never remember an occasion previously when she had been so immediately and so shockingly physically aware of a man's sexuality.

'Oh, must you go so soon?' She pouted again, a little disconcerted to recognise how easily both the pout and the teasing but deliberately flirtatious glance she had given Julian's companion came to her. 'We haven't even been introduced...'

She could sense Julian's surprise at the way she was behaving, and managed to hide her own reservation at her unfamiliar behaviour. Kelly could sense Julian's reluctance to comply with her request, but his companion was already saying with a steely, not to say with a grim note in his voice, 'Yes, Julian, *do* introduce us to your friend...'

'Er... Eve, Brough, may I introduce you to an old friend—Kelly? Kelly, please meet Eve and her brother, Brough Frobisher.'

While Kelly waited for him to expand a little more on the relationship between the other couple and himself she could see from the look in Brough Frobisher's eyes that he was decidedly unimpressed by her flirtatious manner.

At least she had had one of her questions answered, she acknowledged as Harry finally arrived at her side just as Brough was determinedly turning away from her.

Eve and her *brother*, Julian had said.

Ridiculous to feel that dizzying surge of excitement and relief just because Brough Frobisher appeared to be unattached.

'We're on table twelve,' Harry was informing her as he manfully forged a pathway for them both through the press of people making their way towards the banqueting room.

Table twelve was well positioned, with a good view of the top table and close enough to the long row of French windows which opened out onto the terrace to offer the comfort of a cool walk along it should one wish to avail oneself of such a facility.

Curiously, though, as they approached the table a small altercation appeared to be taking place there between a harassed-looking couple, the man red-faced and plainly angry whilst his wife looked flushed and embarrassed.

'*You* told me we were on table twelve,' he was saying to her as Harry and Kelly approached.

'And so we were... At least, that was what Sophie said...' his wife was responding, adding helplessly, 'She must have got it wrong. You'll have to go back and check the table plan.'

As she watched the hapless couple making their way back to the entrance to the room, Kelly couldn't help feeling a little bit guilty. *Was* she being overly suspicious in suspecting Dee's magical sleight of hand might somehow be responsible for their missing seats, especially when she could quite plainly see from where she stood that the place cards the couple had been studying with such bewilderment bore hers and Harry's name?

A middle-aged couple and their daughter, the Fortescues, Kelly realised, were taking their places at the table, and another couple were taking their seats opposite Harry's and Kelly's own, which left three spare seats to Kelly's left. Discreetly she leaned across to study the place cards, her heart thumping just a little bit too fast as she read, 'Mr Julian Cox, Miss Eve Frobisher, Mr Brough Frobisher.' She had no idea just how Dee had managed to get them seated next to Julian, nor did she wish to be enlightened. Dee was turning out to be a master tactician, an expert in the art of gamesmanship and subterfuge.

'Kelly, you're on our table! What a coincidence!' Julian was exclaiming with very evident pleasure as he walked up.

Demurely Kelly said nothing, instead simply smiling at him from beneath down-swept lashes.

Half an hour later, when they had all been served with their main courses, Kelly acknowledged that Julian was even less likeable than she had previously guessed. Ignoring his girlfriend to flirt with her, he had progressed from blatantly sexually motivated compliments to the kind of sensual innuendo which Kelly found teeth-grittingly unwelcome.

Her conscience overcoming her sense of duty, she leaned across the table to ask Eve gently how long she had been living in the town and if she liked it.

'It's very pretty,' was her slightly hesitant response, and Kelly didn't miss the way she looked first at her brother before replying to her, as though seeking either his support or his approval.

Kelly felt distinctly sorry for her. She was no match for a man of Julian's unwholesome calibre, that much was more than evident to her, and Kelly hadn't missed the way she had bitten her lip once or twice when Julian's compliments to herself had pointedly underlined just how sexually attractive he found her.

'What do you do?' Kelly asked her, trying to draw her out a little, but it seemed she had asked the wrong question because immediately the younger woman flushed and looked helplessly at her brother before replying.

'Oh, nothing... I'm afraid my art degree isn't... doesn't...'

Her voice trailed away and Julian cut in boastfully, 'Eve doesn't need to work, do you, my sweet? She has her own income...a trust fund...'

As he spoke he reached for her hand and squeezed it, lifting it to his lips to kiss her fingers in what Kelly considered to be an excessively exaggerated and insincere manner, but to judge from the pretty pink blush that coloured Eve's pale skin she didn't seem to find anything wrong with his manner towards her.

What would she say, Kelly wondered grimly, if she knew that whilst he was kissing her fingers his other hand was resting meaningfully on Kelly's chiffon-clad knee, and she had in fact just had to edge determinedly away from him to stop him from rubbing his leg potentially even more intimately against hers?

He really was totally repulsive, Kelly acknowledged with repugnance as she started to turn towards Harry, stopping when unexpectedly Brough Frobisher entered the conversation, telling her coolly, 'As a matter of fact, Eve works for me. What about you? What do you do?'

Before Kelly could answer him, the Master of Ceremonies called on them for silence whilst their host made a speech.

Gratefully Kelly got to her feet, glad to have the opportunity to shake off Julian's wandering hand. Her dislike of him was growing by the minute—and not just on her own behalf. The minute Julian had mentioned Eve's trust fund Kelly had immediately been aware from his avaricious expression just where the other girl's attraction for him lay. Poor thing, like Beth before her she was obviously too unworldly and naive to see through him, but surely her brother *must* be able to recognise just what Julian was like.

Although he had listened in silence to Julian's conversation throughout the meal, more of an observer than a participator, Kelly had been keenly aware of the intensity of his silent scrutiny of them all. *Was* she being over-sensitive in thinking that he had been particularly watchful where *she* was concerned? At one point, just before the Master of Ceremonies had provided his welcome diversion, Kelly had actually felt as though Brough Frobisher's gaze was somehow burning a laser-like beam right through the table to where Julian's hand was resting on her leg. Not that she had wanted it to be there. She gave a small shudder. He repulsed her now even more than he had done before.

'I can't encourage him. I don't like him. He's loathsome,' she had protested despairingly to Dee last night.

'All you have to do is let him *think* that you're interested in him,' Dee had soothed her. 'All we need is for him to show himself in his true colours so that we can…'

'So that we can *what*?' Kelly had pounced, but Dee had simply given her a mysterious smile.

The speeches were almost over; the Master of Ceremonies had announced that there would be dancing in the ballroom. Hopefully then she would be able to escape Julian's unwelcome attentions, since he would be duty-bound to dance with Eve.

'Your lipstick's all gone and your hair needs brushing,' she heard Julian saying critically to Eve as the speaker sat down.

'I'm afraid Eve doesn't really have much idea about how to dress properly. She isn't into designer clothes. I dare say you didn't have much change out of a thousand pounds when you bought yours?' he questioned, and Kelly knew from the look in his eyes that the news of her supposed inheritance had already reached him via that mysterious 'grapevine' Dee seemed to know so much about. As he spoke Julian's glance slid from Kelly's eyes to her mouth, and he murmured in a much lower voice, 'Mind you, one has to admit the poor darling doesn't exactly have the right kind of raw material…unlike you… Has anyone ever told you that you have the most amazingly sexy eyes…and mouth…?'

Kelly had to fight to suppress the dark tide of colour threatening to betray her feelings. It wasn't embarrassment that was driving the hot blood up under her skin, but anger. How dared he behave so insultingly towards his girlfriend? No wonder she was looking so unhappy. But that was no reason for her brother to give her, Kelly, such a contemptuously angry look. *She* wasn't the one who was responsible for Eve's humiliation.

'I was just going to go to the Ladies to tidy up myself,' she fibbed, smiling warmly at Eve. 'Do you want to come with me?'

'Oh, yes...'

Smiling with relief, Eve got up to accompany her.

'Have you known Julian long?' she asked Kelly shyly as they stood side by side in the elegantly decorated cloakroom, studying their reflections in the mirrors in front of them.

'Mmm...quite a while,' Kelly responded.

'He's a very special person, isn't he?' Eve enthused, her eyes shining with emotion, her expression betraying just how deeply involved with him she was.

Kelly's tender heart ached for her, and she only just managed to resist the impulse to tell her exactly what she thought of Julian Cox and why. Instead she asked, 'What about you? Have *you* known him long?'

'Er, no...not really... That is...' She paused and then said in a breathless rush, 'He's asked me to marry him. Everything's happened so quickly between us that I still can't quite... It's quite a frightening feeling when you fall in love, isn't it?' she asked Kelly with a small, poignant smile. 'This is the first time that I... Brough thinks it's too soon... Julian gets quite cross with me sometimes because he thinks I rely too much on Brough, but he's taken care of me ever since our parents died and...

'I haven't met many of Julian's friends yet,' she confided, changing the subject slightly. 'Julian says that he wants to keep me...us...to himself for a little while...' She smiled and blushed. 'He's so very romantic and loving.'

Oh, yes, Kelly wanted to agree sarcastically. So very romantic and loving that he broke my best friend's heart, just the same way he is probably going to break yours. But caution made her hold her tongue.

How much did Eve know about Julian's relationship with Beth?

Along with the revulsion and dislike Julian had aroused within her was a growing sense of anger and an unexpected surge of desire to protect Eve from suffering the same fate as Beth. Perhaps she herself was a rather stronger and more determined character than she had previously realised, Kelly acknowledged. With every word that Eve spoke she could feel an increasing awareness of how right Dee was to want to have Julian exposed in his true colours, and an increasing desire to help achieve that goal, even if it meant putting herself in an unpleasant, but thankfully temporary, position. Much as it went against the grain with her to subtly encourage Julian's amorous advances, much as she disliked the role she was being called upon to play, there was a real purpose to it.

Checking her own freshly applied lipstick, she gave Eve a warm smile.

'Don't let Julian bully you,' she advised her.

The younger girl's face went scarlet.

'Oh, he doesn't. He isn't… It's just that he's used to women who are so very much more glamorous than me and of course he wants…expects…'

'If he loves you then he must love you just the way you are,' Kelly pointed out, but she could see from Eve's expression that she did not want to hear what Kelly was trying to say.

Perhaps when she saw exactly what kind of man Julian really was she'd realise just how unworthy of her love he was. Kelly certainly hoped so.

Brough frowned thoughtfully as he watched his sister and Kelly weaving their way back through the crowd to their table. Kelly puzzled him and, yes, if he was honest, intrigued him as well.

Having watched the way she behaved towards Julian, subtly encouraging his advances, it would be easy to assume that she was an extremely sophisticated and worldly young woman who was used to using her undeniable feminine sensuality and attractiveness to get whatever she wanted from life—*whoever* she wanted from life, regardless of whether or not the man in question was attached to someone else. But Brough had also observed the way she behaved towards her escort, Harry, and to his own sister, and there was no denying that with them she displayed a warmth, a consideration, an awareness and respect for their feelings that couldn't possibly be anything other than genuine.

One woman, two diametrically opposite types of behaviour. Which of them revealed the real Kelly, and why should it be so important to him to find out? Not, surely, just because the man she was making a play for was the same man her sister claimed to be in love with? After all, there was nothing he wanted more than for something, someone, to make his sister see just how unworthy of her Julian Cox actually was.

Discreetly he studied Kelly. Her dress was expensive, and fitted her as though it had been made for her, but something, some experienced male instinct, told him that she was not quite so comfortable and at home in it as she wanted others to believe. Every now and again she gave a betraying glance down at herself, rather in the manner of a little girl uncertain of the wisdom of wearing her mother's borrowed clothes. As Julian had so admiringly pointed out, she was immaculately groomed, but personally Brough would have rather liked to see her dressed casually in jeans, her skin free of make-up, her wonderful hair soft and tousled and her even more wonderful eyes and mouth...

His eyebrows snapped grimly together as he recognised the direction his thoughts were taking. It was a long time since a woman had attracted him as powerfully or as immediately as Kelly—or as dangerously. On two counts. If she *was* the type of woman she was portraying to attract Julian Cox's attention, then she was most decidedly not *his* type. And if she wasn't...if that unexpected and alluringly enticing chink of vulnerability and uncertainty he had so briefly glimpsed beneath the sophisticated image she was trying to portray was the real Kelly...then that would make it even more imperative that he didn't involve himself in any way with her. His life was already complicated enough as it was, with Eve. One day he would marry, settle down, with a nice, calm, sensible girl—a woman who did not pretend to be something she wasn't.

Of course, there was one way he could probably find out just what sort of woman Kelly really was. The way a woman responded, reacted, to a man's first kiss could say an awful lot about just what kind of person she was, Brough mused.

His frown deepened. What on earth was he thinking? There was no way he could justify that kind of behaviour—or those kinds of thoughts.

His last serious relationship had been when he was in his very early twenties. He had thought himself in love— had thought that she loved him. They had met at university and then she had taken a year out to travel while Brough had stayed at home to be near Eve. When they had met up again both of them had been forced to acknowledge that whatever they'd had had gone.

Since then he had dated...there had been women...but

by the time he had reached thirty he had decided that he must be the kind of man in whom logic and responsibility always won out over passion and impetuosity. And so he was…wasn't he?

'I want to dance with you.' Kelly's heart sank as she saw from the loaded, explicitly sexual way that Julian was regarding her as he spoke to her just how successful Dee's plan had been. There was no doubt just what was on Julian's mind, even without the heavy, lingering glance he gave her breasts.

He was being too obvious, too potentially hurtful to Eve and insulting towards her, Kelly decided as she shook her head and reminded him, 'You haven't danced with Eve yet…'

'I don't want to dance with *her*; I want to dance with *you*,' Julian insisted as he reached out to raise her from her seat.

Unhappily Kelly fought her conscience. This was too much, and inexcusable. Just how much wine had Julian had to drink? she wondered uneasily, wishing that Harry hadn't chosen just that moment to disappear.

'Kelly has already promised this dance to me.'

The interruption from Brough Frobisher was just as unexpected as his coolly uttered, authoritative fib.

Without allowing Julian the opportunity either to protest or argue, Brough came over to her, holding out his hand. Shakily Kelly stood up. She didn't particularly want to dance with him, but dancing with him was infinitely preferable to having to dance with Julian.

Good manners suggested that she ought to thank Brough Frobisher for rescuing her, but to do so would surely be to step out of the role Dee had cast for her and, perhaps even worse, to give him the opportunity to point out that she herself had been actively encouraging Julian to believe that she was interested in him.

'Your sister is very sweet,' she commented awkwardly as Brough led her onto the floor.

'Sweet?' His dark eyebrows lifted as he gave her an appraising look. 'An excess of sweetness can be unpleasantly cloying. I don't consider her to be sweet, rather a little too naive and vulnerable. How long have you known Cox?'

His abrupt question caught her off guard.

'Er...a while... He...we're old friends,' she stammered, boldly remembering her role.

'Old *friends*,' he repeated, stressing the word as he looked hard at her. 'I see.'

Kelly hoped devoutly that he did no such thing.

As they reached the dance floor he touched her lightly on the arm, turning her expertly towards him. The band was playing a slow, intimate dance number, and immediately she felt his arm go round her Kelly tensed.

It wasn't that she wasn't used to dancing in close proximity to a man, it was just that somehow it was unnerving with *this* man—

'Enlighten me,' he was saying to her. 'What exactly is it about Cox that quite patently makes him so attractive to your sex?'

Kelly glanced warily up at him. He was immaculately dressed and she could just catch the scent of the very masculine cologne he was wearing, she noted approvingly. Julian's apparent addiction to very strong and no doubt trendy aftershave was not to her personal taste at all. But despite Brough's elegant grooming she suspected that without the shave he must have had before coming out this evening his very thick and very dark hair must mean that most evenings his jaw must be shadowed and slightly rough to the touch, adding a delicious extra frisson of sensuality to being kissed by him, especially if you were a woman who, like her, possessed slightly sensitive skin.

Appalled by the direction of her own unruly thoughts, Kelly realised that she had still not answered his question.

'Er…Julian likes women,' she told him lamely.

Immediately his eyebrows rose.

'He certainly does,' he agreed silkily. 'Doesn't that bother you? In my experience, most women prize loyalty and exclusivity in a relationship…'

'Julian is simply a friend,' Kelly reminded him sharply.

'A very intimate friend?' Brough pressed.

He was digging too deep, questioning her too closely, Kelly recognised, and in order to answer him she was either going to have to commit herself to more lies or risk betraying the fiction she was creating.

'It's hot in here,' she complained, pulling free of him. 'I need some fresh air.'

It wasn't entirely untrue; she *was* hot and the terrace she could see beyond the ballroom's open French windows did offer a much needed escape from the cause of that heat—which was not so much the air in the ballroom as the presence of the man beside her and her own feelings of trepidation and guilt.

As she headed for the terrace, it didn't occur to Kelly that he would follow her. She could guess from the way he had been questioning her just what he thought of her, and she knew that in refusing to answer him she had equally plainly confirmed those suspicions.

It was a relief to reach the cool shadows of the terrace, and, avoiding the other couples strolling its length, Kelly turned instead to descend the flight of stone steps that led into the garden.

She was almost at the bottom when a sharp stone underfoot caused her to stumble, but instead of experiencing the ignominy of falling to her knees on the gravel pathway she was scooped up in a pair of hard male arms and she heard Brough's voice against her ear telling her calmly, 'It's all right, I've got you...'

He certainly had, and it seemed he had no intention of letting her go, either. Against her body she could feel the heavy thud of his heartbeat as he helped her to her feet but still continued to hold onto her. Disconcertingly her own heart suddenly started to race, and she discovered that she was finding it hard to breathe.

'Did you twist your ankle? Can you put your weight on it?'

'My ankle...' Dizzily Kelly looked up into his eyes, and then at his mouth, and then foolishly she did exactly the same thing again. The effect on her nervous system was like a shock wave of mega-force, a subterranean uprising of such intensity that it blew every fuse on her internal alarm system—and then some.

Unwisely she licked her inexplicably dry lips. What had he said about her ankle? What ankle? Helplessly her gaze clung to his. Surely no man should have such ridiculously long lashes, such darkly intense eyes. She felt as though...as though...

'Kelly. Kelly...'

'Yes,' she whispered in tacit acknowledgement of what she knew was going to happen.

A kiss was simply a kiss...wasn't it? How could she be so foolish, so unaware...so naive as to think *that*? *This* was certainly no mere kiss, this meeting, caressing of her mouth by and with his. But even as she tried to analyse what was happening, to hold onto some protective shred of sanity, the thread holding her, it snapped beneath the weight of what she was feeling. Blissfully she gave herself up to sensation—to the smooth, rough, hot, sweet feel of his mouth against hers, to the swift ascent from careful, hesitant exploration to the dizzying heights of a complete and passionate explosion of need she could feel shaking her body.

'Kelly!' As he whispered her name Brough's hand reached out to touch her face, to stroke tenderly along her jaw, to support her head as his tongue-tip parted her sensuously swollen lips.

'Brough!'

Was that really her whispering his name in a sigh that was all soft yearning and longing, exposing dangerously the tender, vulnerable heart of herself which she normally kept so carefully guarded?

Unable to stop herself, Kelly reached out and touched his jaw with her fingertips. His skin felt cool and strong. Hard, masculine. Shivering in pleasure, she stood still beneath his kiss. His arms tightened around her almost as though he wanted to guard and protect her.

Shyly Kelly opened her eyes, unable to resist the temptation to look at him whilst he was caressing her mouth with the most unbelievably erotic brush of his lips against hers, but to her shock his own eyes were open and he was looking right back at her.

The sensation of looking so deeply into his eyes whilst he kissed her felt like the most intimate experience she had ever had. Her earlier shivers had become deep tremors of intense emotion, and when he stopped kissing her and raised his mouth from hers to look searchingly at her Kelly made a small sound of distress, her fingertips touching his lips in a gesture of silent longing.

This time it was *his* turn to shudder, racked by a surge of male desire so strong and so open that Kelly felt her own body start to respond to it—to it and to him.

This time, when they kissed, she couldn't remain passive beneath his mouth, but returned each caress, mirroring every touch, every sound as they kissed and broke apart, only to kiss again.

'Kelly, are you out there?'

The sound of Harry's worried voice from the terrace above them brought Kelly back to reality. Hot-faced, she stepped back from Brough, not sure whether to be pleased or insulted that he had released her immediately.

His own face was turned away from her as he looked up towards the terrace, and so she couldn't see his expression nor guess what he was thinking until he said coldly to her, 'You're a very popular woman. First Julian and now Harry—but you'll forgive me, I know, if I decline to join the queue; enticing though what you have to offer undoubtedly is, I'm afraid my tastes run to a woman less practised and more genuine...'

Before Kelly could answer him he had gone, plunging past her into the darkness of the garden.

Shakily she turned towards the steps.

'Thank goodness I've found you,' Harry told her as he saw her. 'Dee would have had my guts for garters if I'd let anything happen to you. I'm under strict instructions to take care of you...' He started to frown, and then told her a little uncomfortably, 'It's none of my business, I know, and Dee's not told me what's going on, but Cox isn't a man I'd want any sister of mine to get involved with, and...'

'You're right,' Kelly agreed in gentle warning. 'It *isn't* any of your business, Harry.'

When they returned to their table they were just in

time to see Brough leaving; giving Harry and Kelly a curt nod, he ignored Eve's protests that it was too early for him to leave.

'I've got a meeting at nine in the morning,' Kelly heard him telling his sister.

'Oh, but you haven't forgotten that you promised to talk with Julian? He has something special to ask you, and there's his new venture, too,' Eve reminded her brother anxiously.

Immediately Kelly's ears pricked up. If Julian was looking for someone to finance a new business venture then Dee would certainly want to know about it. But as though he had somehow sensed her curiosity Brough touched his sister lightly on the arm and told her, 'I'm sure that Harry and Kelly aren't interested in our private family affairs. Cox...' He nodded briefly in Julian's direction before telling him, 'I'll arrange for a taxi to collect Eve—if I were you I'd leave your car behind and organise one for yourself.'

Was she imagining it or had he actually emphasised the word 'private', underlining its significance by giving her a cool, distancing look as he did so?

Whatever the case, Kelly could feel her face starting to burn slightly.

There was no point in her trying to deceive herself. From his demeanour towards his sister, she suspected that he was normally a man who regarded her sex with respect and genuine appreciation, even if at times he did allow his natural male instinct to protect anyone whom he might consider to be vulnerable to surface through his otherwise very politically correct manners. But where she was concerned he had displayed the kind of behaviour that was very far from treating her with respect. That kiss they had exchanged, which for her had been an act of heart-shakingly emotional and physical sensual significance, a complete one-off in her life and totally different from anything she had done or experienced before, had for him simply been an endorsement of the fact that her deliberately flirtatious behaviour with Julian meant that she was open to all manner of unpleasant male behaviour.

The kiss, which had seemed so deeply meaningful and intimate to her, had quite obviously for him merely been a reinforcement of his contempt for her, an emotionally barren male reaction to what he must have seen as some kind of casual, careless open invitation from her.

This kind of situation was so alien to her that Kelly had no knowledge of how to deal with it, and her instinctive desire to confront him and challenge his attitude towards her was further complicated and hampered by the role she was having to play.

Anyway, she decided firmly half an hour later as Harry was driving her home, why was she bothering wasting so much time worrying about what Brough Frobisher may or may not think about her? Why indeed! Julian, though, certainly seemed to have taken the bait, as Dee had planned he would. Kelly gave a small shudder of disgust—the heel.

She grimaced a little, remembering the open interest Julian had shown in the pearl earrings and solitaire ring she had been wearing—an inspired addition to her outfit on her own part; unlike her couture gown and earrings, the ring was anything but genuine, but Julian had certainly been taken in by it—just as his unworldly naive victims had been taken in by him. Dee was right—it was time someone turned the tables on him—but, much as she wanted to help her friend, Kelly had to admit to wishing there might be some other way she could do so.

'You, Kelly are suddenly going to become an extremely rich young woman,' Dee had told her. 'All you have to do is let him believe that you're prepared to commit yourself and, more importantly, your future to him. His own ego and his greed will do the rest.'

Kelly hoped that she was right, because there was certainly no way she was going to be able to give Julian any physical, sexual confirmation of her supposed desire for him. No way at all!

CHAPTER FOUR

KELLY looked up as she heard the shop doorbell go. She was expecting Dee. They had spoken on the phone earlier when Dee had announced that she intended to come round to collect the ballgown accessories which had, in fact, been hired from an exclusive dress shop and to discuss what had happened at the ball.

Kelly had had a pleasingly busy morning with several customers. She hoped that Beth *was* going to be able to source a supplier of high-quality glass in the Czech Republic as this morning alone she had promised three potentially interested customers that they were hopefully going to be able to provide them with the sets of stemware they wanted.

'Something different…something pretty…something not too expensive…' had been the heartfelt pleas of their potential customers. Fingers crossed that if Beth's quest was successful they would be able to meet all three requirements.

'Right,' Dee commanded briskly as she walked up to the counter. 'How did the ball go? Tell me everything…'

'Julian was there with his new girlfriend,' Kelly began, pausing before she added quietly, 'I felt so sorry for her, Dee. She's plainly very much in love with him and so young and naive… I hate the thought of doing anything that might hurt her…'

'She'll be hurt much, much more if Julian succeeds in persuading her to marry him, which he's going to go all out to do. His finances are in a complete mess and getting worse by the day. He's desperately in need of money. She's quite wealthy in her own right and then, when you add on the financial benefits which could accrue to him through her brother... But from what Harry has told me Julian was making a very definite play for you...'

'Yes, he was,' Kelly agreed, tracing an abstract design with the tip of her finger on the polished glass counter before saying hesitantly, 'Dee, I'm not sure if I can go on with what we planned. I don't like Julian, and, whilst I like even less what he's done to Beth and what he's doing to Eve Frobisher, I...'

'Would it help if I gave you my solemn promise that on no account and on no occasion would I *ever* allow a situation to arise where you would have to be on your own with him?' Dee asked her.

Kelly stared at her. How on earth had Dee guessed what was troubling her?

'You're quite right,' Dee told her, answering the question Kelly still had to ask. 'I wouldn't want to be on my own with him either, especially if I thought that there was any risk that he might guess what we're up to... Harry is quite aggrieved with me, you know,' she added with a chuckle. 'He not only feels that as your friend and landlady I ought to put you wise to Julian's real character, he also shares your concern on behalf of Eve Frobisher.

'In fact,' she told Kelly ruefully, 'I'm afraid he's rather taken me to task over the whole thing.'

'Does he now know what we're doing, then?' Kelly asked her in some surprise. Instinctively she had felt that Dee was a woman who exercised her own judgement, made her own decisions and played her cards very close to her chest.

'Not entirely,' Dee admitted, confirming Kelly's private thoughts. 'Harry is a sweetie, as solid and dependable as they come. He wouldn't recognise a lie if he met one walking down the street; subterfuge and everything that goes with it is very much alien territory to him, which does have its advantages, of course. He's wonderful potential husband and father material...' She cocked a thoughtful eye at Kelly. 'He's comfortably off, and I know for a fact that his mother is dying for him to settle down and produce children. If you were interested...'

'He's a honey,' Kelly told her hastily, 'but not, I'm afraid, my type.'

Nor, she suspected, was she his, but she rather thought she knew someone who might be. She hadn't missed the anxious and protective looks Harry had been giving Eve over dinner the previous night.

'Mmm... Pity... Look, I've got to dash,' Dee told her. 'When Julian rings you—which he will—I want to know about it...'

'Dee,' Kelly said, but it was too late; the other woman was already heading for the door, ignoring her half-panicky protests.

What was Dee saying? Julian wouldn't ring her. He wouldn't dare. Flirting with her last night was one thing, but...

In her heart of hearts Kelly knew that despite her desire to do the right thing by Beth and the rest of her sex she was secretly reluctant to have anything more to do with Julian. Not because she feared him. She didn't. No. Contempt, dislike, anger...those were the emotions he aroused within her.

Admit it, she told herself sternly ten minutes later as she locked the shop and disappeared into the small back room to have her lunch, 'you just hate the thought of anyone thinking you could possibly be attracted to him. *Anyone*…or a specific someone…a *very* specific someone.

Pushing aside her half-eaten sandwich, Kelly started to frown. Don't start that again, she warned herself. He's not much better than Julian… Look at the way he treated you. Kissing you like that.

Kissing her… Abruptly she sat down, her insides starting to melt and then ache.

Watch it, she warned herself, deriding herself fiercely. It isn't just your insides he's turning to mush, it's your brain as well.

Her frown deepened as she heard someone ringing the shop doorbell. Couldn't they read? They were closed. The ringing persisted. Irritably Kelly got up. There was no way she could finish her lunch with that row going on.

Opening the communicating door, she marched into the shop and then stopped abruptly as she saw Brough Frobisher standing on the other side of the plate-glass window.

Her hand went to her throat in an instinctive gesture of shock as she breathed in disbelief, 'You.'

Shakily she went to unlock the shop door. Brough was frowning as he stepped inside.

'I'm looking for Kay Harris,' he told her abruptly. The sense of shock that hit her was so strong that for a moment Kelly was unable to reply.

'She does work here, doesn't she?' Brough was demanding curtly, looking at her, Kelly realised, as though he doubted her ability to answer him competently.

'Yes. Yes, she does… I do… It's Kelly, not Kay,' Kelly corrected him shakily. 'K is just my initial.'

'You!'

Sensing his reluctance to believe her, Kelly drew herself up to her full height and told him in her most businesslike voice, 'My partner and I run this shop.'

'You paint china?' His disbelief was palpable and insulting.

Kelly could feel her temper starting to ignite. There were many things she was not, and she had her fair share of human faults and frailties, but there was one thing that she was sure of and that was that she was extremely good at her chosen work—and that wasn't merely her own opinion.

'Yes, I do. Perhaps you'd like to see my credentials?' she suggested bitingly.

'I thought I just did—last night.' The long, slow, arrogantly male look he gave her made her face burn and her temper heat to simmering point.

'What is it exactly that you want?' she demanded angrily, adding before she could stop herself, 'If it's simply because you're some sort of weirdo who gets off on insulting women, I should have thought your behaviour towards me last night would have more than satisfied you.'

Kelly knew that she had overstepped the mark. She could hardly believe what she had just heard herself say, but it was too late to withdraw her remarks. Retaliation couldn't be long in coming, she recognised, and she was right.

'If you're referring to the fact that I kissed you...' he began silkily, and then paused whilst he looked straight into her eyes. 'Allow me to say that you have a rather...unusual...way of expressing your...displeasure...'

He didn't say anything more—he didn't need to, Kelly

acknowledged; the expression in his eyes and the tone of his voice along with the masterly understatement of his silky words was more than enough to leave her covered in confusion and angry, self-inflicted humiliation.

'I... You... It was a mistake,' was all she could think of to say.

'Oh, yes,' he agreed dulcetly. 'It certainly was. Now, I'm afraid that I am rather short of time. I have a commission I would like to discuss with you.'

Kelly blinked. All that and he *still* wanted to talk business with her.

Her thoughts must have shown in her face because he explained gently, 'You're my last resort. You have, or so I am told, a very particular and rare skill. It will soon be my grandmother's eightieth birthday. She has a Rockingham-style teaset, a much cherished family heirloom, but some pieces are missing, broken many years ago. The set has no particular material value; its value to her is in the fact that it was a wedding gift from her grandparents. I have managed to find out that Hartwell China bought out the original manufacturers many, many years ago and, whilst they still produce china in the same shape, they no longer produce the same pattern.

'To have one of their own artists copy such an intricate floral design would, they say, prove far too costly—the work would have to be done by one of the top workers, which would mean taking him or her off work they already have in hand. They recommended that I got in touch with you. Apparently there is no one else they would allow, never mind recommend, to do such work.'

'I...I worked for them whilst I was at university,' Kelly explained huskily. 'That was when I discovered that I had some talent for...for china-painting. I would have to see the design... It wouldn't be easy...or cheap...' she warned him.

Against her will she had been touched by the story he had told her, but *she* knew, even if he didn't, just how intricate and time-consuming the kind of work he was describing could be.

'I've managed to cadge one of the tea plates from Nan, and Hartwell have very kindly said that I can use their archive records.'

'Do you have the plate with you?' Kelly asked him.

He shook his head, unexpectedly looking oddly boyish as he admitted, 'I'm terrified of breaking it. I've got it at home. I was wondering if it would be possible for you to call there to see it.'

Kelly wanted to refuse, but her professional pride and curiosity proved too strong for her.

'I could,' she agreed cautiously, 'but it would have to be when the shop is closed. My partner, Beth, is away at the moment.'

'Could you manage this evening?'

'I...'

'I don't have very much time left. Nan's birthday isn't very far away,' he told her.

Kelly sighed. There was no reason why she shouldn't look at the plate this evening.

'I suppose so,' she agreed reluctantly. 'Where do you live? I—' She broke off as the phone began to ring, automatically going to answer it, saying, 'Excuse me a moment...' as she picked up the receiver.

'Hi, Kelly, it's Julian. How are you, you delicious, hot, sexy thing...?'

Kelly almost dropped the receiver as Julian's loud voice seemed to fill the shop. Her face burning with embarrassment, she turned her back on Brough even though she knew that he could well have heard what Julian had said.

'Julian. I...I'm busy...' she protested. 'I...'

'I understand, babe. What you and I have to say to one another needs to be said in private, right?' Julian responded. 'God, but you turned me on last night, doll... I can't wait for us to get together...'

'Julian.' Kelly closed her eyes, as revolted by Julian's conversation as she was by his person. 'Julian, please—' she began. But he wouldn't let her finish, interrupting her to say thickly, 'I'll ring you later at the flat. I've still got the number...'

He had hung up before Kelly could object or protest, leaving her pink cheeked both with anger and chagrin—anger because of Julian's assumption that she, or any other woman for that matter, would be willing to see him when he was supposedly already involved with someone else, and chagrin because Brough could have overheard some of the conversation.

It was to be expected, of course, that he wouldn't let the matter go without comment, especially when the girl whom Julian was supposed to be on the point of becoming engaged to was his own sister.

'I appreciate that custom has it that there's supposedly safety in numbers, but don't you think you could be interpreting its validity just a little too generously?' he asked her smoothly.

'Julian is an old friend,' Kelly reminded him.

The look he gave her could have stopped Linford Christie in his tracks, Kelly felt sure.

'Really? Then I feel extremely sorry for you, not only in your unfortunate choice of *friends* but your misplaced and, no doubt, regularly abused loyalty.'

'Julian is dating your sister,' Kelly felt compelled to remind him defensively.

He had turned to walk towards the door, but now, abruptly, he stopped and turned back to Kelly, and said quietly but with grim force, 'Yes, he is, isn't he?' And then, almost without pausing, he added coolly, 'Shall we say eight tonight? This is the address...'

Kelly was still looking bemusedly at the business card he had placed down on the counter as he closed the shop door behind him.

Why on earth hadn't she said something, objected to his high-handed assumption that she would not merely be free this evening but that, additionally, she would fall in with his plans, agree to his request, especially in view of the way he had spoken to her?

Reluctantly she picked up the card. Kelly had a vague idea where the house was since it was on the same road as a customer who had ordered a special commission from her.

Ten minutes before she was due to re-open the shop, the phone rang again. This time the caller was Beth, ringing from Prague.

'Hi... How are things going?' Kelly asked her eagerly.

'Not too bad, in fact really quite promisingly. I've been given several contact numbers, and I'm due to drive out of the city tomorrow to visit a crystal factory.'

'And you're managing okay, despite the language barrier?' Kelly asked her. This had been one of Beth's main concerns about her trip and Kelly was anxious to know how her friend was coping.

'Oh, I've got an interpreter,' Beth told her.

Kelly frowned. The offhand tone of Beth's voice was both unfamiliar and slightly worrying.

'And she's helping you, visiting factories with you...?'

'*She* is a he,' Beth told her shortly. 'And as for *helping* me...' There was a small pause. 'Honestly, Kelly, men. I'm totally off all of them. Just because a person has a fancy degree and a whole string of letters after his name, that does *not* give him the right to try to tell *me* what to do. And as for trying to force me to visit factories that *he's* chosen, with tales of theft and gypsies—'

'Beth.' Kelly interrupted her in bewilderment. 'I'm sorry, but I don't understand.'

'Oh, it's all right, I'm just letting off steam. It's Alex, the interpreter. He's half-English, as it turns out, and his grandparents left Prague for political asylum in the west when his mother was a child. Alex returned after the revolution to search for his family and he's stayed on here.'

'Sounds like he's been confiding rather a lot of personal history to you for someone you don't get on with,' Kelly told her wryly.

'Oh, he tells me what he wants me to know. He's insisting that I visit a glass factory run by his cousins, but I'm not inclined to go. He obviously has a vested interest in anything I might buy. I've managed to track down somewhere that produces this most wonderful design I've seen, and he's acting all high and mighty and trying to tell me that it's all a con and that the stall-holder saw me coming a mile off. He says there *isn't* any factory where they've told me to go and the glass I wanted to buy couldn't have been genuine. He says it's a well-known ploy to get hold of foreign currency that is often worked against naive people like me...

'Oh, but Kelly, you should have seen this glass. It was wonderful, pure Venetian baroque, you know the kind of thing, and it would lend itself beautifully to being gilded for the Christmas market. I even thought that if the price was reasonable enough we could commission some special sets, hand-painted and gilded for special celebrations—weddings, anniversaries…you know the kind of thing…'

Kelly laughed as she listened to her friend's excited enthusiasm. It was wonderful to hear that note back in Beth's voice again, and even more wonderful that she hadn't even asked once about Julian Cox.

'Anyway,' Beth was continuing determinedly, 'somehow I'm going out to this factory by myself. I'm planning to give my guide, and for that you can read jailer, the slip. It's obvious what he's up to,' she told Kelly scornfully. 'He just wants to secure our business for his cousins. He claims that their factory could probably reproduce the glass if they had a copy of it…'

'Mmm… Well, if that's the case, it might be worthwhile sketching the glass and seeing if they *can* reproduce it.'

'Never,' Beth asserted fiercely. 'There's no way I'm going to have Alex dictating to me… No. I've seen the glass I want and I know where to get it, and I'm determined to get an exclusive supply of it and at the right price. After all, if we did commission Alex's cousins, what's to stop them selling our design elsewhere, putting up the price to us because they know we want it? Look, I must go; Alex is picking me up in half an hour. He's insisting on making me walk over the Charles Bridge, and since it's raining today he says it should be relatively free of other tourists.'

'Sounds fun,' Kelly teased her, smiling as she said goodbye and hung up. The others would be so pleased to hear that Beth seemed to be getting over Julian Cox.

CHAPTER FIVE

As HE let himself into the hallway of their rented house and blinked at the teeth-jarring hard yellow paint of the room, Brough reflected that he would be glad when they could finally move into the large Georgian farmhouse he had bought several miles outside the town and which was presently undergoing some much needed renovation work. It had been empty for three years before Brough had managed to persuade the trustees of the estate of the late owner that there was no way anyone was ever going to pay the exorbitant price they were asking for it.

'If they don't sell it soon, they'll be lucky to have anything there worth selling,' he had told the agent crisply. 'It's already been empty and unheated for three winters, and if the government gives the go-ahead for the new bypass the area will be swarming with protestors just looking for an empty house to take over and make themselves comfortable in.'

Buying the house, though, had simply been the beginning of a whole spate of difficult negotiations. The property was listed, and every detail of his planning applications had to be scanned by what had felt like a never-ending chain of committees, but now at last the approved builder had started work on the property, and, with any luck, he should be able to move into it within the year, the builder had assured him cheerfully on his last site inspection.

For now, he would have to live with the last owner

of his present house's headache-inducing choice of colours.

'Brough, is that you?'

He grimaced wryly as Eve came rushing into the hallway, her face pink with excitement as she told him breathlessly, 'Guess what? Julian rang; he's going to be free this evening after all, so he's taking me out to dinner. Oh, Brough, I was so afraid he was going to be angry with me when you insisted that you couldn't help him with his new venture.'

As he listened to her Brough could feel himself starting to grind his teeth. There was no point in wishing that his sister had a more worldly and less naive outlook, nor in blaming his grandmother and the old-fashioned girls' school she had insisted he send her to for the part they had played in her upbringing. He might just as well blame their parents for dying—and himself for not being able to take on the full responsibility for bringing her up without his grandmother's help.

He knew how upset his grandmother would be if she knew how ill-prepared the select, protective girls' school she had chosen so carefully for her had left Eve for the modern world, and some day in the not too distant future Brough was afraid that his sister was going to have her eyes opened to reality in a way that was going to hurt her very badly.

As he'd thought a number of times before, there was no point in him trying to warn Eve about Julian Cox. She had a surprisingly strong, stubborn streak to her make-up, and was very sensitive about both her own independence and her judgement. To imply that Julian was deceiving her, that she was totally and completely wrong about him in every single way, was almost guaranteed to send her running into his arms, and not away from them, which would have been bad enough if what she stood to lose from such an event was her emotional and physical innocence—more than bad enough. But Eve stood to inherit a very sizeable sum of money from their parents' estate when she reached her twenty-fifth birthday, and Brough was convinced that Julian Cox would have no compunction whatsoever about marrying her simply for that reason alone.

Brough had had Julian's financial affairs thoroughly investigated. To describe them as in total disarray and bordering on the legally fraudulent was no exaggeration, nor was his emotional history any less murky. But, of course, Eve wouldn't hear a word against him. She considered herself to be in love.

'Oh, I'm so pleased. He was awfully upset this morning after you told him you really couldn't help him... That was mean of you,' she reproached Brough.

'On the contrary, it was simply good business sense,' Brough told her dryly. 'I know how you feel about him, Eve but...'

'Oh, Brough, please don't start lecturing me,' she begged him. 'Just because you don't want to fall in love...because you don't have someone to share your life with...someone special...that doesn't mean... I love him, Brough,' she said simply.

Brough sighed as she went upstairs. He wished he could find some way to protect her from the ultimate inevitability of having her heart broken, but he suspected that even if he were to confront her with incontrovertible evidence of Cox's real nature she would simply close her eyes to it.

Women! There was no way of understanding how their minds and, even more, their emotions worked. Look at Kelly. A bright, intelligent, beautiful young woman who was apparently as oblivious to Cox's faults as his own sister. Not that he thought that Kelly's other choice of male was any better—but for very different reasons. Harry was quite obviously an extremely estimable young man, the kind of man whom he would have been only too pleased to see dating his *sister*, but, as a partner for a woman of Kelly's obviously feisty and quicksilver personality, surely a totally wrong choice. She needed a man who could match the quickness of her brain...who could appreciate the intelligence and artistry of her work...who could share the passion that he could sense ran so strongly through her at the very deepest level of her personality... A man who...

Abruptly he caught himself up.

Nothing he had experienced in his admittedly brief contact with Kelly had indicated that she had the kind of insecure, needy personality that would make her a natural victim for a man like Cox.

Eve, on the other hand, if he was honest, desperately needed to feel loved and secure, to have a partner who would incorporate into their adult relationship the kind of protective, emotional padding she had missed from the loss of their father and experienced in a different way at school. Eve needed a man who would treat her gently, a man with whom she could have the kind of relationship which he privately would find too unequal. The woman he loved would have to be his equal, his true partner in every aspect of their lives. There would have to be complete and total honesty and commitment between them, a deep, inner knowledge that they would be there for one another through their whole lives—he too had suffered from their parents' death, he acknowledged wryly.

And Eve was wrong about him not wanting to fall in

love…to marry. At the end of his present decade lay the watershed birthday of forty, comfortably in the distance as yet, but still there on the horizon. When he thought of himself as forty, it was not particularly pleasant to visualise himself still alone, uncommitted…childless… But the woman he married, the woman he loved…

Unbidden, the memory of how Kelly's lips had felt beneath his flooded his body, sharply reminding him that if a male's sexual responses were at their fastest and peak in his teens, then they could still react with a pretty forceful and demanding potent speed in his thirties—disconcertingly so.

The dichotomy he had sensed within Kelly at the ball which had so intrigued him had turned to a more personal sense of irritation this afternoon. Did she really think he was so lacking in intelligence…in awareness…that he couldn't see how alien to her personality her relationship with Julian was? What the hell was it about the man that led a woman like her to…? It was almost as though he held some kind of compulsive attraction for her or had some kind of hold over her.

In another age it might almost have been said that he had cast some kind of spell over her—as she was beginning to do over him?

Kelly paused in the act of picking up her keys. In the close confines of the flat's small entrance hall she could smell the scent of her own perfume. Defensively she told herself that wearing it was simply second nature to her and meant nothing, had no dark, deep, psychological significance, that the fact that she was wearing it to, and for, a meeting with Brough Frobisher meant absolutely nothing at all.

She wasn't a woman who was overly fond of striking

make-up, nor strictly styled hair, but she did like the femininity of wearing her own special signature scent, even if normally she wore it in conjunction with jeans and a casual top.

Tonight, though, those jeans had been exchanged for a well-cut trouser suit—not for any other reason than the fact that wearing it automatically made her feel more businesslike. And that was, after all, exactly what this evening's meeting was all about—business. And as for that small spurt of sweet, sharp excitement she could feel dancing over her vulnerable nerve-endings, well, that was nothing more than the arousal of her professional curiosity.

Hartwell china always evoked special memories for her. It had been the Hartwell china she had seen on a visit to a stately home as a girl which had first awoken her interest in the design and manufacture of porcelain, and it had been the Hartwell factory where she had first had her actual hands-on experience of working on the physical aspect of copying the designer's artistry onto the china itself. And so it was only natural that she should feel this surge of excitement at the thought of seeing a piece which sounded as though it was extremely rare.

It didn't take her very long to drive to the address Brough had given her. Rye-on-Averton was only a relatively small and compact town, virtually untouched by any effects of the Industrial Revolution and still surrounded by the farmland which had surrounded it way, way back in the Middle Ages.

Parking her own car and getting out, Kelly carefully skirted the expensive gleaming Mercedes saloon car parked in the drive and climbed the three steps which led to the front door. Brough opened it for her virtually as soon as she rang the bell.

Unlike her, he was unexpectedly casually dressed in jeans and a soft cotton checked shirt.

The jeans, Kelly noticed as she responded to his non-verbal invitation to come into the house, somehow or other emphasised the lean length of his legs and the powerful strength of his thigh muscles.

As a part of her studies at university she had, for a term, attended a series of lectures and drawing classes on the human body, and whilst there had been required to sketch nudes, both male and female, but that experience was still no protection against either the images which inexplicably filled her thoughts or the guilty burn of colour which accompanied them.

What on earth was she doing, mentally envisaging Brough posing, modelling for a classical Greek statue? That kind of behaviour, those kinds of thoughts, simply were not her.

'It's this way,' Brough informed her, the cool, clipped sound of his voice breaking into the dangerous heat of her thoughts as he indicated one of the doorways off the hall.

The yellow paint in which the hallway was decorated made Kelly do a slight double-take, a fact which Brough obviously noticed because he commented dryly, 'Bilious, isn't it? Unfortunately its shock effect doesn't lessen with time.'

'You could always redecorate,' Kelly pointed out austerely, refusing to allow herself to feel any sympathy with him, even in the unfortunate colour of his walls.

'Not really. This house is only rented. I'm only living here until the one I've bought has been renovated.'

'Oh, so you've moved into the area permanently, then?'

Kelly berated herself furiously as the question slipped out, her curiosity getting the better of her, but to her relief Brough made totally the wrong connection between her question and its motivation as he responded even more dryly, 'Yes, we have, so I'm afraid you can't look to our removal from town as an easy way of removing my sister from your lover's life.'

'It isn't necessary for me to do any such thing,' Kelly denied furiously through gritted teeth, momentarily forgetting her allotted role.

'Eve believes he intends to marry her. How do you feel about that?' he challenged her.

'How do you feel about it?' Kelly sidetracked.

'He's a liar and a cheat and most probably guilty of financial fraud as well,' Brough told her bitingly. 'How the hell do you think I feel about it?'

'She's *your* sister.'

'Strange,' he continued softly, 'you don't look particularly surprised—or shocked. Perhaps you *like* the idea of having a married lover, especially one whose wife is both extremely rich and extremely in love.'

'No. That's not...'

Immediately she realised what she was saying, Kelly stopped.

'That's not what?' Brough goaded her. 'Not what you want? He's *your* lover...'

'And Eve is *your* sister,' Kelly pointed out again quickly. 'My relationship with Julian is no one's business other than our own. If you dislike him so much, *disapprove* of him so much, why haven't you told Eve so?'

'She's too much in love to listen to me or to anyone

else. What *is* it you see in him? What possible attraction can he have for any woman when he...?'

'Why don't you ask Eve?' Kelly suggested.

Ridiculously, dangerously, she was actually starting to feel sorry for him. It was plain how worried he was about his sister, and with good reason, and it was equally plain that he felt helpless to do anything to alter the situation. Even so, she couldn't resist punishing him just a little, both for what he thought about her and what he had said...and done...

'It's obviously hard for a man to see just what it is about Julian that appeals to our sex. Perhaps you feel jealous of him.'

'Jealous...? Look, just because last night I *kissed* you, that doesn't mean—'

'I mean jealous because Eve loves him,' Kelly interrupted him shakily.

'You wanted me to look at this plate,' she reminded him, anxious to return their conversation to a much more businesslike footing.

'Yes. It's in here,' he told her, ushering her into a large, high-ceilinged room which was painted a particularly unpleasant shade of dull green.

'Hideous, isn't it?' he agreed, correctly interpreting her thoughts. 'The owner must be colour blind—or worse. You should see the bedrooms; the one I'm occupying is painted a particularly repulsive shade of puce.'

'Puce...? I don't believe you,' Kelly protested. 'No one would paint a bedroom that colour.'

'If you want to see for yourself I'll show you afterwards...'. Brough started to say, and then stopped to study Kelly's bright pink face with interest.

'Now there's an interesting conundrum,' he mused

sardonically. 'Why should a woman who openly admits that she is sleeping with another woman's boyfriend blush at the mere mention of a completely altruistic visit to another man's bedroom? It *was* my bedroom I was suggesting you view,' he added gently, 'not my bed...'

'I was *not* blushing,' Kelly protested. 'It's just...it's just...it's very warm in here...'

'Is it?' Brough asked, adding, 'Then what, may I ask, are these?'

Before she could stop him he was running a hard fingertip down the full length of her bare arm, right over the rash of goose bumps which had lifted beneath her skin when they'd entered the room's unheated atmosphere. And what made it worse was that the brief and totally sexless stroke of his finger had made the goose bumps even more prominent—and not just her goose bumps, she acknowledged, mortified by the unwanted discovery that her nipples were inexplicably pressing very hard, tightly aroused, against the constraining fabric of her bra.

Instinctively she turned away from him, lifting her arm in what she hoped was a natural and subtle gesture which he wouldn't guess was designed to conceal the evidence of her body's extraordinary behaviour from him.

He had seen it, though, seen it and been both disgusted and angered by it, she recognised, if the look she could see in his eyes was anything to go by.

My God, but she had got it badly if even the mere fact of talking about Cox could arouse her body like that, Brough fumed as Kelly turned her flushed face and aroused breasts out of his eye-line.

It had been bad enough when he had simply wanted to protect and rescue his sister from the man, but now...

'The plate's over here,' he told Kelly curtly.

Silently she followed him, keeping her distance from him as he unlocked the small corner cupboard and removed the plate, but as he walked over to her and she saw it she couldn't resist giving a small cry of pleasure, closing the distance between them so that she could take the plate from him and study it more closely.

'Oh, it's beautiful,' she enthused as she traced the design lovingly with her fingertip. 'Almost Sèvres in style and execution...'

'Yes, that's what they said at the factory. They suspect that the whole set might have been a showpiece set made by a particularly gifted apprentice. Apparently, when they finished their time in apprenticeship the artists were often given the opportunity to do something to act as a showcase for their skills.'

'Yes, I know,' Kelly agreed absently, barely able to take her glance off the plate. 'Oh, it's lovely—so detailed and intricate.'

She stopped and shook her head.

'What's wrong? Don't you think you can copy it?' Brough asked her.

Kelly paused.

'I don't know,' she admitted. 'It's very complex, and the gold leaf work alone would be so expensive in materials... I... Can't Hartwell recommend anyone else to do it for you, someone more experienced?'

Brough gave her a level look.

'According to them there *isn't* anyone more experienced,' he told her quietly.

To her annoyance Kelly knew that she was blushing again.

'I... I... It's very kind of them to say so, but...'

'They also told me that you turned down a very lucrative and secure contract with them to go into business by yourself.'

'I…I like being my own boss,' Kelly told him quietly.

'Even though it doesn't pay you anything like as well as working for them would have done…?'

'Money isn't that important to me,' Kelly admitted after a small pause. There followed a very stiff, very pregnant silence during which Kelly recognised that she had said something wrong, but was not sure what.

'I suppose you don't agree with that kind of outlook at all,' she challenged him when the silence had made her skin start to prickle. 'I expect *you* feel that when a person doesn't exploit their…talents to the best possible financial advantage, then—'

'On the contrary,' Brough interrupted her firmly. '*I* feel extremely sorry for anyone who feels obliged to accept a way of life, a means of living, that doesn't make them happy.'

'But you can't believe that earning money isn't of prime importance to me,' Kelly insisted.

'What I can't believe is that a woman holding the views you've just expressed would in any way consider a man like Julian Cox to be a good partner for her,' Brough corrected her.

'I…I didn't come here to discuss my relationship with Julian,' Kelly told him tautly, handing the plate back to him as she did so, giving it a last lingering look of regret. There was nothing she would have loved more than to copy the design and replace the missing pieces of the teaset, especially under the circumstances Brough had outlined to her. But she couldn't do anything that would bring her into closer contact with him. There was too much risk involved in far too many different ways.

But before she could vocalise her decision, Brough

himself was speaking, telling her coolly, 'We don't have much time left before my grandmother's birthday, so I've arranged for us to visit the factory on Wednesday. They told me when I was there that you'd need to collect the unpainted china from them and get supplies of paint.'

'Wednesday? But it's Monday today; I can't possibly…' Kelly began.

But he was already overruling her, telling her, 'I know what you're going to say and I've asked Eve if she will stand in at the shop for you for the day. She's agreed. And before you say anything you needn't worry—she did a stint at Harvey Nicks during her last year at school.'

'Harvey Nicks?' Kelly exploded, adding pointedly, 'This isn't Knightsbridge…'

'No, it isn't,' he agreed. 'We'll need to get a pretty early start, so if I pick you up at, say, eight I can drop Eve off at the same time.'

'Just a minute,' Kelly objected. 'I haven't agreed that I'm going—'

'What's wrong? Are you afraid that Cox might object to you spending the day with me?'

'This has *nothing* to do with Julian,' Kelly told him angrily.

'Good. So I'll pick you up at eight on Wednesday, then,' Brough repeated cordially as he walked over to the door and held it open for her.

There was no way she was going to be able to make him understand that she wasn't going to Staffordshire with him, Kelly recognised, irritably marching straight past him and heading for the front door, where he caught up with her and commented dulcetly, 'I take it you've decided to accept my word about the colour of my bedroom walls…'

Kelly shot him a fulminating look. 'The colour of your bedroom walls, be they puce, chartreuse or vermilion, is totally and absolutely of no interest to me,' she told him.

'Vermilion,' Brough mused. 'The colour of passion. Interesting that you should suggest it...'

'*Suggest* it? I did no such thing.' Kelly seethed. 'What do you think you're *doing*?' she demanded as, instead of opening the front door, he very gently and totally unexpectedly placed his hands on her upper arms and turned her round.

'I'm going to make you a cup of cocoa before you go home,' he told her, adding suavely, 'It warms the blood and soothes the passions. The Aztecs used to believe it had aphrodisiac powers, as did the Regency bucks. There's no point in you rushing back. Julian is out with Eve.'

'What's that got to do with me? I've got a deskful of paperwork needing attention, and anyway, I *loathe* cocoa,' she told him pettishly.

'A glass of wine perhaps, then,' he suggested.

Kelly started to shake her head, and then for some reason found that she was nodding it slowly instead.

'This way,' he told her, directing her further down the hallway and into another room, which was a cross between an office and a study, comfortably furnished with a couple of deep armchairs and a huge desk which dominated the space in front of the window.

'For Christmas the year before last, Eve rented for me a row of vines in France. The idea is that you get the wine from your own vines and you can, if you wish, take part in some of the preparation of the wine. Surprisingly, it's rather good...'

'So you'll what?' Kelly asked him. 'Buy the vine-yard?'

An unexpected smile tugged at the corners of his mouth.

'Not this particular one,' he admitted. 'But it's certainly an idea. I wouldn't have an objection to a life of viticulture and semi-retirement... Tuscany, perhaps, close to one of those unbelievably visually breathtaking medieval towns...'

'It sounds idyllic,' Kelly responded enviously, without thinking, and then bit her lip, telling him curtly, 'Look, I really can't stay. Paperwork isn't really my strong suit and...'

'I understand,' Brough accepted. His face was in the shadows but there was no mistaking the stiffness in his voice. Quite patently he was angry with her again, Kelly decided, suppressing a soft sigh. So why should she care either what he thought or what he felt? This time, as she headed for the front door, he made no attempt to persuade her to stay, simply opening it for her and formally thanking her for her time.

As he watched her until she was safely inside the car, Brough wondered what on earth had possessed him to reveal that long-held dream of his to her. What possible interest could it be to her, and, more disturbingly, why should he want it to be?

She was an enigma, a puzzle of unfathomable proportions, and he was a fool for even beginning to think what he was thinking about her.

As he went upstairs and switched on the light in his puce-walled bedroom, his glance rested on the neat white line of his bed. He had been lying when he had told her that it was his bedroom he had been inviting her to see and not his bed. Already, with remarkably little effort at all, he could picture her lying there in it, tucked securely beneath its protective sheets as they outlined the warm curves of her body, holding out an invitation which she mirrored as she held out her arms to welcome him.

Eve hadn't had a good night. She and Julian had had an argument, a small altercation which had blown up out of virtually nothing, simply her innocent comment that Kelly was a very attractive and vivacious woman and that she and Julian were obviously very good friends. But Julian had reacted as though she had accused him of some crime, exploding into a rage so intense that he had actually frightened her.

Shocked and in tears, she had run from his flat, ignoring his demands to her to come back as she'd fired the engine of her car, and here she was now, her car parked in the town centre as she walked unhappily along the riverbank, desperately trying to avoid looking at the entwined pairs of lovers enjoying a romantic stroll along the river path.

'Eve... Eve...'

Instinctively, she stopped as she heard the male voice calling her name, her breath catching in her throat as she recognised Harry hurrying towards her.

'I saw you as I walked over the bridge,' Harry told her with a warm beam as he indicated the bridge she had just passed, his smile fading as he saw her miserable expression. 'What is it? What's wrong?'

'Nothing,' Eve fibbed, but his concern, his sympathy and most of all his sturdy male warmth and reassurance were too much for her already shaky composure, and as she spoke she gave a small hiccuping sob and a tear ran betrayingly down her face.

'It's Cox, isn't it?' Harry guessed, revealing an intuition which would have surprised his relatives, who considered him to be good hearted enough but a trifle lacking in anything requiring mental agility and speed.

'We've had a row,' Eve admitted, immediately adding protectively, 'It was my fault. I...I mentioned Kelly and that made him angry... I shouldn't have brought up the subject. Of course he's entitled to his past and to...'

She stopped as Harry gave a fierce snort of disapproval.

'Of course you're upset,' he comforted her. 'You've every right to be, especially after the way...'

'He was flirting a little with Kelly at the ball,' Eve agreed, guessing what he was going to say. 'But I know that they're old friends and Julian is such an attractive man...'

Harry gave another snort.

'Oh, I know that you probably don't like him. After all, Kelly is your girlfriend.'

'No, she isn't,' Harry told her promptly. 'I don't have a girlfriend...haven't ever really wanted one until... I escorted Kelly because my cousin asked me to...'

'Oh, I see. So you aren't actually going out with Kelly, then?' Eve asked him ingenuously.

Harry shook his head. 'Nice girl but not my type,' he told her.

Inexplicably, as they walked, Eve discovered that she had moved so close to Harry that when they had to pass another couple it seemed the most natural thing in the world for him to shield her protectively by placing his arm around her.

It was very pleasant to be treated as though she was so fragile, so vulnerable and valuable, Eve acknowledged. It made her feel very safe and very protected...

It made her feel happy. Nothing like as happy as she was with Julian, of course, she decided loyally as Harry gently drew her into the protection of a small grove of trees just off the river path.

'Now look,' he told her firmly, 'you mustn't let Cox upset you. He's damn lucky to have a lovely girl like you…damn lucky…'

'Oh, Harry, *I'm* the one who's lucky,' Eve corrected him. 'I'm just plain and ordinary, but Julian…'

'You're no such thing' Harry contradicted her immediately. 'You're beautiful, Eve,' he told her huskily as he looked at her mouth. 'Thought so the moment I saw you…'

An odd quiver of sensation ran right through her body as she recognised the way Harry was looking at her mouth. She might be naive, as she was constantly being told, but she wasn't *that* naive. She was woman enough to know when a man wanted her all right…and when one didn't.

Julian hadn't wanted her tonight. He had pushed her away when she had tried to snuggle into his arms.

'Harry,' she whispered huskily.

'Don't look at me like that, Eve,' he groaned, adding gruffly, 'I want to kiss you so damn much… In fact, I'm *going* to kiss you,' he announced boldly.

Going into Harry's arms was like going home, Eve decided blissfully, all warm and cosy and safe. Happily she turned her face up to his and waited.

She didn't have to wait very long.

His kiss was everything she had known it would be— gentle, reverential, asking, not taking; and it was something more as well, something entirely unexpected and exciting, she recognised as the tiny quivers darting through her body began to grow and gather strength.

'I shouldn't have done that,' Harry told her harshly as he suddenly pushed her away. 'In fact...'

Without saying anything more he turned his back on her and started to walk very quickly away from her.

Feeling as though she had been completely abandoned, Eve stared after him. *Why* had he left her like that? Had he lied to her about not being involved with Kelly? She knew instinctively that Julian had done so when he had told her that Kelly meant absolutely nothing to him. She wasn't completely blind. She had seen the way Julian had been watching Kelly at the ball, but she loved Julian so much...far too much to give him up... Far, far too much to enjoy kissing another man... Hot-cheeked, she pressed her hands to her face. What on earth had she been doing? And why?

It was no wonder, really, that Julian had been so out of sorts and cross, she decided compassionately as she made her way back to her car. It had been a big disappointment for him, poor darling, when Brough had refused to finance his new venture.

She had tried to tell him tonight that she had absolutely no influence at all over Brough's decision, and then he had started to ask her about her own inheritance and she had had to tell him that she couldn't touch a penny of it until she was twenty-five.

'That's four years away,' he had exploded irritably. 'What happens if we get married and you need some money to buy a house?'

If they got married...

'I don't know,' she had confessed, adding brightly, 'Maybe the bank would lend me some money against it... I'd have to check with Brough...'

'No! No, don't do that,' Julian had told her hastily.

'Yes, because when we get married I shall move in

here with you, won't I?' she had agreed, blissfully trying to snuggle up against him.

'Yeah…' he had said so unenthusiastically that she had started to frown.

It was then that she had made her first mistake, asking him uncertainly, 'You *do* want to marry me, don't you, Julian? Only I couldn't help noticing at the ball that you seemed awfully interested in Kelly…'

'Kelly's an old friend,' he had told her angrily. 'Not that it's any business of yours…'

Poor darling, of course he was irritable and on edge with all the money worries he was having. It really was too bad of Brough to refuse to help him. Eve's brow creased. She knew, of course, that her brother didn't really like or approve of Julian, but he didn't *know* him the way she did.

CHAPTER SIX

'HI, KELLY, it's Dee.'

Kelly smiled as she recognised their landlady's voice. It was eleven o'clock in the morning and Kelly had just served her third customer and put on the kettle to make herself a cup of coffee.

'Anything to report?' Dee asked her. 'Has Julian been in touch?'

'He rang yesterday,' Kelly told her, 'but I couldn't really talk to him; I had someone here in the shop. You know that Julian is hoping to persuade his girlfriend's brother to finance some new venture he's getting started?'

'*Was* hoping,' Dee corrected her wryly. 'Brough has turned him down.'

How did Dee know that? Kelly wondered curiously.

'Look, we could do with having a meeting,' Dee told her. 'How about lunch tomorrow?'

'Tomorrow? No, I'm afraid I can't,' Kelly told her. 'I'm going to Staffordshire.'

'Staffordshire?' Dee queried sharply. 'On a buying trip? But I thought...'

'No, not that. Actually I'm going with Brough; he's asked me to undertake a private commission for him.'

'And you've agreed?' Dee asked her. 'Be very careful, Kelly. Don't forget his sister is dating Julian and hopes to marry him and he's bound to be extremely suspicious of your role in Julian's life. You haven't told him the truth, have you?' Dee demanded.

'No, of course I haven't,' Kelly reassured her immediately.

'Well, you mustn't. It would ruin everything.'

'I'm not a complete fool, you know, Dee,' Kelly informed her a little irritably. She liked Dee, but sometimes her autocratic attitude irritated her a bit. She wasn't like Beth, who accepted Dee's slight bossiness with placid gentleness even whilst she accepted that the older girl's heart was in the right place and her motives good.

'No, not a complete fool,' Dee agreed dryly, 'but certainly foolish enough to agree to go to Staffordshire with Brough. I understand he's a very attractive man,' she added slyly.

'Not so far as I'm concerned,' Kelly responded immediately, 'but the china he wants me to copy certainly is and, not only that, it's extremely rare and may even be unique. It's a wonderful opportunity, Dee,' she added, warming to her theme, her enthusiasm for the project colouring her voice. 'An almost once-in-a-lifetime chance to work on something very different and very special.

'Oh, Beth rang, by the way,' Kelly informed Dee. 'She's having problems with her interpreter, apparently, but she never said a word about Julian, thank goodness.'

'That *is* good news,' Dee agreed.

'I do feel worried for Eve Frobisher,' Kelly told her.

'You must concentrate on the business in hand,' Dee advised her. 'Eve Frobisher has her brother to protect her interests. Has he said anything about Julian to you, by the way?'

'He's certainly made it plain that he doesn't approve of my relationship with him,' Kelly informed her.

'Mmm... You know, I've been thinking... It could

work to our advantage if you let him think that he might be able to persuade you to have second thoughts about Julian. Men love that—feeling that they're taking charge, doling out advice to some poor, helpless little female. It feeds their egos, and it wouldn't do any harm to get Brough Frobisher on our side.'

'He isn't going to fall for any ''helpless little me' act from me, Dee,' Kelly informed her.

'You don't know until you try it,' Dee told her persuasively. 'There's no saying what helpful information we could pick up about Julian's business affairs via him if he—'

'I *don't* know, because there's no way I am going to try it.' Kelly cut across her comment swiftly. 'Tricking Julian into believing I find him attractive is one thing, lying to Brough is quite another…'

'It is? Why?' Dee asked her interestedly.

'Because I don't like lying to anyone,' Kelly told her sharply. 'The only reason I've agreed to deceive Julian is because of what he did to Beth and to stop him from doing it to anyone else. Persuading Brough to believe that I'm some kind of helpless little creature who needs protecting and rescuing from her own emotions, who can't take responsibility for her own life or her own actions, is just so gross that there's no way I would even contemplate it. Besides, he wouldn't believe me. He'd see through what I was trying to do immediately.'

'He knows you that well after spending…how long…a few hours or so with you, does he?' Dee mused. 'Amazing…'

'He believes that I'm intent on trying to take Julian away from his sister. Let's just leave it at that whilst we're ahead of the game, shall we?' Kelly told her curtly, ignoring her gentle jibe.

'Okay,' Dee soothed her, adding, 'Look, I need to have a word with Anna about her making contact with Julian to offer to lend him the money he needs for this new venture. Now that Brough has turned him down he's going to be too urgently in need of financial backing to question Anna's motivation too deeply, which suits us very nicely. Brough has unwittingly done us a very big favour in turning Julian down.'

'I'm sure he'd be delighted to hear that,' Kelly told her *sotto voce*.

'Oh, by the way, Harry sends his best love,' Dee told her teasingly. Kelly grimaced into the receiver.

'He does?' she questioned, unable to resist the temptation to tell Dee dryly, 'That's odd; he seemed far more interested in Eve at the ball than he was in me. Now there's a match. The pair of them are so well suited they might have been made for one another.'

'Eve loves Julian,' Dee pointed out to her.

'No, what she loves is the man she believes that Julian is,' Kelly corrected her soberly. 'Poor girl, he's going to break her heart.'

'Well, if you're right, Harry will be more than willing to help her to mend it,' Dee told her practically. 'Remember, Kelly, you've got to convince Julian that you want him; that way when you drop him as publicly as he dropped Beth he'll never even guess what's going to happen until it does and…'

'I'm not sure that he'll leave Eve for me,' Kelly warned her. 'Eve believes that he's going to marry her…'

'So did Beth and look what happened to her,' Dee pointed out. 'He's going to be furious when he finds out how we've tricked him, furious and totally and completely humiliated,' she said cheerfully. 'And it couldn't happen to a more deserving man.'

'You really hate him, don't you?' Kelly recognised.

'Yes. I really hate him,' Dee agreed, and she put the receiver down. Kelly thought she heard her saying, But nowhere near as much as I hate myself, but she couldn't be sure, and anyway it was too late to question Dee any further since she had hung up.

Wednesday morning came round too soon. Kelly was awake early—too early, she decided as she watched the sun rise.

It still wasn't too late to refuse to go to Staffordshire but what excuse could she realistically give?

Impossible to tell Brough the truth—that she was afraid of going with him, afraid of what she might say, of what he might guess...of what she might feel... But if she didn't go...

Julian had rung her again last night. Reluctantly she had agreed to meet him for a drink at a local wine bar this evening.

'Julian, you're dating someone else,' she had reminded him coldly, 'and so am I...'

'Harry,' he had scoffed. 'He's no match, no man for a woman like you, Kelly.'

'And I suppose that you are,' she had taunted him, holding her breath at the recklessness of what she was doing.

'Try me,' he had told her, sniggering suggestively. 'I promise you, you won't be disappointed.'

Kelly had been glad that the telephone meant he couldn't see the shudder of revulsion she gave.

'You and I are two of a kind, Kelly,' he had told her thickly. 'We take what we want from life. We're both adventurers, exciting…passionate… I knew that the first time I saw you. I knew then how good we'd be together…'

'When you were dating Beth, you mean,' Kelly had reminded him coldly.

'Beth is history,' he'd told her dismissively. 'But you and I…you and I are *now*, Kelly…'

'You and I are *nothing*,' she had told him.

'Tomorrow night,' Julian had countered. 'Be there, Kelly… You know you want me and I sure as hell want you…'

Want him? Completely revolted both by his conversation and his tone of voice, Kelly had replaced the receiver.

She could just imagine what Brough would have to say.

Brough.

Now why on earth was she thinking about him? she asked herself pointedly as her alarm started to ring. He was almost as bad as Julian Cox, although in a completely different way, of course. He had, after all, misjudged her just as badly.

Eve smiled tentatively at Kelly as Kelly opened the door to her and Brough and they stepped into the shop.

'I'll just run through a few things with you before we leave,' Kelly told her reassuringly. 'Wednesday isn't normally a very busy day so you should be okay, but if you do have any problems—'

'You've got my mobile number, haven't you, Eve?' Brough interrupted Kelly. 'Any problems and you can get in touch with Kelly on that.'

'Thank you, but I have my *own* mobile, Brough,' Kelly told him frostily.

'What I was going to say, Eve, is that I've left you the number of our landlady, Dee. She knows that you'll be working here and she may very well call in to check if everything's okay. She can be a bit daunting, but she's really very kind... She's Harry's cousin,' she added, and then stopped as Eve suddenly went bright red.

'I...I saw him—Harry—the other day when I was walking along the river,' Eve blurted out. 'I...I don't know if he mentioned it, but...'

'No. No, he didn't,' Kelly told her, before adding gently, 'But then, there's really no reason why he should...'

'No. No, of course not,' Eve told her quickly. 'I just meant... Well, I just thought...'

'We really ought to leave,' Brough informed Kelly, frowning slightly as he glanced at his watch. 'The motorway is bound to be busy.'

'I think it's wonderful what you're doing,' Eve told Kelly admiringly. 'I'd love to have that kind of talent,' she added wistfully.

'It's more of a learned skill than a natural talent,' Kelly told her wryly. 'I was just lucky enough to be in the right place to learn it at the right time, and besides, I haven't actually done anything yet.'

'No, but Brough says...' Eve stopped and glanced anxiously at her brother.

What had Brough said? Kelly wondered curiously ten minutes later as he opened the passenger door of his car for her and helped her inside.

She could always ask him, of course. Perhaps later on she would.

The Potteries where the factory was based wasn't too far up the motorway, but Kelly was still feeling extremely apprehensive about the journey. What if Brough used it as an opportunity to take her to task about her relationship with Julian? If he did, then she would just have to remind him—again—that it was none of his business, she told herself firmly as she leaned back in her seat and very deliberately closed her eyes, hoping that he would correctly interpret this as a sign that she didn't wish to talk.

Unfortunately, though, the subtleties of her body language appeared to be lost on him because almost immediately he asked her, 'Tired? I'm sorry we had to have such an early start. We should be able to stop for a short break and a cup of coffee before too long, though.'

He made it sound as though he was taking his ancient maiden aunt out for a Sunday drive, Kelly decided wrathfully, immediately sitting bolt upright in her seat and denying fiercely, 'No, I am not tired, and neither am I unable to travel a distance of less than a couple of hundred miles without the necessity of a comfort stop.'

She used the American phrase very deliberately and pointedly, underlining her comment by adding, 'I'm twenty-four, not seventy-four...'

'I, on the other hand, am thirty-four,' he told her gently, 'and *I* prefer to take life at a reasonably relaxed pace.'

Kelly gave him a surprised look. This was not the sort of comment she expected to hear from a man who had built up a business as successful as Brough's was.

'My parents died in their late thirties,' he told her tersely. 'They were killed in a plane crash. My father had been trying to get to Switzerland for an urgent business meeting and, being unable to get a scheduled flight in time, he'd hired a private plane. They got caught in a bad storm—and that was that.

'Afterwards, I made a vow to myself, a promise that I'd never forget that there was far more to life than meetings, deadlines, and making money. I was nineteen when they were killed, just an adult. Eve was six.'

Only nineteen. Kelly swallowed hard on the large knot of compassion which had lodged in her throat.

'What about you? Do you have any family?' he asked her.

'A brother who lives in South Africa with his wife and their three children. My father took early retirement and my parents normally spend the winter months in South Africa with Jamie and his family and summer at home in Scotland.'

'You're not from Rye-on-Averton? What brought you there?'

'Beth, my partner. Her godmother lives in the town and she suggested to Beth that there was an excellent business opportunity for us there. She was quite right. The shop is beginning to pick up well, and I've had several commissions, but, best of all, the way we divide things between us leaves me enough time to work on my own designs and to accept freelance stuff as well.'

'All in all, a good partnership.'

'Yes, it is,' Kelly agreed tersely. She didn't want Brough to start asking her too many questions about Beth. She had no idea whether or not he knew that Julian had been on the point of getting engaged to Beth when Eve had come into his life, and she could well imagine just what kind of assumptions Brough would make.

Unnervingly, though, he seemed to follow the direction of her thoughts because he suddenly said, 'You've said that Cox is an old friend of yours, but I get the impression from what you've just told me that your business hasn't been established very long.'

'Our accountant told us when we first started that it took three years to establish whether or not a business was going to succeed,' Kelly responded cagily.

She hated having to behave like this, she admitted. According to her family, one of her faults was that she was, at times, almost painfully honest. Prevarication of any kind was anathema to her. So why on earth had she ever allowed Dee to persuade her to adopt a role which even one minute's reflection would have told her was going to be so alien to her that it would be almost impossible to sustain? Because Dee had caught her at a weak and emotional moment, that was why.

Dee, as Kelly was fast coming to appreciate, possessed the dual gift of a very shrewd insight into people's weak points plus an ability to turn them to her own advantage. Not that she could help liking the other woman. She was, intrinsically, a very nice person. Kelly was well aware of the fact that the rent they were being charged was far less than the going amount Dee could have asked for for such a prime site, and then there had been all those little extras she had thrown in. Her concern for them had been almost sisterly and protective in many ways, and Kelly knew that they would never have made the progress they had made without Dee's help, both overt and covert. She had lost count, for instance, of the number of people who had come into the shop commenting that Dee had recommended it to them.

But that still didn't absolve her from the fact that she had deliberately used a moment of weakness to persuade Kelly into a deceit which was becoming, hourly, more stressful to maintain.

Desperate to change the subject, she asked Brough, 'Do you manage to see much of your grandmother?'

'Not as much as I'd like,' Brough admitted. 'Either

Eve or I try to get down to see her at least once a month. As it happens, we're going down the weekend after next; if you'd care to come with us you'd be more than welcome. In fact, it might actually be a good idea; that way you could see the teaset *in situ*, so to speak.'

Go with them...on a family visit...to see his grandmother?

Kelly opened her mouth and then closed it again.

'Oh, I couldn't,' she protested finally. 'There's...'

'The shop; I know,' Brough responded for her.

Had she imagined it or had that really been a note of almost cynical irony in his voice as he shot her a brief sideways glance?

It was impossible... *Anna would always stand in for you...* Hurriedly she closed her mind to the tempting little voice that was reminding her that Anna had made a point of telling her that she was more than willing to take charge of the shop during Beth's absence should Kelly want some time off.

And Brough was right in saying that it would be helpful for her to see the whole of the teaset—when she would already have had the benefit of the archivist's records.

No. No. It was completely impossible, and besides, Brough was quite obviously relieved that she hadn't accepted his invitation, because he had made no attempt to press the matter or persuade her to re-think her decision.

'The last time I drove up here I found a decent pub in a village just off the motorway at the next turn-off. Unlike you, I'm afraid I do need the odd "comfort stop",' he informed her dryly as he swung the car over from the fast lane of the motorway.

Rural Warwickshire was a part of the country with

which Kelly was relatively unfamiliar, and she couldn't quite suppress a small gasp of pleasure as they left the motorway access roundabout and Brough took an exit onto a pretty country road. Farmland stretched to either side of them, and in the distance Kelly could see the gleam of water where a river made its way between tree-lined banks.

The village, which lay concealed just beyond the brow of the hill, was reached via a meandering road which wound down to a cluster of cottages, some of which were thatched, set around a tranquil duck pond.

'Good heavens,' Kelly marvelled as Brough drove in under an archway to the rear of a pub which could quite easily have featured in a film set for a Dickens novel. 'Why on earth isn't this place swamped with tourists? It's almost too perfect...'

'It's an estate village,' Brough explained. 'Originally all the houses, like the land, were owned by the same family, but apparently when the last Earl died the new one, his grandson, decided to sell off the houses, but only to tenants who had family connections with the village.'

The pub was as quaint inside as it looked outside, and there was even a large marmalade cat sitting on an armchair in front of the empty fire.

The coffee room was cosy and prettily furnished, with windows overlooking a paved patio area filled with tubs of flowers.

When the coffee came, it arrived in a large cafetière with, Kelly noted with approval, a choice of both milk and cream—proper milk and proper cream in jugs, not fiddly little plastic containers—and there were even crisp, deliciously scented cinnamon biscuits to go with it.

As she poured herself a cup, Kelly couldn't help but notice how pleasantly Brough spoke to the waitress who had brought in the coffee for them, his manner exactly right, and she was not surprised when the girl gave him a genuinely warm smile before she left.

Kelly had only eaten out with Julian once when, by accident, she had bumped into him and Beth at a local wine bar and he had insisted on her joining them. His attitude then towards the young boy serving them had made her cringe with embarrassment and anger, and she had been unable to look Beth in the eye as she'd wondered how on earth she managed to put up with Julian's arrogant, overbearing attitude.

Kelly might be a thoroughly modern woman, but she still believed that there was a place and a need in her modern world for good manners from both sexes, and she couldn't help feeling not just a warm sense of approval for Brough's behaviour but, far more alarmingly, an additional feeling of pleasure and female pride at being with him and guessing that the waitress thought she was fortunate to be accompanied by him.

'More coffee?' Brough asked her ten minutes later when she had finished her first cup. Regretfully, Kelly shook her head. From the window she could see the river and the pathway that lay enticingly alongside it and, as though he had guessed what she was thinking, Brough commented, 'I thought we could stop here on the way back, perhaps have a bite to eat and a walk round the village, if that appeals to you.'

What could Kelly say? After his earlier display of good manners, the last thing she wanted to do was to appear gauche and ill-mannered by refusing such a pleasantly phrased invitation. It surprised her a little to discover how much she was enjoying this unexpected state of harmony which had arisen between them. When he was not cross-questioning her about Julian Cox, Brough could be very relaxing to be with.

Relaxing…? Who on earth was she kidding? Kelly asked herself a little grimly five minutes later as she checked her appearance in the ladies' cloakroom and reapplied her lipstick. If she was so relaxed then what, pray, were those goose feathers, those distinctive flutters of sensation she could feel giddying around inside her? Those sharp little darts of sensation, of reaction and warning, which kept zipping along her nervous system. If this was relaxed then she would hate to know how it felt to be really on edge in the presence of the man, she derided herself mockingly.

Admit it, she cautioned herself as she replaced the top on her lipstick, he's one very sexy man! So what? She had met sexy men before.

Met them, yes, but reacted to them in the way she was reacting to Brough, no! This was crazy, she told herself sternly. She didn't even like him. Look at how angry he had made her… Look at the things he had said to her…done to her… That kiss for instance…

Hastily Kelly looked away from the mirror and the sudden unexpected pout of her freshly lipsticked mouth.

'Okay?' Brough asked her when she rejoined him in the coffee room. The smile he gave her did uncomfortable things to her heart, causing it to somersault upwards, forwards and then backwards, leaving her breathless and slightly flushed.

'Fine,' she told him crisply, adding in a voice that was designed to show him that so far as she was concerned this was simply a business exercise and that the only thing on her mind was business, 'How long will it take us to get there?'

'Not much longer now,' Brough answered her as they made their way back to the car.

Their destination was familiar to Kelly from the time she had worked there, and as the factory gates came in sight a small, slightly rueful half-tender smile curled her mouth as she reflected on the nervous excitement of the girl she had been when she had first walked through that entrance.

'Nothing ever quite approximates the feeling of earning one's first wage packet, does it?' Brough asked her softly as they drove through the gates. 'I can remember just exactly how it felt to hold *my* first paper-round money in my hand...'

As they shared a look of mutually amused laughter his expression suddenly changed, sobering and clouding slightly.

'It concerns and grieves me that so many of our young people today will never experience the sense of self-esteem earning one's own money brings. We're in danger of creating a society of "haves" and "have nots", not merely in the material sense but in the sense of *owning* one's self-respect and self-worth which, so far as I am concerned, is almost as basic a human need as our need for air to breathe and food to eat. Like love, a strong sense of self cannot be quantified, analysed or bought, but without it our lives are empty and unfulfilled.'

His thoughts, so in tune with her own, made Kelly shiver a little as his words touched a chord within her.

It left her feeling dizzy, disorientated, as though she had somehow strayed off her normal familiar terrain, the feeling both exhilarating and frightening. The thought of what might have been had things been different trembled through her mind. That kind of bond was so rare, so precious, so...so unthinkable and impossible, she warned herself as Brough parked the car and told her mundanely, 'We're here.'

CHAPTER SEVEN

'YOU'RE very quiet. Not having second thoughts, I hope.'

They were on their way back to Rye-on-Averton, the original late-morning meeting with the archivist having turned into a full tour of the factory in addition to an inspection of its archive records, followed by an early dinner as the archivist, delighted to find a fellow enthusiast, had insisted on showing them both some examples of some of the company's rarest pieces as well as advising Kelly on just how she might best mix and colour her paints to achieve an authentic antique tone.

'Not second thoughts about wanting to do the work, just worrying about getting the paint right,' Kelly told him ruefully.

'Mmm...I must admit I hadn't realised that modern paint colours wouldn't be suitable,' Brough acknowledged. 'It's certainly a fascinating and complex business.'

'Yes,' Kelly agreed. 'I thought I knew most of what there was to know about the history of British porcelain, but listening to Frank today I realise just how wrong I was and how little I do know.'

'Mmm...I could see how thrilled he was to be able to talk with you.'

'Well, he certainly couldn't have been more helpful. But, as he says, there really isn't any substitute for seeing the rest of the teaset at first hand for ensuring that I get the colour matches right.'

'It isn't too late to change your mind about coming with us on our next visit,' Brough said.

'I...I'll have to think about it...' Kelly told him.

The evening was already turning to dusk. They had left Staffordshire just before eight o'clock. Frank Bowers had insisted on taking them out to dinner and Brough had taken her to one side after Frank had delivered his half-hesitant invitation, to say quietly to her, 'If it doesn't conflict with any other plans you may have made, I think we should accept. He's plainly enjoyed the opportunity to talk about his work—and I know we did talk about stopping off at the Lion and Swan for a meal and a walk along the river on the way back, but I should hate to disappoint Frank...'

'I agree,' Kelly had responded instantly, and they'd both returned to where Frank was putting away the company records.

'Yes, I understand you'll need to think about the weekend visit,' Brough was telling her cordially now as he swung the car out into the fast lane of the motorway. 'I should hate to interfere with any private plans you might have.'

It was the emphasis on the word 'private' that made Kelly glance warily at him. Was he trying to insinuate that he suspected her of hesitating in accepting the invitation to visit his grandmother because she was either planning to see Julian Cox or hoping to see him? It seemed that, with their return to Rye-on-Averton imminent, the cessation of hostilities between them was over.

Very well, if that was the way he wanted things, she decided hardly, suppressing the unwanted quiver of disappointment that sharpened almost to an actual pang of pain.

'I'm not sure just what you're trying to suggest,' she told him frostily, 'but the *main* reason I can't give you a yes or a no at this stage is because I need to find someone to take charge of the shop for me. *You* may be able to walk away from your business commitments for a whole weekend—I'm afraid that I can't.'

'I'm sorry,' Brough returned equally formally and coolly. 'Forgive me, but I had assumed that since this commission *was* business...'

Immediately hot colour burned a mortified flush up her throat and over her face.

'I realise that,' she retorted stiffly, and of course she did, even if very briefly earlier in the day she had momentarily forgotten.

But, in truth, hadn't there been a few brief but oh, so telling occasions during the day when the sharp line that in the past had always divided her professional life from her personal one had become dangerously blurred—when she had looked at Brough, compelled to do so by something he had said, only to find that it was not the client she was seeing but the man?

And what a man!

Kelly groaned in dismay, lashed by a delicate shiver of sexual awareness. This wasn't what she wanted, what she needed in her life right now.

Her reaction to Brough would have unnerved her even without the added complication of the situation with Julian Cox. When she added to that the already highly combustible mixture of anger and attraction she felt towards Brough, the dangerous extra ingredient of emotional awareness and longing she was confronted with became a potentially lethal cocktail which she knew could destroy her if she wasn't careful. After all, put together all those ingredients and the result was as dangerous as some magical, mystical sorcerer's potion, because the result was quite simply love. And Brough was the last person she could ever allow herself to love. He didn't like her now, so what on earth was he going to feel about her when he discovered—as discover he surely must—that she was deliberately trying to take Julian away from his sister?

She could try telling him, of course, that her motives were truly altruistic, but somehow she doubted that he would believe her, that he would even want to believe her.

'Tired?'

The unexpected concern in his voice brought a small, anguished lump to her throat. Unable to reply without betraying her emotion, she shook her head.

'It's been a long day,' Brough told her, adding ruefully, 'I must admit I had no idea of the complexity of the task I was asking you to take on when I first approached you.'

'It will be a challenge,' Kelly admitted, relieved to be back on a safer subject. 'But I am looking forward to it. My biggest worry is that your grandmother is going to be disappointed. The teaset must mean so much to her... When Frank showed us those jugs this afternoon, which had been in the same family for six generations, and he told us how much each generation had to reinsure them at, it really brought it home to me that it isn't the material value that means so much but the fact that they represent a part of a family no longer there in person, a piece of very personal history...memories...'

'Yes,' Brough agreed soberly. 'I can see from the look in Nan's eyes when she touches her teaset that it's Gramps she's thinking about.'

A little enviously Kelly wondered what it must be like

to have experienced such love, and to still be able to warm oneself by its embers.

What was Brough's grandmother like? What had his grandfather been like? Brough? Her heart gave a small, uneven thump. In thirty years from now Brough could be a grandfather himself. Her heart gave another, even more uneven thud, and then a series of short, frantic, accelerating mini-beats as she contemplated her own future. In thirty years from now how would she feel when she looked back on today? Would the sharp ache of newly discovered love for Brough she had recognised today have dulled to nothing more than a dim memory, or would she be looking back in sadness and regret for what had never been?

They were almost home now, the lights of the town shining in the valley ahead of them as Brough turned off the motorway. Kelly sat in silence beside him as he drove through the quiet streets towards the shop. Rye-on-Averton was a genteel town, its residents either middle-aged or retired in the main. Its wine bars and restaurants, though, were well patronised, as were the shows put on by the excellent local amateur dramatic and operatic societies.

'I'll come up with you,' Kelly heard Brough saying as he parked his car outside the shop.

Immediately she shook her head, but Brough was already climbing out of the car.

'It really isn't necessary,' she said as he opened her car door for her.

The flat had its own entrance, and she had already removed the keys in readiness from her bag and was holding them in her hand, but to her chagrin Brough quietly removed them from her grasp.

'I know this is a relatively crime-free and safe area,

but I'm afraid my grandmother's influence means that I would feel I had failed in my male duty if I didn't see you safely inside.'

So he was only acting out of duty. What had she imagined? she derided herself as she walked silently towards the rear entrance of the flat. That he was insisting on seeing her inside because he wanted to delay the moment when he parted from her for as long as he could? How utterly ridiculous. He probably couldn't wait to see the back of her.

'It's this way,' she told him unnecessarily, indicating the rear ground-floor door.

Stepping past her, Brough inserted the key in the lock and then opened the door for her.

'Thank you...' Kelly started to say as she stepped past him, but it seemed he still did not consider his duty to be fully done, because he shook his head and stepped into the small hallway with her, glancing towards the stairs as he did so.

'Would you like me to come up with you and look around?' he asked her politely.

Immediately, Kelly shook her head.

In the hallway on a small console table was one of the first pieces of china she had painted. She saw Brough looking at it.

'One of your pieces?' he asked her.

'Yes,' she told him. 'The inspiration for it came to me when I was on holiday in South Africa with my family.'

The piece, all greens and blues and surf-whites, always made her think of the magnificence of the Cape's beaches. Such a dramatically beautiful country with such a horrifically cruel history. She touched the curving contours of the piece of china with gentle fingers. It held many happy memories—days when she had played with her brother's children, running in and out of the surf with them, evenings when she had strolled along the beach with her parents and her brother and his wife. Very happy memories. She shuddered a little to imagine what they would think of her current involvement with Julian Cox.

'Are you cold?' Brough asked her, frowning slightly and taking a step towards her just as Kelly, too, stepped forward, away from the table.

Automatically, she put her hand out to prevent them bumping into one another as she shook her head in response to his question, but unwisely, as she did so, her gaze was drawn to his face and then his mouth.

The shape of it had been tantalising her all day—the sharp masculine cut of it, the sensual fullness of his lower lip, the dangerous and somehow illicit knowledge she had of just how it felt to have it moving on her own.

Now, just when she knew she needed to be at her coolest and most in control, her breathing had become erratic, her pulses racing, her pupils betraying the surge of feminine longing that was overpowering her.

Her brain begged her body to behave sensibly, her eyes to break contact, her breathing to slow down and become properly measured, but her senses had become flagrantly disobedient.

Very slowly Kelly lifted her gaze from Brough's mouth to his eyes. It was like gazing into deep waters, so cool that they made her body tremble as though she had touched ice, and yet so hot that her bones felt as though they were going to melt. Every sense she possessed, every centimetre of flesh covering her body, suddenly seemed to have become a thousand times more sensitive than normal, a thousand times more receptive.

She could hear Brough breathing, feel the heat of each breath he drew against her skin, sensing even the tension that coiled like fine wire through his body, feeling just what was burning through him as she gave herself up to the dark blaze of passion she could see in his eyes.

Her body swayed towards him, seeking his strength and offering in return the promise of her own pliant responsiveness, the instinctive age-old body language of woman to man, yielding and promising, whilst at the same time demanding that he show that he had the strength, the manhood, to take up the challenge she was offering and to protect her weakness.

'Brough.' She whispered his name, her eyes heavy-lidded, mysterious, luminous with passion as she turned her face up to his, an enchantress, powerful and strong. Irresistible.

And yet she still placed her hands flat against his chest, as though to deny the promise in her eyes and the desire running through her body, heavy and hot as molten gold.

She could feel his arms wrapping around her, enfolding her, as he drew her close, so close that her hand could feel the wild, fierce, heady drumming of his heartbeat, fast and furious as a cheetah during the chase. Boldly Kelly kept her eyes open. His were hot, dark, deep, glittering with male arousal.

Once again she looked at his mouth, a wild thrill of elation gripping her body. Now she was the hunter, her body tight, coiled, waiting...hungry.

Their mouths met, hers wanton, responsive, and yet at the same time soft and waiting. Brough was kissing her, sliding his hands up over her back, caressing her over and over again, his body hard and powerful against hers. Her own body felt molten and plain, reminding her of glass before it was shaped and blown, liquid running free, waiting to be formed and shaped, a wild natural element that could be coaxed but never forced.

Brough's hands were on her shoulders, gripping them hard as his tongue searched her lips for an opening. Eagerly she gave it to him, her own nails digging into the long muscles of his back.

She was experiencing a wildness within herself, a sensuality she had never encountered before, and it both exhilarated and terrified her. Beneath her clothes her breasts ached and peaked. No need for Brough to even lightly caress them to arouse her need for him, but when he did—!

Was that really her making that low, hungry, almost semi-tortured sound deep down in her throat? Was that Brough growling in fierce exultation beneath his own breath as his thumb-pad returned demandingly to caress and probe the taut peak of her nipple?

She wanted him. Wanted him...wanted him so badly. Wanted to feel his body, his skin, next to hers, his touch, his love...

Kelly made an urgent keening noise deep in her throat, her body arching against Brough's in a sexual mixture of longing and pleasure.

Somehow all the barriers there had been between them, all her doubts and fears, her refusal to believe that it was possible for her to feel like this, for her to love like this, so immediately, so intensely, so unexpectedly were banished, vaporised by the sheer force of her feelings.

Now, here in his arms, she was all feeling, yearning, loving woman, her natural female instincts overturning the conditioning of modern society and its demands. As boldly as some long-ago ancestor might have done, she was recognising and claiming for her own her man and her right to love him.

'Brough.' She whispered his name throatily, a husky purr of aroused pleasure, heavy with sensuous promise shot through with love.

'You feel so good. I want you so much…' Was that *her* saying that, or was it Brough? Was *she* the one reaching for him or was he the initiator of their increasingly passionate caresses? The shadowy confines of the hallway, normally surely the last place she would have ever thought of as romantic, now seemed as private and protected as the most secret of sanctuaries. And it was a dizzying, tantalising thought to know that not so very far beyond its closed door lay her bedroom—her bed.

Her whole body shuddered as it wantonly followed where her thoughts were leading, where she already ached for Brough to lead her. A feeling of the most incandescent joy filled her; a sense of throwing off the past and turning to welcome the future and their love made her feel as though suddenly something unacknowledged deep within her had sprung to life, as though the person she had been before the wonderful, miraculous discovery that she loved Brough had been someone who was only half alive, someone who had been deprived of the true pleasures and meaning of life.

'I don't want you to go…'

As she murmured the words against Brough's mouth she could feel him start to tense; his mouth left her throat, which he had been kissing and nibbling, sending a cascade of tiny erotic shivers all the way from the top of her head to her toes.

'I don't want to either,' he whispered back as his thumb caressed her throat and then her jaw, slowly moving towards her mouth. 'But I must. I'm expecting a call from Hong Kong—I had some business dealings there, which I've sold out of, but there are still some legal ends I need to tie up. And tomorrow I have to go to London to see my accountants. But when I come back…'

As he turned away he paused and then turned back, taking hold of her hand and urging her gently towards him.

'Thank you…' he told her softly.

'For what?' she managed to ask him in a shaky voice.

'For today…and this…and you…' he told her throatily as he bent to place a soft kiss on her half-parted lips.

For *her*… For a moment Kelly felt close to tears. There was so much more about her that he still didn't know. So much that she still had to tell him—especially… But now, when he was on the point of leaving, wasn't the time to start explaining about Julian and Beth.

'I know you're only being like this because you're worried about how much I'm going to charge you for the teaset,' she told him teasingly and a little chokily.

'Aha…so you've seen through my dastardly plot, then,' Brough responded in the same vein.

Suddenly anxious, she clung to him and whispered, 'Oh, Brough, it's all so new, so unexpected. I don't…'

'It's perfect…*you're* perfect,' Brough assured her as he tightened his arms around her and cradled her head against his shoulder. '*We* are going to be perfect…together… Right now, there's nothing I want more than to stay here with you.'

He looked betrayingly towards the inner doorway to the flat and, guessing what he was thinking, Kelly quickly reassured him. 'I know and I understand. You've got your responsibilities, and anyway, perhaps… Everything's happened so quickly, so…'

'I'll call you the moment I get back from London,' Brough promised her huskily.

'There's so much I haven't told you,' Kelly protested as he started to release her.

'Such as?' Brough grinned. 'I've already discovered for myself all that I need to know, and what I have discovered, what I do know...I love...'

'Oh, Brough...'

It was impossible not to throw herself back into his arms and share another passionate kiss with him, and then he was gone, leaving her to touch her fingertips to a mouth that still tingled from the passion of his kiss and to acknowledge with a small, cold shiver that he was wrong, that there were things that he still had to learn.

Would it change what he thought, what he felt, when he learned of her deceit, or would he understand and accept that her deliberate pursuit of Julian had been prompted by loyalty to Beth?

CHAPTER EIGHT

'So you do understand, Dee, don't you?' Kelly asked the older woman anxiously as they sat opposite one another in Kelly's flat.

Kelly had telephoned Dee as soon as Brough had left, despite the fact that it was late evening. The disquiet she had experienced over the role she was playing *vis-à-vis* Julian had coalesced following Brough's departure into a sharp and intense need to free herself from the restrictions that her commitment to Dee's plans were placing on her. There was no way she wanted to deceive Brough, and there was certainly no way she could even pretend now to be anything other than totally revolted by Julian Cox.

'I think so,' Dee confirmed dryly. 'You're telling me that you've fallen in love with Brough Frobisher and that because of that you don't want to carry out your part of our scheme.'

'It isn't that I don't *want* to,' Kelly corrected her quietly, 'it's that I *can't*; and even before I realised how I felt about Brough... I'm not trying to be dramatic, Dee, but there's something about Julian I just don't trust.'

'Join the club,' Dee told her sardonically. 'I don't want to cast a shadow over love's sweet dream, Kelly, and you're certainly old enough and I believe mature enough to be the best judge of your own feelings, but Brough is Eve's brother, and he *does* have a vested interest in monitoring your relationship with Julian therefore.'

Kelly looked at her for several seconds before asking her sternly, 'What are you trying to say? That Brough is deliberately and callously pretending to…to care about me because he wants to leave his sister with a clear field to Julian Cox?'

'No. What I'm *trying* to say is that you would be well advised and wise to be aware that things are not perhaps as straightforward as they could be, that people do have hidden motives and personal agendas for what they do. After all, on the face of it, so far as Brough is concerned, he has a potential rival for your love in Julian, hasn't he?'

'I wanted to explain to him but I just didn't have the chance, and then I decided that I owed it to you to let you know what I intended to do first,' Kelly told her quickly.

She had found it extremely unsettling and disturbing listening to what Dee had to say. Dee was wrong, of course; Brough would never do anything like that… Would he?

'I know you must feel that I'm letting you down,' Kelly told Dee quietly.

'I'm disappointed, yes,' Dee acknowledged, 'but I *do* understand. I have been in love myself, you know, and I do—' She broke off, and to Kelly's surprise she saw that the older girl's face was slightly flushed.

Why?

Dee was only thirty, and what could be more natural, after all, than that she should have experienced falling in love?

'I can't pretend that I don't wish you'd change your mind,' Dee continued honestly, 'but at least Julian seems to be biting on the bait so far as Anna is concerned. Anna was able to ''accidentally' bump into him at yesterday's mayoral function, and vaguely mentioned that she had recently received rather a large sum of money from an insurance policy which had matured and that she was looking for somewhere to invest it with a view to making the maximum amount of profit.'

'You do realise, don't you,' Kelly said a little uncomfortably, 'that I'm going to have to say *something* to Brough about our...about what we planned?'

Dee's eyebrows rose.

'Dear me, it *is* love, isn't it?' she acknowledged dryly. 'I appreciate what you're saying, Kelly,' she responded firmly, 'but I would at least ask you to keep my part in our plans to a discreet minimum. I'm sure your Brough isn't one to tittle-tattle or gossip, but I *do* have a certain position within our local community and I wouldn't want our plans bruited about.

'I personally believe that Julian Cox deserves all that we planned for him and more, that what we intended to do doesn't come to even one tenth of the punishment he deserves, but I have to be honest and admit that there *are* people who might take a very different view, and I certainly don't want to be judged as some sort of melodramatic woman, bent on exacting revenge for some imagined slight...'

'Oh, I'm sure Brough would never think that,' Kelly assured her, so quick to defend her beloved.

'Maybe,' Dee acknowledged, 'but others might.'

'Well, if you prefer it, I could simply say that we'd all agreed that Julian needed to be taught a lesson,' Kelly offered.

'I thought that was what we *had* all agreed,' Dee commented wryly as she stood up.

'One thing that does still worry me,' Kelly told her

as she followed her to the flat door, 'and that's Eve, Brough's sister. She's desperately in love with Julian...'

'And he, by all accounts, is still desperate to secure her—if he can't get you,' Dee concluded. 'I certainly don't envy you *that* relationship, Kelly...Julian Cox as your brother-in-law by marriage.'

'Oh, no, don't say that,' Kelly pleaded with her. 'He'd make Eve so dreadfully unhappy. Maybe I should try to talk to her, warn her...tell her what he did to Beth.'

'Do you think she would listen?' Dee asked her doubtfully. 'Julian's told so many lies, it might be hard to convince her.'

'I've only met her a couple of times,' Kelly said, 'but she strikes me as someone who would think deeply about the situation if we put it to her.'

'Mmm... You and Harry both. He's been singing her praises to me ever since the night of the ball. When are you seeing Brough again, by the way?'

'I don't know. He's going to London on business in the morning, but he said he'd get in touch just as soon as he could.'

'Goodnight, then,' Dee told her as she opened the flat door and stepped out into the fresh air.

Dee had parked her car quite close to the shop, but instead of going directly to it she chose, instead, to walk in the opposite direction through the town and down towards the river.

The walk along the river path had been one of her favourites as a girl. It had been her route home from school and, later on when she had gone to university, it had been one of the first places she had headed for on her return home.

Her family had lived in the area for many generations;

her mother had died shortly after Dee's birth and her father, older than her mother by some eighteen years, had died just before Dee was about to take her degree.

She had returned home to sort out his affairs and to discover that she was an extremely wealthy young woman.

One of the first things she had done with her money had been to make a large, interest-free loan to her uncle in order to enable him to modernise the family farm and buy more land.

Her own father, his brother, had sold his share of the family farmland as a young man, preferring to deal and speculate in the commodities market rather than follow the custom of his forebears, and it had seemed to Dee to be a good memorial to him that she should help her uncle to buy back the land he had sold away from the family. The two brothers had never quarrelled over his decision, and had always got on amicably for two such very, very different people, but Dee, who had inherited her father's intelligence, knew that it was becoming increasingly difficult for small farmers to make a decent living and she had seen that there could come a time when her uncle, for financial reasons, would either have to sell up or rent out his lands.

With the rest of the money she had made several donations to local charities, and then amused herself by finding out if she had inherited her father's gift for making the right investment.

It had turned out that she had.

But, at twenty-one, a girl wanted far more from life than a healthy bank balance, and Dee had had all the normal urges and needs of her sex and age—a man to love and love her, the prospect of a relationship that would last a lifetime and one which included commitment, children…love…

And, for all too brief a space of time, while she had been at university, she had thought she had that relationship…that love…*had* thought…but had thought wrongly. Had made the worst, the most disastrous decision of her life, had prejudiced everything she had, everything she was, because of someone who had proved to be so false, so cruelly betraying that even now she still bore the scars.

She stopped walking, shoving her hands deep into the pockets of her lightweight jacket, and stared angrily up towards the stars.

She had waited a long time for this opportunity to turn the tables on Julian Cox, to get him in a position where he was vulnerable and unable to protect himself…as she had once been. Oh, yes, she had been vulnerable…

Fiercely she bit down hard on her bottom lip. She wasn't being vindictive, she was simply exercising her right to have justice, avenging the wrong which had been done to her, and neither were her motives totally selfish. She *had* been concerned for Beth's pain and heartbreak and, despite what Kelly seemed to think, she was aware of the difficult position she had potentially put her in, and of the heartache that Eve could suffer if no one warned her what Julian was.

She had, of course, assumed that Eve would immediately refuse to have anything further to do with Julian once his involvement with Kelly became public knowledge; Brough would have surely insisted on that for his sister's own sake and, from what she knew of him, Brough was certainly a strong enough character to be able to achieve that end.

It was a pity that Kelly had changed her mind, but the

game wasn't over yet, not by a long chalk. One way or another, Dee was determined that Julian Cox was going to make full recompense for the debt he owed her. *Full* recompense...with interest, the interest at the punitively high rate caused by the sheer extent and weight of the emotional anguish and despair she had suffered.

There was no despair like that of suffering a broken heart, destroyed dreams, the complete desolation of a once promising future.

Determinedly, Dee started to head back towards the town centre. It was time for her to go home. Yes, Kelly's decision was going to cause her a problem, but no problem was insurmountable unless you allowed it to be and she, Dee, was certainly not going to do that.

Where was Brough now? Kelly wondered dreamily as she said goodbye to the customer she had just served. In another five minutes she was going to close the shop for the day and then she was going to go upstairs and indulge in the delicious pleasure of curling up in a chair whilst she relived every second of yesterday, and most especially what had happened after Brough had insisted on seeing her safely inside the flat.

Even now she felt as though it couldn't be real, as though she had to keep mentally pinching herself to make sure she wasn't imagining everything.

She *had* felt guilty telling Dee that she couldn't go on with their plans, but wisely Kelly knew that even without the discovery of her love for Brough she would have found it extremely difficult to continue to practise the deceit her role had called for.

Where was Brough? Still in London? On his way back? When would she hear from him...see him... hold him?

She caught her breath as she heard the shop doorbell ring behind her, and out of the corner of her eye she caught the male outline of the person walking in.

'Brough!'

She turned round eagerly, his name on her lips, only to be swept by a surge of disappointment as she recognised that her visitor wasn't Brough but Julian.

'What happened to you last night?' Julian demanded without preamble. 'We had a date...at the wine bar...remember?'

Guiltily Kelly frowned. She had completely forgotten about that, but even if she hadn't... The last person she really wanted to see was Julian Cox, but since he was here she could at least make it abundantly clear to him just where she stood, and, turning away from him so that he couldn't see her face, she managed a dismissive shrug.

'I changed my mind,' she told him carelessly. 'In fact...'

Summoning all her courage, she turned round and announced crisply, 'In fact, Julian, I think it would be best if you didn't try to get in touch with me any more.'

'What are you trying to say?' Julian demanded furiously, his mouth tightening as he stepped in front of her, blocking her exit. She couldn't do this to him. He had got it all planned—Kelly, with her substantial fortune, unfettered by any access restrictions, was a much better proposition than Eve with her trust fund and her brother, and besides, he wanted Kelly. She excited him in a way that the Beths and Eves of this world could never do.

'I'm trying to say that I think we've both made a mistake,' Kelly informed him as diplomatically as she could. 'You are dating someone else...'

'So?' Julian demanded. '*You* didn't seem to consider

that much of a problem the other night at the ball, nor when I rang you up…'

'Maybe not,' Kelly allowed. 'But since then I've had time to think things through… Eve loves you, Julian,' she told him directly.

To her disbelief, instead of looking embarrassed, he smiled triumphantly.

'You're jealous, aren't you?' he challenged her. 'Well, you needn't be. Eve's a child, Kelly, but you're a woman… The things you and I could do…' he promised her thickly. 'You know what I mean. You want them too. I've seen it in your eyes… Eve is a mistake. It's you I want, Kelly.'

Thoroughly revolted, Kelly tried to step back from him, but the hard edge of the counter was behind her, jarring her back. She looked anxiously towards the door, wishing a customer would walk in and put an end to their unwanted privacy. Unwanted on her part, that was. Julian, far from accepting what she had told him, seemed to be trying to be deliberately obtuse, Kelly recognised. Was he really so vain that he didn't realise how much she loathed him? If so, she would simply have to take a stronger line with him.

'Julian, I meant what I said,' she told him firmly. 'I don't want to see you. If I gave you the wrong idea—'

'*If?*' he broke in, his face changing as he understood the forcefulness of her determination. No way could he afford to let her go, he acknowledged inwardly. When he had first met Eve he had not realised just how much control her brother had over her financial affairs. There was no love lost between him and Brough at all.

'You were giving me the green light, Kelly, all the way to your bedroom door. I want you, Kelly, and I intend to have you.'

'No!' Kelly protested, shocked.

'Oh, come on,' he overrode her. 'You want me too; I can see it in your eyes…your mouth…' As he spoke he reached out and pressed his thumb hard against her bottom lip. 'There's no way I'm going to let you go.'

Taken off guard, Kelly immediately tried to push him away, making a sharp sound of distress.

He actually made her feel physically sick, and not just sick but afraid as well, she recognised as she saw the ugly look in his eyes.

'I want you to leave, Julian,' she told him shakily. 'Now…'

'Oh, you do, do you?' he responded aggressively. 'And what if I choose not to? What if *I* choose to make *you* come good on all those sexy promises you've been giving me, Kelly? What are you going to do about it? How are you going to stop me?'

'What you're talking about is sexual harassment,' Kelly told him bravely. 'If you don't stop threatening me and leave straight away, Julian, I shall report you to the police.'

To her dismay, instead of responding as she'd hoped, he threw back his head and laughed.

'Do you think they'd believe you…after the way you've been coming on to me? Get real, Kelly. You're just being hysterical.'

Hysterical—wasn't that what he had accused Beth of being?

Outrage and panic paralysed Kelly, rooting her feet to the floor as she stood trapped in the maniacal beam of his almost colourless, cold eyes.

Julian was a desperate man, she recognised numbly. He was also *enjoying* her fear, feeding off it, not just emotionally, she sensed with increasing, horrified disgust and fear, but physically as well. Oh, please God, let someone come into the shop and save her, she prayed mentally as she fought not to succumb to the awful, fearful heaviness filling her body. To say that she was afraid in no way came even close to describing what she felt. Her whole body had gone icy cold. She knew, she just *knew*, that Julian meant every word he said, that nothing, nothing she could do or say would persuade him to leave. Now, when it was almost too late, she recognised how much she had underestimated how dangerous he really was.

Brough had been delayed in London longer than he had planned. There had been a couple of time-consuming delays in the finalisation of the transaction with Hong Kong. He had been tempted to ring Kelly just as he left the city, but he had wanted to clear his mind of everything to do with his work before he spoke to her again. And besides, when he told her he loved her he wanted to see the look in her eyes, to hear that wonderful female adorable catch in her breath as she looked at him, to know that she felt the same way that he did.

Impossible now to think that he had imagined that first time he had held her in his arms that he was immune to the risk of falling in love—and besides, *what* risk? Loving her was *heaven…paradise…*the fulfilment of his every previously unacknowledged dream.

He would go home, shower and then drive round and see her…surprise her…

So why, having made that decision, did he suddenly, when he was within a hundred yards of his own driveway, suddenly succumb to an almost overpowering sense of urgency, so strong a need, so immediate and intense, that he drove through a set of traffic lights on

amber and broke the speed limit just to get to her. He
drew up several yards away from the flat and got out,
forgetting to lock his car as he strode quickly towards
the shop.

As he approached the door he could see two people
inside. Kelly was standing with her back half turned towards him so that he could only partially see her face,
her head submissively bent towards the man who was
wrapping his arms around her. To anyone else their pose
might have seemed to be that of lovers, but Brough knew
immediately and incontrovertibly that it wasn't love that
was keeping Kelly immobile in Julian Cox's embrace,
but fear. Just *how* he knew it he didn't stop to question
as he pushed open the door and rushed to Kelly's side,
forcibly thrusting Julian away from her. As he did so he
could see not just the relief and shock in her eyes, but
also an anguished pain that cut right to his heart. His
love, his darling, felt shamed by the fact that she was
being attacked by...

He could quite happily have slowly roasted Julian Cox
over a very, very hot fire, just for that act of violation
alone—he, a man of peace and logic. Brough could see
the fury and the fear in the other man's eyes, and the
urge to punish him, hurt and frighten him, as well as
release his own fury against him, was so strong that for
a second Brough was almost tempted to give in to it.

But over Julian's shoulder he could see where Kelly
was standing, white-faced, her eyes blank with shock,
and instead he released Julian and told him in disgust,
'Get out of here before I give in to the temptation to
forget that non-violence is the making of a truly intelligent man.'

'You've got it all wrong...' Julian started to whine as
he backed towards the door. 'She's the one who's to

blame, not me. She's the one who's been leading me on, coming on to me,' he started to protest, but Brough had heard enough. Grabbing hold of his collar, he virtually marched him to the door and opened it, pushing him through it.

'If I find out you've so much as even tried to speak to her again, I promise you you're going to regret it,' he told Julian in a steely voice.

As Brough locked the door he turned towards Kelly. She was still standing motionless, her face grey-white, her eyes huge and unfocused. *She* was his prime concern now. He could talk to her later, find out later just what had been going on and why Cox had been terrorising her.

At the back of his mind as he walked towards Kelly lay the knowledge that he was now going to have to take very firm action over Julian's relationship with his sister, but right now Kelly was his only priority.

'Kelly... It's all right, my darling, he's gone, you're safe...'

As she heard Brough's familiar, warm voice, Kelly turned her head and looked towards him, towards him but not at him. How could she? How could she *ever* come to terms with the pain, the humiliation, the defilement of what she had just experienced? Julian's verbal attack on her, his threatened assault on her, had left her feeling totally physically shocked and degraded. The thought passed through her mind that if this was how *she* felt how on earth did rape victims feel? How did *they* cope? Julian's abuse of her had come nowhere close to anything like that...

'Come on...I'm taking you upstairs...' she heard Brough telling her. Desperately she struggled to get back to normality, her always keen sense of responsibility reminding her of her duties.

'I can't—the shop,' she began to protest, but Brough overruled her.

'The shop is closed,' he told her firmly, adding more gently, 'You're in shock, my love; there's no way you can work. You need...' He paused and started to frown. 'Who is your GP? I think perhaps that...'

Immediately Kelly shook her head.

'No, no, I'm fine...' Her bottom lip started to tremble. 'Honestly, Brough, I will be fine,' she told him in a thready voice. 'I don't need... I don't want... It was my own fault,' she told him huskily, dropping her head so that he couldn't look into her eyes and see the truth she felt must be clear there. 'I shouldn't have—'

'You shouldn't have what?' Brough interrupted her immediately and fiercely. 'You shouldn't have let him in? No way was it your fault, Kelly. I *saw* what was going on... There was *no way* you were inviting or enjoying what was going to happen.'

The sureness in his voice, the conviction, the trust and the love were too much for Kelly's fragile composure. Hot tears filled her eyes and started to roll down her face as she shook her head.

'Oh, no, please, my love, don't cry,' Brough begged her with a small groan. 'I shouldn't have let him walk away from this... The police...'

'No...no, please. I don't want anything like that,' Kelly protested sharply. 'I just want to forget about it, Brough... I just want...'

She started to tremble violently, reaction setting in as the realisation of what had happened swamped her.

'Come on, I'm taking you up to your flat,' Brough

told her masterfully, holding her gently by the arm and leading her towards the door.

Five minutes later she was standing in her own small kitchen drinking the fortifying mug of coffee Brough had just made her, liberally laced with brandy. She could feel the strong spirit going straight to her head, relaxing her both physically and emotionally, releasing her from the rigid self control she had been exercising ever since Julian Cox had walked into the shop.

'Brough, Julian wanted...' she began huskily, suddenly desperately anxious to tell him everything, to explain to him what she had been doing and why, but before she could finish what she had been about to say she suddenly became very dizzy.

Immediately Brough reached for her, rescuing the half-empty mug she had been about to drop, gathering her in his arms as he told her gruffly, 'I know *exactly* what Cox wanted... He's gone, Kelly. You're safe—forget about him...'

'No, you don't understand,' Kelly protested, but it was impossible to keep on trying to form rational thoughts and make difficult and painful explanations when Brough was holding her so tightly, one hand stroking her hair whilst the other tilted up her chin so that he could look down into her eyes.

'I should *never* have gone home and left you last night,' he whispered rawly to her. 'I certainly didn't want to...'

'*I* didn't want you to either,' Kelly admitted bravely, adding tremulously, 'Oh, Brough, I wanted you to stay so much, but...I still can't quite believe all this is happening...that you and I... It frightens me a little,' she admitted, her tongue as well as her self-control loosened by the potent mixture of shock and alcohol. 'I've never been in love before, never wanted... Loving someone means risking that they might hurt you and—'

'I could *never* hurt you, Kelly,' Brough interrupted her to tell her passionately. 'And I know that you would never hurt me.'

'How *can* you know that?' Kelly protested nervously. 'Brough, there's so much about me that you don't know...'

'Mmm...so much about you that I still have to discover...' Brough agreed softly as his lips started to caress her willing mouth.

'Brough...' Kelly whispered, but it was only a token protest. There was nothing she wanted more than to be held like this by him, kissed like this by him, unless it was to lie naked in bed with him, his body her only covering, his hands caressing her, leaving hers free to explore him...

'Mmm...well, if you're sure that's what you want, I'm certainly not going to argue with you,' she heard Brough saying hoarsely as he gently stepped back from her and turned her to face the kitchen door, and it was only then that Kelly realised that what she had thought were her most private and unspoken thoughts she had in fact spoken out loud to him.

'Oh, Brough...'

Her face pink, she looked helplessly at him, but far from being shocked by the desires and wishes she had expressed he was looking at her as though...as though... Kelly felt her heartbeat start to pick up. Suddenly she was finding it extraordinarily difficult to breathe properly; suddenly her mind was full of the most extraordinarily detailed and sensual images of them both together; suddenly she couldn't wait to make those private wanton thoughts a reality.

It took them almost ten minutes to reach the bedroom, primarily because Brough insisted on stopping virtually every foot of the way to hold her and kiss her and tell her that she was the most wonderful, the most wanted thing that had ever happened to him.

'I never imagined you could be like this,' Kelly breathed in ecstatic pleasure as the look in his eyes confirmed that he meant every romantic word he was saying to her. 'When we first met, you seemed so disapproving…so…'

'So desperately afraid of revealing to you just how totally and completely I'd fallen for you,' Brough admitted softly as he cupped her face and very slowly started to kiss her.

Dizzily Kelly clung to him. They were in her bedroom now, and Brough was very carefully, but *very* thoroughly and determinedly, starting to remove her clothing whilst continuing to kiss her with a passion which caused her heartbeat to slow to a sensuously heavy thud and her body to melt into eager compliance and longing.

This was not how it was meant to be for a modern nineties woman. *She* was supposed to take her own initiative, remove her *own* clothes and expect her lover to remove his with equally mature independence, and when a modern woman did make love it was an open-eyed, clear-minded 'I know what I'm doing and why' thing. Wasn't it?

So *why* was she, who considered herself to be such a thoroughly modern woman, simply standing there, not merely allowing Brough to dictate the pace of their lovemaking but positively *yearning* for him to do so? *Why* was she experiencing this unfamiliar, heady sense of pleasure and excitement, of anticipation and, yes, just a tiny thread of nervousness as well, at the thought of what lay ahead? Why, much as she wanted him, ached for him, *loved* him, did she actually want *him* to be the one, initially at least, to show her how much he loved and wanted her?

Because she loved him enough to do so! Because she trusted him enough! Because there was, after all, something inalienably sweet and precious about admitting, *allowing* herself to be so vulnerably female in his presence, in being able, for the first time since childhood, to acknowledge a need for another person, for their love…their touch…

'Brough…'

She shivered in delicious pleasure as he slid her top away from her body and then gently unclipped her bra, freeing her breasts to his gaze and the softness of the air against them. As she felt and saw her nipples peak into hard, excited, aroused nubs of flesh, Kelly knew immediately what was responsible for their arousal—or rather who. It wasn't cold in her bedroom and, anyway, she undressed in here every night without her body reacting like this.

'Beautiful…beautiful…' Brough murmured thickly as he reached out and gently traced the curve of one breast, brushing its softness with his finger, the lightest of light touches, and yet it was enough to send a sensuous shudder of sensation curling through her entire body.

'Beautiful,' Brough repeated as he bent his head and, cupping her breast very carefully, kissed one erect nipple and then the other, and then repeated the whole process again and then again, and each time his mouth returned to graze and suckle on one swollen point the other ached jealously for the loss of the delicious pressure of his mouth against it.

'Brough…'

Heavy-eyed, Kelly bent her head towards him, leaning its weight on his downbent shoulder. Beneath her cheek she could feel the fabric of his shirt. Quickly she started to pull it free of his waistband, making a little frustrated sound of protest deep in her throat, a small feline growl of longing as she realised that unless and until she unfastened the buttons of his shirt and physically removed it from his body she was going to be denied the sensation of his skin against her own which she craved so much. But if she did that he might have to stop kissing and caressing her breasts in that delicious way.

But somehow Brough seemed to have divined her thoughts, because he gently eased her slightly away from him, kissing her deeply on the mouth as he lifted her hands to the front of his shirt and then, whilst he was still kissing her, placed his own hands over her breasts, gently teasing her erect nipples with his thumbs and fingertips. Already sensitised by the erotic attention of his mouth, they reacted to this extra stimulation by causing such a curling, coiling, tightening feeling to gather deep inside her body that Kelly cried out in soft protest against the intensity of what she was feeling.

Her fingers stilled over the task of unfastening his shirt and then, as the sensation within her body refused to be controlled, her actions quickened, becoming urgent and demanding, her lips pressing tiny hungry kisses against Brough's jaw, his throat, and then lower, following the reckless speed of her fingers as she tugged and wrenched at the recalcitrant buttons, the progress of both her hands and her mouth only halted when she suddenly realised that she had reached the barrier of his belt.

Now it was Brough who was losing control, groaning rawly as he took her hands and guided them over his body. The feel of him even through the fabric of his clothes, hard, hot and aroused, filled her own insides with a heaviness, a dull, unfamiliar ache, and an instinctive knowledge that there was only one way, one way it was going to be eased...satisfied...

Kelly needed no encouragement nor coaxing to remove the rest of his clothes. Now she *was* an all nineties woman, wanting her man and not ashamed for him to know it, proud of her own body, her own sexuality as he stripped the rest of her clothes from it with a fierce eagerness that matched and fed her own longing.

When they were both completely naked she looked at him and then told him breathlessly—and meant it, 'Brough, you are *so* beautiful. So perfect...' Hot-faced with female appreciation, she ran a delicate but oh, so possessive fingertip down the length of him, teasingly avoiding the thick dark shaft of aroused manhood that was almost awesomely powerful to her as a woman—in some ways an almost primitive visual reminder of the human race's sexuality and its genetically encoded gift and goal of ensuring its own continuity—and yet still somehow a reminder of how very vulnerable a man could be, how very much in need of a woman's love and even of her protection of his maleness, of her appreciation of it and of him.

Very, very gently and carefully, caringly, Kelly reached out and ran her fingertip the entire length of the engorged shaft, lovingly circling its tip, smiling a mysterious, sultry, female smile of power and love as she caught Brough's audibly indrawn breath and saw the fierce leap of passion darkening his eyes before he closed them on a helpless moan of aching male pleasure.

'Oh, God, that feels so good,' he told her throatily, and then, opening his eyes, he admitted, 'Too good, Kelly; if you do it again I don't know...'

'You don't know what?' Kelly teased, obliging him with an opportunity to find out as she delicately ran her fingertip back up the way it had just come.

'I don't know whether to kiss you…or…'

Far too quickly for Kelly to stop him, he grabbed hold of her, rolling her down onto the bed and very gently keeping her there as he carefully parted her thighs, kissing the inner flesh of each one before looking up at her uncertain face and smiling tenderly at her.

'No,' Kelly protested, guessing what he was going to do and knowing instinctively that once she felt his lips, his mouth against that most vulnerable and sensuously responsive part of her body there was no way she was going to be able to hold back the response that had been building up inside her ever since their first kiss.

But of course she knew that Brough wasn't going to listen to her denial, and she knew as well that there was no way she really wanted him to do so.

The gentle brush of his lips against the soft mound of her sex was the most blissful, the most sensual, the most erotic and achingly beautiful sensation she had ever experienced, she told herself dizzily. And then, for good measure, she told Brough as well, interspersing the words with soft, husky, imploring pleas for him to stop before…because… Her voice finally trailed away into a soft sob of delirious pleasure as the dragging ache inside her changed shape and texture and form and became a living, pulsing, fiery sensation that exploded sharply inside her in a cataclysmic surge of pleasure which to her surprise left her not drained and empty but somehow feeling as though she was just on the edge of some previously unguessed and undreamed-of new universe of delight, heralded by the tiny but unmistakable little excited pulse that still throbbed inside her body.

Very gently, but very determinedly, she urged Brough towards her.

'I want you,' she told him shakily. 'I want you now, Brough…'

'Now,' he repeated, but he was already responding to her, answering her, his body starting to move within hers slowly and then with gathering pace, gathering force, so that with each thrust he lifted her and carried her a little further, a little closer towards the goal her body now so desperately craved.

'Yes, now,' she whispered back. 'Now, Brough… now…now… Oh, Brough… Brough… Brough…'

She could feel the world exploding around her, the whole universe filling with light and love and Brough.

Brough… Brough whom she loved so much, whom she would always love so much…who loved her…

Satisfied, satiated, Kelly snuggled down into his arms. Sleepily she remembered that there was something she had to tell him, something she had to say…something…

Her eyes were already closed, her breathing slowing…

Tenderly Brough curled her into the warmth of his own relaxed body.

There had been a moment, a heartbeat, just then, when, just before the end, he had felt his eyes start to burn with emotional tears. Strange how, until he had met her, he had never even known how much he had wanted to find her, how desperately he must secretly have been searching for her… How good and right she would feel and how complete she would make his life.

He must remember to tell Eve that when he was trying to explain to her why Julian Cox wasn't the man for her. Kelly!

God, but he loved her…had loved her, he now recognised, the moment he saw her, even though she had been behaving in a way which he now knew was way, way out of character. He started to frown. There were still things they needed to discuss. She had originally claimed Cox as an old friend, but the way he had been behaving towards her earlier had been anything but friendly.

His frown deepened as he heard a familiar sound from the landing where he had left his jacket. Gently easing his body away from Kelly's, so as not to disturb her, he padded towards it, flicking the receiving switch on his mobile phone. An unfamiliar voice on the other end of the line announced that he was Brough's grandmother's GP.

'She's had a fall—a neighbour found her. We've admitted her to hospital, but unfortunately she's developed pneumonia. It can happen with elderly patients…'

'I'm on my way,' Brough told him grimly.

Back in the bedroom, he quickly dressed. Kelly stirred in her sleep and opened her eyes, frowning as she saw what he was doing.

Still half asleep, she questioned anxiously, 'Brough…?'

'It's all right,' he told her. 'Go back to sleep. I've got to go… I'll explain later…'

Her eyes were already closing again. She was exhausted, he recognised, the shock of Cox's attack on her no doubt now taking its toll along with the brandy he had given her and the intensity and passion of their lovemaking.

His mind raced ahead. He would have to tell Eve about their grandmother. But he didn't want the additional delay of driving home. He would call her on his mobile. Dear God, but he hoped Nan was going to be all right. She was a fighter, he knew that, but a serious fall at her age, followed by the complication of pneumonia... No wonder the doctor had sounded so grave.

Quietly Brough let himself out of Kelly's flat and headed for his car.

CHAPTER NINE

'AND you're sure that Nan's going to be all right?'

'Yes, Eve, the doctors say she's over the worst now, and although they want to keep her in hospital for observation they're confident that she's on the mend,' Brough assured his sister gently as he heard the concern in her voice.

He had arrived at the hospital just as his grandmother's pneumonia entered its most critical stage and had sat with her, willing her to draw strength from him and pull through, holding her hand tightly in his, even though the doctor had told him kindly that she was probably not aware of his presence. At one point she had turned her head, opening her eyes as she looked at him, and Brough had felt his eyes smart with tears as she'd called him by his grandfather's, her late husband's, name.

It was now ten o'clock at night, three hours and ten minutes since he had left Kelly. He was longing to speak with her, and longing even more to be with her, but first he had an important brotherly duty to perform.

'Eve, I appreciate that this might not be a good time to tell you this. You know that I've never been exactly happy about your relationship with Julian Cox, but I've no—'

'Brough, before you go any further, there's something I have to tell you,' Eve interrupted him nervously.

Brough felt his heart sink. He knew how loyal she was, and how trusting, how stubborn as well, but surely if he told her that he had actually found Julian attacking Kelly...

'Eve—' he began.

But she overruled him, begging shakily, 'Brough, please let me speak. I'm so nervous about telling you this, but I'm legally an adult now, and we've both talked the whole thing through, and even if you, as my trustee, withhold the allowance from my trust fund from me it wouldn't stop us. We love each other, Brough, and we want to be together. We *have* to be together. Oh, Brough, I love him so much,' she told him, the emotion in her voice so strong that Brough almost felt the air around him humming with it. 'If you'd ever been in love yourself, you'd understand... I don't want you to hate me for what I'm doing, but even if you do...'

Brough closed his eyes and took a deep breath. He hated having to do what he was going to have to do...hated having to destroy her dreams...her love, but what option did he have when he knew what Cox really was?

'Eve,' he said gently. 'I'm sorry, I understand everything you're saying, and you're wrong—I do understand what it means to be in love, to love someone; but you can't marry Julian Cox.'

The silence that followed his announcement was so complete and so intense that for a moment Brough thought she had actually hung up, and then he heard her saying shakily, 'Brough, I'm sorry; I haven't...I didn't... It isn't Julian I'm in love with...'

Now it was Brough's turn to be silent.

Not Cox. Then who? What...?

'It's Harry,' Eve blurted out.

'Harry!' Brough repeated in bemusement. 'Harry—'

'Harry Lawson,' Eve explained, adding ernestly, 'You remember he was at the ball we went to...'

'You mean the Harry who was escorting Kelly?' Brough questioned her sharply.

'Yes. But there's nothing between *them*. He was simply escorting her because his cousin had asked him to,' Eve told him defensively, before adding eagerly, 'Oh, Brough, I love him so much and so, I know, will you.'

'Yes... Yes...I'm sure I shall,' Brough agreed obediently, mentally reviewing what little he knew of Harry. A pleasant, solid-looking young man, phlegmatic in the extreme, Brough would have guessed, reliable, solid, trustworthy, an excellent foil for his sister's far more vulnerable and fragile personality.

A sense of relief began to fill him as he digested what he had just learned.

'Tell me again that Nan is going to be all right,' Eve implored, adding, 'I want to come down and see her, Brough, and I want to bring Harry with me.'

'Leave it a few days, until she's back at home,' Brough suggested. 'She'll feel more like company then, and you know she's going to want to give your Harry a thorough interrogation...'

Laughter bubbled along the line.

'Yes. I've warned him about that already. Brough, we don't want a big wedding...just a quiet family ceremony. Harry says Christmas would be best for him because it fits in best with the farming calendar...'

'We'll talk about it when I get back,' Brough promised her, pausing before asking, 'What about Cox, Eve? Have you told *him* that—?'

'No, not yet,' Eve responded quickly. 'I know I'm going to have to but...' She paused. 'I...*we* wanted to tell you about us first...'

'Well, whatever you do, Eve,' Brough cautioned her, 'make sure you aren't on your own with him when you do tell him—or better still let me tell him for you.'

'No, Brough,' Eve told him gently. 'It's all right. Harry and I will handle this together.'

After he had terminated his call to his sister Brough took a deep breath and walked the length of the hospital car park whilst he assembled his thoughts. What he had just learned seemed nothing short of a small miracle, even if her Harry was rather an unexpected magician. He certainly seemed to have performed some very special magic in his sister's life, Brough recognised ruefully.

Although, technically, as Eve had just reminded him, she was legally an adult, he had always taken his brotherly responsibility towards her very seriously, and now, with one stroke, he was being freed, not just from that responsibility but also from the necessity of worrying about her emotional and financial future security, which meant...

Eagerly Brough reached for his mobile phone and punched in the number of Kelly's flat. Odd how easy it was to memorise certain vital numbers, how they seemed instinctively to lodge themselves in one's memory, he reflected wryly as he waited for Kelly to answer his call.

Five...ten minutes and three attempts later, he was forced to acknowledge that she must have gone out. He glanced at his watch. He wanted to have a further talk with the ward sister before she went off duty. He intended to spend the night in his grandmother's house just in case he should be needed urgently at her bedside. By the time he got there it would be too late to ring Kelly—she would no doubt be in bed and sound asleep—but first thing in the morning...

* * *

After she had replaced the telephone receiver following Brough's call, Eve turned to Harry, her eyes shining with love and relief.

'See, I *told* you he would understand,' Harry chided her lovingly.

'Yes, I know, but he was so…so stern and disapproving over Julian that I thought he'd be bound to think I couldn't possibly know my own mind when I told him I'd realised that I didn't love Julian at all and that you…'

She made a small happy sound beneath her breath as Harry put an end to her speech by kissing her very firmly and very determinedly. That was what she liked…*loved* about her Harry… He understood her so well…*knew* just how she felt…just what she wanted…knew that she was not like the majority of her peers in that she positively *wanted* someone to take control of her life and herself, that she adored having someone to stand beside her and protect her, to guide her masterfully.

But that someone had to be kind and gentle as well… He had to have the intuition and the love to know that the guiding hand she liked on the reins of her life had to be so delicately light that it could never chafe nor hurt her. Julian hadn't been like that. Julian had sometimes been very cruel to her, saying the most cutting and hurtful things…making her cry… Harry would never do that.

'You still have to tell Cox,' Harry reminded her quietly.

'I know,' Eve responded, 'but he frightens me a little, Harry… He keeps on telling me that he wants us to get engaged and he gets very angry when I tell him that Brough won't agree. He says it doesn't matter whether Brough agrees or not… I think he's more interested in my money than me,' Eve admitted in a small voice.

Privately, Harry thought so as well, and Cox was a

fool, in his opinion. He always had been, and not just a fool either, Harry reflected, his forehead creasing as he recalled certain things…certain old items of gossip he had picked up at home. But Harry was not the kind of person to pry into another person's personal life, and if Dee, his cousin, chose to place an embargo on certain events in her life, then he, for one, was quite happy to abide by it.

'Would you like *me* to tell him for you?' Harry suggested.

Immediately Eve's face lit up.

'Oh, Harry, would you…?'

Standing on tiptoe, she kissed him happily and then gave a small feminine gasp as he drew her closer and kissed her back, but much more deeply.

They were going to be so happy together, she and her Harry… She couldn't wait for the babies they were going to have, filling the old farmhouse with their presence and the love they would all share. All houses needed love and she certainly had plenty to give. She had already briefly met Harry's family, not officially as his intended bride because although she and Harry knew how strongly they felt about each other it had only been a *very* short time since they had first met, but she had seen from the looks his parents had exchanged that they had guessed how they felt about one another, and she had known straight away that she would get on well with them. Harry's mother was, in many ways, a younger version of her own grandmother, a plump, motherly woman who would draw her daughter-in-law safely beneath her maternal wing and keep her secure there.

'I'll go and see Cox first thing in the morning,' Harry promised her as he reluctantly released her.

'You could stay here tonight if you want,' Eve suggested daringly. 'Brough won't be coming back and...'

She stopped as she saw the stern look Harry was giving her.

'We agreed that we'd wait until we're married,' he reminded her.

Eve pouted and smiled.

'I know, but I love you so much and... Don't you want me, Harry...?'

The passion in the kiss he gave her was the only answer she needed.

'If I stay now, I'll have to make love to you, and if I do that... The Lawsons have a family tradition that the first child is born nine months virtually to the day of the wedding...I don't want our child to arrive ahead of that day,' he told her simply.

He had such pride, such moral fibre, such strength, Eve decided adoringly as she snuggled closer to him and whispered blissfully, 'Yes, Harry...'

Kelly came out of the darkness of a very deep sleep so abruptly that for a few seconds she was totally disorientated. Why was she alone in bed? Why...?

Frantically she sat up, searching the darkness of the room, and then the dim memory of Brough saying something to her about having to go came filtering back, clouded and fuzzy from the combined effects of the shock- and brandy-induced depth of her sleep.

Shakily she went to get herself a drink of water. Her throat felt dry and her eyes were scratchy and sore. In the cold pre-dawn chill of the kitchen she shivered a little as she stared into the darkness.

Had she and Brough really made love so intensely, so passionately, so poignantly? Had they really exchanged vows of love and commitment, told each other of the depth of their love for one another, or was it all simply a self-created fantasy...a dream? But no, she could feel the difference in her body, and knew that the words reverberating through her mind and her heart had been said...exchanged... Oh, Brough... A little weepily she started to tremble. Where on earth had he gone and why? If only she knew. Why *hadn't* he woken her up properly and spoken to her? Had he really meant what he had said to her, or...?

There was still so much they didn't really know about one another, despite the intimacy they had shared. So much he didn't know about *her*. She had tried to tell him about Julian...to explain...but her explanations had been swept away by the passion of the moment. What had he thought when he had walked in and discovered Julian with her like that?

Her thoughts began to chase one another around inside her head until she felt sick and dizzy with the weight of them, clasping her head in her hands as she protested aloud, 'No... No... Stop...'

It was too early for her to get up, and yet she knew if she went back to bed she wouldn't be able to sleep. After walking around her bedroom, touching the pillow where Brough's head had lain and then lifting it to her face to breathe in the scent of him and press the comfort of it close to her hot face, she reminded herself that she was a mature adult woman and that this type of fevered, frantic behaviour belonged more properly to early adolescence. Wearily she walked back into the sitting room, and then frowned as the things she had brought back from the Hartwell factory caught her eye.

Half an hour later she was blessedly engrossed in the records she was studying.

Now, the prospect of painting the new pieces for Brough's grandmother didn't just appeal to her artistically but emotionally as well. How typical of Brough, *her* Brough, that he should think of doing this, and typical too that he should search so assiduously to find someone, the *right* someone, to do the work for him.

How fitting…romantic even…that it should have been his quest to replace the missing pieces of a teaset which had originally been a wedding present for his grandmother that had brought them together, Kelly decided dreamily, determinedly ignoring the small, unwanted voice that insisted on reminding her that they had first met because of Julian Cox. That might have been their first meeting, but their *first mutual* realisation of their feelings for one another had been brought about by the Hartwell china, and when she told their grandchildren about it it would be that day together she would tell them about.

Their grandchildren.

A tiny shiver struck her. *Was* she taking too much for granted, reading too much into what Brough had said, the way he had held her…touched her…? When he had spoken of love had he merely been speaking of an emotion, a desire of the moment, and not meant it as she had done—that his feelings were so profound and deep that they were a commitment for life?

Suddenly her small doubts, tiny minnows nibbling at the sure structure of her belief in his love for her, had become a swarming shoal of destructive piranha eating greedily into and devouring her confidence.

Where was Brough? Why had he gone like that? She had a vague memory of him bending over her and speaking to her, but now, when it was crucially important to do so, she just couldn't remember what exactly it was he had said. Something about having to go…but why? Because once the immediate passion of the moment had been spent he had had second thoughts about loving her? Or had, perhaps, her declaration of love for him come too soon and, even worse, been unwanted? *Had* she assumed too much…*loved* too much?

Outside dawn was lightening the sky. Sternly she told herself that there was no point in allowing herself to think so destructively. Only Brough knew the answers to her questions. Only Brough could assuage her doubts. But where was he? She had his home telephone number; she could always ring him.

She looked at the telephone, her fingers itching to pick up the receiver and dial his number, but it was still only six o'clock in the morning. What if her worst fears were correct? What if he *had* regretted the intimacy they had shared? How would he react when he heard her voice, an unwanted intrusion into his privacy, and an even more unwanted reminder of something he might prefer to forget? And how would *she* feel, knowing that he didn't want to speak to her?

Give it time…give *him* time, she urged herself.

Six o'clock. Brough stretched and grimaced as he turned over in the small bed in his grandmother's spare bedroom. It was far too early to ring Kelly and too soon to leave for home. He wanted to check with the specialist that his grandmother was truly on the way to recovery before he did that, and they had told him at the hospital last night that he couldn't see the specialist until ten o'clock in the morning.

He would ring Kelly before he left the hospital to come home, he comforted himself. God, but he missed her…wanted her. He frowned as he remembered the look of fear and revulsion on her face as Julian Cox held her. There was something that just didn't jell, that just didn't ring true to her character about her whole relationship with Cox—something he could sense without being able to analyse properly. It was obvious that she loathed him, but at the ball she had been actively flirting with him.

Brough frowned.

'We're old friends,' she had told him dismissively when he had challenged her, her whole attitude towards him almost aggressive. In a way that an animal was aggressive when it tried to cover up its fear?

Brough knew with a gut-deep instinct that there was no way Kelly, *his* Kelly, could *ever* have done anything so directly opposed to her open, straightforward nature as to be deceitful. It simply wasn't her. And neither would he have thought it would have been her ever to be even remotely attracted to a man like Julian Cox. It wasn't his own male ego or vanity that made him think that. He simply knew that she was too sensitive, too aware, too intelligent to be attracted by a man who held her sex in such obvious contempt.

But maybe, just maybe, it *was* possible that a much younger and more impressionable and vulnerable Kelly might have been unable to see through the façade that Cox was so adept at throwing around himself. His own sister, after all, had fallen for it, but that didn't explain why Kelly had been flirting so heavily with Cox on the night of the ball.

Wide awake now, Brough closed his eyes and tried to collect his thoughts. What was he doing? Whatever may or may not have happened in Kelly's past, it *was* her past. She had no need to make any explanations or apologies for it to him. He loved her as she was and for what she was, and if she *had* made an error of judgement...

An error of judgement? By allowing Cox to be her lover? The vicious kick of emotion he could feel in his stomach was an all-male gut reaction, but just as immediate and even more powerful was an instinctive awareness that there was no way Kelly would ever have shared that kind of intimacy with Julian Cox. Brough had no idea how he knew that...he just knew it. And, knowing it, he owed it to her and to their love to allow her privacy over the whole issue of just what role Julian Cox had played in her life prior to their meeting.

Whatever it may or may not have been, there was one thing Brough was one hundred per cent sure of: it most certainly didn't give Cox the right to behave towards her in the way he had been doing, half frightening the life out of her, bullying her.

Suddenly Brough was even more anxious to get back to her. Half past six... He was sorely tempted to ring her, but the things he wanted to say to her were so intensely personal that they simply could not be said over the phone.

Eve had told him that she and Harry wanted a Christmas wedding. Well, they could most certainly have it, but his own marriage to Kelly was going to take place first. Well, so far as he was concerned it was. Kelly, he suspected, might take a bit of persuading. She took her responsibilities to her partner, Beth, very seriously; that much was obvious.

Six forty-five. Brough groaned, quickly calculating how long it was going to be before he could get back to Rye-on-Averton and to Kelly.

'Are you awake?' Eve whispered softly to Harry.

Sternly he sat up in bed and looked at her. She might

have been able to persuade him that he should stay overnight with her, but he had been very firmly determined
that they would sleep in separate rooms, and they had.
Eve was so sweetly naive that she had no idea of just
what she was doing to his self-control, curling up at the
bottom of his bed like that in her soft white nightdress,
her long hair flowing down her back.

'What are you doing in here?' he demanded.

'I came to talk to you…I couldn't sleep,' she answered, whispering excitedly, 'Oh, Harry, I'm so
happy…' Her face suddenly clouded. 'When are you
going to see Julian?'

'Nine o'clock,' Harry responded promptly, 'and then
you and I are going out to celebrate.'

As she looked down at her bare left hand he followed
her line of thought and told her gruffly, 'I've got my
grandmother's ring… I'd like you to have it, but if you
don't like it…'

'Oh, I'm sure I shall,' Eve breathed, pink-cheeked.
'Oh, Harry,' she repeated, flinging herself into his arms,
'I'm so excited. I still can't quite believe what's hap-
pening…'

Seven o'clock. Dee pushed back the duvet and padded
over to her bedroom window. Beyond it she could see
the soft rolling countryside, the fertile acres which had
been tended by her ancestors for so many generations.

Once, those ancestors had been as fertile as the fields
they tilled, but she and Harry were the only descendants
in their generation, a poor crop yield indeed. Harry
would marry, of course, and hopefully would produce
sons and daughters to continue the family tradition. She
would never marry nor have children since through her

own experience as a motherless girl she had formed very strong views on the need of a child to have the loving support of both its parents. An old-fashioned view in this day and age, perhaps, but it was hers and she had the right to have it—just as she had the right to choose whether or not to yield to the demand of her own fast-ticking biological clock.

Yes, the future of their family was solely dependent on Harry. It needn't have been that way. There had once been a time when... But what was the point in dwelling on that now? Unbidden she had a sharp mental image of Julian Cox. Her whole body stiffened as a surge of pain gripped her.

She had waited for such a long time for the chance to punish Julian Cox for what he had done...to punish him in a way which would ensure that he suffered just as she had suffered...but once again it seemed that he was evading that justice, escaping it. There was no point in her being angry with Kelly. Love was a powerfully potent force. No one knew that better than she, but it wasn't over yet; there was still Anna's role to be played. Julian still needed money and he needed it desperately now. Brough had already refused to invest any money with him, thus closing down that avenue of escape to him. But Julian could still marry Eve and thereby gain access to her money.

But Brough was his sister's trustee, and once Kelly told him what Julian had done to Beth it was Dee's guess that Brough would never allow Julian to marry his sister. Julian was in debt up to his neck and sinking fast...very fast...

So maybe everything wasn't lost after all. Julian might have been clever enough technically not to break the law, but he had certainly come very close to doing so.

Through the people she had hired, Dee had discovered a vast hidden tangle of false names and hideaway companies, all of which could be linked to him if, like her, you used a little creative thinking. He might deceive others but he couldn't deceive her. There were the aliases with the same initials as his, the clever use of his mother's maiden name and the names of people now dead.

No, legally he might be able to laugh in the faces of his victims as he challenged them to claim restitution from him, but morally— But what did Julian know of morals? What did he care about the good name of others, about their pride in it, their shame at losing it? Nothing.

A bitter smile curled her mouth as her eyes closed on a wave of sharp pain.

Her father had been such a proud man. Distant and old-fashioned towards her in many ways, perhaps, but always, always scrupulously honest in everything he did...*everything*. But he was dead now, and it was pointless to dwell on how much closer they might have become once they had been able to meet as adults. That chance was gone, destroyed...like her option to marry and have children; stolen from her...

Stop it, you're getting maudlin, she warned herself sharply. It was time for her to get up. She had work to do. The markets in Hong Kong would soon be closing. She had investments there she needed to check on.

Julian enjoyed gambling on the futures market. Or at least he had done until recently, when he had begun to sustain such heavy losses, outsmarted and outbid, outbought and outsold by a shadowy rival who seemed to second-guess his every thought. Poor Julian!

When he woke up this morning it would be to find

that his investments had sunk without trace, that the profit he had been so in need of making had become a loss.

Suddenly Dee began to feel better.

CHAPTER TEN

WHITE-FACED, Julian stared at the screen of his computer, a sick feeling of shock and disbelief coagulating his blood.

He had woken up two hours ago, his tongue thick with yesterday's alcohol and his head throbbing. That bitch Kelly thought she was so clever; leading him on and then dropping him, but he'd get even with her. But first that hot tip he had picked up yesterday from his informer had sounded such a sure thing. He had bought heavily into it, using all his last reserves, but this morning when he had gone to check the market he had hardly been able to believe his eyes. The stock was gone, wiped out, finished, and with it everything he owned. *Everything.*

He pushed the computer screen off his desk with such violence that it hit the floor. He picked up the keyboard and flung it against the wall of his office in an attempt to relieve his panic and fury. What the hell was he going to do? He *had* to have money by the end of this month. He *had* to. And it wasn't just a matter of the banks calling in his loans and stopping him trading.

A long time ago Julian had hit on and discovered how easy it was to persuade gullible and often naively managed small private charities to accept his offer of free investment advice. Eagerly they had accepted, co-opting him onto their boards, offering him access to their monies, only too glad to have him remove from their shoulders the burden of managing their investments. Just so long as he provided them with an income which increased from year to year they were happy and didn't enquire about their capital…

And that was exactly what he had done…until now… Never mind the fact that their capital was long since gone, used to fund his own lavish lifestyle, used to make investments so perilously on the outside of mere risky that no one else would touch them; just the excitement he had got from backing these outsiders had given him more of a buzz than sex and even drugs ever had.

Of course, the empty coffers of some of those early and rather clumsy siphoning-offs of funds had quickly come to light, but luckily he had been able to place the blame elsewhere and convince people that *he* was not the one responsible for the foolish investment and subsequent loss of their money, and he had even had the signatures of his co-investors to prove it. He had always been rather good at forging other people's signatures. The first time he had put his skill to a financial advantage had been when he had stolen a 'friend's' cheque book.

Those had been good days; fortune had favoured him and his investments and it had been no problem to move money from one place to another as and when it was needed. But now things were different. The markets were running against him and he had made heavy losses…too heavy… He needed money and he needed it urgently. It was all Kelly's fault. He had gambled heavily on being able to persuade her to allow him to advise her, on how best to 'invest' her inheritance. But now she had dropped him—made a fool of him—and no woman did that.

It was a pity that Eve didn't have access to her capital, and Brough certainly wasn't going to be easy to persuade to allow her to have full control over it; but still, it was better than nothing.

The sweat of fear that had soaked his skin was beginning to disappear and, with it, his earlier panic. He was worrying too much and too soon. What he needed was something to calm him down, help him relax…a drink…

He went to find the bottle of gin he had discarded in the kitchen the previous evening and then stopped as he heard his doorbell ring.

It was just gone nine o'clock.

It had been well gone ten o'clock when Brough had seen the specialist, who had declared very reassuringly that his grandmother would make a full recovery, and then Brough had gone from his office to his grandmother's bed to spend his allocated fifteen minutes with her. Kelly would be in the shop by now. Hurrying outside the hospital, he reached for his mobile phone.

Kelly had just opened the post when she heard the phone ring. As she reached for the receiver her heart started to beat very fast, her face flushing a soft pink, but to her disappointment her caller wasn't Brough but Beth.

'Hi… How are you?' her friend and partner asked her.

'I'm fine; how are you?' Kelly returned automatically.

'Not so good,' Beth responded. 'I'm still trying to fix up a visit to that factory I told you about.'

As Kelly listened to her friend's enthusiastic voice she suddenly heard the sound that warned her that a second caller was trying to get through on her line. Was it Brough? Even if it was, she could hardly cut Beth off in mid-sentence, she acknowledged frustratedly as her friend paused for a brief breath before continuing, 'Look, the reason I'm ringing is that I've decided I'm going to stay on in Prague for some more time. It could take me a while to track down this factory, and I'm determined to do it, Kelly, even if I have to learn the language to make myself understood,' she told her friend with unusual fierceness. 'I don't care how much Alex tries to put me off... I *want* that glass. Look, I'm intending to move into a cheaper hotel for the rest of my stay, but I don't know which one yet. I'll give you a ring once I've sorted something out.'

'Oh, Beth, you will take care, won't you?' Kelly begged her. 'If your interpreter doesn't think it's wise—'

'He's just being awkward and difficult,' Beth assured her firmly. 'I'm an adult, Kelly, not a child,' she added with un-Beth-like grittiness, saying before Kelly could raise any further objections, 'Look, I have to go; I'll be in touch. Bye...'

Frowning a little, Kelly replaced the receiver. Beth was obviously determined to track down this elusive factory, but her determination seemed so at odds with her normal gentle, almost passive behaviour that Kelly was a little puzzled by it. She certainly seemed to thoroughly dislike her interpreter, who, from what she had said, seemed to be doing his best to be extraordinarily obstructive.

Nervously Kelly dialled the numbers that would allow her to check her answering service.

Her heart started to thump as the recorded voice announced that she had one message.

'Hear message?' the tinny voice asked.

'Yes,' Kelly whispered, her throat suddenly constricted.

'Kelly, it's me, Brough. I need to talk to you...see you... I should be home around eleven-thirty; could you possibly call round? I'd come to the shop, but what I want to say I'd prefer to say in private... Bye now.'

'Repeat?' the tinny recording was demanding rather bossily. 'Repeat?'

'No. No...' Kelly responded automatically.

What did Brough mean? What *was* it he wanted to

say to her? Her mouth had gone dry and her heart was thudding heavily in a drumbeat of doom.

He *had* changed his mind, made a mistake... That was what he wanted to say to her and *that* was why he wanted privacy in order to do so. He *didn't* really love her at all.

Kelly started to shiver, causing the customer who had just walked into the shop to exclaim sympathetically, 'Oh, my, you do look poorly! It's not this virus that's been going round, is it? I should go straight to bed if I were you.'

If only the cause of her pain *were* merely a virus, Kelly reflected after her customer had gone. What time was it now? Eleven-thirty, Brough had said, his voice sounding remote and grave. He wouldn't have asked her to go round...

She would have to close the shop; it was too late to get someone in to take over from her. It would be the earliest lunch hour in history, she decided miserably. There was no point in trying to deceive herself or give herself false hope. Brough was only confirming what she herself had been thinking. He had had second thoughts, realised that her feelings were much, much stronger than his, and now he wanted to make the situation completely clear to her. That was the way he was. He wasn't the kind of man simply to walk away without any explanation.

He was sorry, he would tell her. He didn't want to hurt her. What they had had had been good...very good...but for him it had simply been a one-off and not, as she had obviously believed, the basis, the foundation, for a lasting relationship or a permanent commitment.

Five past eleven... She would leave at eleven-fifteen... Plenty of time for her to drive to where Brough was living. She reached mechanically for a cloth so that she could pass the time in polishing some of the items they had on display, but her hands were shaking so much she put it down again. In her present state of agitation she was likely to do more harm than good.

Julian stared drunkenly at the screen of his computer which he had picked up off the floor. His system had crashed...just like the whole of his life. The last thing he had expected when he'd opened the door to his caller two hours ago had been to discover Harry standing on his doorstep. The other man had asked him quietly if he could come in. Automatically, Julian had agreed.

'There's something I have to tell you,' Harry began calmly as Julian led him into his untidy, dusty sitting room, shaking his head when Julian offered him a drink, saying mildly, 'Rather too early for me...'

'It's never too early...' Julian responded boastfully as he poured himself another gin.

He had no idea what Harry wanted. He only knew the other man vaguely and totally despised him. Harry represented everything that he himself loathed.

'Eve has asked me to come and see you,' Harry began quietly. 'She and I are getting married...'

Julian stared at him in disbelief. Was he trying to play some kind of joke on him? He searched the other man's face, a slow sensation of sick realisation creeping like death along his veins. This was no joke.

'What the hell are you saying? She's marrying *me*,' Julian told him furiously.

Harry said nothing but just continued to look steadily at him.

'No! No! I don't believe it,' Julian insisted, starting to shake his head, trying to dispel the clouds of panic swamping him. 'I want to see her...talk to her...'

'I'm sorry, but I don't think that would be a good idea,' Harry told him politely.

'*You* don't think…?' Julian gave him an ugly look. 'Eve is *my* girlfriend. We're all but engaged, dammit, and—'

'She was your girlfriend,' Harry agreed quietly, 'although…' He stopped and gave Julian a steady look. 'It seems to me that you rather took her for granted. Perhaps if you'd valued her a little more…as she deserves to be valued…'

'Oh, my God, now I've heard it all—*you* telling *me* how to treat a woman…' Julian gave him a contemptuous look and tossed back the last of his drink. 'What the hell do *you* know about women? Nothing…' he jeered. 'She loves *me*; she told me so… She's besotted with me…' he boasted.

Harry said nothing, refusing to retaliate, simply watching him with a look in his eyes that goaded Julian into walking unsteadily across the floor and pouring himself another drink.

'You can't do this to me…and don't think I don't know who's behind it. It's that precious brother of hers; he never wanted—'

'This has nothing to do with Brough,' Harry corrected him. 'Eve and I are in love…'

'Eve in love…with you? Don't make me laugh. She loves *me*.'

She did love him. She had told him so in a soft, nervous little voice, her eyes big with wonder and excitement. It had been so easy to trick her into believing he had fallen for her. She was so trusting… She hadn't even questioned the fact that he hadn't taken her to bed.

'I respect you too much,' he had told her untruthfully.

The truth was that his drinking and the intense pressure of his lifestyle meant that sex was the last thing on his mind, the last desire he had. It took a woman like Kelly to arouse *that* need in him, not a babyish innocent like Eve.

Julian *knew* that it was her brother who was behind her decision to drop him. Brough had guessed that Julian was after her money, of course. Julian gave a small mental shrug. So what? He didn't give a damn what Brough had or hadn't guessed, and as for preferring Harry to him... That was ridiculous...impossible...

'I don't believe you... I'm going to see Eve—talk to her,' he announced, walking unsteadily towards the door, but oddly, when he got there, Harry was standing in front of it, barring his way.

'No, I'm sorry, but you're not,' Harry told him calmly.

Julian looked drunkenly at him.

'What is this? You can't stop me...'

Harry stood solidly in front of the door, simply looking at him. A little to his own surprise Julian discovered that he was actually backing off. What the hell was he doing? He wasn't afraid of Harry.

'I think you'll find it would be best for everyone concerned if you simply accept the situation,' he heard Harry saying gently to him, to his utter amazement.

'People will soon forget. After all, it isn't as though you were actually engaged, and neither Eve nor I shall say anything. People will simply believe that the two of you drifted apart. It happens all the time.'

Julian swayed and focused vacantly on Harry's face. What the hell was he trying to suggest? That he, Julian Cox, was in danger of being humiliated by people thinking that Eve had dropped him? No way!

'Eve mentioned that you have business interests in Hong Kong. I've heard it is a fascinating part of the world, even more so these days... Have you ever been there? I haven't myself... Farming doesn't combine well with travelling...'

Julian continued to gape at him.

Was Harry actually daring subtly to suggest to him, to *warn* him, that he should leave town...? No, it was impossible. Harry simply wasn't like that. He didn't have the nerve...nor the subtlety. No, he was imagining it, Julian assured himself. The other man was too unworldly to know that there was no way Julian could visit Hong Kong right now, not with the money he owed out there, the enemies he had made.

'I'll let myself out,' he heard Harry saying mildly. When he reached the front door, Harry turned to him and commented quietly, 'I should keep off the drink for a while if I were you.' Then he turned round and opened the door to leave.

Now as he sat staring blindly at the screen in front of him, Julian couldn't believe it. His life was in chaos, *ruins*... He had been counting on Eve and her inheritance. By God, but she wasn't going to do this to him. No way... He could soon make her change her mind.

He needed a drink. He lurched over to the kitchen worktop, frowning impatiently when he saw the empty bottle. Well, he would just have to go out and buy some more, wouldn't he? He still had enough money for that...he could still afford to buy himself a *drink*...to get drunk... By God, yes, he could still afford to do that, and once he had...

As Julian opened his front door the brilliance of the bright morning hit his eyeballs in fiery darts of pain. Oblivious to the looks on the faces of other pedestrians, he started to stagger towards the centre of the town. His car was parked outside the house, but some vestige of self-preservation warned him that it would be extremely unwise for him to drive.

Kelly too had made the same decision, but for very different reasons. It wasn't drink that made her aware that her reactions were simply not good enough for her to drive anywhere safely. She was trembling from head to foot as she opened the shop door, dreading her coming interview with Brough, and yet knowing that she was too proud to ring him up and simply tell him that it wasn't necessary for him to say anything; that she had already guessed what he wanted to tell her and that she understood.

Pride, was it? Was she *sure* it wasn't more of a desperate, anguished yearning on the part of a woman far too deeply and vulnerably in love to deny herself the masochistic pleasure of spending some last precious minutes with the man she loved?

It seemed to be adding an even finer edge of cruelty to her unhappiness that it should be such a wonderful day, the sun shining, the air soft and fresh, people walking about dressed in light clothes, smiling...

As she turned the corner at the bottom of the street she could see across the town square to the river, glinting happily in the sunshine. Rye-on-Averton was such a pretty town that normally just to walk through it lifted her spirits, but not today—no, definitely not today.

Head down, fighting to hold back the tears threatening to overwhelm her, Kelly walked quickly to Brough's house.

She was less than five yards away from it when she suddenly heard someone calling her name. Lifting her head, she froze as she recognised Julian Cox staggering towards her from the opposite direction. He was quite obviously drunk and looked totally repulsive, she decided as she saw his stubbly jaw and creased clothes.

'Kelly... What are you doing here...or can I guess? Come crawling round after Brough, have you? What happened? Dropped you, has he?' he tormented her jeeringly. 'Well, what did you expect? Surely you aren't really stupid enough not to guess what he was up to? He wanted to draw you off me because of his sister. That was all... Didn't you guess? Surely you must have realised that a man like him would *never* look seriously at someone like you, someone who's been to bed with half the town... Not that he minded getting a taste of what you've got to offer himself... He told me that...said he might as well have full value for his money...'

Julian had gone straight from his house to the supermarket, where he had discovered, contrary to his belief, he did *not* have enough money on him to buy any alcohol. Infuriated, both by this and Harry's interview with him, he had, instead of going home, headed for Brough's house, intending to try to persuade Eve to see reason and change her mind. She would more than likely be on her own at this time of day and he was pretty sure he could persuade her to listen to him.

But just as he had reached the house he had seen Kelly approaching it from the opposite direction, and immediately he had remembered just how she had rejected him and how, because of that rejection, Brough Frobisher had humiliated him—and, no doubt, brought pressure to bear on Eve to end their relationship.

All the fury and vindictiveness caused by this suddenly found a target in Kelly. What better way of getting back at Brough than by destroying his relationship with Kelly? If he knew anything about women—and he did— she would never stay if he told her that Brough had discussed her sexually with someone else.

Now, looking at her face, he knew he had been right—God, he was enjoying hurting her, making her pay for rejecting him.

'Did you really think he wanted you?' he taunted her cruelly. 'How could he? He saw the way you were all over *me* at the ball... He's a proud man, our Brough...far too proud to want *my* leavings...'

Brough had not made as good time coming back as he had hoped. Some unexpected road works had held him up and then, to make matters worse, he hadn't been able to park his car outside his house but had had to leave it much further down the street.

It was already gone half past eleven. Quickening his stride, he turned the corner to see Kelly standing outside the house with her back to him, facing Julian Cox. What the hell was he doing...?

Immediately Brough started to run.

Julian, who was facing him, saw him first, smirking triumphantly at him as he reached them, taunting Brough drunkenly, 'How did it feel having my leavings?' He waved his arms towards Kelly. 'She's pretty good, I know, but just in case you're interested I can recommend someone even better... They say that an enthusiastic amateur is better than a professional any day, I know, but...'

Kelly made a small, tortured whimper of protest but both men seemed to be ignoring her.

'Well, you saw for yourself at the ball how it was,' Julian continued tauntingly. He was beginning to enjoy himself now. The effects of the drink he had consumed earlier were beginning to wear off, sharpening his instincts. Kelly looked white and sick. Oh, yes, he really was enjoying this.

'Of course, Kelly and I are old mates. She and I had a little thing going when I was dating her partner, Beth. Kelly's like that. She *prefers* a man who belongs to another woman, don't you, my pet? She says it adds to the enjoyment…gives it an extra kick of excitement for her…and she certainly likes her excitement, does our Kelly. Has she…?' He used a phrase which horrified Kelly and made her face burn with shame. She couldn't bring herself to look at Brough. How could she defend herself against Julian's charges without going into lengthy explanations? And besides, what was the point? She already knew that Brough didn't want her, didn't *love* her as she did him.

Not returning her love was one thing, she reminded herself in anguish, but having him receive this kind of information about her, knowing how it *must* affect his judgement of her and his future memories of her, was quite another.

'It's okay, though,' Julian continued laconically. 'I've put her in the picture about Eve and she knows that you were just using her to draw… All you really wanted was to get her out of my life… Is…she in, by the way? I promised her I'd take her out this morning to choose an engagement ring.'

As he spoke Julian stepped determinedly past Kelly, almost knocking her over.

'I agree with what you said about her,' he commented loudly to Brough. 'She's really just a good one-night lay.'

Suddenly, as Julian looked into Brough's eyes, the drunken fumes momentarily cleared from his brain. He had, he recognised sickly, made a bad mistake—a dangerous error of judgement. But it was too late for him to have second thoughts now, he realised as the contempt in Brough's eyes became a seething fury.

Kelly couldn't bear to hear any more. Without turning to look at Brough she started to walk and then to run desperately away, ignoring the concerned stares of passers-by as she ran, head down, along the street, back in the direction she had come.

Brough watched her like someone turned to stone.

'I need to see Eve, Brough,' Julian started to plead whiningly.

Cold-eyed, Brough turned to look at him. 'Eve is marrying Harry,' he told him. 'You're not wanted here, Cox, and if I find you *anywhere* near my sister for *any* reason...'

'Are you threatening me?' Julian began to bluster as he knew he had gone too far in venting his rage against Kelly.

'No. I'm *telling* you,' Brough said softly. 'And, by the way, you've wasted your time coming here. Eve isn't here; she's gone to visit her in-laws-to-be. Now, if you'll excuse me I—'

'I wouldn't waste your time going after Kelly,' Julian interrupted him, grinning. 'Everything I said about her was true. But you must have found out what she's like for yourself by now. She doesn't make a man waste time; I'll give her that. Pretty energetic in bed, isn't she? Pity she's not been a bit more exclusive about how she hands it out...'

Julian never saw the blow that hit him, he certainly felt it, though, as he dropped to the floor, trying to stem the blood pouring from his nose. He started to curse but Brough had already gone.

Instinctively Kelly headed for the river path and its protective seclusion.

She *couldn't* go back to the shop, not just yet, and there was nowhere else, no *one* else, she could go to—not like this...

Oh, but it had hurt, hurt more than anything else in her life, knowing what Brough must be thinking about her. None of Julian's crude accusations were true, of course—at least not in the way *he* had said them.

Apart from a brief, immature adolescent relationship with the boy who had been her first lover, there had been no one else in her life other than Brough, and certainly no one else in her bed. But how on earth could she prove that to Brough?

He might not love her but at least he had liked her, *respected* her, and she couldn't bear to think of him now carrying an image of her that Julian had painted for him. But even if she could bring herself to face him and explain, why *should* he believe her?

The river path was empty of other walkers, and Kelly's fast pace had slowed as the thoughts started to tumble around in her head.

'Kelly!'

The shock of hearing Brough's voice behind her made her stumble, but immediately he was beside her, catching her up in his arms.

'*Why* did you run off like that?' he demanded as her body stiffened defensively in his hold.

Agitatedly Kelly shook her head. The shock of him suddenly appearing, never mind what being held so close to him was doing to her nervous system, was too much for her to cope with.

'Those things that Julian said—it wasn't...I never... You have been the only one—' Kelly stopped, unable to go on.

She could feel Brough's tension, and when he lifted his hand to raise her chin so that she was forced to look into his eyes Kelly felt as though she would die from the pain of what she was expecting him to say, but to her shock what she saw in his eyes wasn't contempt and rejection, but love and tenderness and, along with it, anxiety.

'Kelly, I don't understand. You surely don't think I could *possibly* place any credence on what Cox was saying?'

Kelly stared at him.

'You didn't…you don't believe him?' she whispered.

'Of course not. How could I? What kind of man do you think I am?' he demanded, his expression changing, darkening. 'I certainly don't need a man like Cox to tell me *anything* about the woman I love. I can learn about her for myself, and what I have learned…'

The woman he *loved*. Kelly felt as though her heart was going to burst with joy.

'You *love* me?' she asked him huskily.

He was still frowning.

'Of course I do. You *know* that. I told you… Kelly… Kelly, darling, please don't cry,' he begged her as he drew her closer. 'Please, please don't cry, my love…'

'You *left* me,' Kelly wept, more out of relief and joy than unhappiness; after all, what possible reason was there for her to be unhappy *now*, with Brough's arms around her, Brough's words of love ringing so sweetly in her ears, Brough's lips so close to hers?

'I *had* to,' Brough told her. 'I'd had a phone call to say that my grandmother had been taken into hospital. You were so deeply asleep I couldn't bear to waken you…'

'Your *grandmother*,' Kelly repeated, instantly asking anxiously, 'Oh, Brough, what…? How…?'

'She's fine… She had a fall followed by pneumonia but she's well on the way to recovery now and very much looking forward to meeting you.'

'You've told her about me?' Kelly asked him shyly. 'Oh, what…?'

'I told her you were interested in seeing her teaset,'

Brough teased her, relenting when he saw the uncertainty still clouding her eyes.

'I told her I love you and that I want you to be my wife,' he told her huskily. 'She can't wait to meet you and I've promised that I'll do my best to persuade you to come with me when I drive down to see her tomorrow...'

'Oh, Brough...'

'You're crying again,' he chided her.

'It's because I'm so happy,' Kelly assured him. 'Say that again...'

'What, that you're crying?'

'No...what you said about loving me and wanting to marry me,' Kelly told him softly.

'I love you and I want you to marry me,' Brough repeated dutifully, but before Kelly could respond to him he was cupping her face and kissing her tenderly and slowly, and then not tenderly at all as her emotions caught fire and she clung passionately to him, returning the demanding pressure of his mouth, her whole body singing with joy as it recognised just how much he truly loved and wanted her.

'Brough, about Julian...' Kelly began slowly when she had finally managed to persuade him to stop kissing her.

'What about him? He means nothing to us; he has no place in our lives, our future,' Brough pointed out.

'No. But, yes, he does have a place...sort of...in *my* past,' Kelly told him carefully, adding hastily, 'Oh, no, it's not that we were ever lovers.' She gave a small shudder. 'I couldn't...he's loathsome...and I... Well, as a matter of fact, you've been the only...that is... There was a boy when... Brough, how can I explain about Julian if you keep on kissing me?' she protested shakily.

'You don't have to tell me anything about your past,' Brough told her quietly.

'You are the person you are, Kelly, and that includes everything and everyone in your past that has gone to make up that person, that Kelly—*my* Kelly. Without those experiences you wouldn't be the Kelly I love so much... You didn't really think I'd place any credence on those ridiculous lies that Cox was telling, did you?' he asked her, obviously pained that she might have done.

'I... I...I thought, after the way you left me, that you'd had second thoughts about...about us. And then, when I got your telephone message, I thought you wanted to see me to tell me that...that it was...that I was...that there wasn't any future for us...'

Kelly bit her lip as she heard the incredulous sound he made, but she was determined to finish what she had to say.

'I...' She raised her head and looked him firmly in the eye. 'When you and I met at that ball, I *was* flirting with Julian, and it was because of that that I thought you might think...'

'What I thought that night was that even though I knew nothing at all about you there was something odd about your behaviour, something that somehow didn't ring quite true, something alien and quite patently uncomfortable for you in your behaviour towards Cox.'

'You felt all that but...but you kissed me as though—' Kelly began, but Brough stopped her.

'That was an experiment,' he told her boldly. 'I was curious about you, about the...er...discrepancies in your behaviour and the person I sensed you were, and I was curious about... I felt that if I kissed you I would immediately be able to tell—'

'You're fibbing,' Kelly interrupted him. 'How could you tell anything from just one kiss?'

'I could tell that I was falling in love with you,' Brough told her wryly, silencing her before continuing, 'It did puzzle me that you should be acting in a way that was quite plainly out of character for you,' he admitted quietly. 'But I decided that whatever your reasons for doing so, they were *your* reasons. You are a woman, adult, mature, perfectly capable of making your own decisions and doing whatever you decide is right for you. I have no right nor reason to question those decisions, nor would I want to do so,' he told her gravely. 'As I've already told you, Kelly, I love the person you *are*, and whatever you choose to do or not to do...'

'I did it for Beth,' Kelly told him quickly. 'It was Dee's idea...'

Briefly she explained what they had planned to do.

'Beth... So that was the girl Cox was seeing before he met Eve. Cox told Eve that she was obsessed with him and that—'

'No way...' Kelly told him indignantly. '*He* was on the verge of getting engaged to Beth when he met Eve and then he told poor Beth that she had imagined everything...that he had never said he wanted to marry her. But Beth's not like that. She's gentle and sweet, a passive, loving...'

'Rather like my sister, in fact,' Brough concluded grimly.

'A little like that,' Kelly agreed. 'But of course Beth didn't have any money...' She sighed. 'I'm sorry if I sounded unkind...'

'No, you're only corroborating my own thoughts,' Brough told her. 'However, fortunately that's not a problem we need to worry about any more, since Eve has informed me that she is in love with Harry and that they intend to get married at Christmas. Christmas, apparently, is a perfect time for a marriage in the farming community…'

'Harry…? I knew he was attracted to her,' Kelly admitted. 'He's Dee's cousin. That was why he was escorting me at the ball.

'Brough, what are you doing?' she demanded as Brough turned her round and, tucking her into his side, proceeded to walk briskly back in the direction they had just come.

'I'm taking you home with me,' he told her firmly, and then added huskily, 'Do you realise it's almost twenty-four hours since I made love with you?'

'Brough,' Kelly protested as he took her back in his arms and proceeded to show her just how long a time he felt those hours had been.

'Kelly…' he teased her softly as he nibbled at her bottom lip and felt the sweet response of her body and herself to his caresses.

'I've got to go back and re-open the shop,' she told him.

'Why?' Brough demanded. 'There's no point; all its stock has just been sold.'

'What…what are you talking about?' Kelly demanded in bemusement. 'Who…? What…?'

'I'm talking about the fact that if the only way I can get you to myself is to buy every piece of stock in your precious shop, then that's exactly what I shall do,' Brough told her rawly.

'You can't do that,' Kelly protested. 'It will cost you a fortune…'

'Yes, I can. I'm a very rich man,' Brough assured her sweetly, adding huskily, 'The richest and happiest man in the world now I've got you, my love, my precious only one true love.

'My grandmother's already nagging me about a white wedding.'

'Cream…' Kelly murmured, nuzzling closer to the promising intoxication of his mouth. 'Cream suits me better…'

'Mmm… Well, there's no way I intend to wait until Eve gets married…'

Kelly's heart gave a funny little jump.

'It takes at least three weeks for the banns to be read, and my family will have to come back from South Africa…'

'Mmm… Well, that certainly won't take three weeks, but I hear what you're saying. How about we make it the same time as Nan's wedding anniversary, which is several weeks away? I know it would mean a lot to her if you and I chose the same wedding day…'

'It sounds perfect,' Kelly told him happily.

'It *is* perfect…like you…perfect in every way…and don't you ever forget it,' Brough told her huskily as he drew her even more deeply into his arms.

EPILOGUE

'TRY not to feel too bad that things didn't work out,' Anna tried to console Dee gently. 'We may not have been able to reveal Julian in his true colours, but at least Beth seems to be getting over him. She never mentioned him once the last time she rang me, and in fact she seemed far more concerned about the problems this interpreter's causing her than her broken engagement. And just think, if it hadn't been for *you*, Kelly and Brough might never have met...'

Dee gave her a rueful look.

They were sitting in the pretty conservatory at the back of Anna's house, Anna's cat purring loudly on her knee whilst her little dog begged hopefully for crumbs of the home-made biscuit Dee was eating.

'I wish I could be more like you, Anna,' Dee told her in a rare admission of self-criticism. 'You have such a peaceful acceptance of life...'

'Maybe now,' Anna agreed with her gentle smile, 'but not always. When I first lost Ralph, my husband...' She paused and shook her head. 'But that's all in the past now.' She looked thoughtfully at Dee before continuing quietly, 'Have you ever thought, Dee, that it might be time for *you* to put Julian and whatever...?' She stopped and bit her lip as she saw the storm clouds beginning to darken Dee's magnificent eyes.

'No. Never. There's no way I can put Julian in the past until—'

Abruptly Dee stopped. Close though she had become to both Kelly and Anna these last few weeks, there were still some things she just couldn't bring herself to discuss with them, some confidences she couldn't even make to gentle, understanding Anna.

'It isn't over yet,' she said fiercely instead, reminding Anna, 'At least he's taking the bait in *our* trap.'

Their trap? Wisely Anna said nothing. Something that went far, far deeper into Dee's past than her relatively recent friendship with her own goddaughter, Beth, was motivating Dee in her need to see Julian get his just deserts.

'Julian's already made overtures to you, hinting that he could put you in the way of a highly profitable investment opportunity, hasn't he?'

'Yes, he has,' Anna agreed.

'Excellent. We'll get him yet, and when we do...'

'When we do, what?' Anna pressed her gently.

Dee turned to her, her eyes bleak with an anguished pain that touched Anna's tender heart as she told her grimly, 'When we do, we'll expose him for the liar and the cheat that he is! The liar, the cheat and the murderer,' Dee emphasised.

The *murderer*? Anna was too shocked to say anything, and Dee was already getting up, pausing only to give the waiting dog the titbit she had saved for him before turning to hug Anna and tell her, 'I'll be in touch. There are a few arrangements I need to make to ensure that you'll have sufficient cash available to properly tempt Julian. I think probably that fifty thousand pounds should do it...'

'Fifty thousand pounds!' Anna gasped in protest. 'Oh, Dee, so much. But...'

'It's nothing,' Dee told her quietly. 'Nothing compared with the cost of a man's life.

'Don't worry,' she reassured Anna as she saw her anxious face. '*You* won't be in any danger.'

No, maybe *she* wouldn't, Anna acknowledged as she watched Dee drive away ten minutes later, but what about Dee? Ridiculous though she knew other people would find it, in view of Dee's uncompromisingly self-assured attitude, Anna actually felt very protective towards her. No one could look into those tortoiseshell-coloured eyes and see, as she, Anna, had so briefly seen, the pain and anger that sometimes lurked there, without doing so.

And Anna knew all about pain and anger and, yes, there was guilt too. Emotions these women shared, but both chose to hide their pain from those around them.

LOVER BY
DECEPTION

by

Penny Jordan

CHAPTER ONE

PAIN, anger and guilt—right now, looking at his twenty-two-year-old half-brother, Ritchie, Ward felt them all.

'Why on *earth* didn't you come to me if you needed money?' he demanded tersely.

The sunlight through the narrow, almost monastic window of Ward's study touched Ritchie's hair, turning it to bright gold.

Ward already knew that when Ritchie raised his head to look at him his blue eyes would be full of remorse.

'You've already done so much, given me so much,' Ritchie told him in the quiet, well-modulated voice that was so very much his own father's, Ward's stepfather's.

'I didn't want to bother you, to ask you for any more, but this postgraduate year in America would just be so valuable,' he told Ward earnestly, and then he was off, completely absorbed as his enthusiasm for his subject, his studies, overwhelmed his earlier guilt.

As he listened to him Ward looked at him steadily, his eyes not blue like Ritchie's and his stepfather's, but instead a dark iron-grey, the same colour as those of the tough young apprentice who had fathered him forty-two years ago and who had then lost his life before he, Ward, was out of nappies. He'd been killed in an industrial accident which had had more to do with him being the victim of a greedy employer's refusal to make sure that he was operating proper safety standards for his workforce than any genuine 'accident.' That had been in the days before such incidents were fully mon-

5

itored, when any compensation for the loss of a life, a husband, a father, was at the discretion of the employer rather than a matter for the law.

Ward's mother had received nothing—less than nothing since; following her young husband's death she had had to leave the company-owned terraced property they had lived in and she and her baby son had had to move to another part of the northern town where they lived to make their home with her own parents. Baby Ward had been left with his grandmother whilst his mother earned what little she could cleaning.

It had been through her job cleaning the local school where Ward went that she had ultimately met her second husband, Ritchie's father.

She had spent a long time discussing with Ward her hopes and plans and the changes they would make to both their lives before she had accepted the proposal of the gentle English teacher who had fallen in love with her.

Neither of them had expected that their marriage would result in the birth of their own child and Ward could well understand why both of them should have been so besotted with their unexpected and precious son.

Ritchie was his father all over again. Gentle, mild-mannered, a scholar, unworldly and easily duped by others, not through any lack of intelligence but more because neither of them could conceive of the extent of other people's greed and selfishness, since these were vices they simply did not possess.

It had been thanks to his stepfather and his care, his love, his *fatherliness*, that Ward had been persuaded to stay on at school and then, later, to start out and found his own business.

He was, as others were very fond of saying, very much a self-made man. A millionaire now, able to command whatever luxuries he wished since the communications business he had built up had been bought out by a large American corporation, but Ward preferred to live simply, almost monastically.

A big lion of a man, with broad shoulders and the tough-hewn body and bone structure he had inherited from his own father and through him from generations of working men, gave him a physical appearance of commanding strength and presence. Other men feared him—and their women...

His dark eyebrows snapped together angrily, causing his silently watching half-brother to wince inwardly and wish that he had not been so foolish.

Only the other week Ward had had to make it sharply plain to the wife of a business colleague that despite her obvious sensuality and availability he was not interested in what she had to offer.

Ward had grown up with a mother who was everything that a woman should be—tender, loving, gentle, loyal and trustworthy.

It had come as an unpleasant awakening to discover how rare her type of woman actually was.

His wife, the girl he had fallen in love with and married at twenty-two, had shown him that. She had left him before their marriage was a year old, declaring that she preferred a man who knew how to have fun, a man who had time and money to spend on her.

By that time Ward had been as disillusioned by marriage as she, tired of coming home to an empty house, tired of having to search through empty cupboards to throw himself a meal together, but tired most of all of a woman who gave nothing to their relationship or to him but who took everything.

Even so, it had given him very little pleasure five years later to have her feckless husband come begging him for a job.

More out of disgust than anything else he had not just given him one but had made the couple a private, non-repayable 'loan.' He could still remember the avaricious look he had seen in his ex-wife's eyes as she'd looked around the new house he had just moved into, assessing the worth of the property, of the man who could have been hers.

Small wonder, perhaps, that she had had the gall to dare to come on to Ward behind her new husband's back, claiming that she had loved him all along and that their divorce, her desertion of him, had been an aberration, a silly mistake. Even if he'd had the misfortune to still love her, which fortunately he did not, Ward would not have taken her back. It was in his genes, his tough northern upbringing and inheritance, to prize loyalty and honesty above all else.

Their marriage was dead, he had told her starkly, and so too was whatever emotion he had once felt for her.

He hadn't seen her since, nor had he wished to do so, and since then he had opted for a woman-free lifestyle, but that of course did not mean that he didn't have his problems, and he was being confronted with one of them right now.

When Ritchie had won a place at Oxford, Ward had proudly and willingly offered to finance him. Ritchie was, after all, his half-brother, his family, and Ward himself could never forget the help and support his stepfather had given *him* when he was first getting started.

His parents, *their* parents, were retired now, his stepfather, older than their mother by nearly fifteen years, in poor health, suffering from a heart condition, which meant that he had to live as quietly as possible, without any stress. Which was why...

'Why the *hell* didn't you *tell* me you needed more money?' he reiterated to Ritchie explosively now.

'You'd already given me so much,' Ritchie repeated. 'I just couldn't—didn't...'

'But for God's sake, Ritchie, surely your intelligence, your common sense *must* have told you that the whole thing was a scam? No one, but no one, pays that kind of interest or gets that kind of return. Why the hell do you think they were using the small ads?'

'It just seemed to be the answer to my problem,' Ritchie told him. 'I had the five thousand that you'd given me in the bank, and if it could be turned into virtually ten in a matter of months and I could get a holiday job as well...' He stopped uncomfortably as he saw the way Ward was shaking his head and looking skyward in obvious angry disbelief.

'It seemed such a good idea,' he insisted defensively. 'I had no idea...'

'You're dead right you didn't,' Ward agreed grimly. '*No* idea whatsoever. You should have come to me instead... Tell me again just what happened,' he instructed his half-brother.

Ritchie took a deep breath.

'There was an ad in one of those free news sheet things. I just happened to pick it up. I forget where. It said that anyone interested in seeing real growth and profit on their capital should apply to a box number they quoted for more details.'

'A box number.' Ward raised his eyes skyward a second time. 'So you, with the common sense of a lemming, applied.'

'It seemed such a good idea,' Ritchie protested again, a hurt look in his eyes. 'And I just thought…Well, Dad's always going on about how lucky I am to have you behind me, helping me, financing me. How he and Mum couldn't have afforded to give me any help to go up to Oxford and the fact that I don't have to finance myself with part-time work means that I'm free to study properly, and sometimes that makes me feel…Well, I hate thinking that Dad's comparing me to you and finding me wanting and that my classmates reckon I'm spoiled rotten because I've got *you* to bankroll me.'

Ritchie found wanting? Ward's frown deepened. He admired and respected his stepfather, yes, and loved him too, but he had always been sensitively conscious of how far short he must fall of the kind of ideals on which his gentle, unmaterialistic stepfather had founded his life.

'Anyway,' Ritchie continued, 'eventually I had a phone call from this chap and he told me what to do—said that I should send him a cheque for five thousand pounds and that he'd send me a receipt and a monthly statement showing the value of my investment. He also said he'd send me a portfolio listing where my money had been invested.'

'And did he, by any chance, also tell you just *how* he was able to offer such a reality-defying rate of growth and profit on this investment?' Ward enquired with awful ominous calm.

'He said it was because he cut out the middle man and that due to all the changes going on in certain overseas markets there were good opportunities there for those who knew the markets to make a real killing…'

'Indeed, and he, out of sheer generosity, intended to share that knowledge with anyone who happened to respond to his ad. Was that it…?'

'I…I didn't enquire into his motivation,' Ritchie responded with desperate dignity and a betrayingly flushed face.

'Oh, I know I ought to have done, but Professor Cummins had just told me that if I took this extra year out to get an additional qualification in the US, then I'd have a much better chance of success if I ever decided I wanted to apply for a fellowship over here, and he had just asked me to do some research for him for a series of lectures he was giving in America. God knows why he chose me. My grades…'

'He chose you for very much the same reason that our enterprising entrepreneur and financial crook chose you, Ritchie,' Ward told him with cool sarcasm before prodding his half-brother.

'So, to continue, you paid over the five thousand pounds you had in your bank account, and then what?'

'Well, for the first two months everything went well. I got statements showing an excellent return on the investment, but then the third month I didn't receive a statement, and when I eventually rang the number I'd been given I was told that it was unobtainable.'

He looked so perplexed that in any other circumstances Ward, who had a good sense of humour, would have been tempted to laugh a little at his naivety, but this was no laughing matter. This was a young man who had been deliberately and cold-bloodedly relieved of five thousand pounds by as shrewd a fraudulent operator as Ward had ever come across, and he had met his fair share of the breed in his time, although needless to say none of them had ever taken *him* in.

'How surprising,' was the only comment he allowed himself to make.

Ritchie raised stricken eyes to his and muttered, 'I know. I know what you're thinking but...Well, at first I just thought it was a mistake. I wrote to the address on the statements but my letter came back ''address unknown'' and since then...'

'Since then your friendly investment manager has proved that it isn't just money he can magic away into thin air?' Ward suggested dryly.

'I really am sorry, Ward, but I...I had to tell you...I haven't even got enough money left to cover myself this term now, never mind next, and...'

'How much is it going to cost you to pay for the rest of your year's living and studying expenses?' Ward asked him point-blank.

Reluctantly Ritchie told him.

'And how much for your year in the US? And I want the full cost of it, please, Ritchie, not some ridiculous guestimate because you're too proud to tell me the full amount.'

Again, this time even more reluctantly, Ritchie gave Ward the figure he wanted.

'Right,' Ward announced, opening a drawer to his desk and removing his cheque book, which he promptly opened, writing across the top cheque an amount which not only covered the sum Ritchie had disclosed but included a very generous allowance over it as well.

So much so that when he handed Ritchie the cheque the younger man gasped and coloured up to the roots of his fair hair, protesting, 'No, Ward, I can't. That's far too much... I...'

'Take it...' Ward overrode him firmly and then glanced at his watch before adding casually, 'Oh, and by the way, I've decided it's time you had a new car. I've got the keys for you so you can leave the old one here; I'll dispose of it for you.'

'A new car? But I don't need one; the Mini is fine for my needs,' Ritchie protested.

'For yours, yes, but your father isn't getting any younger. I know how much he looks forward to your visits home and how much he worries, and we both know that that isn't good for him. He'll feel much happier if he knows you're driving something that's safe...'

Shaking his head, Ritchie accepted the set of keys his elder brother was extending to him. There was no point in arguing with Ward. No point whatsoever. As he smiled his thanks into his brother's austerely handsome face he wished, not for the first time, that he could be more like him.

Only the previous term, when Ward had come down to visit him, one of the other students in his year, a girl—the prettiest and most sought after girl on the campus—had commented breathlessly to him that Ward was just so-o-o hunkily sexy, and Ritchie had known exactly what she meant.

There was an energy, a power, and *maleness* about Ward that somehow or other set him apart from other men. He was a born leader and he possessed that magical spark inherited from his forebears which Ritchie knew he could never, ever possess, no matter how many academic qualifications he obtained.

After his half-brother had left, Ward picked up the small folder he had brought with him. In it were the statements Ritchie had referred to. Frowningly Ward studied them. He would check out the stock they cited, of course, but he knew already that they would either be completely fictitious or, if real, never actually bought. That was how this kind of scum worked.

Heavens, but you'd have thought that a young man with Ritchie's brains would have known immediately that the whole thing was a scam. There had been enough warnings over the years in the financial press about this type of thing, but then Ritchie was studying the classics and Ward doubted that he had ever read a financial article in his life.

His father was similarly naive and had been hopelessly out of place in the large, sprawling urban jungle of a school where he had taught and where Ward himself had been a pupil. Ward had perfectly understood what his mother had meant when she had told her son gently that one of the reasons she wanted to accept Alfred's proposal of marriage was that she felt he needed someone to look after him properly.

Ward could still remember how some of the other boys had mocked and taunted him because their softie of an English teacher was now his stepfather, but Ward had soon shown them the error of their ways. He had been big and strong for his age, with a tongue that could be just as quick and painful as his fists when it needed to be.

Ward had grown up in an environment where you had to be tough to survive, and the lessons he had learned there had equipped him very well when it had come to surviving in business. But now those early thrusting, exhausting years were over. Now he never needed to work again.

He got up and walked over to stare out of the window. Down below, the Yorkshire moors rolled away towards the town. The stone manor house he had made his home was considered by many to be too bleak for comfort, but Ward just shrugged his shoulders at their criticism. It suited him. But then, perhaps, he was a bleak person. He certainly was one it wasn't advisable to try to cheat.

He looked again at the statement. He suspected that J. Cox and A. Trewayne, whoever they might be, were by now very safely out of reach; that was the way of such things. But the streak of stubbornness and the drive for justice that were such a strong part of his personality refused to allow him to dismiss the matter without making at least some attempt to bring them to book.

Now that he had sold his business, his time was pretty much his own. There were certain calls upon it, of course. He made regular visits to his parents, who were now living happily and genteelly in the spa town of Tunbridge Wells. He took a very vigorous interest in the local workshop he had founded and funded which taught youngsters the basic mechanics of a wide range of trades—thus not only providing them with some skills but also providing older men who had been made redundant with a new job which gave them a renewed sense of pride in their trades.

It was a project to which Ward devoted a considerable amount of his time, and he had no time for shirkers. Everyone accepted onto it, whether as a teacher or a pupil, was expected to work and work hard. Tucked away at the back of Ward's mind was the possibility that, should the right opportunity arise, it might be worthwhile establishing an eclectic workforce comprising the best of his young trainees and encouraging them to work both as a supportive group and on their own.

'Ward, you can't finance the apprenticeship of every school-leaver in Yorkshire,' his accountant had protested when Ward had first mooted his plans to him.

But Ward had shaken his head and told him simply, 'Maybe not, but at least I'll be able to give some of them a chance.'

'And what about those who are simply using your scheme, your generosity—the ones who are using *you*?' his accountant had asked him.

Ward had merely shrugged, the movement of his big shoulders signifying that they were broad enough to take such small-mindedness and greed. But if either his accountant or anyone else had ever dared to suggest that he was an idealist, a romantic at heart who wanted only to see the best in everyone, to help everyone, Ward would have dismissed such a statement instantly with a pithily scathing response.

He frowned as he studied the papers Ritchie had given him again and then flicked through his phone book, looking for the number of the very discreet and professional service he sometimes used when he wanted to make enquiries about anyone. As a millionaire and a philanthropist he was constantly being approached for financial help, and whilst Ward was the first man to put his hand in his pocket to help a genuinely deserving cause or person he was street-wise enough to want to make sure that they *were* genuinely deserving.

Whilst he was waiting for his call to be answered, his attention was caught by some papers awaiting his attention on his desk.

They carried his full name—once the bane of his life and the cause of many a childhood scuffle; where he had grown up there had sometimes been only one way of convincing his jeering taunter that the name Hereward did not mean that he was a victim or an easy target for the school's bullies.

Hereward.

'Why?' he had once emotionally demanded of his mother.

'Because I like it,' she had told him with her loving smile. 'I thought it suited you. Made you different...'

'Aye, it's done that all right,' he had agreed bluntly.

Hereward Hunter.

Perhaps deep down inside his mother had been motivated by much the same impulse that had driven the absentee father in Johnny Cash's famous song 'A Boy Named Sue.' She had known, not that it would make him different, but that it would make him strong. Well, strong he undoubtedly was, certainly strong enough to ensure that J. Cox and A. Trewayne paid back every penny they had gulled from his naive half-brother, even if he had to up-end them and shake them by the seat of their pants to make their pockets disgorge it.

A single bar of sunlight streaming in through the narrow window of his office touched his thick dark brown hair, burnishing and highlighting the very masculine planes of his face. His eyes were as cold and dark as the North Sea on a stark winter's day when he told the girl who answered his call whom he wanted to speak with.

Oh, yes, J. Cox and A. Trewayne were most definitely going to regret cheating his half-brother. Legally it might be possible to pursue them through the courts for fraud, but Ward had already decided that they merited something a little swifter and more punitive than the slow process of the law.

Like the bullies who had tried it on with him at school, their type relied on their victim's vulnerability and fear—not, of course, fear of violence, but of being publicly branded either foolish or, even worse, financially incompetent. And that fear prevented the truth of what these con men were doing from being disclosed.

Well, they were soon going to discover that in trying to con *his* half-brother they had made the biggest mistake of their grubbily deceitful lives.

CHAPTER TWO

'ANNA! Hello! How are you?'

As Anna Trewayne heard the pleasure in Dee's voice her heart skipped a small, uncomfortable beat. Dee wasn't going to sound anything like so happy once Anna had broken the news to her that she had to break.

Unhappily, she wondered whether the three of them—Dee, Kelly and herself—would have taken the decision they had taken to try to bring to book the man who had so nearly destroyed the life and broken the heart of the fourth member of their closely-knit quartet—her own god-daughter, Beth—if they had known just how things were going to turn out.

Kelly, the first of them to pit herself against Julian Cox and reveal him as the cheat and liar that he was, even with Dee's encouragement and backing, had in the end not been able to go through with their plan to unmask him by pretending to be a rich heiress. Yes, Julian had shown an interest in her, and, yes, he had also made overtures to her whilst still paying court to his existing girlfriend. But then Kelly had fallen in love, and, as Dee had generously acknowledged, there had been no way she could have continued with their plan to unmask Julian once Kelly had fallen in love with Brough and he with her.

And so Dee had announced that they would take their plan to stage two, which meant that she, Anna, had had to intimate to Julian that she would like his financial advice. She had, she had told him when they had met

19

up, a sizeable sum of money she wanted to invest to produce a good return.

Coached by Dee, who had also supplied the fifty thousand pounds Anna supposedly wanted to invest, Anna had listened wide-eyed and apparently naively whilst Julian, true to form, had informed her that he knew just the deal for her and that all she had to do was to write him a cheque for fifty thousand pounds and relax.

'Fifty thousand pounds, Dee,' Anna had protested when she had reported this conversation to her. 'It seems such a lot…'

'Not really.' Dee had stopped her firmly. Although at thirty-seven Anna was Dee's senior by seven years, Dee's mature and businesslike manner often made Anna feel that she was the younger one.

As a foursome they were perhaps a disparate group, she recognised. Beth, at twenty-four, was a dreamer, gentle and easy-going, which was what had made her such an easy victim for Julian Cox.

Kelly, Beth's friend and business partner in the pretty shop they ran in the small town of Rye-on-Averton, where Anna had encouraged them to move and open up a business, was much more vivacious and impetuous. Brough and she would make a very good couple, Anna acknowledged.

Dee was their landlady; she owned the building which housed the shop and the flat above it where both girls had lived until Kelly had met Brough. Dee's father had been a very well thought of local entrepreneur and had been on several local charity committees until his unexpected death just as Dee had been about to leave university. Immediately Dee had changed her plans, and instead of pursuing her own choice of career she had come home to take up the reins of her father's business. It had been Dee who had been the prime motivator in their decision to bring Julian Cox to book for the way he had humiliated and hurt Beth, although Beth herself was still unaware of this decision.

'We won't say anything about any of this to Beth,' Dee had informed them. 'It wouldn't serve any useful purpose and it could even do some harm, especially now that she seems to be getting over Julian and putting what happened behind her.'

'Yes, she does. She's tremendously excited about this glass she's found in the Czech Republic,' Kelly had agreed, and Anna had been too relieved to hear that Beth was getting over the pain that Julian had caused her to want to protest or argue.

It had been Dee's idea to persuade Beth to visit Prague on a buying trip after the break-up of her relationship with Julian Cox.

Since her return Beth had thrown herself into the shop with a determination and single-mindedness which had rather surprised Anna, who was more used to her god-daughter's dreamy habit of allowing others to take a leading role in things.

Perhaps she felt that now that Kelly was soon to be married it was down to her to become the senior partner in their business, Anna decided. She herself was the oldest member of the quartet; Beth's mother was her own cousin, which was how she had originally come to be asked to be Beth's godmother. Both families were based in Cornwall and had been for several generations.

At twenty-two Anna had married her childhood sweetheart, Ralph Trewayne. They had been so much in love. So very happy together. Ralph had been a quiet, gentle boy, their love for one another a very youthful, tender one. What it might have grown into, how it would have weathered the tests of time, they'd never had the opportunity to find out. Ralph had been killed; drowned whilst out sailing. They had only been married a very short time and after his death Anna had been unable to bear the sight of the sea or the memories it brought her and so she had moved here to Rye to make a new life for herself. Rye was inland and the river that ran close by was shallow and placid. Even so, Anna had deliberately chosen to buy a house outside the town, and with no views from any of its windows of the river.

Dee had commented on this once in some surprise when the subject had been raised. 'Well, this house is certainly in a lovely spot, Anna, but most people who move to Rye look upon properties in a riverside location as being in a prime position.'

Anna had seen that Dee was curious about her decision but she had simply not felt she had known her well enough at that stage to confide her feelings to her.

'This house suits me,' was all she had felt able to say. 'I like living here.'

'Well, you've certainly made a very comfortable home of it,' Dee had responded approvingly.

Ralph had been very well insured, and financially Anna was comfortably off. She had never had any desire to remarry. Somehow it would have seemed a betrayal, not so much of their love, which had now faded to a soft, fuzzy, out-of-focus memory she could sometimes scarcely believe was hers, but of the fact that Ralph was no longer alive, that his life was over, cut off cruelly short. And yes, a part of her somehow felt guilty because she *was* alive and he wasn't.

She was sad not to have had children but she enjoyed living in Rye. She liked the town's quiet pace and the beauty of its surrounding countryside. She enjoyed walking and was a member of a rambling club. Needlework was one of her hobbies, and she was currently working on a communal project involving a tapestry depicting the history of the town.

For the past five years she had been doing voluntary work, helping to provide community care for the elderly, and through her friendship with Dee she had found herself being co-opted onto several charity committees.

'I'm not quite sure I shall be very much use,' she had protested when Dee had first asked her to join one of them.

That had been in the early days of what had then been more of an acquaintanceship than a friendship, and Anna, who was normally rather retiring and reticent about making new friends, had surprised herself a little at the speed with which she had become so close to Dee. Despite Dee's outward air of self-sufficiency, Anna sensed there was an inner, hidden vulnerability about the younger woman that touched her own sensitive emotions. She liked Dee and she respected her and she acknowledged that it was Dee's energy and insistence that had encouraged her to become more involved with the town and its activities.

'Nonsense,' Dee had told her sternly. 'You undervalue yourself far too much,' she had scolded Anna, and, with Dee's encouragement, Anna had even taken the step of starting to train for voluntary counselling work. What was more, she had surprised herself by discovering how instinctively skilled she was at it.

She had her cat and her dog, and her small circle of friends, and all in all she was quite satisfied with her gentle, compact way of life. Yes, it might lack excitement and passion and love, but Ralph's death had caused her so much pain and despair that she had been afraid of allowing herself to love another man.

All in all, until Julian Cox had become involved in their lives, she had considered herself to be very content. And now here she was, feeling anything but content, dreading having to give Dee the bad news. She knew there were those who considered Dee to be too businesslike, too distant, but Anna knew there was another side to Dee—a softer emotional side.

Taking a deep breath, she announced, 'Dee, I'm afraid I've got some bad news. It's about Julian Cox and...and the money...your money...'

'He hasn't backed out of advising you on investing it, has he?' Dee asked her sharply. 'Although it has taken some time to lure him in, I thought he'd well and truly taken our bait.'

'No. He hasn't backed out,' Anna told her, 'but...'

She paused and cleared her throat. There was just no easy way for her to tell Dee this.

'Dee, he's disappeared, and he's taken the money, your fifty thousand pounds, with him.'

'He's *what*?'

'I know, I'm sorry; it's my fault...' Anna began guiltily, but Dee stopped her immediately.

'Of course it isn't your fault. How could it be? I was the one... Tell me exactly what has happened, Anna.'

Anna took another deep breath.

'Well, I did as you'd said, and I told Julian that I'd got fifty thousand pounds to invest and that I wanted a good return on it. He said he knew just the right kind of investment for me. He also suggested that we keep things very informal. He said that the deal he had in mind was an off-shore thing—something to do with

Hong Kong—and he said that the less paperwork involved, the better the profit would be for both of us.

'I did try to ring you to get your advice but you...'

'I was in London on business. I know. I picked up your message, but even if I'd been here it wouldn't have made any difference because I would most certainly have told you to go ahead.'

'Well, I agreed to what Julian was suggesting and wrote him the cheque. I thought that the mere fact that it would have to go through my bank account and his would be proof that he had had the money. He said he'd be in touch. I hadn't really intended to ring him at all— after all, it was only last week that I gave him the cheque—but then I bumped into Brough's sister Eve with your cousin Harry and she just happened to mention that she had seen Julian at the airport. Apparently he was just getting out of a taxi as they were getting into one. She said that he didn't see them and...

'Anyway, I don't know why, but I just got a feeling that something wasn't quite right so I rang Julian. His telephone had been cut off and when I went round to his address his place was up to let. I tried his bank and all they would tell me was that they had no knowledge of his whereabouts. Brough's made some enquiries, though, and he's discovered that Julian has closed his account.

'No one seems to know where he's gone, Dee, or when he's coming back and I'm very much afraid...'

'That he won't *be* coming back,' Dee finished grimly for her.

'I think you're probably right, given what we know about his precarious finances. With fifty thousand pounds in his pocket he could quite easily have decided to cut his losses here, and dodge his debts, and simply

start the whole dishonest game afresh somewhere else.'
Anna bit her lip.

'Dee, I'm so sorry…'

'It's not your fault,' Dee assured her immediately. 'If
anyone's to blame, it has to be me.'

'What are we going to do?' Anna asked her anxiously.

'What *you* are going to do is relax and stop worrying,' Dee told her gently. 'As for what I shall do…I'm
not sure yet, Anna. God, but it makes me so angry to
think he's getting away with what he's done absolutely
scot-free. The man's only a hair's breadth away from
being a criminal, if indeed he isn't legally one, but it
isn't so much the actual money he's cheated other people out of that—'

Dee broke off and Anna could hear the emotion in
her husky voice as she continued shakily, 'It's the damage he's done to other people, the hurt and harm he's
caused.'

'Well, Beth seems to be recovering from her heartbreak over him now.' Anna tried to console her.

'Yes,' Dee agreed. 'But it isn't just—' She stopped
abruptly, and not for the first time Anna had the distinct
impression that there was much, much more to Dee's
determination to unmask Julian Cox than just the heartache he had caused Beth. She knew better than to pry,
though. Dee was an extremely proud woman, and a
rather vulnerable one behind that pride. If she wanted
to confide in her Anna knew that she would do so, and
until, or unless, she did so Anna felt that she had no
right to probe into what she guessed was an extremely
sensitive issue.

'Perhaps Dee and Julian were an item once,' Kelly
had once mused to Anna when they were discussing the

subject. 'Perhaps he dropped her in the same way he did Beth.'

But Anna had immediately shaken her head in denial.

'No. Never. Dee would never be attracted to a man like Julian,' she had told Kelly firmly. 'Never.'

'No. No, you're right,' Kelly had agreed. 'But there must be something.'

'If there is and if she wants to tell us about it then I'm sure she knows she can,' Anna had pointed out gently then, and a little shamefacedly Kelly had agreed that Dee was entitled to her privacy and her past.

'Dee, I feel so guilty about your money,' Anna repeated unhappily now. 'I should have realised... suspected...'

'There's no way I want you to feel guilty, Anna. In fact...'

Dee paused and then continued quietly, 'I rather suspected that something like this might happen, or I thought he might be tempted to try to abscond with the money. What I didn't allow for was that he would do it so openly or so fast. You aren't in any way to blame,' she added firmly. 'His situation must be even more desperate than I thought for him to have behaved so recklessly. After this there's no way he can come back, not to Rye. No way at all.

'What are you doing this weekend?' Dee asked, changing the subject.

'Nothing special. Beth's going down to Cornwall to see her parents. Kelly and Brough are away. What about you?'

'My aunt in Northumberland hasn't been too well again so I'm going to go up and see her. Her doctor wants her to have an operation but she's afraid that if she does she might not recover, so I thought I'd try to talk to her and make her see sense.'

'Dee, do you think we'll be able to track Julian down?'

'I'm not sure,' Dee told her soberly. 'If I know Julian he'll have gone somewhere where he can't be touched by European law and it probably isn't just *our* fifty thousand pounds he's taken with him.'

For a long time after she had said goodbye to Dee and replaced her telephone receiver, Anna stood silently in her conservatory, ignoring the indignant miaows of her cat, Whittaker, as he wove round her legs. Beth's mother, her cousin, had suggested that it was high time she paid a visit home to Cornwall. Perhaps she should, Anna acknowledged. The time was past now when the hurt of going back to the place she had once loved so much, knowing it had taken the life of the man she loved, had been too much for her to bear.

Their love had been a gentle, very young and idealistic kind of love, the intimacy between them a little awkward and hesitant, both of them learning the art of loving together, and what hurt more than anything else now was knowing that Ralph had never been allowed to reach his full potential, to grow from the boy he had in reality still been to the man he would have become.

She could barely remember now how it had felt to love him, how it had felt to be loved by him. Try as she might she could hardly conjure up now those nights they had lain in one another's arms. They seemed to belong to a different life, a different Anna.

No, there was no reason really why she shouldn't go back. She had forgiven the sea a long time ago for stealing her love. But had she forgiven herself for going on living without him?

She might not be able to recall his image very clearly any more but she could still vividly recall the look of anguish and resentment in his mother's eyes on the day of his funeral. It had told her, without the words being spoken, how bitterly his mother resented the fact that she was still alive whilst her beloved son was dead. How distressed, how guilt-ridden that look had made Anna feel. Now her guilt was caused by the fact that her memories of Ralph and their love were so distant that they might have belonged to someone else. She had loved him, yes, but it had been a girl's love for a boy. Now she was a woman, and if the vague but so sharply disturbing longings that sometimes woke her from her sleep were anything to go by she was increasingly becoming a woman whose body felt cheated of its rightful role, its capacity for pleasure, its need for love...

Anna drew in a distressed, sharp breath. She knew quite well that it was her ongoing training as a counsellor that was bringing to the fore all these unfamiliar and uncomfortable feelings, but that didn't make them any easier to bear.

Watching as Brough kissed his fiancée, Kelly, she had actually experienced the most shockingly sharp pang of envy. Not because Brough loved Kelly. That couldn't be the reason. Brough, much as she liked him, was simply not her type. No, her envy had been caused by the most basic feminine kind of awareness that her womanhood, her sexuality, was being deprived of expression.

But what did that mean? That she was turning into some kind of sex-starved middle-aged stereotype? Her body stiffened at the very thought, pride lifting her chin. That she most certainly was not. No way!

Her cat, seeing that his mistress wasn't going to respond to his overtures, stalked away in indignation. As she continued to stare out of the window Anna's soft blue-grey eyes misted a little.

At thirty-seven she still had the lithe, slender figure she had had at eighteen, and her hair was still as soft and silky, its honey-coloured warmth cut to shoulder-length now instead of worn halfway down her back. Ralph had used to run his fingers down its shiny length before he kissed her.

Anna gave a small, distraught shudder. What was the matter with her? She had met men, plenty of them— nice men, good men—in the years of her widowhood, and not once had she ever come anywhere near desiring any of them.

How irrational and unsolicited it was that her body should suddenly so keenly remember what desire was, how it felt, how it ached and urged, when her mind, her emotions, remained stubbornly resolute that they wanted no part in such a dangerous resurgence of her youthful sensuality.

'Yes. I'm sorry, I'm coming,' she acknowledged as Whittaker's protesting wails suddenly intruded on her thoughts.

CHAPTER THREE

HUMMING exultantly beneath his breath, Ward checked the last signpost before his ultimate destination. Rye-on-Averton.

It sounded such a middle England, respectable sort of place, but at least one of its inhabitants was anything but honest and trustworthy.

He hadn't been able to believe his luck when the agents he had employed had informed him that, whilst they could find no trace of Julian Cox, who according to their enquiries had, in fact, left the country and apparently disappeared, his partner, Anna Trewayne, had been traced to the small English town of Rye.

They had even been able to supply Ward with an address and a telephone number, as well as a considerable amount of other pertinent information about Ms Trewayne.

Widowed, childless, outwardly she appeared to live a life of almost boring propriety and respectability. Ward knew otherwise, of course. He could picture her now. She was in her late thirties and no doubt struggling to hold onto her youth. She probably possessed a certain amount of surface charm—a useful tool for helping to persuade vulnerable men to part with their money. Her make-up would be too heavy and her skirts too short. She would have sharp eyes and a keen interest in a man's bank account and, of course, a very shrewd business brain—but not, it seemed, shrewd enough to warn her to do what her erstwhile partner had done and dis-

31

appear whilst the going was good. Perhaps she even had plans to continue with their 'business' on her own.

Perhaps he was a chauvinist but for some reason Ward felt an even greater sense of revulsion and outrage towards the woman who had cheated his half-brother than he had done the man. An avaricious, heartless woman. Ward had a deep sense of loathing for the breed. His ex-wife had, after all, been one of them.

He dropped the speed of his powerful, top-of-the-range Mercedes to turn off the bypass and into the town.

Nestled in a pretty green valley, it had an almost picture-book quaintness. Mentally he compared it to the grimy, run-down, inner-city area where he had grown up and then grimaced. No haggard-faced, old-before-their-time, out-of-work men gathered on the corners of *this* place. No gangs of testosterone-driven youths with nothing in front of them, no way out of the underclass environment that trapped them, roamed these clean, tree-lined streets.

Ward saw a parking area up ahead of him alongside the river and he pulled into it. Time to study his map. As he switched off the engine he was conscious of the beginnings of a tension headache. He picked up the street directory map he had brought with him. A few seconds later Ward jabbed his forefinger triumphantly onto the map as he found the place he was looking for.

Anna Trewayne lived a little way out of town, her house solitary, without any neighbours, but then, no doubt, a woman of her ilk would not want the complications that curious neighbours could bring.

As he reversed his car back into the traffic Ward's expression was bleak.

Anna was in the garden when Ward arrived, the sound of his car stopping on the gravel drive causing her to

put down the basket she had been filling with flowers
for the house and frown a little anxiously.

She wasn't expecting any visitors, and the car, like
the man emerging from it, was unfamiliar to her.

Expecting her visitor to announce himself at the front
door, Anna turned to slip into the house through the
still open conservatory door, but Ward just caught sight
of her flurried movement out of the corner of his eye
and, wheeling round, started to walk swiftly towards
her, calling out to her, 'Just a minute, if you please, Mrs
Trewayne; I want a word with you.'

Instinctively Anna panicked. Both the way he was
walking and the tone of his voice were distinctly threatening and she started to run towards the protection of
the conservatory, but she wasn't quite fast enough and
Ward caught up with her just as she reached the door,
grabbing hold of her wrist in a grip that almost made
her flinch at its strength.

'Let me go... I...I have a dog...' Anna told him,
issuing the first threat that came into her mind, but just
as she felt his grip starting to slacken Missie came trotting round the corner, her small, furry body quivering
with welcome as she rushed happily towards Anna's
captor.

'So I see,' he agreed sardonically. He started to lift
his free hand and immediately Anna reacted, her fear
for her little dog far, far greater than her fear for herself.

'Don't you dare hurt her,' she told him fiercely, holding out her own free arm protectively to Missie.

The little dog, a bundle of white fluff, had been a
rescue dog, bought as a puppy and then abandoned
when the family who'd owned her had decided that her

small, sharp teeth were doing too much damage to their home.

Anna had taken her in, trained and loved her, and Missie adored her.

Ward frowned his surprise. Odd that a woman of her type should ignore her own danger just to protect her dog. Not that he had intended to hurt the little creature, and Missie seemed to know it.

Ignoring her mistress's frantic attempts to shoo her away, she was happily investigating the stranger's shoes, and then, as Ward extended his hand towards her, she jumped up and licked it, wagging her small tail approvingly.

'Look, I don't know who you are or what you want,' Anna began nervously, 'but—'

'But you *do* know Julian Cox, don't you?' Ward slipped in quietly.

'Julian.' Anna went pale. Was this man someone Julian had sent to demand more money from her? Had he perhaps guessed what they were doing?

As he watched the blood drain from her face Ward experienced a disturbingly unfamiliar—and unwanted—sensation. All right, she might not look anything like he had imagined. Her skirt was calf-length, all soft and floaty, and as for her make-up—well, she had to be wearing some, surely? No woman of her age could have such a soft, pink, kissable-looking mouth naturally, could she? And her hair had to be dyed, he decided triumphantly, whilst as for that air of frightened vulnerability she was projecting—well, that was, no doubt, as false as the colour of her hair.

'Don't bother lying to me,' Ward announced sternly. 'I know you know him and know something else as

well. I know just what the pair of you have been up
to…'

'The p-pair of us…?' Anna repeated, stammering a
little. 'I…'

'I've got the evidence here,' Ward told her curtly,
releasing Anna's wrist as he reached into the inside
pocket of his suit.

As she rubbed her tender wrist Anna wished that she
had the courage to risk slamming the conservatory door
and locking him on the outside of it, but a quick, fleet-
ing glance at him warned her of the danger of doing
anything so reckless. For a start there was the size of
him. He was…he was huge, she decided. So tall, over
six feet, and so…so *big*. Not fat…no, not that. She
could feel her face growing hot as her feminine instincts
conveyed the message to her that the male body, under
its quietly dignified suiting, owed its size to hard-packed
male muscle and the kind of physique one might normally associate with a man who spent a lot of his time
working physically hard. His hair was thick and dark
brown, tinged unexpectedly with gold at the ends where
the sun had caught it, giving him an almost leonine
look.

'This *is* you, isn't it?' he demanded as he turned the
paper he was holding towards Anna, jabbing his forefinger at a name printed on it.

Anna's eyes widened as she saw that it was her own.

'Yes. Yes…it is…' she admitted, her face burning
hotly as she saw from the look he was giving her that
he hadn't, after all, missed the discreet female inspection she had been giving him. Trying to ignore him, she
forced herself to read the document. What on earth was
it?

Anna blinked and stared hard at what he was holding,

her heart starting to pound heavily. In front of her on the paper she could see her own name quite plainly, and just as plainly beneath it was written the word 'partner.' What on earth did it mean? Why on earth had Julian Cox untruthfully and surely illegally claimed her as his partner? Anna had no idea. All she could assume was that he had done it because he'd felt it added weight and credibility to whatever he had been planning. Or had he perhaps known that something like this could happen and, in that knowledge, had deliberately set her up to act as a fall guy? Anna wondered queasily. He was, she knew, perfectly capable of that kind of deliberately dishonest behaviour.

The words of denial and protest springing to her lips were ruthlessly suppressed. Could this be the breakthrough, the evidence of Julian's fraudulent deceit which Dee had striven so hard to find? She needed time to think, Anna decided, time to consult Dee and tell her what had happened, and, most of all, she needed that all-important piece of paper. But as she reached out to take it, as though he sensed what she was about to do, the man stepped back from her, determinedly folding it and putting it back in his pocket.

'Well, your partner might have been clever enough to disappear, but you, it seems, were less wise—or perhaps more arrogant,' Ward challenged softly.

Arrogant!

Anna couldn't believe what she was hearing.

'How does it feel, knowing that you have deprived other people of their money; that this house, the clothes you wear and the food you eat are, no doubt, paid for out of other people's pockets?' Ward demanded with scornful anger. 'Nothing to say?' he queried. 'No protests of innocence? You *do* surprise me.'

He would be even more surprised if he knew the truth, Anna reflected, but would he believe her if she tried to tell him? From the look on his face, somehow she doubted it. But if he thought she was going to stand there and allow him to revile her verbally...

Tilting her head so that she could look straight into his eyes, she told him firmly, 'Look, I'm sorry if you feel that you've been cheated...' She paused. Something about his attitude made her so angry that she felt physically weak at the knees. At least, she supposed it must be anger; after all, what else could it be?

She smiled sweetly before saying, very, very gently, 'However, surely the fact that you were being offered such an exceptionally high rate of interest on your investment must have alerted you to the fact that something might not be quite...genuine...?'

Ward could scarcely believe his ears. Was she actually daring to tell him that it was his *own* fault he had been cheated; that *he* had been guilty of either a lack of intelligent caution or an excess of simple greed?

Her head barely touched his shoulder. She was as fine-boned as a little bird and he guessed that he could have spanned her waist with both his hands and picked her up off the ground without straining his breath, and yet she stood there and had the audacity to challenge him!

Reluctantly Ward acknowledged that she had guts. Certainly more than her partner. By heaven, though, she was cool and calm—both virtues that he admired.

Abruptly he pulled himself back from the dangerous brink he was teetering on, reminding himself of just what she had done.

'I'm sure it would have,' he agreed grimly. 'I pride myself on being able to spot a phoney a mile off. As it happens it isn't me the pair of you gulled—but then, of course, you know that already.

'Does the name Ritchie Lewis mean anything to you?' he shot at Anna.

'No…I've never heard of him before,' Anna told him honestly, starting to frown as she questioned, 'But if you didn't invest money with Julian then what are you doing here?'

'Ritchie is my half-brother,' he told her impatiently, demanding bitingly, 'Have you any idea just what you've done? Ritchie should be studying, not worrying about the loss of five thousand pounds. No, of course you haven't,' he told her scornfully. 'I'll bet you've never strayed out of your cosseted, comfortable little world. Of course you don't know what it is to suffer pain, disappointment—'

'You're making judgements about me without knowing the first thing about me,' Anna interrupted him swiftly, her gentle expression suddenly replaced by one of pride and anger.

'Oh, but I do know the first thing about you. I know that you're a liar and a cheat,' Ward returned softly.

Anna gave a sharp gasp.

'Well…nothing to say?' Ward demanded.

'I…I don't intend to say anything until…until I've spoken to my legal advisors,' Anna fibbed, suddenly gaining inspiration from a recent television series she had been watching.

'Your legal advisors? They're no doubt as guilty of sharp practice as you and your precious partner,' Ward told her bluntly. 'Well, let me tell you here and now, there's no way I'm going to let him or you get away with this. You owe my half-brother five thousand pounds and I intend to make sure you pay it back.'

'You do?' Anna was impressed. Dee would love to meet this man, she knew. Here at last was someone who was prepared to stand up to Julian; to pursue him, Anna was certain, to the furthermost corners of the earth with relentless determination.

Even so, there was something about his attitude towards *her* that had got her hackles rising in a way she could never remember anyone else doing.

'Er…what you have to say is extremely interesting, Mr…er…'

'Hunter,' Ward supplied briefly. 'Her— Ward Hunter.'

Ward Hunter. Well, at least now she had his name. She could pass it on to Dee along with the information he had given her and then she could leave him and Dee to pursue Julian Cox together.

Suddenly Anna had a brainwave.

'You say you want me to repay your half-brother's money. I'm afraid I don't have five thousand pounds here at home with me. Could you call back, say, tomorrow…?'

Ward stared at her. Now what was she up to? One minute she was claiming she knew nothing about the money, the next she was accusing him of deserving to be cheated, and now here she was calmly and coolly announcing that she would repay him. She was even more dangerous than Ward had first suspected.

'Why should I believe you? You could pull the same disappearing stunt as your partner.'

'Leave the country, you mean.' Anna looked down at where Missie was lying on the conservatory floor. 'No. I couldn't do that,' she said simply and ridiculously.

Ward found that he believed her. She might be quite

happy to cheat his brother and goodness knew how many others, but he had seen the love in her eyes when she looked at her dog. She wasn't going to abandon her.

'I could, of course, give you a cheque now,' Anna suggested sweetly. The look he gave her in return almost made her want to laugh.

'Which your bank would, no doubt, refuse to honour,' he told her, shaking his head. 'No, I don't think so. I want the cash…'

'Then you will just have to wait until tomorrow,' Anna told him firmly.

'Very well, then,' Ward agreed. 'I'll be here at nine sharp.'

'Nine? But the bank doesn't open until ten,' Anna protested.

'Exactly,' Ward responded smoothly. 'I can hardly allow you to take the risk of travelling there and back alone with such a large sum of money. I shall come with you.'

'Come with me…?' Anna's outrage momentarily overwhelmed her. 'Perhaps you'd like to stay the night and keep me chained to your side,' she said acidly, only to flush bright red as she saw the look in his eyes.

Ward was as startled by the bright pink glow of her cheeks as Anna was. It would have been much more in character for her to have deliberately flirted with him, to have flaunted her sexuality and drawn his attention to it rather than to betray such embarrassment. It was just another one of her tricks, of course, and one she had no doubt used to good effect in the past on the more vulnerable members of his sex. He could well imagine how easily a man might feel tempted to rush to protect and cherish her. She was so tiny, so fragile…and yet, at the same time, so determinedly and so ridiculously feisty.

Angrily he turned away from her, warning her as he did so, 'Don't even think of not being here because I promise you, wherever you go I shall find you.'

He had just started to walk back to his car when Missie suddenly darted out from behind Anna and ran after him, whining pathetically.

Immediately he stopped, turned round and dropped down to fuss the little dog. From his kneeling position he looked up at Anna and growled, 'Poor little thing. She deserves better—someone worthy of her loyalty and her trust, someone who knows what those things mean and values them, respects them.'

And then, before Anna could say a word, he got to his feet and strode towards his car.

Of all the nerve! What an arrogant, insensitive block-head of a man, Anna fumed once he had gone. Nursing Missie on her lap and chiding her for her treachery, she told the dog severely, 'Well, I certainly feel sorry for his wife.'

His wife. Heavens, but it must take an awful long time to caress every inch of that big hard chest, and heaven knew how much coaxing and cajoling it must take to get that hard mouth soft enough to kiss it. And as for his oh, so high moral principles... What must it be like to have to break through that stern, austere bar-rier to get him to react emotionally, to drive him out of control with longing and desire? If he were to wrap his arms around *her* she would be lost in them, Anna re-flected. It would be like being mauled by a lion. Was his body hair as soft and delicious to touch as her old teddy's? Did he growl, too, if you pressed his middle?

Anna gave a little giggle, her eyes dancing with

amusement. Oh, but there was so much of him. A woman would have to be either very brave or very foolish to risk falling in love with him. He had been so antagonistic towards her, so ready to believe the worst...and yet, at the same time...Sternly she reprimanded herself.

'Down you go. I need to ring Dee,' she told Missie, gently dislodging her from her lap.

Anna's heart sank when she listened to the message on Dee's answering machine. She had, she informed her callers, gone north to see her aunt.

Anna had the number of her mobile but when she tried it there was no reply. Well, she would just have to try again later, she decided. Heavens, but Ward Hunter had been so rude, so aggressive. She just hoped she had been right in thinking that paper he had could be used against Julian Cox. She certainly had never given Julian permission to name her as his partner, and his doing so had been a blatant piece of fraud on his part. Mulling over what she had learned, Anna headed for her kitchen.

She was an enthusiastic cook but she was the first to admit that there was much more fun in cooking for others than in cooking for herself, which was one of the reasons she enjoyed her work with the elderly so much. Which reminded her...

She would make herself something to eat and then she would go outside and finish her gardening before it got too dark.

Half an hour after leaving Anna, Ward was booking into a local hotel. It had been a warm day and he was beginning to feel in need of a shower and something to eat. After the porter had gone he looked a little disparagingly around the room. He had booked into the first hotel he had come across. Luxurious living was something Ward could either take or leave. He liked good things, appreciated them, and had a good eye for quality, but the comfort of a five-star hotel with a highly recommended restaurant was the last thing on his mind right now.

God, but she was the most distracting, deceitful, downright dangerous woman he had ever met.

When the sunlight had shone through that long skirt thing she had been wearing, revealing slim, surprisingly long legs, it had been all he could do to drag his gaze away.

It couldn't possibly have been deliberate, and neither could the way her soft stretch tee shirt top had clung to the warmly rounded outline of her breasts as she'd bent so protectively towards her ridiculous little dog.

Her bare arms had been softly pale, just barely sprinkled with pretty freckles, and Ward had had to fight an overwhelming urge to run his fingertip all the way up the soft flesh of one of them from her wrist right up past her breast. She had smelled distractingly of roses and honeysuckle and there had been a piece of clematis in her hair that he had itched to reach out and remove.

He had wanted to hold her, stroke her and shake her all at the same time, so confusing and conflicting had been his reactions to her.

One reaction had been uncompromisingly plain, though. His jaw tightened irritably. He was forty-two and he couldn't remember the last time his body had given such an impromptu display of its potent maleness.

Thankfully he had managed to control it before *she* had seen what was happening.

Ward swallowed hard. There was a print on the bed-room wall, a cornfield bright with red poppies, and, for one logic-defying moment, he could almost breathe in the field's summer scent, feel the itchy sharpness of it against his bare skin, the sun hot against his naked body as he wrapped Anna's equally naked form in his arms. Her flesh felt so soft, her breasts delicious mounds of femininity, creamily pale, throwing into prominence the erotic, contrasting darkness of her nipples. He touched them with his fingertips and heard her indrawn breath of pleasure, saw the eager, wanton look in her eyes as she commanded him, 'Kiss them, Ward. I want to feel you mouth against me.'

Ward closed his eyes. The little triangle of hair be-tween her thighs felt so unbelievably silky soft.

'Ward, I want you so much…' he heard her whisper.

Ward opened his eyes. Damn her. What *was* she, some kind of witch? Well, she wasn't going to bewitch him. *No way*. His body felt hot and tense, aching with angry desire. Very deliberately he ran the shower cold. That should put a damper on such dangerous thoughts, amongst other things!

That was all the dead-heading done. Now all she needed to do was to put everything away and then she could go and have a bath. Heavens, she was tired. Her whole body ached. A little guiltily Anna flushed. It wasn't just the gardening she had been doing that was causing that ache. Now, where was that hoe she had been using—a long-handled one especially useful for recalcitrant weeds? Tiredly Anna stepped backwards, and then cried out in pain as she inadvertently trod on the hoe and the handle came up and hit her right on the back of her head.

*   *   *

Missie whined unhappily. Why was her mistress lying in the middle of the lawn ignoring Missie's anxious little cries and licks...?

Ward pushed away the room-service meal he had ordered, half-eaten. It was no good. He simply didn't trust that woman. By morning she could be heaven alone knew where. Quickly Ward gathered up his coat and his keys, almost running out of the hotel towards his car.

Missie greeted his arrival with excited, relieved little barks. Ward frowned. The house was in complete darkness, even though it was now dusk, and the conservatory door was open. Where the devil was Anna?

Missie showed him, standing anxiously beside her unconscious mistress, her little tail beating the ground as she looked trustingly up at Ward.

On the ground Anna gave a little moan and started to open her eyes.

'Oh, my head hurts,' she cried out, tears filling her eyes.

'It's all right; you've bumped it. Don't move. I'm going to call for an ambulance,' Ward told her grimly.

When Anna had moved her head he had seen the dark patch of drying blood staining her hair and he could see a smear of blood on the handle of the hoe, too.

'Who are you?' he heard Anna asking him fretfully.

He checked before he started to dial the emergency services number on his mobile phone and stared at her.

'Don't you know?' he asked her.

Tearfully Anna looked at him.

'No, I don't.' She started to shiver as she told him frantically, 'I don't know anything.'

Without answering her Ward quickly dialled 999.

* * *

'She seems to have lost her memory,' he told the paramedic some fifteen minutes later after they had carefully lifted Anna into the ambulance and out of earshot.

'It can happen,' he told Ward. 'She could be concussed. We'll know more once we've done some proper tests. I take it you weren't with her when it happened?'

'No…No, I wasn't…' Ward agreed.

'You say her name's Anna Trewayne, and you're…?'

'Ward Hunter,' Ward supplied.

'So you're not married.' The other man gave a brief, dismissive shrug. 'If you'd like to follow us to the hospital in your car, I'm sure the consultant will want to talk with you.'

'But I'm not…' Ward began, but the man was already jumping into the ambulance and it had started to pull away.

After bundling Missie into his own car and closing the conservatory door, Ward followed it. After all, what else *could* he do with Missie looking so imploringly at him?

'If you'd just wait here, Mr Hunter, the consultant will be along to see you in a moment.'

Anna had been whisked away on a stretcher the minute they had entered the hospital's casualty department, and now, so far as Ward could glean from the busy desk in the foyer area, the consultant had finished examining her and she was in a bed on one of the wards.

'Mr Hunter?'

Nodding, Ward held out his hand to the consultant.

'How is she?' he asked without preamble as the other man ushered him into a small cubicle off the main foyer area.

'Well, so far as we can ascertain she hasn't sustained

any serious damage. There's a considerable amount of bruising and some external bleeding, but fortunately there aren't any signs of internal bleeding. We'll want to keep a check on her for the next few weeks, but that can be done via her GP.'

The consultant glanced at his watch and frowned. He should have been off duty three hours ago but an unexpected emergency had kept him at the hospital, which was how he had come to be there to examine Anna.

'She's regained consciousness fully now and since there aren't any obvious problems we can discharge her and let her go home.'

'On her own?' Ward queried. He suspected that, like many others, the hospital might be short of beds and, although he knew the consultant would never have discharged Anna if he wasn't confident that it was medically safe to do so, Ward certainly did not feel, judging from what he had seen, that she would be anywhere near strong enough yet to cope by herself.

The consultant's eyebrows rose, his voice suddenly a few degrees cooler as he heard the criticism in Ward's voice.

'I take it you *will* be there with her?' he responded.

Him?

Ward was just about to deny any such thing when the consultant continued carefully, 'Of course, there is this added problem of her temporary loss of memory—it's a complication which does occur sometimes with head injuries. Fortunately, in our experience, the patient's full memory eventually returns in almost one hundred per cent of cases. In Anna's case, it just seems to be her recent memories she isn't able to recall. She knows her name and her family background, for instance, but she was unable to tell us what she had done today or who she had seen; the last memory she seems to recall is over several months ago.'

'She's lost her memory?' Ward started to frown, and the words 'and you're sending her home' trembled on his lips, but he controlled himself long enough to suppress them. Had Anna been a member of his own family, right now he would have been ruthlessly bypassing the harried man in front of him and insisting not just on a second opinion but on Anna being referred to a private hospital.

Anna, though, was not a member of his family. Anna was *nothing* whatsoever to do with him—apart from the fact that she owed him five thousand pounds.

'Of course, if she should start to complain of suffering any kind of head pains, double vision, sickness, that kind of thing, then bring her straight back in.'

'If she should... Is she *likely* to?' Ward demanded tersely.

'Not so far as I am able to judge,' the consultant assured him.

'And you say that she will regain her memory...'

'I should think so. Although, of course, I can't say when. Sometimes patients experience a flashback and total recall; other times their memory returns in stages.'

The consultant's bleeper started to go off. He was already turning away, his body language indicating that he was a busy man.

Damn, Ward cursed under his breath as he watched him hurry down the corridor. *Now* what was he supposed to do? Realistically he owed Anna nothing. Quite the opposite. And he had a perfect right to walk out of the hospital and leave her to sort out her own problems. Realistically, perhaps, but what about morally...?

Morally...

What about *her* moral obligations to his half-brother and the others she had cheated?

So she was a liar and a cheat; did that mean he had to descend to the same level of callousness? Ward asked himself quietly. He might not want to help her but it simply went against his whole character for him to walk off and leave her in her present condition.

'Mr Hunter?' a nurse enquired, coming up to him. 'The consultant has already informed Anna that she can go home. She's just getting dressed, so if you'd like to come with me...'

As he turned to follow the nurse onto the ward, a sudden thought struck Ward—a possible escape route from the unwanted chore of taking charge of Anna until she either regained her memory or someone more appropriate turned up to take over from him.

Stopping abruptly, he asked the nurse curtly, 'This amnesia—I don't suppose it could be...imaginary...could it?'

'Imaginary amnesia?' The nurse gave him a sharp look. 'Sometimes we *do* have patients who fake memory loss for one reason or another, but our consultant here would soon detect any sign of *that* in a patient. Why do you ask?' she questioned him curiously. 'Do you have some reason to suppose that Anna is faking her amnesia? Occasionally we have patients who have suffered such intense trauma that their only possible escape route is to pretend that it has never happened, but in Anna's case...'

'No. No...' Ward hastened to reassure her. Good grief, the next thing he knew the nurse would probably be accusing him of causing Anna's trauma.

'I can assure you, Mr Hunter,' the nurse said tartly, 'that if Anna has been diagnosed by our Mr Bannerman as suffering from temporary amnesia, then temporary amnesia is *exactly* what she *is* suffering from.'

They had reached the entrance to the ward now and Ward could see Anna standing forlornly beside her bed, her expression anxious and strained.

No matter what she might have done, Ward couldn't help feeling a small surge of compassion for her. To be unable to remember even the most basic detail of one's current life was not a position he would want to be in.

Anna's eyes lit up as she saw the nurse. Obviously she recognised *her*, Ward decided, and then he realised with a sharp frisson of unfamiliar emotion that it was *him* she was looking at, not the nurse.

'Ward?' She said his name uncertainly and tremulously, her eyes more grey than blue and stomach-achingly haunted.

'You recognise me?' he demanded, ignoring the small, disapproving shake of her head the nurse was giving him.

Immediately Anna's mouth trembled betrayingly.

'No, I don't.' She shook her head. 'But Nurse James told me your name. She said I could go home,' she added, her eyes brightening and then darkening again at this thought.

The nurse had slipped diplomatically away, leaving them alone together.

'I...I'm sorry I don't remember you,' Ward heard Anna telling him softly, biting her lip before continuing in a small rush, 'But in a way I do. I can sense...feel that...that there's something very special between us...'

She started to flush a little, her glance meeting Ward's and then sliding away almost shyly.

'You can sense that?' Ward queried, his voice suddenly disconcertingly gruff when he had intended it to sound sarcastic.

'Yes. Yes, I can,' Anna confirmed. And then, to Ward's bemusement, she reached out and touched his face very gently with her fingertips, the look on her face one of tender joy.

'I know that I can't recognise or remember you at the moment, Ward, and I can understand how hard that must be for you. I know how concerned you are about me.'

A pair of dimples suddenly appeared at either side of her mouth as she smiled teasingly at him.

'The consultant told me how you'd interrogated him about me...'

God, but she looked so heart-achingly vulnerable. The trust in her eyes, in her touch, made Ward's throat close up. He shuddered to think of the appalling and dangerous situation she could have found herself in with someone less honourable than himself.

'I'm so glad you're here with me, Ward,' Anna confided. 'It feels so odd not being able to remember...so frightening. Mr Bannerman told me that you aren't my husband...'

'No,' Ward agreed shortly.

'But we *are* partners. He said you'd told the ambulance staff that,' Anna continued.

Ward ground his teeth. He had told them no such damned thing. *They* had made the assumption that he and Anna were a pair, because their laughable urgency in getting her to hospital had not given him any opportunity to correct their misinterpretation of his presence at her house.

'How much exactly can you remember?' he demanded brusquely.

Uncertainly Anna stepped back from him, her hand dropping away. Ridiculously he felt oddly bereft, as though a part of him had actually enjoyed having her touch him.

'Everything, and then nothing since some time early this year.' Anna gave him a painful smile. 'I can't remember how we met or when, how long we've been together.'

Her eyes filled with tears which she immediately tried to blink away, her fingers twisting her wedding ring in agitation.

'Well, don't worry about it,' Ward told her, trying to comfort her. 'The consultant says you'll get your memory back fully eventually. Come on, let's get you home,' he added, starting to guide her towards the door, but, to his consternation, instead of preserving the small distance he had placed between them, Anna closed it, snuggling up to his side and slipping her arm through his.

'Home. Well, at least I know where that is.' She stopped, her face shadowing again. 'Where do *we* live, Ward? I can't remember.' Ward could see the panic darkening her eyes. 'I know where *my* house is, but...'

'That's where we're going,' Ward told her.

What the hell was he doing? Ward asked himself as he guided her out to his car. Why the *hell* hadn't he simply told the consultant the truth? Now just look at the situation he had got himself into. Anna quite plainly thought they were lovers, which was ironic when he thought of the real relationship between them, and that was bad enough. How the hell he was going to manage to fabricate answers for the questions she was bound to ask him he had absolutely no idea.

When he had given in to his chivalrous, protective

male instinct and the moral code instilled in him by his mother and his stepfather, he hadn't realised the complications it was going to cause. But what was taxing him even more than that was the apparent total change in Anna's character. Did bumps on the head and amnesia do that? Could she have changed at a blow from an avaricious, self-seeking, heartless flirt, who preyed on the innocent and unaware, into this gentle, vulnerable, tender-eyed woman who made no pretence of being anything other than thoroughly relieved to be able to lean on him?

He had heard that blows to the head could cause bizarre behavioural changes, but not, surely, quite like this?

It was one o'clock in the morning now. Ward had, to say the least, had a challenging day, and right now he simply didn't have the energy to pursue the issue.

Ultimately, of course, he was going to have to tell Anna the truth—if she didn't regain her memory in the next few days he would have no option but to do so— once he had tracked down someone close to her who could take responsibility for her, of course. There was no way he could simply walk out and leave her in her present condition. And, of course, whilst he stayed close to her there was no way she was going to be able to disappear without repaying Ritchie's five thousand pounds.

'Oh, *this* is your car!' Anna exclaimed in obvious surprise as they reached the Mercedes and Ward unlocked it. Ward frowned. Why was she so surprised? It was an expensive car, yes, but then, to judge from what he had seen of her home, her own living standards must be reasonably comfortable, and from what he knew of her lifestyle she was surely not the type of woman who would be unfamiliar with things such as luxury cars. Far from it, he would have suspected.

Suddenly Anna saw the little dog curled up on the back seat of the car and immediately her face broke into a delighted smile.

'Oh, Missie,' she breathed.

'You recognise her,' Ward commented unnecessarily.

'Oh, yes,' Anna confirmed. 'I got her last year; she'd been abandoned and...' She paused. 'I know she's mine, Ward, but *when* was last year? I...'

To Ward's consternation her eyes filled with tears again.

'It's all right, you *will* remember.' He tried to reassure her, opening the passenger door of the car and urging her towards it, but Anna had other ideas. Ward was totally unprepared when she turned to *him* instead of the car and buried her head against his shoulder. She whispered, 'Hold me, Ward—oh, please, just hold me...I'm so frightened.'

Uneasily Ward hesitated. *This* wasn't something he had taken into account at all. He was, generally speaking, a man who prided himself on keeping his head in any kind of crisis—or at least he had been—but there was something about the soft warmth of Anna pressed so trustingly against him that caused the normal logical thought processes of his brain to be thrown into complete disarray.

'It's all right, don't worry, I'm here...'

Even as he heard himself saying the words, Ward knew that he had crossed a fateful Rubicon, but he told himself he was far too practical a person to listen to the unfamiliar inner voice warning him of danger.

How, after all, could *he* be in any possible danger? He knew exactly what kind of woman Anna really was and when she got her memory back she would be throwing him out, not *herself* into his arms.

Her hair smelled of roses and Ward could feel her trembling slightly as he held her.

Instinctively he lifted his hand to her hair to stroke it and then dropped it again.

'I think perhaps we haven't been together all that long,' Anna told him several seconds later, half laughing and half embarrassed as she moved away from him. In the illuminated car park Ward could see that her face was prettily flushed and that she looked both amused and self-conscious, her mouth curving into a slightly rueful smile.

She told him, 'That's what my body says, anyway, judging by the way I'm reacting to you. I don't think I'd still be trembling in your arms quite so—so intensely if we were long-time lovers.'

Trembling in his arms. Ward closed his eyes and swallowed—hard.

'We did meet only recently,' he admitted a little hoarsely as he helped her into the car.

It was, after all, the truth. He just hoped she wouldn't ask him how recent 'recently' actually was, but fortunately, when he got into the driver's seat, she was too busy hugging Missie to ask him any more questions.

As he drove Anna home, Ward's mind was busy. He would have to call at the hotel tomorrow and pay his bill. But what about his clothes? He hadn't known how long he would need to be in Rye so he had packed a suitcase, but there was hardly enough in it if he was supposed to be living with Anna; he would need rather more than what he had.

And then there was his own life. Fortunately he had his laptop with him, and even more fortunately there

was no one in his life who was likely to question his
absence. He would have to ring Mrs Jarvis, though, his
twice-weekly cleaner, to warn her that he wasn't going
to return home for a while.

Anna closed her eyes and leaned her head back against
the head-rest.

It felt so odd not being able to remember properly.
She knew who she was and where she came from; she
could remember quite clearly her family, her friends,
her way of life here in Rye and the tragedy which had
originally brought her here. But meeting Ward, their life
together, the events of the last few months and even
Ward himself—these were all things of which she had
no memory whatsoever.

The consultant had explained to her that she had suffered a blow to her head through standing on a garden
hoe.

'You were concussed, and although there was what
looked like a lot of blood fortunately no real damage
was done.'

'Apart from the memory,' Anna had reminded him.

'Apart from that,' he had agreed. 'Try not to worry
too much about it. It *will* return.'

'But when?' Anna had asked him anxiously.

'I'm afraid that's impossible to say,' he had told her.

'Will I...will I have to stay here in hospital?' Anna
had asked him anxiously.

'No,' he had assured her. 'Although if there wasn't
someone at home to look after you it would be different.'

Someone at home. Ward. The man who had brought
her here to the hospital.

Anna felt oddly breathless and dizzy just thinking

about him, her heart starting to race. He was so big, so masculine. Her skin started to heat as she realised the direction her thoughts were taking. Heavens, surely a woman of her age shouldn't get so giddily excited just thinking about her partner...her lover...

Ward... So familiar to her in some ways—she had immediately felt at home in his arms, recognised his scent, his feel—and yet a complete stranger to her in so many others. She was going to have to learn all about him all over again. Where had they met and when? Did he have a family? Had he ever been married? Did he have children?

Tomorrow she would ask him, Anna decided tiredly as Ward swung his car between the gates to her house.

At least she could recognise and remember that! She had no idea why Ward was living with her here. Why had she and Ward decided that they should live in *her* house? They must have had a reason—but she had to admit that she was pleased that they were living here. Having to contend with a house she couldn't even remember would have been far too daunting a prospect right now.

CHAPTER FOUR

'YOU sit down; I'll put the kettle on and make us both a drink.'

'No, Ward, let me do it,' Anna insisted. They were both in her kitchen, Missie tucked up happily in her basket whilst, next to her, the huge cream and brown cat, Whittaker, stretched languidly in his.

On the point of insisting that she needed to rest, Ward suddenly remembered that he would be expected to know his way around Anna's kitchen *and* the rest of her house.

'Well, if you're sure you'll be okay,' he agreed. 'I'll just get your stuff out of the car and take it upstairs.'

Anna had refused to put the blood-stained jacket she had been wearing back on and the hospital had also supplied her with some ointment to put on the broken skin of her scalp. On the pretext of disposing of them he could have a brief look round the upstairs of the house and familiarise himself with its layout, Ward decided.

In the morning before Anna woke up he would also have to slip out to the hotel, but that was a problem he could worry about then.

He had collected everything from the car and was halfway upstairs when he heard Anna calling out urgently to him. Dropping her jacket and the ointment, he rushed back to the kitchen.

'What is it?' he demanded abruptly. 'Are you ill? Do you feel sick? Are your eyes—?'

'Oh, Ward, I'm sorry…it's nothing like that,' Anna assured him remorsefully. 'I just wanted to know how you like your coffee…I'm afraid I can't remember…'

'Strong, black, no sugar,' Ward told her curtly.

Hell, for a moment he had feared…He closed his eyes and then flinched in shock as he felt Anna's lips brush his jaw.

'Thank you,' he heard her whisper tenderly.

She was thanking him?

'For what?' he asked her almost brusquely, opening his eyes and moving back from her, determinedly avoiding her, turning his head to look into those oh, so dangerous blue-grey eyes.

'For being here…for caring…for being you,' Anna told him softly.

The look in her eyes, so trusting, so…so giving…made Ward gulp.

It just wasn't possible that a simple blow on the head could so totally transform a person's personality—was it?

'Oh, I'm sorry,' Anna said, sleepily stifling a second yawn. They had finished their coffee and Ward had insisted that she was to stay where she was, sitting at the table, whilst he cleared up.

Although she lived alone, Anna's house was a comfortable size. She came from a large extended family and when Beth and Kelly had first moved to Rye she had been only too delighted to put them up. Her house had four good-sized bedrooms and her own large bedroom had its own separate bathroom.

Downstairs, in addition to the large kitchen with its pretty dining conservatory which she had added, there was a more formal dining room, a pretty sitting room and a drawing room. Too much, perhaps, for one person, and certainly far larger than the pretty little cottage she and Ralph had started married life in.

She had bought the house with some of the money she had received from Ralph's life insurance policies—the rest of the money, quite a considerable sum, had been invested. She had been upset at first at the thought of touching it, had even suggested that it ought more properly to go to Ralph's parents, but both her own and Ralph's family were comfortably off and, in the end, she had listened to them and had accepted that they were probably right in saying that Ralph would have wanted her to have the money. Although Anna suspected that neither of Ralph's parents, especially his mother, would ever feel totally comfortable in her presence because of the memories she brought back, both of them had been genuinely determined that the proceeds of the insurance policy Ralph had taken out when they married should go to Anna.

It was a mother's love for her child that caused Ralph's mother to be so anguished whenever she saw Anna, not the money, and Anna, always so sensitive, could appreciate just how she must feel, just how she herself might feel in the same circumstances.

Her own father was an architect and until Ralph's death she had worked for him as his personal assistant. He had understood why she had felt she had to leave Cornwall, even though he had told her how much he was going to miss her quiet efficiency.

The house was decorated with the same quiet good taste exhibited by her clothes and her whole way of life, and Ward, who was still trying to come to terms with the powerful surge of desire he had felt earlier on when she had touched him, couldn't help contrasting her manner with his ex-wife's.

She had never, so far as he could recall, voluntarily reached out to him in the way that Anna had just done, and when he had tried to bring a little tenderness into their relationship she had pushed him away, declaring, 'Don't be so soft.'

Soft. Him. Well, he might have been then, but he certainly wasn't any more. And he most definitely wasn't soft enough to forget just exactly what kind of woman Anna Trewayne really was.

'You're tired,' he told her shortly as she stifled another yawn. 'Why don't you go to bed?'

'What about you?' Anna asked him uncertainly.

'I'll be up later,' Ward told her, deliberately turning away from her so that she couldn't see his face.

It was so obvious that Anna assumed they would be sharing a bed, and just as obvious that there was no way he could allow that to happen. For one thing…well, he lived alone and normally slept in the raw, and he was used to having the whole of his large king-sized bed to himself. If he rolled over in his sleep, Anna, tiny little thing that she was… And besides— But he didn't want to allow himself to think the highly personal and explosively dangerous thoughts that were crowding his brain—thoughts which were of a far, far too intimate and sensual nature.

He heard Anna's chair scrape over the floor as she got up. Even with his back turned he knew that she was walking towards him.

'Good—goodnight, then,' he heard her saying a little breathlessly. Automatically he turned round. Anna was smiling tremulously up at him, lifting her face, her *mouth* towards his, plainly expecting to be kissed.

Who the hell was he trying to kid? Ward asked himself angrily. *This* was the reason why he didn't want to share a bed with Anna... The harshly guttural sound of protest he had been about to make was lost as he wrapped his arms around her and bent his mouth to hers.

'Mmm... Oh, yes...' Anna breathed delightedly as she wriggled closer to him. 'Oh, yes... Oh, Ward!' Blissfully she leaned into him. How could she possibly have forgotten *this*? She could feel her whole body reacting to Ward's kiss, right down to her toes which were curling sensuously into her shoes.

Experimentally she caressed his bottom lip with her tonguetip, her own body trembling with excitement as she felt him shudder. She suddenly felt like someone who had discovered undreamed-of treasure. Ralph, love him though she had, had *never* made her feel like this, but she felt no guilt. The relationship she had with Ward had already passed through those turbulent, traumatic waters, such feelings obviously resolved before they— *she*—had committed themselves to one another as lovers.

Anna might not be able to remember how or when they had met, or the nature of their courtship, but she knew herself and she knew just how powerful her feelings, her *love* must be for her to have become so intimate with him.

She must have experienced this rapture, this intensity, this total compulsion to abandon herself to him sexually and emotionally with him before, many times, but right now she couldn't recall those times, which must be why what she was feeling was so headily thrilling and exciting. She wanted desperately to touch him.

Touch him? She practically wanted to tear his clothes

off, she acknowledged ruefully, but he was already lifting his mouth from hers, his voice satisfactorily strained with emotion and desire as he told her thickly, 'The consultant said you had to rest...'

'Did he? I don't remember,' Anna teased him mischievously, but she still obediently let him go and started to make her way out of the kitchen, pausing only to fuss Missie and Whittaker.

Ward didn't dare to allow himself to relax until he was sure she had gone.

He couldn't remember the last time he had felt like this.

No, he didn't think he had *ever* felt like this. She had caught him off guard, that was all, he assured himself, and he'd have had to be made of stone not to respond to her. She was, after all, an extremely attractive woman, an extremely *sensual* woman—an extremely sexually experienced woman?

She had been instantly responsive to him, her body language making it plain just how much she wanted him, but earlier on this afternoon, despite what he knew about her, he had somehow gained the impression that she was not someone who was sexually promiscuous. There had been an innate feminine fastidiousness about her, a delicate hint of determined hauteur. And yet just now in his arms...

It had been all he could do not to show her just what she was doing to him, and there had even been a moment when, if he hadn't let her go, the urgency and intensity of his desire for her would have had him practically tearing the clothes off her—and that was something he had most certainly never come anywhere near wanting to do...ever...with any woman...

When he had met his ex-wife he had been full of

romantic ideals. He had put her up on something of a pedestal, respecting her. The thought of making love with her had made him go dizzy with longing, but when it had eventually happened, physically satisfying though the experience had been, emotionally it had been lacking in something.

He had told himself that the fault lay with him in that his expectations were too idealistic and unrealistic. Five minutes ago, holding Anna in his arms, he had discovered that they weren't.

Upstairs, in her bedroom, Anna undressed quickly. She wanted to be showered, all clean and sweetly scented, when Ward came to her.

This might not be their first time, but it would be the first of the *new* memories she would make with him and she wanted it to be very special. Not just for herself, but for Ward as well. She must have given him such a dreadful fright.

In her bathroom she had found a serviceable cotton robe and beneath her pillow there was an equally serviceable cotton nightdress. Frowningly she studied them. Surely she didn't wear *these* when she was with Ward?

Quickly she checked her drawers. It was odd how she knew automatically which ones held her underwear. It was all as dismally plain as her nightwear. Puzzled, she checked again. Instinctively she knew that for Ward she would have wanted to wear the most deliciously feminine things she could find, silky satin wisps of delicately coloured fabric, lavishly trimmed with lace, nothing vulgar or too provocative—she knew she wasn't the type for that—but surely, during the course of knowing him, she must have bought *something* to tease and tempt him with? If so, it certainly wasn't here.

Disappointed, she went back to the bed and climbed in. Well, if it was a choice of wearing that boring cotton nightdress or nothing, she'd take the nothing, thank you very much!

How long would Ward be? Not long, surely? A tiny shiver of nervous excitement ran through her. She felt almost like an old-fashioned virginal bride, madly in love with her husband, but also, at the same time, a little apprehensive about the intimacies that lay ahead.

Downstairs Ward waited half an hour and then another half an hour. The house was silent. Anna must surely be asleep by now?

Very quietly he crept upstairs. Her bedroom door was half open; he could see her lying to one side of the bed, thankfully asleep. She looked oddly forlorn and alone.

His mouth dry, Ward hurried past, pushing open the door to the bedroom furthest away from Anna's.

He had a quick shower, but no shave—his razor was still at the hotel, of course. If, in the morning, Anna questioned his desire to sleep in a different room he would tell her that the consultant had advised it—make up some story about him suggesting that it might be an idea for the two of them to put their intimate life on hold until Anna had recovered her memory.

Tiredly, Ward climbed into bed.

Anna woke up abruptly; her heart was pounding very fast and she was trembling. She had been having a frightening dream, but what about she could not remember. Her head ached a little and, whilst the nightmare fear had left her now, another much sharper fear had taken its place. What if she *never* recovered her memory? What if…?

'Ward. Ward?' She turned anxiously to the other side of the bed, only to discover that Ward wasn't there.

Thoroughly agitated, Anna pushed back the bedcovers. Where was he? She hurried out onto the landing. Whittaker, the cat, was just about to make his way into the end bedroom through the open door.

'Oh, no, you don't,' she chided him, padding after him and scooping him up. He was forbidden to sleep on the beds and well he knew it—but Whittaker's naughtiness was forgotten as she glanced into the room and realised that Ward was asleep in the bed.

What on earth was he doing in here? Bemused, but thoroughly relieved to have found him, Anna put the cat down and hurried over to the bed. He must be exhausted, poor man. She wouldn't wake him. Instead she slipped in beside him, cuddling as close to the warmth of his body as she could.

Mmm…he felt so good. *She* felt so good, so safe, so loved…so happy….

'Mmm…' Ward turned over in his sleep, his body instinctively accommodating the slight curve of Anna's, his arm curling round her, his leg, with genetically programmed male possessiveness and protection, moving to pin her gently to his side.

Happily Anna snuggled even closer. She wasn't quite asleep and the temptation to press a soft, delicate kiss against the muzzy warmth of his chest proved irresistible, and so too did the temptation to stroke her fingers through the soft mat of body hair tangled there.

'Just like a teddy bear', she marvelled softly under her breath, and then frowned. The words held a familiar echo, a vague ethereal recollection, but the harder she tried to grasp it, the fainter it became. Her agitation had woken Ward, though; she could feel his fingers tensing on her upper arm.

'Oh, Ward, you feel so good,' she whispered happily to him. 'Kiss me,' she begged him huskily.

Abruptly Ward became fully awake. What on earth was Anna doing in bed with him?

'Anna...' he began, but Anna had grown impatient of waiting for him to obey her command and she was already pressing her soft mouth against his, her lips warm and tender, clinging to his as her tonguetip traced their shape.

'Oh, Ward, I can't believe this is real,' she told him ecstatically. 'I'm just so lucky.'

He could feel her breasts pressing against his bare chest, her nipples provocatively hard. To his own horror Ward felt his hand lifting to cup one of them and caress it. Beneath her breath Anna gave a small, sucked-in sigh of pleasure and Ward felt her body start to arch against his own. Shockingly she was as naked as he was himself, her only covering the soft, silky triangle of body hair which right now was pressed tormentingly against his body. She was still kissing him, holding his face in her hands to keep him still as she pressed eager little kisses against his mouth.

Oh, God, he wasn't going to be able to stand much more of this; his body was already...

Ward gave an anguished groan as Anna, plainly aware of his arousal, moved her own body with simple directness to accommodate it.

That was *it*... It was no good, no *use* trying to pretend that he didn't want her, no use either trying to control that wanting when she was doing everything she could to encourage it. Ward almost cried out aloud as he felt her lift her hips so that she could press herself even more closely against him.

'Ward…' she whispered against his mouth.

Helplessly Ward felt himself succumb.

She felt too tiny, too fragile, to roll underneath him. He was afraid he might hurt her, so instead he moved the other way, lifting her with him so that she was lying on top of his body, their mouths still locked eagerly together.

Unable to stop himself, Ward ran his hands down the length of her body, cupping the delicious mounds of her buttocks, pressing her even deeper into his own flesh.

Anna moved wildly against him.

This was heaven, wonderful, unbelievable; her whole body was sighing with pleasure and love. Ward's hands swept round the front of her body and cupped her breasts.

They felt so heavy, taut with their need to be kissed and caressed. Almost as though he knew how she felt Ward urged her towards him, licking the swollen areolae that surrounded them, first one and then the other until Anna was wild with pleasure, trembling from head to foot, lost in the ecstasy of what she was feeling.

'Oh, yes, Ward, do that…do *that*,' she encouraged him throatily as he started to kiss each nipple, the sensation radiating through her body like nothing she could ever remember experiencing, but of course she *must* have experienced it before.

He could feel her stomach muscles tensing, locking, her pelvis lifting, and a sensation that came from lower, deeper within it, starting to grow and pulse out a rhythm that she instinctively began to respond to, her whole body moving against Ward's in time to it.

Ward knew he had totally lost control. There he was,

forty-two years old, and for the first time in his life he knew what it was to experience total abandonment and compelling, urgent desire. He wanted to possess Anna, absorb her completely into himself, devour her. Lost in the sensation that suckling on her nipples was giving him, he heard her cry out as his teeth accidentally grated against her sensitive flesh. Cursing himself, he stopped immediately, but as he started to release her Anna held him where he was.

'No. Don't stop,' she told him passionately. When Ward looked into them her eyes weren't grey any more but blue—the richest, hottest blue he had ever seen in his life. He groaned and reached out for her, cupping her face and drawing her down against him so that he could kiss her mouth.

Whilst he was doing so Anna moved eagerly against him and did what she had been aching to do ever since she had looked down the hospital ward and seen him walking towards her. As he felt her gentle fingers taking hold of him Ward closed his eyes. A small sob of sharp pleasure clogged his throat. He knew he should draw away, stop her, but he also knew that there was no way he was going to. There was something so unbearably erotic about having her guide his body into her own, something so heart-rockingly sweet about the absorbed expression on her face as she did so that his will-power just melted. She felt so good—hot, wet, her flesh surrounding his.

Anna gave a small moan of exquisite pleasure. It felt so good having Ward inside her. She moved experimentally against him and then caught her breath as he responded to her tentative movement. Wide-eyed, she focused on him, watching as he reached out and took hold of her, his hands just below her waist. Now it was his turn to take control, to set the pace of their love-making, to move *her* to the rhythm of *his* desire, and Anna couldn't believe how much she loved him doing so, how much she revelled in the fiercely sweet pangs of pleasure she could feel with each movement of his body inside her. Slow at first, slow and careful, and then harder and deeper and then deeper still, until…

'Ward. Ward…' Anna sobbed his name as she reached her climax and felt the release of Ward's body within hers, the hot, powerful surge of it leaving her dizzy with feminine smugness and satisfaction. Exhausted, she leaned her head on his chest and closed her eyes in mute happiness as she felt his arms close around her.

What on earth had he *done*? Ward berated himself furiously as he automatically responded to Anna's unexpressed need and drew her down against him, holding her in his arms. What had happened to his will-power, his self-control, that same self-control that had enabled him, with very little prior difficulty, to refuse to give in to the temptation of satisfying his sexuality? He had lost count of the number of times in the past he had turned away from the opportunity to have a brief fling or even begin a new relationship. The scars left by his marriage had disillusioned him too much for him to want to risk a second failure. His pride and his idealistic moral code meant that he had never been tempted to indulge in sex for its own sake…

And yet here he was, his body relaxed and at peace, still washed by the soft echoes of the pleasure the woman sleeping beside him had given him. And, even worse, that pleasure had aroused the kind of emotional response in him that he knew to be ironically farcical.

He actually felt protective of her, tender towards her; he actually *wanted* to hold her, to go on feeling the slender warmth of her body next to his own.

How could he, when he disliked and despised her, when everything he knew about her dictated that she was the last woman he could ever possibly love?

It was virtually impossible that her amnesia could have been faked, the nurse had told him, and she had obviously meant it, but *Ward* wasn't suffering from amnesia and he knew perfectly well that alongside the animosity that had crackled between them the first time they had met there had also been a very dangerous surge of mutual physical attraction. He also suspected that it was that which had led to Anna believing that they already shared a relationship, a past—and a bed...

However, that still did not explain how the woman he knew as a fraud and a cheat could suddenly be metamorphosed into someone so tender, so giving, so open and loving that she had literally taken his breath away.

No one had ever said the things to him that she had said, shown him so openly that he was desired and loved.

Loved!

His heartbeat stilled, and then started up again with heavy, potent, leaden strokes.

His body tensed.

What on earth was he going to do?

CHAPTER FIVE

'GOOD morning.'

Ward struggled to sit up, pushing his hand through his hair as the events of the previous night came flooding back.

'I've been awake for ages,' Anna told him, sitting up too, her face alight with love and happiness as she reached over to kiss him.

Ward groaned as the duvet slipped down, revealing the soft globes of her breasts. His fingers itched to pull it up again and cover her nakedness but Anna seemed to have no such inhibitions, pressing herself lovingly against him in a way that was so totally devoid of any manufactured kind of provocation or deliberate intent that Ward was helpless to prevent his body's response to her.

'You should have woken me,' Ward told her tersely, returning her kiss as perfunctorily as he could before saying, 'I'll go down and make us both some tea. How are you feeling, by the way?' he asked her. What was it the consultant had said he had to watch out for? Headaches, dizziness, blurred vision, nausea...

'Wonderful,' Anna told him softly, making no attempt to hide the smile curling her mouth. 'Totally, absolutely wonderful... Let's leave the tea for a while,' she added meaningfully, closing the distance he had put between them, her eyes suddenly shadowing a little as she confessed, 'All this between us feels so new to me, Ward. I...I still can't quite believe that it's really...that

I've been lucky enough to have met you. I know I must have told you all of this before, but after Ralph's death I felt so, so afraid that I...I didn't want to let anyone else into my life in case...in case...' She stopped and shook her head. 'The pain and shock of losing Ralph like that was...' She frowned. 'I felt so guilty as well. He was so young...alive one minute and then the next gone, and it seemed to me that it was safer not to let myself love anyone else ever again.

'He'd only taken the boat out on an impulse. Normally I'd have gone with him, even though I never really liked sailing that much. You can't grow up in Cornwall, though, and not know how to sail, or how important it is to respect the sea,' she added in a shaky voice. 'The coastguard said he must have been hit by a freak wave. He was an experienced sailor, cautious and not the sort of person who ever took any kind of risk.

'We were going to have dinner with his parents that night. I waited and waited and...'

She stopped, unable to go on, and Ward frowned. He had known from his enquiries that she had been widowed young and by a sailing accident, but he had assumed that her husband's death had been a result of some drunken revelry on the part of a group of young idiots. Now it seemed he had been wrong. The picture Anna had just painted for him was a very different one indeed, and there was no mistaking the emotion in her voice when she talked about her young husband.

'I don't know how I met you or why I changed my mind. I've always been so protective of my...my emotions...' She gave him a small smile. 'I can't pretend that I don't know exactly why, as a lover, you were able to turn over my decision to stay single...'

The dimples he had seen last night reappeared briefly

as she made this rueful disclosure. 'But what *does* puzzle me is how I ever came to let you get close enough to me for *that* to happen... I've never...How *did* we meet, Ward...?'

'The consultant said we were to let your memory return naturally,' Ward told her.

What she had just said to him had had a far more profound effect on him emotionally than he wanted to acknowledge—a very profound effect indeed.

'You must have loved him—Ralph—a lot,' he heard himself say gruffly. Well, better to keep her talking about her precious Ralph and the past than to run the risk of having her question *him* about *their* relationship again, and if he got out of bed as he had originally planned she would see, realise—

It shook him that he, a man who prided himself on his hard-headed pragmatism, should be so intensely and physically affected just because a woman smiled at him and said, 'Wonderful.'

'Well, yes, I did,' Anna agreed, but she was frowning slightly. 'It all seems so far away from me now and we were so very young. Our love for each other was... We grew up together and we'd always been a pair; people expected that we would marry. Our parents were friends and, whilst no one put any pressure on us to do so, and none of our parents would have wanted us to marry someone we *didn't* love, there was a sense of it being the right thing to do.

'Please don't misunderstand,' she begged him. 'We were very happy together, very content, but there was no... It wasn't like it is with you,' she told him huskily, lifting her glance to his as she added, 'But then I must have told you all of this before... What about you, though? Were you...have you been married?'

'Yes, briefly,' Ward told her tersely, 'but my marriage wasn't... It was a mistake for both of us.'

'Do you still love her?' Anna asked him hesitantly. Ward stared at her.

'Still *love* her?' He threw back his head and gave a bitter shout of laughter.

'No, I do not. For a long time after the divorce I think I probably hated her but, eventually, that died. If she was greedy and self-seeking, concerned only with her own wants and desires, then it was my fault for not realising it before we got married, and if she didn't like the fact that she was married to a workaholic who didn't have time to go out clubbing or throw his money around, then that was hers. The truth is that we both married a person who didn't exist. I accepted that she wasn't the woman I'd thought a long time ago.'

'You've forgiven her for her part in the break-up of your marriage,' Anna guessed wisely, 'but I don't think you've ever quite forgiven yourself.'

Ward was astounded. Her simple, direct statement was so true and yet no one else had ever recognised how he had felt, how much he blamed himself for making the wrong marriage.

'At least we didn't have any children.'

'You didn't want them?' Anna asked.

'*She* didn't want them,' he told her quietly.

'Ralph and I... We were so young and at first when he died I longed passionately to have a child, and sometimes even now...'

She gave a sad smile.

'Of course, I have my god-daughter, Beth. She lives here in Rye.' She paused. 'Oh, I'm sorry, you'll know all about her, of course.'

'Mmm…' Ward was deliberately non-committal but his brain was starting to work overtime.

If Anna had family here in town then surely it wouldn't be very long before they made contact with her. Then what was *he* going to do?

'I do hope that she and her friend Kelly will be able to continue making a success of their shop,' Anna continued chattily. 'Both of them have been spending quite a lot of time away on buying trips.

'I've helped out at the shop occasionally but I haven't been able to as often as I would have liked because of my other obligations.'

Her other obligations.

Ward's pulse quickened. Did she mean her partnership with Julian Cox? How could he question her further without arousing her suspicions?

'Mmm… I know you have a very busy life,' he agreed.

Anna frowned.

'Do I? I…' Her face suddenly crumpled. 'Oh, Ward, *I* don't know…I can't remember.'

He could hear the panic in her voice.

'When Mr Bannerman questioned me he said the last positive memory I had which he could date was some months ago. It was the weekend before Easter and it was my turn to do Meals on Wheels. Beth had invited me over for dinner…' She was beginning to look and sound increasingly distressed and Ward acted instinctively, reaching out towards her, intending only to calm and reassure her, but as she had done before Anna responded by wrapping her own arms around him.

Shivering a little, she begged, 'Oh, Ward, hold me, please… I feel so muddled… My head… My thoughts…'

'Then don't think,' Ward chided her.

'Don't *think*…' Anna had started to relax a little bit. She turned her head so that she could look into his eyes, and whispered against his mouth, 'Don't think…? Then what shall I do instead?'

It was a totally unnecessary question because she was already doing it—kissing him with such sweet fervour that Ward felt the back of his throat sting with raw emotion. No one had ever treated him like this, touched him like this, either physically or emotionally.

'Mmm…you taste nice,' Anna told him.

'So do you,' Ward responded gruffly. He could feel her nipples harden as they pressed against his chest. His own body was already aroused and eager.

Closing his eyes, he gave in to the swift tug of desire that ran through him like molten heat, dissolving the steel barrier of his self-control.

This time he knew exactly how to touch her and how to arouse her. She murmured blissfully when he kissed the side of her neck, her eyes tightly closed as she lay in his arms and encouraged him with soft, sensual little whispers of praise and love.

When it was her turn to touch him she was a little more hesitant, a little bit shy.

'I can't remember just what you like,' she told him uncertainly, her eyes grave and anxious.

'I like whatever you like, whatever you want to do,' Ward told her gently, and as he said the words he realised just how much he meant them.

'You might have to…to show me,' Anna warned him shyly, but they soon discovered he did not.

Anna seemed to know instinctively just where his body was most sensitive to her touch, and his throat arched tautly like a strong bow under the gentle assault of her open-mouthed kisses. His nipples turned into small, hard-tipped channels of pleasure that galvanised his whole body as she slowly kissed and then sucked on them. Now he knew just *why* she had trembled and arched so ecstatically against his hands when he had caressed her like that, but when she trailed her fingertips over the flat plane of his belly and bent her head to rim a fiery circle of pleasure around his navel Ward very quickly stopped her, his breath so tortured and hoarse that she looked anxiously at him.

'Come here,' he begged her rawly, exclaiming as he reached for her, 'You're a witch, do you know that? No one has ever made me feel like you do…made me want like you do…need like you do…' He groaned as he positioned her beneath him, shuddering wildly as he saw how eagerly and generously her body moved to accommodate him. There was such a generosity about her, such a sensuality, coupled with such a lack of wantonness that Ward was totally bemused by her.

'If I'm a witch, then you are definitely a magician,' Anna told him breathlessly several seconds later as her body quickened frantically to the fierce pace of his. The sex she and Ralph had shared had been pleasant, nice, but it had been nothing like this…nothing whatsoever. She had heard, of course, read, realised, but she had not known…never felt…

Oh, how could she have forgotten this? How could it have ever slipped from her memory? She was sure she would think of it and of Ward as the very last breath of life slipped from her body.

Anna had no idea she had said the words aloud at the summit of her climax until afterwards, until after she had felt the fierce, hot spurt of Ward's satisfaction spilling sensually into her body.

'You are the most...' Ward began as his lips gently grazed the length of her throat. He stopped and Anna looked at him, smiling through her emotional tears.

'I still can't quite believe we've got this, Ward,' she told him shakily. 'I still can't quite believe that it's real, that we've got each other. It just seems so wonderful, so magical...and I feel...' She touched her fingertips to his lips, her smile deepening as he couldn't resist catching hold of them and sucking slowly on them.

'I feel so blessed,' she finally told him sincerely. 'So very, very blessed.'

Blessed, but once she knew the truth she would feel *cursed*, Ward acknowledged.

She touched his jaw with her free hand.

'Mmm...you need a shave,' she commented.

Ward knew she was right; he could already see the slight rash his overnight stubble had caused on the fair skin of her breast.

'Er...yes...' Suddenly he was totally alert. 'I...I left my stuff in my car. I'll have to go and get it and whilst I'm up I may as well go and get a paper as well.'

'Oh, but I thought you said you'd brought your things in last night,' Anna objected.

'Er...yes, I did...but not my razor...'

'Oh, well, if you are going out for a paper, why don't I come with you and—?'

'No! No...' That was the last thing Ward wanted. Getting a paper had simply been an excuse to allow him to drive over to the hotel, pay his bill and collect his things.

'No. The consultant said you had to rest,' he reminded Anna more gently. 'I'll get the paper and then we'll have something to eat and...'

'What day is it?' Anna asked him, suddenly anxious.

'Sunday,' Ward told her promptly, glad to have her ask a question he could answer honestly.

'Oh, so you don't need to be at work. What is your job, Ward?'

'I don't have one,' he told her. 'At least, I sold out my business interests some time ago, and now I've got some consultancy work to do from time to time and my investments…'

'Investments.' Anna started to frown, her forehead crinkling. 'Oh, that rings a bell. I…'

Whilst Ward held his breath she shook her head regretfully.

'No, it's gone…gone… Is *that* how we met?' she asked him curiously. 'Did you come to advise me on my investments?'

Ward just about managed to conceal his reaction. He advised *her* on investments!

'I'm not telling you anything,' he responded. 'Remember…'

'I know… The consultant said it would all come back naturally,' Anna agreed with a sigh. 'You go and get your paper, then. Oh, and would you bring one for me?'

Bring one for her? Which one? Naturally he was supposed to know which paper she would read.

Whoever had made that comment about deceit and tangled webs had certainly known exactly what they were talking about, Ward decided grimly as he got out of bed.

CHAPTER SIX

TUCKING the newspapers he had just bought under his arm, Ward quickened his step as he hurried back to his car. It had taken him rather longer than he had planned to check out of the hotel and make his way back to Anna's home. He only hoped that the paper he had bought for her would be to her taste. It had seemed a fairly safe bet; his mother read it.

He had almost reached his car when his attention was caught by the display of fresh flowers at a small outdoor stall.

Ward hesitated, looked at the blooms, turned away and made to walk past, but then changed his mind and turned to walk in the direction of the stall.

The friendly young woman who had served him was certainly a persuasive salesperson, he acknowledged ruefully ten minutes later as he opened the boot of his car to place the newspapers and the bouquet of flowers he had just bought in it.

He had no idea what Anna's taste in flowers was but there was no denying that the artistically arranged assortment of soft cream blooms spiked with dark green foliage and varying shades of lilac to deepest purple, both looked and smelled attractive.

It was only when he was in the car and on his way back to Anna's home that he thought to question just what he was doing buying a bouquet of flowers for a woman whom he claimed to dislike and despise.

He had bought them because it was the sort of gesture

she would probably expect, he told himself defensively. That was all. There was no more personal meaning behind the gesture. After all, it wasn't as though he had bought her red roses, was it? His actions certainly hadn't been inspired by any kind of tender feelings for her. That was impossible. Wasn't it? The very thought that he might be guilty of such uncharacteristic behaviour made Ward scowl darkly.

He was still scowling five minutes later when, having retrieved everything from the boot of his car, he walked up to Anna's front door and rang the bell.

Anna had used Ward's absence to good effect; she had had a shower, dressed in a pair of soft chambray trousers and a comfortable white shirt and then she had gone downstairs and started to prepare their breakfast.

When she opened the front door to him, the first thing that Ward could smell was the appetisingly rich aroma of freshly ground coffee; the second, as she leaned forward to take the flowers he was handing her, was Anna's perfume.

It must be because he was hungry that he had experienced that peculiar heart-stopping moment of dizziness, Ward decided as he closed the front door behind himself.

'Flowers. Oh, Ward, they're so beautiful,' Anna breathed ecstatically. 'And you chose my favourites… Oh, Ward…' Her eyes were bright with happy tears as Anna looked up at him. 'I was just thinking again when you were gone how very, very lucky I am.'

Ward closed his eyes and turned away from her so that she wouldn't see his expression. By rights he ought to feel pleased that she was exposing her emotions to him like this; that she was putting herself in his power, in a position where, ultimately, he would have the ability to humiliate her. But for some reason what he did feel was a confusing mixture of anger and pain—anger because she was so recklessly and foolishly leaving herself unprotected and at his mercy, and pain...

Ward had no idea why he should feel pain and, what was more, he didn't want to know.

'You could have used your key, you know,' Anna was telling him conversationally as she led the way back to the kitchen.

His key!

Ward opened his mouth to tell her that he didn't possess a key to her house and then closed it again.

'You've got time to go up and have a shave before breakfast,' Anna told him, pausing before saying ruefully, 'I didn't know...what you'd like, but I have to confess there isn't much choice. I must have planned to go shopping yesterday, I think.'

Anna had been dismayed to discover how little there was in her fridge to satisfy the appetite of a man the size of Ward. Somehow, even without the benefit of her memory, she doubted that he would be happy to eat the simple breakfast of bio yoghurt and raw fruit which she knew instinctively she preferred. There was wholemeal bread and eggs and, to her relief, she had found some smoked salmon in her freezer along with a leg of lamb. They could have the lamb for lunch and then tomorrow she would shop for proper man-filling food. Odd. What an odd thing memory was; she knew, for instance, exactly where the shops were and how to cook, but she had no idea of Ward's culinary tastes.

'I'll have whatever's going,' Ward told her almost brusquely. At home he lived and ate simply. He could cook, when he had to, but eating solitary meals did not encourage him to spend time in the kitchen preparing them so he normally relied on ready-prepared super-market ones or ate out.

Whilst he was upstairs, Anna arranged her flowers, humming happily to herself. They really were beautiful, her favourite colours, and she quickly coaxed them into a lovely soft, relaxed display.

Upstairs in the bedroom they had shared the previous night, Ward deliberately ignored the now neatly remade bed. He still couldn't understand how he had come to behave in the way he had.

To simply say that the opportunity she had presented had been too much of a temptation for him to resist was too simplistic and just didn't lie easily on his conscience. He had always been so controlled, so in control of himself and his desires. From both his mother and his stepfather he had learned the value of respecting both himself and others. Casual sex, once he had been past the experimental eagerness of his extreme youth, had simply never been something which held any appeal for him.

He swallowed hard as he made his way to the bathroom with his razor. Even now, just thinking about last night made him feel…made him want… Ward clenched his jaw. Well, what he wanted he certainly could not have, he informed himself sternly. Last night had been a mistake which wasn't going to be repeated tonight.

But Anna thought that they were lovers and she would expect them to share a bed, he reminded himself.

Maybe, but that didn't mean that he had to *touch* her, did it? It didn't mean that he had to stroke her silky skin or kiss her soft mouth; it didn't mean he had to…

Hell!

Why on earth had he started to think about that—about her? It had been an accident, an error of judgement, something that should never have happened and most certainly would never ever happen again.

'I hope you like smoked salmon and scrambled eggs,' Anna told Ward ruefully as he came into the kitchen. He looked so handsome, all freshly shaved and smelling subtly of something tangy and slightly citrusy. She was glad he wasn't the kind of man to wear a heavy, ostentatious aftershave, but even though he looked and smelled good now there had been something very special and erotic, something deeply personal and intimate about the way he had smelled—and tasted—last night.

Anna blushed a little as she realised where her thoughts were taking her—and why.

Heavens, if Ward were to suggest that they forget about breakfast and feast off one another instead, she knew she would be very easily persuaded to agree. The way she had behaved last night was totally outside her own experience of herself, and she had to confess that once she had got over the shock of her physical desire for Ward she had positively enjoyed the liberating experience of exploring her own sensuality.

Smoked salmon and scrambled eggs. Ward's eyes lit up and his mouth started to water; it was one of his favourite breakfast dishes.

'Wonderful,' he told Anna warmly, unable to take his eyes off her face as he saw the pretty way she started to blush. Surely this wasn't how a woman of her type should behave, blushing just because he had shown approval of her choice of breakfast?

Anna could have told him that it wasn't so much that that was making her skin colour up so rosily as the fact that she felt so euphorically happy, so sensually sensitive and aware that she was very tempted to ignore the habit of a lifetime and take the initiative by suggesting boldly to him that they take their breakfast back to bed.

Instead, she told him a little breathlessly, 'I…er…found a bottle of champagne. It's in the fridge. If you could open it we could have Buck's Fizz…'

Champagne!

Ward's eyebrows rose.

'It…I…'

What was his voice implying? Anna wondered. That she was being extravagant, both emotionally and financially, going over the top, perhaps? It was so frustrating not being able to rely on her knowledge of him, her previous experience with him, to judge what his reactions meant or what his views were.

'It doesn't matter if you'd rather not,' she began hesitantly, and then changed her mind. Honesty was a vital component of any relationship so far as she was concerned, even if sometimes it had to be softened a little with tact.

Her head held high, she told Ward, 'I wanted to make this special. Memorable.' Her face flushed rosily again as she added truthfully, '*You* made last night so very special for me. I may not be able to recall the memories, the special times we've already had together, Ward, but at least I can make sure that the new ones we're creating now are good ones. For me, this morning will be a first celebration of our love for one another and our relationship. Although perhaps the champagne *is* a little excessive…'

She paused and gave him a wry smile. 'If you'd rather not…'

For a moment Ward was too caught off guard to speak. The words she had used, the emotions she had just expressed, had made him shockingly, shamingly aware of just what he had done.

But *she* wasn't really the person she now appeared to be, he reassured himself fiercely. In reality the words she was saying to him meant nothing; the emotions she had expressed just did not exist, *could* not exist in the woman he knew her to be. But how could she possibly manufacture such a very different personality from her own? Ward had to admit that he didn't know and that perhaps he should have questioned the hospital consultant a little more thoroughly.

By rights he knew full well that the last thing he should be doing was toasting a relationship, a *love* that simply did not exist with Buck's Fizz, whilst eating *à deux* with a woman who was completely unaware of the real situation between them, but as he looked into Anna's eager, happy face Ward knew that there was no way he could disappoint her.

They ate their breakfast in Anna's sunny conservatory, with Missie curled up in her basket and the cat, Whittaker, basking in a pool of sunlight.

'I'll help you clear up,' Ward offered when they had finished. Smiling at him, Anna got up. She had put his flowers on a small side table and as she caught sight of them her smile deepened. Instead of starting to clear the table she walked to Ward's side and leaned over him, one hand on his shoulder, the other very gently, hesitantly almost, touching his face as she bent her head to kiss him.

'Thank you again for my beautiful flowers,' she told him softly.

It wasn't a passionate or intimate kiss, just the soft brush of her mouth against his—nothing really, Ward would tell himself angrily later, and certainly no reason for him to reach out and slide his arms around her body, pulling her onto his knee, his mouth fastening hungrily over hers, one arm cradling her against his body whilst he lifted his free hand to slide it behind her head so that he could hold the nape of her neck as his mouth fed greedily on hers.

Anna almost felt as though she would swoon with delight.

When she had made that abrupt decision to kiss Ward she had hoped, of course, that he would respond, reciprocate, but the intensity of his response had exceeded even the most adventurous of her hopes. She forgot that she was thirty-seven years old, that she was a woman whose desires were far more cerebral than physical. Her mouth opened beneath Ward's, her tongue twining sensuously with his. Beneath the hand she had originally placed against his chest to steady herself she could feel the suddenly accelerated thud of his heartbeat. The still warm air of the conservatory was filled with the sound of their breathing and the soft, frantic endearments Anna was whispering to Ward against his mouth.

Already her body was starting to ache with need for him, all the wild, sweet, wanton feelings she had experienced with him before rushing back over her.

The soft weight of her body pressing against him combined with the responsive murmur of her voice as she responded to his kiss was too much for Ward's precarious self-control. His mind might deplore what he was doing, but his body was working on a very different agenda.

His hand shook as he unfastened the buttons of Anna's shirt and then slipped it off her shoulder so that he could kiss the fragrant warmth of her skin. A tiny rash of goose bumps betrayed her responsive reaction to him and through the sheer transparency of her ivory-coloured bra he could see the dark burgeoning of her nipples.

Now it was his turn to vocalise his desire, and Anna shivered deliciously beneath the warm gust of his breath against her breast as he whispered her name.

As Ward bent his head down towards her, a shaft of sunlight touched the exposed nape of his neck, burnishing his thick dark hair, highlighting not just his masculinity but also an unbearably poignant vulnerability which touched Anna's emotions so intensely that her eyes filled with tears.

Very gently she stroked his exposed nape, almost as a mother might a child. Mother and child—immediately the images her thoughts conjured up sent a shocking surge of emotion right through her body. What had Ward been like as a child? What would it be like to have his child?

Ward's mouth nudged aside the fabric of her bra, his tonguetip circling urgently around her nipple. Anna shuddered wildly as her body reacted compulsively to his touch, all thoughts of anything other than what was happening between them forgotten. Ward's mouth covered her nipple, hot, wet, tugging urgently on her eager flesh.

Anna's dining chairs, charming though they were, had not been designed for the use they were currently putting them to and, although she had impatiently tugged Ward's shirt free of his trousers, right now Anna needed far more intimate contact with his body than their present situation allowed.

'Ward… Ward…' she whispered frantically in his ear. 'Let's go upstairs…to bed…'

The sound of her voice brought Ward back to reality. What on earth was he *doing*? Yes, what was *she* doing? his body protested as he slowly released Anna's nipple and slid the silky fabric of her bra back over her damp breast.

As Anna slid shakily off his lap Ward knew he had to do something—say something—and quickly, because if—*once* they were upstairs... His body was already very powerfully making its protest felt. It wanted Anna right back where she had been, or, even better, where she had been last night—in his bed, in his arms, her body clothed only in the heat generated by their mutual desire. But Ward couldn't afford to give in to the dictates of his body, no matter how urgently it was expressing them.

Instead, he caught hold of Anna's hand whilst determinedly keeping some distance between them.

'Anna...' When she looked at him like that he lost all sense of what he wanted to say; all he could do was shake his head and tell her bluntly and hoarsely, 'I can't...'

He *couldn't*! Anna's eyes widened. What on earth...? And then she flushed as she realised what he must mean. They weren't a young couple at the height of their sexual powers, after all, and last night and then this morning they had—

It was different for a woman. She didn't need...she could... But then Ward had...

As he saw the uncertain, discreet little look she gave his body Ward suddenly realised what Anna was thinking.

A little wryly he wondered how she would react if he were to tell her that not only was he perfectly capable of making love with her but that if he took her to bed now he doubted that *once* was going to satisfy the fierce, pulsing ache which was tormenting a body almost incandescent with desire for her. The barrier which was preventing him from making love with her wasn't a physical but a moral one. But he could hardly tell her that! And perhaps it might be a good idea to make sure that he was not confronted with any more temptation.

To that end, as soon as they had finished clearing away after their meal Ward said to Anna, 'It's a nice day; I was wondering if you would like to go out somewhere, perhaps for a drive or a walk…'

'Well, we could possibly do both,' Anna answered. 'We could call at the garden centre; I noticed when you were out this morning that I must have been working on planting up some containers when I had my accident and I obviously need some more plants to finish them off. There's a good garden centre on the other side of town, and since it's not far from the river we could park the car and walk along the river path, if that appeals to you.'

At the sound of the word 'walk' Missie, who had been lying in her basket, jumped up and started to bark excitedly.

'Looks like the decision's already been made for us,' Ward told Anna ruefully.

'What are your hobbies?' Anna asked him hesitantly half an hour later when she was seated beside him in his car as he drove in the direction she had described to him.

'Work, work and more work,' Ward told her dryly and honestly. 'I like walking,' he added equally truthfully, 'but I'm afraid I seldom make time to do any even though my farmhouse is right up in the hills.'

'You're a workaholic, but you said you were retired,' Anna pointed out, confused.

'Yes, I am, sort of… I sold up my company but I'm still involved in consultancy work.'

'You mentioned investments before,' Anna remembered, her forehead crinkling as she gave a small shiver. For some reason the word 'investments' made her feel anxious and tense, as though a large shadow had been cast over the warmth of the sun shining so brightly outside the car.

Ward gave her a quick look. Was she going to start remembering, and what was she going to do if she did— no, *when* she did? he corrected himself sternly. When she did he would be only too relieved, because then he could insist on her repaying Ritchie's money and then once that was done he could walk away from her and get on with his own life.

'Is that how we met? Were you…did you advise me on my investments?' Anna asked him uncertainly, repeating her earlier question to him. She didn't understand why the subject should make her feel so unhappy and ill at ease.

'Hardly,' Ward told her curtly, unable to stop himself from adding, 'Investment advice is the *last* thing *you'd* need or want from anyone.'

Confused, Anna was just about to ask him to explain his cryptic remark when she realised they were coming to a roundabout and that she'd have to give him directions. By the time they were on the right road, a small inner voice of caution had warned her that some things, like Pandora's box, were best left unmeddled with. Maybe she and Ward had quarrelled over the subject; maybe he had offered her advice and help and she had been too independent to take it. Whatever the case, she would be much better able to deal with it once her memory had returned, she told herself firmly.

Ward wondered suspiciously why Anna was not pursuing the subject and demanding to know more. *Had* she remembered? Instinctively he knew that she couldn't have done, but who knew how far back in her past her double dealings went? Who knew how long she had been cheating and deceiving others?

'Here we are; it's this lane on the left,' Anna told him, directing his attention to the entrance to the garden centre.

At Anna's suggestion Ward remained in the car with Missie whilst she went to get her plants. Although she would not have dreamed of saying so to him, Ward's cryptic remark to her had left her feeling hurt and confused, her manner towards him noticeably cooler than it had been, Ward was aware as she gently refused his company. This was a woman who would never descend to angry arguments or sullen silence but who could, nevertheless, very firmly retreat into her own space when she felt the need, Ward recognised, unwillingly admiring her distancing air of dignity as she quietly closed the car door and walked away from him.

Everything about her spoke of gentleness and dignity, of a woman who put the needs of others above her own, a woman whose behaviour was governed by a slightly old-fashioned moral code, a code which he acknowledged was very similar to his own. And yet she had still joined forces with Julian Cox in his despicably fraudulent activities. On her way towards the store, Ward was not surprised to see her stop to aid an elderly couple who were having trouble lifting an unwieldy pot plant into the boot of their car.

CHAPTER SEVEN

WARD glanced frowningly at his watch.

Anna had been gone for over half an hour, having told him she would be about ten minutes.

He looked at Missie. She was fast asleep, curled up on the blanket on the back seat of his car. Checking that a window was open enough to let in fresh air for her, he climbed out of the car and locked it, setting out in the direction Anna had taken.

He found her less than five minutes later, standing next to a car filled with plants. She had her back to him and her face was turned up towards that of the man standing next to her, who, if his besotted expression was anything to go by, was thoroughly enjoying the experience. As Anna's soft laughter rang out, Ward was suddenly stabbed by a surge of dislike for her male companion that was so strong, it literally momentarily deprived him of breath.

Angrily he told himself that the feeling pounding through him was caused merely by his apprehension that Anna's companion might inadvertently have said something to her to make her suspicious of his own supposed relationship with her, thereby foiling his plans to punish her, and that it had nothing to do with something more personal—something, in fact, which was far, far more dangerous.

Anxiously he hurried towards Anna but, as Ward approached her, the man with her reached out and touched her arm, drawing her closer to him in order to allow someone to pass her. As he saw the man put his hand on Anna's arm, a murderous flash of emotion sliced through Ward. Without knowing how he had got there he suddenly discovered he was standing at Anna's side, his gaze challenging the other man's right to touch her.

'Oh, Ward!' Anna exclaimed. His appearance at her side had both startled her and somehow made her feel a little guilty. 'I'm sorry I was so long,' she said, mistaking the cause of his black-browed look. 'There was a long queue at the till and then I was just on my way back when I bumped into Tim.'

As Anna started to introduce them Ward forced himself to respond to the other man's uncertain smile.

He knew from the look in Anna's eyes that she had no suspicion whatsoever that he wasn't who she thought him to be, but for some reason his angry anxiety refused to subside, and so did his dislike of the man at her side. What was the matter with him? he asked himself irritably. Anyone would think he was jealous. *Jealous*. The very idea was ridiculous...laughable, impossible. He never got jealous. In fact he didn't have a jealous bone in his body.

'I'm sorry you had to wait so long.' Anna apologised again quietly once they were on their own.

She was silent after that as they walked back to the car but Ward was well aware that she kept watching him, looking at him.

'I only came to look for you because Missie was getting fretful,' Ward told Anna untruthfully as they approached the car. Anna said nothing but Ward could see the quick look she gave the peacefully sleeping dog as he placed her plants into the car boot.

Ten minutes later, as they headed silently for the river path, Missie tugging a little impatiently on her lead,

Ward acknowledged that he had perhaps overreacted. Had the situation been different, had they been a real couple, he might have been able to lower his pride enough to admit his jealousy, but how could he admit to feeling jealous about a woman he didn't even like, never mind love?

It was just his natural male instincts coming to the fore, he tried to tell himself as he helped Anna over the stile that led to the footpath.

As they walked side by side along the river, Anna acknowledged how daunting she was beginning to find the fact that she knew so little about Ward. His anger had confused and upset her. It had seemed completely at odds with the way he had behaved towards her previously. Was he, perhaps, a very impatient man?

She watched as he paused whilst a young woman with three young children and two dogs went through the turnstile ahead of them. One of the dogs and the youngest child had to be coaxed through. Ward waited patiently, even offering to hold one of the dogs' leads for the harassed young mother, who flashed him a grateful smile. Not the action of an impatient man, Anna admitted as she instinctively moved closer to him, her hand touching his arm in a gesture of female possession. The young woman meant no harm, but even so…Anna was both surprised and a little bewildered by the strength of her own feelings.

Her eyes flashed a little as she saw the way Ward was smiling at the young mother. How dared he look at her like that, smile at her like that…*flirt* with her like that?

Her head had begun to ache and she felt tired.

'I think I'd like to go back to the car,' she told Ward woodenly. Without waiting for his response she turned round and started to walk quickly in the direction she had just come, both ashamed of and overwhelmed by her own emotions.

As he drove them back to Anna's house, Ward reflected inwardly that Anna had every right to be annoyed with him. He *had* overreacted in the garden centre, but admitting his fault and his jealousy would mean admitting emotions he couldn't possibly allow himself to feel. He was losing track of the real reason for his presence in Anna's life, her home…her bed… His body was confusing and betraying him with its passionate response to her.

By the time they reached her house Anna's head was pounding nauseously, but a headache was no excuse for her behaviour. How *could* she have been so jealous of that poor, harassed young mother? She could sense that ordinarily such emotions were totally foreign to her and yet she *had* experienced them and that confused her. Even frightened her, she admitted to herself.

The telephone was ringing as they walked into the house. Anna went to answer it, one hand massaging her aching temple as she recognised her god-daughter's voice.

'Beth! How are you?'

'Fine…and you?'

Anna hesitated for a moment. She just didn't feel up to coping with Beth's concern and questions if she told her the truth.

'I'm fine,' she fibbed.

'I meant to ring earlier,' Beth told her, 'but I didn't get back until this morning. The family all send their love, by the way. Mum said to remind you that it's their silver wedding soon; she's planning a big party and, of course, she wants you there.'

Anna released her breath slowly. Beth must have been home to visit her parents in Cornwall. No doubt she, Anna, *had* known about her trip even though she couldn't remember .

'Look, I must go. We'll talk again soon,' Beth was saying, and before Anna could reply the younger woman was saying goodbye and ending the call.

In the living room of the accommodation above the shop, Beth closed her eyes and gave a small sigh.

She knew she had been a little abrupt with Anna, but her godmother was always so intuitive and aware that Beth was afraid she might guess... Quickly she scanned through the post she had picked up on her way in, her body tensing as she saw the airmail envelope from Prague.

Her mouth went dry as she ripped it open. Inside was a copy despatch note for some of the pottery she had bought for the shop during her buying trip to Prague earlier in the year. She was still waiting for the gorgeous reproduction antique crystal. Only the previous week her partner, Kelly, had mentioned that it was disappointing that it had still not arrived.

'When exactly is it coming? What exactly did happen about that?' she had asked curiously.

'Soon,' Beth had told her quickly, crossing her fingers behind her back. 'Very soon.'

She had been conscious of the searching look Kelly had given her. They had known one another since university and she was just grateful that Kelly's newly engaged status meant that she was too involved with her new fiancé to probe too deeply into the delayed arrival of the Czech crystal. It had been bad enough having her stupidity over Julian Cox made public without...

Angrily Beth closed her eyes. Her emotions were still too raw and sensitive. It was just as well that Kelly was out of town with Brough, visiting his family. Her godmother's voice had sounded a little strained on the telephone. If she had hurt her feelings by being distant with her recently, she would have to find a way of making it up to her...later...when she felt more able to. For now she intended to avoid her godmother as much as she could. The last thing she wanted was for Anna to guess...To guess what? That she had made a fool of herself over a man a second time?

'What is it? What's wrong?' Ward asked Anna sharply as he saw the way she was massaging and rubbing her temple. She looked very pale, very heavy-eyed.

'I've got a headache,' Anna told him warily.

'A headache!' Immediately Ward was at her side. 'Since when? Why didn't you say something? Do you feel sick? Can you—'

'Ward, it's a headache, that's all,' Anna snapped, immediately regretting her small loss of patience when she saw his expression.

Mindful of what the consultant had said to him, Ward watched her grimly. The last thing he wanted to do was panic her, but...

'Come on,' he told her quietly, taking hold of her arm.

'Where are we going?' Anna protested. 'I was just going to put the lunch on...'

'Hospital,' Ward told her, ignoring the second half of her statement.

'Hospital? Why? I...'

'The consultant warned me to be alert for any symptoms such as a headache, nausea, or blurred vision,' he told her gently.

'It's just a headache…that's all… I haven't got blurred vision.' Anna started to panic but she still allowed Ward to guide her out to the car.

Luckily the hospital's casualty department was relatively quiet, and even more fortunately the consultant who had seen her last night was actually on duty. At Anna's insistence Ward remained with her whilst the consultant questioned her and then examined her.

'Hmm…' he announced when he had finished. 'Are you normally prone to headaches?' he asked Anna.

'Sometimes… I do get the odd tension headache,' she admitted.

'I tend to think that this is what this one is,' he diagnosed. 'So far as I can judge there certainly isn't anything to indicate that it might be anything else. You say that so far you haven't remembered anything of the time that you've lost…no flashbacks…?'

'No, nothing,' Anna told him dispiritedly.

'You see, I *told* you it was just a headache,' she said tiredly once they were back in the car.

'I know, but it still had to be checked out,' Ward responded.

She had looked so forlorn, so…so sad, sitting there whilst the consultant asked her if she could remember anything yet, that Ward had ached to take hold of her, to wrap his arms protectively around her and tell her that everything was all right, that she was safe; that it didn't matter a damn to him if she never remembered… That he would—

Anna gave a startled gasp as he changed gear almost viciously, throwing her against her seat belt.

'Sorry,' he muttered, avoiding meeting her gaze as he swung the car into her drive.

Once they were back in the house Ward went straight upstairs. He had seen some headache tablets in the cabinet in the bathroom. Removing two, he went back downstairs and filled a glass with water.

Anna had her back to him as she placed the lamb in the roasting tin. Going up to her, he tapped her on the shoulder and handed her the glass and the tablets, saying quietly, 'Take these. They might help.'

Tears blurred Anna's eyes. She was so unused to having anyone look after her, take care of her...love her. To her own consternation as much as Ward's, her whole body started to shake as her emotions overwhelmed her.

Pushing past Ward, she dashed upstairs. This was ridiculous. She was behaving idiotically.

Ward caught up with her just as she pushed open her bedroom door.

'Anna, what is it? What have I done?' he demanded worriedly.

What had *he* done. Anna shook her head.

'It isn't you, it's me,' she told him through her tears. 'This morning, on the footpath...that young mother... I was so jealous, but I don't get jealous, and you were just helping her, but I thought...I felt... For a moment I wanted...' Anna stopped, too ashamed of herself to go on.

'I hated her, Ward,' she finally admitted huskily. 'I hated the way she smiled at you and...and the way you looked back at her...I wanted...'

Ward stared at her.

'Was *that* what caused your headache?' he demanded.

Anna gave a small smile.

'No, the headache was already there, but it did cause me some *heartache*,' she admitted ruefully. 'Ward, I was so jealous…'

Ward took a deep breath. Her honesty and her bravery compelled him to be equally open with her.

'I was jealous too…earlier…in the garden centre. That man…Tim…he was touching your arm and I wanted to…I could have…'

'You were jealous of Tim and not angry because I had been so long? Oh, Ward, Tim is just a friend and he's very happily married…' Laughter gurgled in Anna's throat. 'You couldn't possibly have been jealous of him…'

'And you couldn't possibly have been jealous of that poor young woman.'

Somehow or other Ward discovered he had taken Anna in his arms and now she was nestling happily against his body, lifting her tear-stained face to his.

'I suppose the trouble is that our love is still so new that we aren't quite sure of one another yet. Our feelings are still very…very intense…very…passionate…' Anna concluded, her voice dropping to a whisper and her glance following the gentle touch of Ward's fingertip as he started to trace the shape of her jaw and then her mouth.

Anna's lips parted on a small, beatific sigh. Ward's fingertip met the soft breath she expelled. It sent a shaft of fierce pleasure right through his body. Anna moved her head a little, capturing his fingertip in her mouth. Very, very slowly she started to suck on it.

Ward felt as though his insides had been turned to pure molten pleasure. Honesty was a very dangerous aphrodisiac, he decided dizzily as Anna gave a little

moan of pleasure before starting to nibble on a second
finger.

'Have you any idea just what that is doing to me?'
Ward grumbled despairingly.

'Mmm…No… Why don't you tell me?' Anna invited
seductively.

'Well, it might feel a little bit like this,' Ward
obliged, instigating a little bit of seduction of his own
by nibbling gently on her neck.

'Mmm…' Anna sighed appreciatively, closing her
eyes.

'You know, you really do wear too many clothes,'
Ward whispered thickly to her several seconds later as
he helped to correct this sartorial error by removing her
shirt.

'Mmm… I could say the same about you,' Anna
agreed huskily. If Ward responded so satisfactorily to
just the delicate touch of her mouth against his fingers,
then how would he react if she repeated that caress on
other more sensitive parts of his body? Anna wondered
daringly.

She and Ralph had never really experimented with
sex. They had both been a little shy and almost formal
with one another in their lovemaking, but now Anna
was beginning to discover a spirit of sensual adventure
within herself that both bemused and excited her. Her
fingers tugged impatiently at Ward's buttons whilst she
nuzzled the warm flesh of his throat. His skin smelled
just as it had done last night—slightly musky, warm and
very, very male.

'Mmm…you taste good,' Ward told her, echoing her
own thoughts about him as his lips started to caress the
soft curve of her breast.

Anna had no idea just how long it took them to remove each other's clothes; she only knew that once they had she couldn't stop herself from openly feasting her gaze and then her hands and mouth on Ward's body.

Initially he was tempted to stop her. He wasn't used to a passive role, but Anna was gently insistent.

'I've never been like this before,' she told him quietly.

'How do you know,' Ward questioned her, 'if you can't remember?'

'I just *know*,' Anna told him simply, and against all logic, as he looked into her eyes, Ward believed her.

There was nothing practised or artificial about her touch, and Ward controlled his own desire to watch her tenderly as she explored his body with absorbed concentration.

'Everything, *all* of you, is just so perfect,' she whispered, pink-cheeked, at one point, giving him an indignant look when Ward started to laugh.

'Twenty years ago I might, *just might*, have been tempted to believe you,' he said. 'But now...' His laugh, warm and uninhibited, shook his body.

'It's true, though,' Anna protested, injured. 'You are perfect—to me...'

'Aha...' Ward began, but Anna stopped him.

She demanded huskily, 'Ward, were you really jealous of Tim?'

'Really,' he confirmed steadily, holding her gaze before adding truthfully, 'Very!'

Anna gave a small loving sigh.

'You don't have any need to be, you know,' she told him frankly. 'I never thought I'd ever feel like this.' She paused. 'Did you...*have* there been...?'

'No...not now,' Ward replied promptly. 'My mother...' He stopped abruptly.

'Tell me about your family, Ward,' Anna encouraged, her fingers playing with the soft, dark hair that covered his chest.

'No, there isn't very much to tell, and no, you haven't met them,' Ward answered. This was a subject he didn't want to pursue but Anna obviously wasn't going to be sidetracked.

'Tell me about your home,' she insisted. 'Have I seen it?'

'No!'

Ward reached up and drew her down against his body, cupping her face as he started to kiss her. It might be a good way of silencing her, he acknowledged several seconds later, but it still possessed dangers of its own. He had already told himself that, no matter what the temptation, he was not going to succumb to it or make the same mistakes he had made last night, but Anna's fingertips were gently stroking down the length of his body and just the thought of how it would feel to have them caressing the most intimate part of him was enough to make him give a small gasp of awed awareness.

'You're so big,' she told him, wide-eyed, as she touched him.

Ward looked at her a little suspiciously but there was no trace of any guile in her expression. In fact, if he were a vain man, he could, he acknowledged, be very, very susceptible to the look in Anna's eyes, urgent now as she studied his body.

'And you're so…you're so you,' he told her thickly as he reached out for her.

After that it was a long time before either of them said anything remotely intelligible, although neither of them seemed to have any difficulty in interpreting the other's whispered words of pleasure and incandescent delight.

'Oh, Ward,' Anna whispered, torn between emotional tears of release and happy laughter as she lay trembling in Ward's arms in the aftermath of their lovemaking.

'Oh, Ward, what?' he demanded wryly.

'Oh, Ward, I'm just so glad that you're a part of my life, that I met you, that you're here with me... like...like this...' Anna told him softly.

Ward paused for a moment.

'No more than I am,' he told her gruffly.

For a moment Ward could hardly believe what he had said. His admission had been tantamount to a declaration of love. What the hell was he doing... thinking...feeling...?

'Ward?'

He tensed as Anna suddenly shot up in bed, her voice anxious. What had happened? Had she suddenly recovered her memory? Was she...?

'What is it? What's wrong?' he asked her tersely.

'I never fed poor Missie and Whittaker. Oh, and the lamb's still waiting to be cooked...'

'Stay here,' Ward told her masterfully. 'I'll go down and sort everything out.' He was only gone a couple of minutes, and when he came back he was smiling broadly.

'What is it?' Anna demanded suspiciously as he climbed back into bed beside her. 'Why are you smiling like that?'

'I think you can forget about the lamb,' he told her jovially. 'Oh, and Missie and Whittaker *don't* need feeding either.'

Anna guessed immediately what had happened.

'Oh, no. They've eaten the lamb,' she wailed.

'Oh, yes, I'm afraid they have,' Ward chuckled. 'They must have got tired of waiting for us and decided to help themselves.'

'Oh, but Ward, there isn't anything for *us* to eat,' Anna complained.

'Who needs food?' Ward responded recklessly.

'Mmm…Who needs anything else when we've got what we've got?' Anna agreed dreamily.

CHAPTER EIGHT

'AND so as I was saying, Anna, if you could swop with me and do my next week's Meals on Wheels rota, I would—'

Anna's visitor broke off, her eyes rounding in surprise, her face going pink as Ward came strolling into the kitchen.

'I've changed the tyre on your car. Just as well I noticed that you'd got a slow puncture,' Ward told Anna.

'Er...Mary, this is Ward, my...my friend...' Anna said hastily, correctly interpreting the curiosity in the other woman's face.

'Oh, yes...I see... Your...friend...I didn't know. I...er... Look, I really must be going. Nice to have met you...er...Ward...'

'What was all that about?' Ward asked Anna after Mary had gone.

'She wanted me to change rotas with her for her Meals on Wheels,' Anna told him.

Ward started to frown.

It was three days now since he had moved in with Anna and so far she had shown no signs of her memory returning—and so far, too, he had shown no signs of keeping his promise to himself and putting a safe distance between them.

In fact...

He grimaced to himself, remembering the way Anna

108

had coaxed him last night, whispering to him, 'It's silly you sleeping in this bed and me having to…'

'The consultant said you needed to *rest*,' Ward had reminded her stoically.

'Mmm…but how will you know if I get a bad headache or something in the night if we aren't sleeping together?' Anna had asked him teasingly.

There had been no contest, of course, and this morning he had woken up with Anna tucked neatly into the curve of his body, and then… But that wasn't the complication which was making him frown now. Sooner or later someone was going to question his appearance in Anna's life and he couldn't afford to have that happen, not at this stage. When Anna got her memory back then he would be able to deal with whatever accusations she chose to make against him. After all, he had to point out her own culpability, but until then…

The sight of an oil smear on his last clean shirt reminded him of something else. Coming to a sudden decision, he told Anna quietly, 'I need to go home for…for a few days—check my post, make a few phone calls…'

'Oh, yes, of course…'

Even though she tried hard to conceal it Anna knew that her feelings must be showing on her face. She hated the thought of being without him and she knew she would miss him dreadfully.

'I'd like you to come with me,' Ward added quickly.

'Go with you…?' Anna's eyes widened. 'But what about Missie and Whittaker?'

'They can come too,' Ward assured her.

Go with him. See his house. Perhaps meet his friends… Anna's heart gave a small skip of pleasure.

'Oh, Ward, yes, I'd love to.' She beamed happily.

*   *   *

'What's all this about Anna and this man she's got stay-ing with her?' Kelly asked Beth curiously.

'What man? I don't know what you're talking about,' Beth replied as she stared incredulously at her friend and partner. 'It can't possibly be true... We'd have known. Anna would have told us. Besides, she just isn't...she just doesn't...'

Beth paused and looked at Kelly.

'She just isn't like that.'

Kelly knew exactly what Beth meant. It wasn't that Anna wasn't a desirable or attractive woman—she was—but there was an air of shyness about her, an air of...of purity, for want of a better word. Kelly acknowl-edged that that made it hard to imagine her even flirting with a man, never mind letting one move in with her.

'There must be a mistake,' Beth protested uneasily.

'Not according to Mary Charles. Apparently she saw him up at the house when she went to see Anna and Anna actually introduced him to her as her "friend."'

The two young women eyed one another specula-tively.

'Dee might know,' Beth volunteered. 'She and Anna have become quite close recently.'

'Dee *might* know,' Kelly agreed, 'but she's in Northumberland with her aunt.'

'Oh, yes, of course; I'd forgotten.'

Kelly gave Beth a thoughtful look. Beth had become increasingly remote and preoccupied recently, and if Kelly hadn't known better she would almost have imag-ined Beth was concealing something from her. But Beth simply wasn't that type, just as her godmother wasn't the type to have a live-in man 'friend.'

'Do you think one of us should go up and see Anna?' Beth asked eventually.

Kelly pursed her lips.

'Well, of course, Anna's private life is really none of our business. However... I'll have a word with Brough and see what he thinks,' she offered.

'Mmm...Brough will know what to do,' Beth agreed.

Her godmother wasn't a wealthy woman but she wasn't a poor one either and, as Beth knew to her cost, there *were* men around who were all too eager to take advantage of a vulnerable woman. Look at the way she had deceived herself over Julian Cox, letting herself be persuaded that he loved her when all he had really been interested in was the money he'd thought she was going to inherit.

Mind you, she had certainly learned her lesson there and she would certainly *never* make that mistake again. The best way to treat men was with the same lack of real emotion with which they treated women. There was, after all, nothing morally wrong about enjoying sex for its own sake, about using a man in the same way that men used women... Beth gave a small toss of her head. No, there was nothing wrong with that at all, despite what a certain person seemed to think.

'Beth, come back,' Kelly commanded her friend wryly.

Flushing a little guiltily, Beth collected her thoughts. 'Mary is bound to have got it wrong,' she told Kelly. 'The man she saw was probably just a friend of Anna's.'

'Mmm... I expect you're right,' Kelly agreed.

'Brough, I'm worried about Anna.'

Brough looked up from the papers he had been read-ing to study Kelly's concerned face.

'Why, what's wrong with her?' he asked her calmly. 'If she's not well…'

'No, it isn't anything like that,' Kelly told him quickly, shaking her head. 'It's…well, she's disappeared, Brough, and no one seems to know where she's gone. I went up to the house yesterday. It's all closed up. There was no sign of her, or of Missie or Whittaker either.'

'Perhaps she's decided to have a holiday,' Brough suggested reasonably, but Kelly shook her head even harder.

'No, not without telling someone. Oh, I wish that Dee was here,' she told him fretfully.

'Have you asked Beth if she knows anything?' Brough asked her.

'She doesn't,' Kelly informed him. 'Not that there's much point in trying to discuss anything with Beth these days. She seems to be living in a world of her own. Something happened to her in Prague,' she stated positively, briefly switching her thoughts from Anna's disappearance to Beth's unusual behaviour. 'But I don't know what and every time I try to get her to open up to me she shuts me out. She's worrying about something, I can tell.

'Oh, Brough, I'm so worried about Anna. It just isn't like her to disappear like that without telling anyone.'

Brough put down his papers and walked over to her, her distress making him frown a little.

'She's run her own life ever since she was widowed, Kelly,' he told her gently.

'Yes, I know that, and I know what you're thinking as well,' Kelly informed him accusingly. 'You think I'm being irrational and over-emotional. Well, perhaps I am a little, but, Brough, I can't help worrying.'

She paused and then looked at him before announcing, 'Julian Cox has disappeared as well.'

As she saw the look of angry distaste that crossed her fiancé's face, Kelly wished that she hadn't had to bring up the subject of Julian Cox. Brough had every reason to dislike the other man—they both did—and normally he was the last person Kelly would have wanted to talk about—after all, he had nearly destroyed their love—but her concern for her friend overrode her natural inclination to avoid the subject.

'I heard it in town and Harry confirmed it. It seems he left town whilst we were away, without any kind of warning, leaving all manner of debts behind him. No one has the least idea where he's gone.'

'The further the better so far as I'm concerned,' Brough told her grimly.

Harry was his sister Eve's fiancé and cousin to Dee.

It had been Dee who had been instrumental in bringing Brough and Kelly together, and because of that Brough had decided to overlook her other and far less beneficial manipulation of people and events in her determination to win the war she was waging against Julian Cox.

'Brough, you don't think that Anna's disappearance has anything to do with Julian, do you?' Kelly asked him uncertainly.

Brough's eyebrows lifted. 'Surely you aren't suggesting that Anna's fallen for him, in view of what she knows about him—'

'Of course not.' Kelly interrupted him impatiently. 'I didn't mean that at all.' She looked serious. 'What I meant was, what if…?' She stopped, unable to put into words her frightening suspicions.

'Brough,' she whispered, her throat dry, 'what if he

made her go with him? You know how desperate he was for money.'

'But surely Anna isn't *that* wealthy? I know she's comfortably off, but—Kelly, what is it?' he demanded sternly. 'There's something you aren't telling me, isn't there?'

Kelly was torn between her loyalty to her friend and her concern for her. In the end her concern and Brough's seriousness won.

'Dee and Anna were trying to trap Julian into betraying himself. He'd hinted to Anna in the past about needing a loan, so... Well, to cut a long story short, Anna let him believe that she had quite a large sum of money she wanted to invest...'

There was an ominous silence before Brough said quietly, 'I see. Well, that puts an entirely different complexion on the matter. Have you spoken to Dee about Anna's disappearance?'

Kelly shook her head.

'No. She's in Northumberland.'

'Hmm... You know, it seems to me, Kelly, that there's far more behind Dee's desire to punish Julian Cox than she's ever revealed to the rest of you.'

'Yes, I think you're right,' Kelly agreed. 'I've often wondered myself, but...'

'She's never given you any hint?'

'No, nothing. In fact—well, Dee isn't the kind of person who encourages you to ask personal questions. I did wonder initially if at some stage Dee might have fallen for him herself, but I just can't see it.'

'No, neither can I,' Brough agreed.

'Perhaps Harry might know something; after all, he is Dee's cousin.'

'Well, he might, but what's more important right now

is finding out exactly what's happened to Anna. Who else is likely to know where she could have gone, apart from Beth?'

'Well, either Dee or yourself—but there's still something I haven't told you, Brough. When Mary Charles went to see Anna recently, there was a man there with her.'

'A man?' Brough gave her a blank look.

'Yes. Mary seemed to think… Well, apparently Anna introduced him to her as a "friend."''

'A friend…?' Brough looked blank and a little irritated. 'What does *that* mean?'

'I mean friend with a capital F. Which means…'

Kelly stopped. What was the point of trying to explain the nuances of female conversation to her fiancé— a mere man? Brough wasn't listening anyway. Instead he was asking her, 'Did this…this Mary Charles say what this man's name was? If she did, we could get in touch with him and check if he knows anything about Anna's disappearance.'

'Well, yes and no. She says that Anna introduced him to her as Ward but that she didn't give his surname.'

'Oh, that's very helpful.' Brough looked exasperated. 'You do realise, don't you, that if Anna is having a…relationship with this man, this Ward, whoever he may be, she might have her own reasons for choosing not to discuss it or him with any of you?'

'If that was the case she wouldn't have introduced him to Mary, would she?' Kelly countered, and then added, 'Besides, that's just not Anna; she isn't like that. She's shy, Brough, and…and cautious. I really am worried about her,' Kelly told him quietly. 'We both know how…how violent Julian can be. If something went

wrong and he discovered that Dee and Anna were trying
to trap him…'

'Mmm… Well, the first thing we should do is to get
in touch with Dee and find out if *she* knows anything
about Anna's plans and this unknown friend of hers.'

'I thought you said you lived in an old farmhouse,'
Anna gasped as Ward brought his car to a halt in the
courtyard of the stone-built building which was both far
larger and far more formidable than Anna had visual-
ised.

'It is—or rather it was,' Ward told her.

It looked more like a cross between a manor house
and a small fortress, Anna decided as Ward opened the
car door for her, and even inside the enclosed courtyard
the air was noticeably cooler than it had been back in
Rye.

When she said as much to Ward, he reasoned dryly,
'That's because we're several hundred metres higher
here. The house was built originally by a family of rich
wool merchants from York. It had been left empty for
several years before I bought it.'

'It's rather isolated,' Anna felt bound to point out.

They had driven for what had seemed like miles
through empty countryside, climbing all the time, before
reaching their destination, but Anna had to admit there
was something bracing and exhilarating about the wide
emptiness of the sky above them and the rolling landscape of the Dales around them.

'Well, it certainly doesn't encourage casual visitors,'
Ward agreed, and Anna could tell that he considered
that an advantage.

If it had been her home she would have softened the
austerity of the courtyard with tubs of plants and wall

baskets, Anna decided as she waited for Ward to retrieve her case from the boot of his car.

'This way,' he instructed her, leading the way to a heavy and very old oak door.

The passage it opened onto was narrow and dark, stone-flagged and icy cold. Anna shivered as she waited for Ward to switch on the light. When he did she could see that, whilst the walls and the floor were meticulously clean, they presented an appearance of unwelcoming austerity. Only one door led off the passage into a large, well-equipped kitchen. Anna looked with relief at the well-made wooden units and the large burgundy Aga. The room was large enough to hold a good-sized oak table and the stone floor had been softened by a couple of rag rugs.

'This is lovely,' she told Ward appreciatively.

'My mother's choice,' Ward informed her. 'She said I'd never get anyone up here to cook or clean for me if I didn't provide them with a decent kitchen.

'I'll show you over the house and then we'd better have something to eat.'

They had stopped for a snack on the way to Yorkshire but Anna had been too excited at the thought of seeing Ward's home to eat very much.

Half an hour later her excitement had faded, to be replaced by a mixture of complex emotions. Seeing Ward's house—she could not call it a home—had almost been like studying a blank canvas. None of the rooms Ward had shown her, not even his own bedroom, betrayed anything of his character. Even the room where he worked was as austere as the rest of the house.

There was nothing wrong with the house itself. Its rooms were well proportioned, its views awesomely stunning, the furniture sparse but of good quality. It was just that the house was so sterile. It had no life, no warmth...no heart, and as she looked at Ward Anna suddenly felt unbearably sad for him. The house was so...so loveless. Had it been hers...

Anna allowed herself to daydream for a few minutes. That huge master bedroom he had shown her needed softening with fabrics that were sympathetic to the age and character of the house, not pretty chintzes, of course, but there were other fabrics—damasks, rich velvets in ruby-reds, imperial blues, warm golds, cool linens in sky-blues and watery greens—that would complement the landscape.

The single ceiling lights needed replacing with lamps and wall lights. The large plain white bathroom needed thick, fluffy towels. The dull brown carpet needed replacing with something lighter and richer. The big double bed needed a rich, dramatic cover; the sofas in the television and drawing rooms needed heaping with piles of cushions. The bare walls cried out for paintings, the empty surfaces of the furniture for bowls of flowers and family photographs.

Family photographs!

That was what this house needed, what it lacked. It lacked a family. It lacked love, as perhaps Ward had lacked it before they had met one another. A huge lump filled Anna's throat. She loved him so much, ached for him so much. She only had to see this house to know that there must have been a time in his life when he had felt very unloved.

As Ward watched the expressions chasing one another over Anna's face, he realised that he had seen them before. His mother's eyes had held that same look of loving compassion when she had gently tried to persuade him to move closer to her and his stepfather.

'I like it here,' he had told her stubbornly.

'But, darling, it's so…so bleak,' she had sighed.

Ward had shrugged away her criticism. It might seem bleak to her. To him it felt merely private, secure…safe.

'I'll take your things up and put them in the guest room; it's got its own *en suite* bathroom and if you want to have Missie and Whittaker up there with you…'

The spare guest bedroom. Anna looked at him in surprise. She had naturally assumed that she would be sharing *his* room, *his* bed.

Ward could see what she was thinking but this time he was prepared. He had had the long drive north to think about the situation and he had decided what he must do—and say.

'Ecclestone is a bit old-fashioned,' he told her, 'and I wouldn't want Mrs Jarvis to get the wrong idea about our relationship.'

It was, after all, the truth. He certainly didn't want his cleaner carrying tales back to the town that he and Anna were a couple. His mother still had contacts in the area, and sooner or later the news would get to her ear, and when it did…

It was no secret to Ward that his mother very much wanted him to marry again and have a family—not for her sake, as she was always quick to reassure him whenever she raised the subject, which was virtually every time she saw him, but for his own. If she thought for one moment that there was a woman in his life she would move heaven and earth to keep her there—permanently!

It was, though, also true that Ward did not relish the thought of being the subject of local gossip. He had endured enough of that when his marriage had broken up. But that, of course, was not the real reason why he wanted them to have separate bedrooms!

It was sweet of Ward to want to be so protective and chivalrous, Anna acknowledged, but she would still rather…

'We are both mature adults,' she reminded him gently. 'And both free to…to choose what we do with our lives.' She looked at Ward gravely but she could sense that he wasn't going to change his mind.

It would, she knew, be relatively easy to persuade him to change it. If she went over to him now, for instance, and started to coax him, touch him, *seduce* him… But she simply wasn't that kind of woman. She wanted Ward to want her, to be proud of desiring her, to want her love so recklessly that he simply didn't care what other people thought. And, after all, if he really felt so strongly about other people's views and about her, then he could always ensure that no one had any reason to gossip about them. There was nothing to stop them from making public vows of the commitment they had surely already made to one another privately.

Maybe they had not known one another very long, but it must be long enough for Anna to be very sure of *her* feelings, long enough for her to know that if Ward were to ask her to marry him she would say yes.

'What would you like to do tomorrow? We still haven't been to Lindisfarne, and then there's—'

'Couldn't we just stay here?' Anna asked Ward gently. She had been in Yorkshire for three days now and every day Ward had insisted on taking her out.

They had spent a day in York, which she had loved, and another in Harrogate. Ward had driven her miles through the Dales, delighting her both with his knowledge of his home county and the sights he had shown her. They had eaten magnificent Yorkshire high teas in York and in Harrogate's famous tea shop, and delicious lunches in traditional village pubs in the small Dales villages, sumptuous dinners in restaurants boasting many prestigious awards. But all Anna really longed for was to be alone with Ward, with a simple meal of nothing more exotic than bread and cheese washed down with a bottle of wine, and with the knowledge that he wanted and loved her. That was what she wanted.

Yesterday, after a delicious lunch, they had walked, climbing the moorland track until they found a sheltered spot to rest surrounded by empty moorland and out of sight of any curious eyes. Anna had longed for Ward to take hold of her, kiss her, make love with her, the way he had done in Rye, and for a second she had thought he would. She had stumbled on a piece of stone and he had reached out to steady her, asking, 'Are you all right?'

When she had nodded she had seen the way his gaze slid to her mouth and stayed there. Her heart had started thumping, her body quivering with longing for him. He had moved closer towards her so that she could feel the warmth of his body, and her mouth had become dry with arousal and tension. Automatically she had licked her lips. Immediately Ward had released her, turning away from her, but as he had done so she had thought she heard him groan.

Now Anna longed for the courage to be bolder, to be able to express her longing for him openly, but it simply wasn't her nature. She was finding her loss of memory increasingly frustrating; without any proper knowledge of the history of her relationship with Ward to guide her she had no idea how to deal with the present situation.

He didn't want people to gossip about them, he had told her, and, naturally, it had pleased her that he should be concerned for her reputation, but she was beginning to feel as though their relationship existed in some kind of vacuum. It had no past, or at least none that *she* could remember, nor did it seem to have any future, or at least not one which Ward wanted to discuss with her.

Anna shook her head, trying to disperse her uncomfortable thoughts. Perhaps it was the bad dreams she had been having these past two nights that were making her feel so on edge and uneasy. None of her dreams seemed to make any sense; they were a confusing mixture of images, faces, scraps of conversation, untidily woven together with her own emotions of despair, fear and anger. In them she could hear Ward's voice, raised and angry, but the words he was speaking to her made no sense, nor did her frantic anxiety over money, her desperate physical searching for it.

All in all, Anna was beginning to question whether she had made the right decision in agreeing to come north with Ward.

Turning his back on Anna, Ward walked over to the sink and looked out of the window. His heart was thumping heavily, too heavily; keeping Anna at arm's length was proving even more difficult than he had imagined.

Yesterday on the fell he had been so tempted to take her in his arms and kiss her, so very, very tempted, and he had seen from the baffled, hurt expression in her eyes that she couldn't understand why he had not done so.

He was growing tired of having to remind himself

just why he had brought her here. After all, what was five thousand pounds to him? He could easily afford to lose ten times that amount of money. It was his own stiff-necked pride that had brought him to this impasse. If he hadn't been so determined to make her repay Ritchie, he wouldn't be in this situation now.

If he had any sense he would get the car out and drive her home right now. After all, she had friends, a god-daughter, who could look after her until she recovered her memory. It wasn't *his* responsibility to take care of her. What did he actually owe her? Nothing. *She* was the one who owed *him*…five thousand pounds.

But, despite the logic of his thoughts, Ward knew that he did have an obligation towards her. He should never have allowed her to believe that they were lovers and, if he hadn't been so furiously angry with her, so determined to make her admit that she had lied to him when she had denied being Julian Cox's partner, he would never have done so. His own deceit was going to cost him an awful lot more than a mere five thousand pounds. It was going to cost him a lifetime of pain and guilt and regret, Ward acknowledged.

'Ward?'

He stiffened as he heard Anna's voice directly behind him. Anna took a deep breath as she waited for him to turn round. She knew what she had to say, what her pride demanded that she say, but that wasn't going to make it any easier.

'Ward, I think it's time I went home,' she announced quietly.

Somehow Ward managed to suppress his instinctive cry of denial, his instinctive refusal to allow her to go…to leave him.

'Very well,' he heard himself saying harshly. 'If that's what you want.'

'It is,' Anna lied.

Through the kitchen window she could see the court-yard. It was raining, a dull, steady downpour from clouds which had masked the tops of the hills she could see from her bedroom, cloaking the landscape in mist.

'I'll go upstairs and pack,' she added, stepping away from Ward and turning her back to him.

'The car needs petrol; I'll go down into town and fill the tank whilst you're packing,' Ward told her shortly.

Anything, anything, to put a safe distance between them. If he stayed, he knew he wouldn't be able to stop himself from begging her to change her mind.

They were treating one another like strangers, Anna thought despairingly as he picked up his keys and headed for the door. But then, in many ways, wasn't that what he was to her? A stranger and her lover. But he hadn't been her lover these last few nights. He had kept her at a distance, in a separate room.

Her case was packed but Ward still hadn't returned. Anna tutted as Whittaker jumped out of her arms and through the open door into Ward's study.

Irritably she followed him inside, calling him back. There were some papers on Ward's desk. He had been working the previous evening after their return from dinner. He had been in a quiet mood all evening, un-communicative with her, and distant, and eventually she had gone to bed without interrupting him.

Whittaker jumped up onto Ward's desk, refusing to come to her. Tiredly Anna scolded him as he sat down on Ward's papers.

'You are a bad cat,' she told him ruefully as she

leaned across the desk to pick him up. Absently she glanced at the papers he had been seated on, more to check that he hadn't left them covered in paw-prints than for any other reason, then she froze as a name leapt off the printed page in front of her.

Julian Cox!

Anna ignored Whittaker's miaow of protest as she gripped him tightly. The room spun round her, going dark, dissolving in a terrifying vortex of fractured images and memories.

Julian Cox.

She could see him, hear his voice. She started to tremble with reaction and fear. She had lost Dee's money to him, her fifty thousand pounds. He had frightened her with his constant phone calls, asking her when he could have the money she was supposed to be investing with him. There had been something almost unbalanced and dangerous about him, as though he was a man close to going totally out of control.

Anna had wanted to tell Dee how she felt but she hadn't wanted to let her down, so she had suppressed her anxiety, with disastrous results. Perhaps if she had spoken up Dee would still have her money.

The black mist was starting to clear, Whittaker's plaintive miaows bringing her back to reality. What she had just experienced had been a flashback and resurgence of her missing memory, Anna recognised as her body shook with cold and reaction. Her skin felt clammy, drenched with an icy sweat; she felt nauseous and her head ached.

Julian Cox.

She could remember now, but what had he to do with Ward? It was like lifting the newly formed scab off a vicious wound, opening the door to a dark cellar, know-

ing that what lay as yet unseen was something potentially threatening and frightening.

Anna forced herself to look a second time at the paper on Ward's desk, and this time she deliberately read
it.

When she had finished, her face was chalk white.

It was a report on Julian Cox and her as co-partners
in an investment company.

Totally in shock, Anna walked into the kitchen,
Whittaker following at her heels. Beside the Aga Missie
was curled up in her basket. She jumped up as her mistress walked in and raced to the back door.

Walk time!

Anna stared at her blank-eyed and then automatically
opened the door, following Missie out into the courtyard
and then beyond it.

It was still raining but Anna neither noticed nor cared
as she followed Missie up the steep hillside; she was
totally absorbed in the traumatic chaos of her thoughts
and the return of her memory.

She and Ward weren't really lovers at all. He had
come to see her, claiming that she had cheated his
brother out of money. Anna could remember it all.

The path she was following climbed steeply; her
clothes, her hair, her skin were drenched in rain, but she
scarcely noticed. All around her the landscape was now
clothed in a wet white mist, but Anna trudged on, placing one foot in front of the other like an automaton.

Ward didn't love her—he didn't even like her; but
he had gone to bed with her, let her think…let her believe… Anna bit back the anguished sound that bubbled
in her throat.

Oh, God, why? Why had he done it? To punish her,
hurt her. Anna felt sick with shock and disbelief. Up

ahead of her Missie barked and a startled rabbit suddenly shot across the path virtually under her feet, almost causing her to stumble.

Anna called out to her dog as she raced after the rabbit, but Missie ignored her, her small white body quickly melting into the surrounding mist-covered landscape.

Anna's teeth started to chatter. It was almost impossible to believe it was summer, she felt so cold.

She called out to Missie again and then waited, listening, but all she could hear was the anxious thudding of her own heartbeat. A patch of slightly thicker mist caught her eye; swiftly she walked towards it, letting out a small protest of dismay when it dispersed without revealing her errant dog.

'Missie,' Anna called again, and was rewarded with an excited bark.

Thankfully, she turned towards the sound. She had lost the path now, and the hillside beneath her feet was rough with tussocks of grass and boulders. She almost stumbled on one of them but managed to save herself just in time, wincing as she realised that she had scraped the hand she had put out to prevent herself from falling.

'Missie,' she cried out anxiously, hearing the sound of her own voice bounce back to her in the mist.

This was crazy. She couldn't possibly be more than a few minutes from the house, but she couldn't see further than a few inches in front of her nose and she couldn't recognise anything either. It made sense that if she went uphill she would be going further away and if she went down she had to be going back.

Half an hour later, her hands and clothes muddy from a series of stumbles, her heart pounding and her legs aching, Anna acknowledged that she had absolutely no idea where she was. Logically she ought to have reached the house long ago, but no matter how hard she tried to pierce the gloom of the mist all she could see was mist. A darker shadow suddenly loomed out of the hillside, making her scream in fright until she realised it was only a sheep—a sheep hotly followed by Missie.

'Oh, Missie.' She scolded the little dog in relief. 'Where have you been, you naughty dog?'

She had a terrible pain in her head, a knife-like ache that was making her feel sick and dizzy. Missie wriggled in her arms and broke free.

Anna called to her to come back. She had to sit down, her legs felt so shaky and weak. The grass felt wet, but no wetter than her damp clothes. She was cold as well, but the cold on the outside of her body was no worse than the dreadful icy chill inside it.

How could Ward have done that to her?

Anna closed her eyes, trying to put her chaotic thoughts into some kind of order. She could remember that first meeting with him quite clearly—his anger, their argument. She could remember, too, seeing him again in the hospital. A low moan of pain escaped her as she recalled what she had said to him.

How *could* she have done that? What on earth had possessed her?

But he hadn't corrected her. He had let her… Oh, the exquisite memory of what she had believed—how he must have relished it, knowing the humiliation that lay ahead of her once she regained her memory—the self-inflicted humiliation.

Dry-eyed, Anna stared into the mist. She was lost and alone but she didn't care. She didn't care if no one ever found her. In fact, she decided, it would be far better if they didn't. How on earth was she going to face people now? How on earth was she going to face *Ward*? She had humiliated herself utterly and completely—and he had let her. And she had thought him so wonderful, so caring, so upright and honest.

Anna started to laugh, a wild, high-pitched sound, only partially muffled by the thickening mist.

CHAPTER NINE

WARD had been gone much longer than he had planned. He had bumped into an old friend of his mother's in the garage, an elderly widow who had been having an anxious discussion with the mechanic about the state of her small car.

Automatically Ward had gone to see if she needed any help. It had turned out that the mechanic was trying to explain to her just why he considered her small car to be unfit to drive, but, as she had explained tearfully to Ward, she couldn't manage without it nor afford to replace it.

After soothing her over tea in a nearby café, Ward had driven her home. He had then gone back to the garage where he had questioned the mechanic and given him certain instructions. After he had gone, the mechanic had shaken his head and told the apprentice, 'Weird guy. He only wants me to replace that Mini with the one we've got for sale—and he's paid cash for it—but he wants us to re-spray it the same colour as the other one. I warned him what it would cost but—' he gave a brief shrug '—he said he wasn't concerned about the cost… Like I said—weird…'

Ward had his apology and his explanation ready for Anna as he drove into the courtyard, but she wasn't, as he had expected, waiting for him in the kitchen, annoyed by his tardiness. Her cat was there, though. Ward stroked him absently as he walked past him and into the hallway.

His study door was open, the report he had been reading the previous night still on his desk. He went in and picked it up. Last night he had made himself re-read it just to remind himself of exactly what Anna was, but it hadn't worked. He had still gone to bed aching for her, longing for her, missing the soft, sweet weight of her in his arms. How was it possible for him to feel like that in such a short space of time, to miss her so intensely in his bed that he was constantly waking up, searching for her? It had been less than a fortnight since he had first met her, for God's sake.

Less than a fortnight, hardly more than a week. No time at all, but more than time enough to change his whole life.

Abruptly he picked up the report, tore it in half and then in half again, needing an outlet for the anger he could feel building up inside him.

The house felt quiet and still…empty…just the way he liked it—just the way he *used* to like it! He called out Anna's name sharply, warned by some prescient instinct even before he had taken the stairs two at a time and pushed open her bedroom door to discover her suitcase but no Anna.

It took him less than ten minutes to search the house from top to bottom.

No sign of her. So where was she?

In the kitchen the cat was lying triumphantly in Missie's basket. Ward frowned. Where was Missie?

He glanced through the window, his heart starting to thud.

Surely Anna hadn't taken her out for a walk in this?

He raced back into the courtyard calling both Anna and Missie's names as he pulled on a thick waterproof country jacket.

She must surely have recognised how dangerous it was to walk *anywhere* in this mist. Even he, who knew the hills around here like the back of his hand, would have thought twice. It was the easiest thing in the world to get lost…

He found Missie first. She came flying towards him out of the mist, barking excitedly, flinging herself at him. She was wet and her white coat matted with mud.

Ward hugged her fiercely.

'Where is she, Missie?' he demanded thickly. 'Where's Anna? Where is she…?'

When he put her down Missie stared at him and wagged her tail.

'Where is she, Missie?' Ward begged. 'Find Anna. Find her.'

The dog ran off uncertainly and then ran back to him.

Ward's heart sank. Anna could be anywhere out there. Anywhere.

'Anna… Anna…' He cupped his hands together and called her name.

And then he heard it, the eerie, almost inhuman sound of someone laughing, so faint that at first he thought he must have imagined it.

Straining his ears, he listened, hurrying as fast as he dared in the direction of the faint sound.

'Anna! Anna!'

Silence.

Ward cursed. At his feet Missie whined and then barked excitedly. Ward tensed hopefully, but she was only barking at a stray sheep.

'No,' he told her sternly as she made to chase it, but Missie wasn't listening to him.

'Missie,' he called as she ran off, then plunged into the thick mist behind her, cursing her under his breath.

She was barking again, having no doubt caught up with the lumbering sheep. Ward could just about make out the shape of her up ahead of him. He hurried after her and then stopped abruptly as he saw why she had stopped.

Anna was sitting there on the hillside, looking as calm and unruffled as though she were sitting in the kitchen of her own home.

'Anna!'

'Hello, Ward,' she greeted him quietly.

'Anna!'

Relief poured through him as Ward hurried up to her.

'What are you doing? What happened? Are you all right?'

In his anxiety Ward didn't notice the way Anna was gripping her hands together to control the way she was shaking. She had heard him calling out to her and she had known that sooner or later he would find her and that once he did... But her head ached so much, *hurt* so much, that there was no way she could even think about what she ought to say to him. It was so much easier simply to say nothing, simply to let him take charge and urge her to her feet whilst he demanded to know why on earth she had gone for a walk in such dangerous conditions.

'I didn't realise,' she told him emotionlessly. 'I followed Missie...'

Her eyes felt heavy and she wanted to close them. She started to shiver violently.

Her body felt like ice but her face was flushed—almost feverishly so, Ward recognised in concern as he guided her carefully back towards the path.

'Are you sure you're all right?' Ward demanded anxiously once they were back in the farmhouse kitchen.

'You don't look well. Perhaps I should get a doctor out…'

'No,' Anna responded sharply. 'No. I'm fine… Besides, we're leaving anyway, aren't we?'

'Leaving?' Ward looked at her grimly. 'Not until you've had a hot bath and something to eat, we aren't,' he told her firmly.

'I've packed all my clothes,' Anna objected.

'Then I'll *un*pack some for you,' Ward told her, adding sternly, 'You're soaking wet, Anna; you can't go anywhere like that.'

Ward was growing increasingly concerned about her. She seemed so cold and distant, so unlike her normal warm, loving self. He should never have left her alone for so long. Anything could have happened to her out there on the moors. As it was, she would be lucky if she didn't end up with a severe cold, if not something worse, and it would all be his fault.

Anna started to shiver convulsively. Ward cursed under his breath, sweeping her up into his arms.

'What are you doing? Put me down,' Anna objected, but Ward refused to listen to her.

The *en suite* bathroom off his own room had a huge whirlpool bath, which his mother had persuaded him to install.

'They're wonderful for rheumatism,' she had told him.

'But I don't *have* rheumatism,' Ward had pointed out.

'Not yet,' she had agreed. 'But you aren't getting any younger, you know, Ward.'

It had been a dig at the fact that he wasn't married, that he hadn't provided her with any grandchildren; Ward knew that but he had still installed the bath. Not that he often used it. He preferred to shower, but right now he was mentally blessing his mother for her interference as he kicked the bathroom door shut behind him and carefully placed Anna down on her feet.

'Ward…' Anna began to protest as he started to run the bath and fill it with hot water.

But then she stopped speaking as she was seized by another violent fit of shivers that made her teeth chatter. Ward had rolled up the sleeves of his shirt to fill the bath and Anna noticed distantly how the light glinted on the soft fine hair on his arms. He was such a masculine man, such a *male* man, and she had felt so very, very safe in his arms. She gave a small sob and closed her eyes, only to open them again as she felt Ward's hands on her body, tugging at her clothes.

'Anna, for heaven's sake,' Ward protested as she started to push him away.

'I can undress myself,' she told him fiercely. 'I will undress myself,' she added pointedly. 'When you've gone…'

Ward wasn't going to argue. She was behaving very oddly, but the longer she stood there in her soaking wet clothes the greater her chances of becoming ill.

Shrugging, he walked past her and opened the bathroom door.

Anna waited until he had closed it behind him before inspecting it. No lock. Her lips tightened, her eyes suddenly bleak. She wasn't really afraid that he was going to come back or try to force himself on her. After all, he had had the opportunity to have as much sex with her as he could have wanted these last few days and he had totally ignored her. She gave a bitter, mirthless smile.

Was there no end to her humiliation at his hands?

First he encouraged her to betray herself to him in the most intimate way possible and then he rejected her.

Bitterly she tugged off her clothes and then stepped into the hot water, gasping a little as its heat touched her icy cold skin. The bath really was huge, easily large enough for two people, even when one of them was as big as Ward.

Ward!

Anna closed her eyes as two tears dripped down her face. Angrily she reached for the button that turned on the bath's water jets. What was she crying for? She hated him…hated him…

'Anna…?'

Ward paused outside the closed bathroom door as he called Anna's name. No reply. Anxiously he opened the door and then stopped.

Anna was curled up on the bathroom floor, fast asleep, wrapped in a towel. With her hair damp and her face free of make-up she looked so young, so vulnerable, so…so lovable.

His throat raw with emotion, Ward leaned down and picked her up. Sleepily she opened her eyes and whispered drowsily, 'Ward…'

'Shush, it's all right. Go back to sleep,' Ward told her gently as he carried her through to the bedroom and placed her on his bed. Carefully tucking the duvet round her, Ward faced the truth. He loved her and there was no way he could ever let her go. No matter what she might have done. It was so odd, but now that his fight to deny how he felt about her was over and he had lost he actually felt almost euphoric with relief, as though a huge weight had been lifted from his shoulders.

What he was thinking, feeling, planning was contrary

to everything he had always believed in, and yet all he could feel was a tremendous surge of joy that he was finally free to admit his love for her.

Once he was sure she was comfortable he went back downstairs. Missie and Whittaker still had to be fed and he had some work he might as well do whilst he waited for Anna to wake up.

For the rest of the day Anna drifted in and out of an uneasy sleep. Several times Ward went up to check on her, reluctant to wake her but anxiously checking her skin and her pulse just in case she had a temperature.

He ate a solitary evening meal. Outside the mist had started to lift. The house was quiet but not empty. Not any longer, not any more.

Humming lightly to himself, Ward went upstairs again. Anna woke up as the bed depressed beneath Ward's weight when he got in beside her.

'Ward.'

'Mmm…' he acknowledged as he reached for her, wrapping his arms tightly around her as he drew her down against his body—his very male and totally naked body, Anna recognised in shock. She wanted to tell him not to touch her, not to lie to her and deceive her, but Ward had already started to kiss her, gently at first and with such false tenderness that her eyes filled with tears.

'Don't cry, don't cry,' she heard him whisper softly. 'You're safe here with me, Anna. You're safe now. Everything's all right…'

Everything *wasn't* all right. Anna knew that, but her body was turning traitor on her and Ward's kisses were growing increasingly intense and passionate.

She tried to resist him and she might have succeeded, but she couldn't resist *herself*. She wanted him so…loved him so… Her heart gave a painful jolt against her ribs.

'You're shivering,' Ward told her huskily. 'Are you cold? How do you feel? Are you all right?'

Anna knew that she wasn't shivering, she was *trembling*, and the cause of her tremors wasn't any residual cold from being trapped on the misty hillside but something much more immediate and personal. In fact, the cause of them was lying right beside her, holding her, stroking her arms with pseudo-tender, caring little caresses as though he wanted to comfort her with his own body heat. What was it about men that allowed them to behave so differently from women? He didn't love her, didn't even *like* her, and *he* certainly wasn't blinded to the truth by any amnesia, and yet here he was, holding her, touching her, making love with her as though…as though…

Only her pride prevented Anna from blurting out that she had regained her memory; that she knew everything. Her pride and the sure knowledge that if she did so now the admission would be ignominiously accompanied by her tears, her anguish and pain that he should have treated her so callously and so cruelly. Surely, no matter what her supposed crime, to have done what Ward had done was a punishment far, far in excess of any true form of justice.

'Anna…'

Perhaps if she just closed her eyes and lay still he would stop touching her, withdraw from her and leave her alone. Anna knew that she couldn't trust her own voice to tell him that she didn't want him, and she certainly couldn't answer any of the questions he might try to ask her.

She didn't want him. Behind her closed eyelids Anna

felt her eyes burn with acidly bitter shaming tears. She couldn't lie to herself. She *did* want him. She wanted his tenderness, she wanted his touch, she wanted his *love*.

How could she, when everything he had allowed her to believe was a fiction?

Anna didn't know; all she *did* know was that her emotional response to him was so strong that it defied all logic. Her body, so sensitively attuned to his touch, was already responding to him and she simply didn't have the will-power to stop it.

And anyway, what was the point? she asked herself in aching resignation as he gently kissed her mouth, his hand slipping from her arm to her breast.

Why not add this one last memory to the others she already had? Why not *really* punish herself for her stupidity, her vulnerability, by giving in to the longing she could feel flooding her body like a form of sweetly venomous death?

With a small, painful sigh Anna turned towards Ward.

'Mmm…'

Bleakly she felt the warmth of his body enveloping her as he nuzzled the soft, tender flesh of her throat.

She put out a hand defensively. Beneath it she could feel the fine silk of his body hair. Her heart started to beat very fast; in a way it was almost as she had imagined drowning might be, easier to succumb, to give in than to try to fight feelings which only grew stronger with every breath she took.

'Oh, but I've missed you,' she heard Ward telling her throatily. 'These last few nights without you here, beside me.'

Anna forbore to mention that it had been *his* decision that they should sleep apart.

She gave an involuntary shudder as his thumb tip caressed her nipple… Immediately he bent his head and kissed it gently, and then less gently, until Anna was writhing achingly against him, powerless to stem the hot flood of feeling that roared through her like a forest fire. Her body, aware now of the pleasure he could give it, was way, way, beyond the control of her mind, her own desire, her own love a force that defied any kind of logic she tried to use to rein it in.

Instinctively she reached out to touch him, her body melting with pleasure as she felt his taut shudder of response. He might hate her, resent her, despise her, but he still wanted her. The savagely bitter shaft of acid pleasure that knowledge brought her told Anna just how destructive her feelings were, and as though to reinforce her own anger against herself she deliberately stroked her fingertips down the length of his body, touching him more boldly and more intimately than she had previously done without his own encouragement.

If she had expected Ward to stop her or withdraw himself from her she had been wrong. Instead he seemed to positively revel in the bold control she had taken of their lovemaking, groaning hoarsely deep in his throat, his eyes opening wide as he focused on her face.

'That feels so good,' he told her rawly. He was breathing heavily, his body filming with a light sweat that smelled mustily erotic. To Anna, who had always known she was almost a little too fastidious, the knowledge that her instinct was to bury her face against him and breathe in the pheromone-charged sensuality he was exuding was almost, in its way, more shocking than knowing how much she wanted him, how much her own disobedient, wanton body ached for the culmination of his lovemaking.

Beneath the soft pads of her fingertips his erection felt hard and muscular. Even without looking at him she knew how he would look, could remember the inexperienced awe with which she had first observed his body. Ralph's body had been that of a very young man, albeit firm and well-muscled. Ward possessed a much more raw and potent masculinity, a man fully grown in every sense of the word, Anna acknowledged as she explored and then caressed him with her fingers.

If so far in their 'relationship' she had taken from him a pleasure she had had no right to have, then now, tonight, she intended to repay *that* debt in full. Her sense of pride and honour demanded it.

In the darkness Ward moaned softly.

'I shouldn't be letting you do this,' he told her softly. 'I should be the one...'

'I *want* to do it,' Anna told him truthfully. This way at least she had some control over herself—and over him. What she didn't want to admit to herself was that there was a sharply sweet pleasure for her in what she was doing, in knowing she was giving him pleasure. Her own body was even reacting to it, responding to it, as though it too had been aroused and caressed.

'No, Anna, no more,' she heard Ward begging her gruffly as he took hold of her hand and gently removed it from himself, at the same time drawing her down against him and kissing her with open-mouthed passion.

Unable to stop herself from responding, Anna clung to him.

She wasn't sure which of them it was who was trembling the harder now, Ward or herself. She only knew that her body barely needed the assistance he gave it as he moulded it to his own, and it certainly needed neither coaxing nor teaching to accommodate the urgent thrust of his flesh against her own. If anything her body was even more sensitively responsive to him than it had been before, quickening, tightening even with his first eager movement into it. Somewhere, at the back of her mind, Anna knew she was in the very gravest danger and that it was wrong for her to feel so complete, so at one with a man with whom she could not possibly have any future. The beauty of what they were creating together was nothing more than a sham and deception. The agonised pleasure she could hear in Ward's voice was just another lie, like the love words he was whispering to her now as their bodies trembled in dizzy release.

'I love you, Anna,' he told her huskily as he cupped her face and kissed her. 'I love you.'

Anna waited until she was sure he was fast asleep before carefully sliding out of his bed. She knew what she had to do. Downstairs in the kitchen Whittaker and Missie were sleeping in their baskets and Ward's car keys were on the table. It was almost as though fate had at long last decided to help her.

Anna's final act after she had loaded her pets and her suitcase into Ward's car was to pull out her cheque book. Five thousand pounds was a lot of money to give away in payment of a debt she didn't even know about but it would be worth it. With the cheque she left a brief note:

'I've remembered everything. I shall leave your car at York station and post the keys back to you. This cheque repays the money you *believe* I owe your half-brother. Last night repays any debt I *might* have owed you.'

As she climbed into Ward's car and started it she blessed the manufacturer for its near-silent engine. There was no chance, of course, that Ward would come after her or try to get in touch with her.

All she had to face now was her friends at home. What a pity Mary Charles had had to call round when she had, but even harder to live with than her friends' curiosity would be her own shame and pain.

Ward woke up at first light, automatically reaching for Anna. When he discovered she wasn't there he waited for a few minutes, thinking initially she might be in the bathroom, and then, when there was no sign of her, he threw back the bedclothes and hurried downstairs.

He saw her note at the same time as he realised that the animals and their baskets had gone.

As he picked it up and read it, the blood left his face. His hand trembled as he picked up Anna's cheque, but it was the line she had written about repayment of any debt she might have owed him that he concentrated on most.

He glanced at the clock. Half past six. If she had driven to York that must mean she intended to go home by train. With a fast car he could be there before her. But he didn't have a fast car; he didn't have *any* car.

Cursing under his breath, he froze as the telephone rang abruptly. As he reached for the receiver his heart slammed fiercely against his chest. It could only be Anna; it had to be, ringing at this time. She must have realised, had a change of heart. But the tearful woman on the other end of the line wasn't Anna, it was his mother.

'Ward, it's Alfred; he's in hospital with a suspected heart attack. Oh, Ward, I'm so afraid for him.'

'Don't worry, Ma, I'll be with you as soon as I can,' Ward assured his mother.

He would have to ring the local taxi firm and get them to drive him to York. Where the hell were his spare car keys? In his desk drawer!

The last thing he did before he left the house was to tear up Anna's note—and her cheque.

CHAPTER TEN

'I TAKE it there's still no word from Anna?' Dee asked
crisply. She and Beth and Kelly were seated upstairs in
the flat above the shop. Dee had only arrived home late
the previous evening in response to Kelly's anxious
telephone call about Anna's disappearance.

'Nothing,' Beth responded.

With a wary look in Beth's direction Kelly asked
uncertainly, 'Dee, do you think this man Mary saw her
with *could* have anything to do with Julian Cox?'

'With Julian? Why should he have?' Beth asked
sharply.

Warningly Dee shook her head at Kelly. They had
agreed that there was no point in adding to the distress
Beth had suffered over Julian's treatment of her by telling her what they had planned to do.

'Julian tried to borrow money from Anna,' Dee answered calmly. It was, after all, true.

Beth looked shocked.

'Oh, but surely that doesn't mean...' She stopped,
and then whispered shakily, 'You don't really think that
Julian might have done something to *hurt* Anna, do
you?'

'He didn't think twice when it came to hurting you,
did he?' Dee reminded her caustically.

'Does *anyone* know where he's gone?' Beth asked
worriedly. She had hardly given Julian Cox a thought
since her return from Prague. Her infatuation with him

and the pain he had caused her seemed unimportant now.

When was she going to hear from the factory about her crystal? She had invested far more than she could really afford in the consignment of crystal she had bought, recklessly almost quadrupling her original order, and she had used every spare bit of capital both she and Kelly had to pay for it in defiance of a warning to her that she would be well advised to give her business to the factory *he* had recommended to her. Did he *really* think she was so much of a fool? She'd known perfectly well that this man who'd been acting as her guide and interpreter was bound to be being paid by the factory owners—relatives of his—to direct potential business their way.

Her body tensed as she remembered how angry he had made her. Oh, but he had been so arrogant, so sure that he was right. She had been determined to show him that she didn't need his advice, that she was a modern, independent woman. People were often deceived into thinking that, because her nature was essentially so gentle, Beth could be pushed around, but beneath that gentleness she possessed a fortifying streak of stubbornness. Alex had challenged her and she had met that challenge—more than met it. But at what personal cost…?

'Beth!'

Guiltily she realised that Kelly was speaking to her and that she ought to be thinking about Anna and not her own problems.

'I agree that Julian has behaved very badly, but if Anna has disappeared—' She shook her head. 'No, I can't see him being involved in anything like that.'

Dee listened in silence. It was just as well that her

aunt had been virtually recovered when she'd got Kelly's phone call—she *had* been planning to return home later in the week anyway, and to come back a couple of days earlier hadn't been any problem.

Beth might believe that Julian couldn't be involved in Anna's disappearance but she didn't know him as well as Dee did, despite the fact that Beth and he had once been on the point of becoming engaged.

Julian had no regard for the feelings or the safety of others. His greed was such that he simply didn't care who he hurt and harmed, or how. Despite all the enquiries she had made whilst she had been staying with her aunt, she had found no evidence of Julian's whereabouts.

She had, at one stage, thought she had traced him as far as Hong Kong, which would make sense since she knew he had business dealings there, but if he was still there now there was certainly no official trace of him.

Could Anna have gone away with this mystery man Mary Charles had seen?

'She *could* have,' Beth answered, and Dee realised she had asked her question out loud. 'But why hasn't she told us about him if he is her lover? It's just so out of character for her—and we've only Mary Charles's word for it that they are—involved!'

'If he isn't her lover then who is he?' Kelly asked practically.

'The husband of one of her friends, perhaps?' Beth suggested, her forehead pleating in a small frown. 'Someone she had got round to do some work for her—a gardener or handyman, perhaps.'

'Mmm… Mary was adamant that when Anna introduced him to her as a "friend" she meant friend with a capital F.'

'Perhaps we *are* making too much fuss. Perhaps she just decided to go away for a few days without telling any of us,' Beth offered, but she knew she sounded as unconvinced as she felt. Guiltily, she remembered that when she had last spoken to her godmother on the telephone she had been impatient to end the call. Perhaps if she *hadn't* been Anna might have said something to her that would have given them some clue as to where she might be.

'Her car's still at the house,' Kelly pointed out.

'But Missie and Whittaker aren't there, you said?' Dee questioned her.

'Well, I couldn't see or hear them.'

'Hmm... Well, it's all very odd. You don't think she could have gone to Cornwall to see your family, do you?' she asked Beth.

Beth shook her head.

'No, I rang home yesterday and I know that my mother would have said if Anna had been there. I didn't ask her outright because I didn't want to start worrying her; she and Anna have always been close.'

'What are we going to do?' Kelly asked the other two, but it was Dee she was looking at.

Dee pursed her lips.

'If we haven't heard anything by tonight, there's only one thing we can do: we shall have to inform the police.'

'You think it's that serious, then, do you?' Beth faltered. Dee's eyes were bleak.

'Possibly,' was all she would allow herself to say.

Ten minutes later as she drove home, though, she was glad that Beth and Kelly couldn't see into her mind and read her thoughts. She knew that Kelly was curious about why she, Dee, should hate Julian Cox so much, and she knew too that Kelly suspected that there was far more to her hatred of him than just his treatment of Beth.

And she was right.

But it was not Kelly but Anna whom Dee had been increasingly tempted to confide in and talk to about the private demons that drove her. Anna might lack Kelly's vibrant immediate response to things but she possessed her own quiet brand of strength and sometimes Dee yearned to be able to lean on someone else's.

She knew that people found her self-possessed and even a little challenging, but they didn't know what had made her that way, nor why she *had* to be that way.

To confide in anyone, even Anna, would be to risk inflicting terrible damage on someone she had loved very, very dearly and there was no way she could do that, so the burden she had carried on her own for so long was one she would have to go on carrying, and if some people thought her hard and unfeeling, unfeminine, then so be it.

And now, of course, she had another burden to shoulder. If something *had* happened to Anna, how much responsibility did *she* bear for it? *Was* Anna's disappearance connected with the trap they had set for Julian Cox? Had the fifty thousand pounds he had so cleverly snatched from beneath their noses not been enough? Had he come back for more, or perhaps sent someone else? She had promised no harm would come to Kelly and Anna through her plans, so the pressure and guilt were mounting by the minute.

Loath as she was to involve the police—for several reasons—Dee knew she had very little option. Surely Anna's disappearance could have nothing whatsoever to do with Julian Cox, but that made Dee even more anxious for her safety and not less.

How often had she seen articles in the press about women—and it was nearly always women—who had disappeared under mystifying circumstances? In some cases the body was found later… In some it wasn't. Dee's knuckles turned white as she gripped the steering wheel of her car.

'Please God, no,' she whispered. 'No.'

She couldn't go home, she just could not, Anna decided tiredly as she got off the train and wearily thanked the porter who helped her with her luggage and her pets. She felt empty, drained of all emotion. The long train journey with its numerous changes and stops had given her plenty of time to think—and remember—and not just plenty, but too much.

If she went home there would be questions for her to answer, people for her to see, and she could not bear it—Ward might even try to get in touch with her, if only to charge her for the use of his car, she reflected bitterly.

There was a row of waiting taxis outside the station, and she hailed one of them.

Once she was settled inside, Missie on her knee, Whittaker in his carrying cage, the driver turned round and asked her, 'Where to, love?'

Where to? Good question… Anna closed her eyes and then, almost as though the words were being spoken for her, she heard herself giving him Dee's address.

Dee was upstairs lying in the bath, her eyes closed, her body still and relaxed but her mind furiously busy, when Anna's taxi arrived. Her bath had, for Dee, always been a place of safety and retreat, a place to regroup her energies and marshal her forces. As a teenager, trying to come to terms with so many different emotions at once, so many physical changes within herself, she had found the bathroom a place in which she could be alone without feeling guilty about shutting her father out. They had always been so close, just the two of them on their own since her mother's death, but with her teenage years had come an instinctive female awareness that now she was moving into the new territory of her own womanhood.

She had been so protective of her father, sensing his solitude, his loving absorption in her life. Where, previously, his had been the only company she had wanted, now she was increasingly experiencing a yearning for the company of her own age group, for female friends with whom she could share the mystery and excitement of what was happening to her. And yet, at the same time, she had sensed how hurt her father would be by her alienation from him. Side by side they had battled it out; her loving daughterly desire to protect him and her growing need to spread her own wings.

There had been many hours spent in the bathroom worrying about what she should do: go on to university as she so longed to do or stay at home with her father.

In the end it had been her father himself who had resolved her dilemma for her—wiser and more aware than she had guessed—telling her firmly how disappointed he would be if she did not finish her education and go to university.

Dee was lost in her thoughts and her memories of the past when the doorbell rang and, at first, she was tempted to ignore its summons. Then, reluctantly, she acknowledged that perhaps she ought to see who it was, pulling on her robe as she opened the bathroom door and padded quickly downstairs.

'Dee.'

Frowning slightly, Dee peered through the frosted glass of her front door and then, realising just who her visitor was, she quickly unlocked and opened it, exclaiming thankfully, 'Anna! Come in!'

Still semi-dazed with shock, Anna followed Dee into her hallway.

It was a relatively warm day but she had started to shiver, her eyes blank and unfocused as she allowed Dee to take hold of her arm and virtually guide her into the kitchen.

'Sit down,' Dee commanded her firmly, relieving her of Whittaker's cat box and deftly removing Missie's lead from her hand at the same time.

Something very distressing had obviously happened to Anna, Dee recognised as her initial relief at seeing her standing outside her front door was swiftly replaced by concern.

'We've been wondering where you'd got to,' she told Anna chattily as she filled the kettle.

Instinct was warning her not to make too much of a drama of Anna's reappearance, nor to bully her into immediate explanations.

Instead, as she made them both a cup of tea, she kept up a stream of light, inconsequential chatter, telling Anna that she had recently seen both Beth and Kelly, watching her as she did so to see how she reacted, but apart from a brief flicker of her eyelids Anna remained almost motionless. She was not, perhaps, actually catatonic, but she had most certainly undergone some kind of severe trauma, Dee realised, and she, after all, knew all the signs of acute emotional shock.

There were some things you never forgot, some experiences that never faded.

Now, as she put Anna's cup of tea down in front of her, she saw that the other woman was simply staring into space.

'Anna,' she said gently, touching her arm. 'What is it? What's happened? What's wrong?'

What was wrong?

Anna focused despairingly on Dee's face.

'I... I...' Slowly her face crumpled and her body started to shake.

Instinctively Dee put her arms around her, holding her comfortingly.

'If it's about Julian and the money...' she guessed. She knew how distressed Anna had been about the fact that Julian had outwitted them both.

'No. No...' Anna shook her head and then stopped.

'Then what is it? What's wrong?' Dee asked her gently.

Anna put a trembling hand up to her face. She still wasn't sure what she was doing here in Dee's kitchen or really why she had come. All she did know was that she simply could not go back to her own house.

'Dee, I've been such a fool,' Anna told her dully. Tears welled up in her eyes. 'I should have known, guessed, but instead...' She gripped her hands into angry fists, her body shuddering in self-loathing. 'I don't know what came over me...or why...'

Patiently Dee waited, listening to her incoherent utterances for several minutes before coaxing, 'Anna, why don't you start at the beginning and tell me everything?'

'Everything...?' Anna's face changed colour, going pink and then white. 'I can't...tell you everything,' she said flatly. 'Some of it.' She paused and shook her head.

'Oh, Dee, I just don't know what I'm going to do, how I'm going to get over…'

How I'm going to get over Ward, she had been about to say, Anna recognised, but she had managed to stop herself. How many times did she have to remind herself that the Ward she had believed she loved simply did not exist? In reality, there was no Ward, no lover for her to get over.

'Tell me,' Dee repeated softly.

Slowly, haltingly at first, Anna started to explain what had happened.

'He did what?' Dee demanded flatly in disbelief when Anna explained about the mistake at the hospital and how she had assumed that Ward was her lover.

'He…this man, this stranger, who less than twelve hours previously had been threatening you…actually allowed you to believe that you and he were lovers…?'

The furious outrage in Dee's voice made Anna bite her bottom lip.

'I've been thinking about it over and over again,' she told Dee in a low voice. '*I* was the one who assumed that we were lovers. *I'm* to blame for that and—'

'You were suffering from amnesia,' Dee reminded her grimly.

'He knew perfectly well what the real relationship— if it can be called a relationship—was between you. He should never…' She stopped, her eyes flashing with contempt. 'Of all the underhanded, conniving…'

'I thought he loved me,' Anna told her shakily, 'but all the time he actually *hated* me, loathed me…'

Closing her eyes, she placed her hand over her mouth to silence the sobs of emotion she could feel rising in her throat.

'I never suspected anything; I truly believed…'

Dee watched her silently. She didn't want to upset Anna by questioning just how far the deception had gone. It appalled her to know that Anna had been victimised, and in such a cruel and dangerous way, and she could well understand why her friend felt that she didn't want to return to her own home where she would be on her own.

'What I don't understand is how on earth anyone could possibly justify such behaviour,' Dee breathed furiously when Anna had eventually told her everything. 'What possible motivation could he have had?'

'He wanted his half-brother's money back,' Anna told her quietly.

She was beginning to feel slightly more in control now. Telling Dee what had happened, painful though it had been, had had a cathartic effect on her, helping to ground her a little better and make her feel more like her normal self instead of as though some unfamiliar stranger was inhabiting her body and her emotions.

'He did *that* to you for money?' Dee demanded savagely.

'No, not just for *money*,' Anna told her, shaking her head. 'I think there must have been a certain degree of revenge and punishment in it for him...'

'What? How could *anyone*...?' Dee began, but Anna shook her head, giving Dee a small, painful smile.

'*We* did,' she reminded her dryly. 'Or at least we tried to with Julian...'

'Oh, yes, but that wasn't the same thing at all,' Dee protested quickly. 'There's no way anyone could compare *you* with Julian. You weren't in any way responsible for Julian's scams...'

'You and I might know that, but Ward...' She

paused, and had to swallow hard before she was able to continue speaking. 'Ward thought I was.'

'But to deceive you like that. To…'

'To pretend that he loved me? Take me to bed?' Anna gave a brief mirthless laugh. 'He did actually try to insist that we had separate rooms. I was the one who…' She stopped again.

'Oh, Dee,' she wept. 'I feel so…so degraded, so…so—' She broke off. There were some things that were just too painful to discuss.

'Well, at least you're back and you're safe; that's the main thing,' Dee told her briskly. When she saw Anna's face she touched her arm a little awkwardly and told her gruffly, 'I know you won't think it possible right now, but eventually time will soften… You'll feel…it won't seem so bad as it does right now. After all, you're over the worst, you've experienced that already, so, logically, things can only get better.'

Anna gave her a small wry smile.

'What did he say when you confronted him, when you told him that you knew the truth?' Dee asked her. 'Did he express any kind of remorse, try to make any kind of explanation or apology…?'

'No…' Anna began, and then, when she saw Dee's outraged expression, she told her shakily, 'I didn't confront him. I…I just left him a note saying that I'd remembered everything; that I knew… I couldn't bear… I just wanted to get away, Dee,' she told her. 'You see…' She paused and a single tear rolled betrayingly down her pale face. 'You see…' Despairingly she twisted the damp tissue she was holding in her fingers. 'I really thought I loved him; I really believed… He seemed so…so right,' she told Dee helplessly. 'Being with him felt so right… It was as though…it was as though he filled in all the missing pieces of my life, as though he completed it and me in a way that I'd never dreamed I could *be* complete. It was as though he… Even now I can't really believe… It all seems like a dream…'

'Nightmare, more like,' Dee told her angrily as she leaned over to take her in a protective hug.

Anna smiled sadly. It was crazy, humiliating and dangerous, she knew, but deep down inside she knew that a part of her was always going to ache and long for him, that that part of her which he had touched so vibrantly and brought to life so immediately and intensely was always going to yearn for him. No amount of righteous anger, of bitterness and contempt, or logical emotional response to what he had done, was ever going to completely wipe out of her memory the sweetness of what they had shared, even though she now knew it had been a poison-tipped sweetness.

But that was her secret, her cross to bear for the rest of her life.

'I'd love to have him here right now to give him a piece of my mind,' Dee told her with angry contempt. 'To do something like that, to you of all people…'

She saw that Anna's eyes were filling with tears again.

'Come on,' she told her gently. 'Let's get you upstairs and in bed. You look exhausted.'

'No. I'm fine,' Anna protested, but she still obediently followed Dee towards the stairs.

'So how is Anna now?' Kelly asked Dee anxiously. 'What did the doctor say? Is she…?'

'She's fine,' Dee assured the other girl, tucking the telephone receiver under her chin so that she could stroke Missie, who was as anxious about Anna as the rest of them were. 'The doctor has given her the all-clear medically; he said, though, that she needed to rest as she's obviously undergone a tremendous amount of trauma.'

At Anna's specific request, Dee had kept the details of Ward's role in what had happened to her to an absolute minimum. So far as Kelly and Beth knew, Ward was simply someone who had stepped in to help her after her accident and subsequent loss of memory—a good Samaritan, so to speak, even though it had practically choked Dee to have to refer to him as such.

'Did she say why she went away—or where?' Kelly asked Dee curiously.

'Oh, she just felt like a few days away,' Dee responded airily and, she hoped, dismissively enough not to further arouse Kelly's curiosity, but despite her outwardly relaxed manner inwardly Dee was seething with fury over the way Ward Hunter had behaved towards her friend. How could he possibly have thought she was the kind of woman who would get involved in anything even vaguely underhand? Anna was the type of woman who panicked if she couldn't get a parking ticket out of the machine and instead left a message plus an IOU for the car park attendant—and, even if he had thought she was involved in some kind of criminal activity with Julian Cox, to have done to her what he had done...

Dee closed her eyes as she replaced her telephone receiver after Kelly's call. Why, why were they the way they were? For every man like her own father and Kelly's Brough there were ten—no, a hundred—who seemed to deliberately go out of their way to hurt the woman they professed to love. Dee carried her own scars from the war she believed existed between the sexes, but that was another story.

A little ruefully Dee admitted that she had perhaps been rather heavy-handed, in more than one sense, with the large brandy she had insisted on Anna drinking earlier in the evening, but it had had the desired effect and now Anna was getting some much needed sleep. The trauma of her temporary amnesia was something that anyone would find difficult to come to terms with, never mind the added misery and anguish Anna had been caused, Dee reflected as she checked that Anna's pets were secure in their new temporary home.

She still had some financial reports to read before she went to bed. The responsibility of handling her father's complex financial empire was one she took extremely seriously. His death had been totally unexpected, and it had thrown her head-first into relatively unfamiliar work, but Dee had felt she owed it to him to become familiar with it and to ensure that his business interests generated enough money to service his varied philanthropic activities.

The only changes she had made were such that his financial generosity to the various charities he had helped had been made public, so that other people would know, as she had known, just what a very special and caring man her father had been.

There were times when she still missed him very badly. If he could see her now, would he be disappointed in her? she wondered. He had been a little old-fashioned in some ways, and she knew he would have wanted her to marry and have children. But how could she do that? There was enough of him in her for her to know that she could only make that kind of commitment to someone if she truly loved them and was loved by them in return. And how could that ever be possible when she didn't believe that love, the kind of love she had dreamed of as a young girl, actually existed? Love was simply a word used to cloak far more practical and less ideological emotions. Love, or rather the promise of it, was just a weapon men used against women.

'I love you,' they said, but what they meant was, 'I love myself.'

'You'd better watch it,' she mocked Whittaker playfully. 'There aren't many males brave enough to come into this house!'

CHAPTER ELEVEN

'How is he?'

Ward put down the article he had been reading as his mother came out of his stepfather's hospital room, closing the door behind her.

Instantly his mother's face broke into a relaxed smile.

'He's feeling much better. The specialist just wants to have a few words with him and then he... He saw the specialist this morning and he's confirmed that it wasn't a heart attack after all. They've got all the test results back now and he thinks the pain was caused by anxiety.

'You know how your stepfather is, and he's been worrying about this trip Ritchie is planning to make to America...'

Ward made a small, explosive sound before getting up and reassuring his mother.

'There's no need for him to worry about *anything*...'

'I know that, dear, but you know what he's like. He feels it isn't fair that you're having to finance Ritchie through university when you...'

She stopped and Ward gave her a wry look.

'When I what? When I had to work my own way through life? Ma, for heaven's sake, surely he doesn't think I begrudge Ritchie the chance—'

'No. No, of course he doesn't,' his mother reassured him quickly. 'He knows how fond you are of Ritchie, Ward,' she told her elder son, placing her hand on his arm. 'We both do. You've done so much for all of us.

I just wish... You really ought to marry again, you know,' she told him gently. 'Have children... I know that...' She stopped and then looked at him intently.

'You've met someone, haven't you? Don't deny it, Ward. I can see it in your eyes...'

Ward was too taken aback to deny her maternal perception, stating curtly, 'I don't want to talk about it, and anyway—' He broke off, his mouth hardening.

Perhaps it wasn't really surprising that his mother had guessed about Anna. After all, he had barely stopped thinking about her from the moment he had read her note. Even in his most anxious moments for his stepfather, Anna had still been there in his thoughts, tormenting him, haunting him.

He had tried telling himself that everything he had done had been justified; that he had owed it to Ritchie and her other victims to do what he had done, but, instead of being able to focus on her crime, all he had really been able to do was remember how she had felt in his arms, how she had smelled, tasted, *been*, and how much he was missing her, how damnably much.

'Tell me about her,' his mother insisted with firm maternal authority.

Ward glanced towards his stepfather's closed hospital-room door, but it was obvious that no help or rescue was going to come from that area.

'There isn't anything *to* tell,' he informed his mother brusquely. 'Oh, you needn't look at me like that.' He gave a bitter laugh. 'It's not what you're thinking; it's no match made in heaven, Ma, far more like one made in hell.'

His skin darkened slightly as he saw the look of mingled despair and compassion in his mother's eyes.

'She's a liar and the next damned thing to being a

thief,' he told her baldly. 'By rights there's no way I should feel about her the way I do, but…' He stopped and shook his head. 'And, even if she felt the same way about me, which now that she knows…' He stopped again.

'Tell me,' his mother repeated.

'You won't like it,' he warned her grimly.

Twenty minutes later, when he had finished, his mother's face was pale.

'You're right,' she told him in a strained voice. 'I *don't* like it. Oh, Ward,' she burst out painfully. 'How *could* you do such a thing? That poor girl. What *must* she have felt?'

'That poor girl?' Ward exploded. 'Ma, she's the one—' He stopped, pushing his fingers into his hair. 'If anyone needs your sympathy then…'

'Ward, she must have been so hurt and shocked. To have believed you loved her as much as she obviously loves you…'

'Hang on a minute… What makes you think she loves me?' Ward demanded sharply.

'But it's so obvious,' his mother replied gently. 'If she didn't love you she would never have… Ward, of *course* she loves you,' she told him severely.

'Ma, you're behaving as though…' He hesitated and shook his head in frustration. 'I told you. The reason I went to see her in the first place was because…'

'Because she cheated Ritchie out of five thousand pounds,' his mother agreed serenely. 'Yes, I know. But, Ward, have you thought she could have had a reason for her behaviour? There could have been mitigating circumstances…'

'For what's damn near fraud?' Ward demanded scornfully. 'Ma…'

'Is it really so important what she did, Ward?' his mother asked him quietly. 'You've as good as said yourself that you love her. I know that she must love you.'

'Of course it's important,' Ward told her harshly. 'If a person is inherently dishonest, how can you have a trusting relationship with them? How could I ever...?'

'Ward, I've never told you this, but when I first knew your stepfather there'd been a spate of thefts from the school—only small amounts of money were involved, but they were thefts nonetheless. *I* knew and so did your stepfather that all the circumstantial evidence pointed to me being the thief. Your stepfather had every reason to believe that I *was* a thief, but he still put his feelings for me and the fact that he had fallen in love with me above all the logical facts that indicated that I was responsible for taking money from the school.'

'But you weren't the thief,' Ward pointed out grimly, 'and Anna...'

'Ward, you aren't listening to me,' his mother told him gently. 'Just as you aren't listening to your heart. You should do. Sometimes it gives a much truer message than one's brain.

'Go and see her,' she counselled him. 'Go and see your Anna, Ward, and tell her what you've told me. Tell her that you love her.'

He wasn't going to, of course. What was the point? He had already made a complete fool of himself over her once, telling her that he loved her, but fate had intervened, giving him a second chance to get his life back under his own control, giving him a second chance to listen to the logical, analytical messages of his brain rather than the emotional ones of his heart.

No, he wasn't going to pay any attention whatsoever

to what his mother had said, to what he himself was feeling…

So why, just as soon as he had assured himself that his stepfather was on the mend, was he driving far too fast along a motorway which would not take him home to Yorkshire but instead to Rye?

Because his mother was right, that was why. Because he loved Anna and he couldn't let her go without at least seeing her one more time.

One more time. Just who was he kidding? Ward asked himself with grim black humour.

He loved Anna, and he loved her so deeply and so intensely that… That what? That he was prepared to abandon his principles and his beliefs for her? That he thought he could totally suspend reality and pretend that she had not done what they both knew she had done?

And what of Anna herself? What if she did not *want* to change? What if she enjoyed cheating and deceiving? What if he took her his offer of amnesty and a completely new beginning and she threw it back in his face?

But somehow Ward could not imagine the Anna he had come to know and love so intimately ever behaving like that. She had shown such tenderness and compassion, such concerned awareness for the feelings of others, that it would, quite simply, be totally out of character for her to do that kind of thing.

But had he actually known the real Anna? Perhaps her blow on the head had affected *more* than just her memory. What was he trying to persuade himself to believe? Ward asked himself scornfully. That Anna had undergone a complete personality change? Now he was venturing into the realms of fantasy.

But still, when the opportunity came half an hour

later for him to switch motorways and drive straight home, he made no attempt to take it.

'Are you sure you really feel well enough to be home?' Dee asked Anna sternly as they stood in Anna's kitchen.

'Dee, I'm fine,' Anna responded gently.

Dee had tried every argument she could think of to persuade Anna to change her mind and stay on as her guest instead of going back to her own house, but Anna had remained obdurate and Dee had finally been persuaded to drive her home.

'I have to get my life back to normal some time,' she had responded with a brisk lack of self pity when Dee had suggested that perhaps she needed more time to come to terms with what had happened, before returning home where she would be on her own.

'I think it is much better that I should get back into the swing of things sooner rather than later,' Anna insisted now. 'Not that I don't appreciate all that you've done for me,' she told Dee warmly. 'Without you...' She stopped and shook her head. 'It's made me feel so much better just having someone to talk things over with, and I'm grateful to you as well, Dee, for keeping what I've told you between the two of us. It's bad enough that I've made such a complete fool of myself anyway...'

'I'm sure that Kelly and Beth would have understood,' Dee told her quickly and truthfully.

'Yes. I know they would, but... Beth seems to be over Julian but she's changed...she's different. There's something on her mind, something that's worrying her, but whatever it is she just doesn't seem to want to talk about it.'

'Mmm... I must admit I *have* noticed that she does

seem to be rather preoccupied lately,' Dee agreed, 'but I'd put that down to the problems she seems to be having with this stuff she ordered when she was in Prague.'

'Oh, dear, has she still not received that order?' Anna asked her. 'Poor Beth; I hope it arrives soon. I know she was counting on it to boost her sales.'

'Mmm... Well, she's got time yet,' Dee reminded her.

'You've been such a wonderful friend to all of us, Dee,' Anna praised her. 'You've helped us all and—'

'Helped you?' Dee interrupted her dryly. 'Have I? *I* was responsible for nearly turning Kelly and Brough against one another, and now it's because I involved you in lending Julian money that this Ward Hunter has behaved so badly towards you...'

Anna looked quickly at Dee. There were still times when she tended to forget that Dee was actually younger than her, times when all of them tended to lean on her, but Anna recognised that Dee too had her moments of insecurity, her moments of vulnerability.

'You are a good friend,' she reiterated softly now. 'A very good friend, Dee. I just wish...' She stopped and looked searchingly at her. 'I don't want to pry but...this thing between you and Julian Cox. There's more to it than you've ever told any of us, I think...'

Anna waited, holding her breath, wondering if Dee would take the opportunity she was trying to give her to confide in her as Anna had done in her, and, for a moment, she thought her patience was going to be rewarded as Dee began hesitantly, 'Yes, there is, and...'

'And...?' Anna encouraged.

Dee looked away from her.

'I can't... It isn't anything really,' she told her dismissively, and Anna knew that there was no point in trying to press her any further. She knew something else as well, she acknowledged a little sadly as Dee announced that she would go out to the car to bring in the rest of Anna's things, and the shopping they had just bought. She knew that Dee was lying to her.

She couldn't make Dee confide in her, but what she could do, Anna decided as she gave in to Dee's insistence and agreed that, yes, perhaps she would go upstairs and rest on her bed for a while, was to make sure that if Dee did ever need her—for any reason—she was there for her.

'Look, I've got to go and do some supermarket shopping,' Dee told her. 'If there's anything that you want I could get it for you and we could perhaps have lunch here together…'

Anna hesitated before accepting Dee's offer. She was perfectly well enough to go and do her own supermarket shopping now that she was home, but if she was honest she knew that if anyone were to ask her the kind of questions she could not bring herself to answer… It was still too soon, her emotions still too raw.

'I shan't be long,' Dee assured her, heading for the door.

The last thing she felt like doing was sleeping, Anna admitted after Dee had gone, but nevertheless she lay down on the bed and closed her eyes, opening them quickly a few minutes later as the telephone beside the bed rang. Reaching for the receiver, she said, 'Hello?'

'Hello,' she heard a woman's voice responding warmly. 'Am I speaking to Anna Trewayne?'

'Yes, you are,' Anna confirmed. 'But who—?'

'My name is Ruth. I'm Ward's mother…'

Ward's *mother*! Anna nearly dropped the receiver; her heart was thudding frantically, her immediate instinct being to replace the receiver and blot out the woman's soft, warm voice. But as though she had guessed what Anna was thinking Ruth begged her, 'Please listen to me, Anna. Please…'

Dazed, Anna did as she had requested.

Ward's mother, as Anna soon discovered, had a very good understanding of her son, his bad points as well as his good ones.

'I'm not trying to make excuses for him, and certainly do not intend to make his apologies for him,' she told Anna firmly. 'But what I do want to say, Anna, is that he loves you very much.'

'He didn't love me at the hospital when he allowed me to believe that we were lovers,' Anna countered quietly.

'No,' his mother agreed immediately. 'He didn't love you then, but, after all, he didn't know you then.'

'He deliberately and callously took advantage of my vulnerability,' Anna pointed out remorselessly.

'Yes,' his mother conceded, without attempting to defend him. 'And the fact that he believed you had done the same thing to Ritchie in no way excuses that behaviour,' she added firmly.

On her end of the line Anna smiled rather ruefully at that quick and very sure maternal thrust.

'Why are you telling me all of this?' she asked Ward's mother eventually.

'Because I'm a woman as well as a mother,' she came back immediately. 'And I know that as a woman you need to know that your own instincts and feelings didn't betray you. That what you and Ward shared *was* real and that he *does* love you.'

'I love you,' he had told her after making love with her, and in the bitterness of discovering how he had deceived her Anna had considered those words to be as much a fiction as everything else he had told her. But what if they had not been? What if they had been the truth—still were the truth?

'Has he asked you to tell me all of this?' Anna asked her challengingly.

'No. Ward's a very proud and independent man. He won't like what I've done at all.'

'So why have you done it?' Anna asked her.

There was a brief pause before his mother, sounding heart-rendingly like a female version of Ward, told her seriously, 'Because I wanted to know myself what the woman my proud and picky elder son has fallen so completely in love with is like.'

'And you can tell that from a phone call?' Anna derided gently.

'*You* could tell *you* loved him through your amnesia,' his mother retorted, before adding wisely, 'Our sex have very well-attuned emotional instincts.'

'And what you're saying is that because I love him I should just ignore what he's done, the way he's behaved…'

'Certainly not,' Ward's mother returned with a touch of asperity. 'All I wanted to do, Anna, is to tell you plainly and simply that Ward loves you. I'm his mother; my natural instinct is to help and protect him—despite the fact that at forty-two he's more than adult enough to take charge of his own life and to make his own decisions.'

'And if I hadn't told you that Ward got it wrong, that I had absolutely nothing whatsoever to do with Julian Cox's shabby schemes, that I was as much a victim of him as your Ritchie, then how would you have felt?'

'No different,' Ward's mother told her promptly and,

Anna could tell, truthfully. 'And to tell you the truth it pleases me more than you can imagine that Ward has been forced to admit that he loves you even though he thinks that you *are* in cahoots with Julian Cox. I'd begun to despair of him ever letting down his guard with anyone, or ever allowing himself to listen to his emotions. Had he produced some perfect woman he had chosen to become involved with because he thought she would make him a good wife, I would have been very upset. Ward needed to be shown that he's only human, that his emotions cannot be controlled or contained. The fact that he thinks so badly of you and yet still loves you so much...' She paused and then laughed before adding wryly, 'Of course, I don't pretend not to be very, very pleased to hear that my darling and oh, so idiotic son has got it so very, very wrong... I can't wait to meet you for myself, Anna...'

Then it was Anna's turn to laugh.

'Don't count your chickens,' she warned her a little shakily. 'Ward may have told *you* that he loves me and that my supposedly nefarious behaviour hasn't destroyed that love, but that doesn't necessarily mean he's going to do anything about it, nor that I would want him to,' Anna felt bound to point out a little hardily.

'Oh, but he will,' his mother told Anna very positively, pausing again before admitting, 'I don't believe in interfering in my sons' lives—at least not normally—but during our...er...discussion it struck me that in the heat of the moment Ward might have been, shall we say, a little irresponsible—neglectful of the consequences of what he was doing...'

It took several seconds for what she was saying to sink into Anna's consciousness fully, but once it had she sat bolt upright on her bed, her face flushing a hot pink with the recognition that Ward wasn't the only one who had perhaps behaved irresponsibly.

'Oh, but that's…' 'Impossible,' she had been about to say, but of course it wasn't, and what was more… Anna took a deep breath. Suddenly her bedroom seemed to be filled with sunshine. Suddenly she felt absolutely on top of the world; suddenly that world had become a wonderfully exciting place.

A baby… Why on earth hadn't she…?

'There's just no way Ward would ever turn his back on his child or its mother,' Ward's mother told Anna quietly. 'But there is one point I should make, I think, Anna. When you do tell Ward the truth about your relationship with Julian Cox, don't be surprised if he isn't as pleased and relieved to hear it as you expect. He *will* be pleased, of course, but he's also going to feel very much at a disadvantage with you because of it, and very ashamed of his own misjudgement of you. It will be one thing for Ward to offer you the generosity of his understanding of your errors, but he will find it very hard to accept your generosity over his.'

'Yes,' Anna agreed simply, knowing what Ward's mother had told her was perfectly true.

When she replaced the receiver she felt so elated and excited that she could barely contain her emotions. She wanted to get up, get dressed, sing, shout, laugh. Ward loved her… Ward had never meant to humiliate or deceive her; he had simply seized the moment, just as she had seized him!

A baby…

Anna made a soft crooning sound of pleasure beneath her breath.

Dee was just about to turn into Anna's drive when she saw the large Mercedes behind her, signalling to do the same. Frowning, she stopped her own car and got out. She knew that Anna wasn't expecting any visitors. Warily she approached the now motionless Mercedes.

Its driver was instantly recognisable to her from Anna's description.

'Where do you think you're going?' she demanded angrily.

Ward stared at her. Who on earth was this virago?

'I was actually intending to visit Anna—not that it's any of your business,' he returned coolly.

The young woman standing in front of him was quite plainly on the warpath but Ward had no idea why she should be—nor did he wish to find out. All he wanted to do was to see Anna, to hold her in his arms, to tell her how much he loved her...

Dee stared at him. She could scarcely believe the man's effrontery.

'Don't you think you've already done enough, *hurt* her enough?' she demanded furiously. 'I know exactly who you are *and* what you've done, and if you think for one minute that Anna could want to see you...'

Ward frowned.

'She's discussed me with you?'

'She's told me *everything*,' Dee informed him acidly.

Ward's frown deepened. This very angry young woman standing in his way wasn't a complication he had expected.

'Where *is* Anna?' he asked Dee curtly, looking past her towards the house.

'She isn't here,' Dee fibbed. 'She's gone away. And even if she was here,' she told Ward fiercely, 'there's no way she would want to see you after the way you've lied to her, deceived her...'

'Just a minute,' Ward objected grimly. 'I had my reasons for doing what I did.'

'If by "reasons" you mean your erroneous belief that Anna was involved in one of Julian Cox's scams, then I have to tell you that you got it completely wrong,' Dee told him scornfully. 'Anna was as much a victim of his deceit as your brother.'

Ward stared at her.

'I don't know what you're trying to say, but I know for a fact that Anna and Julian Cox were partners.'

'Don't you mean you know for a fact that you saw a piece of paper *claiming* that they were partners?' Dee queried fiercely. 'It's a pity you didn't check your facts a little more carefully. Had you done so you might have discovered the truth.'

'What truth?'

'The truth that Julian Cox simply used Anna's name without either her knowledge or her permission.'

'If that's true then why didn't Anna tell me that herself?' Ward questioned Dee.

'Perhaps she would have done so had she been given the chance and had she not been suffering from amnesia,' Dee told him frostily.

Ward studied Dee's set face. There was no doubt that she was speaking the truth.

'If *you* had been honest with Anna, if you'd told her at the hospital just who you were and why you were there, no doubt in time, when she had regained her memory, she could have told you just how wrong you were in assuming that she was Julian's partner.'

Ward paused for a moment before retaliating hotly, 'If that's the truth, then why didn't she tell me when she had the opportunity the first time we met?'

Now it was Dee's turn to pause.

'She didn't tell you because she wanted to speak with me first,' she told him reluctantly.

'To speak with you?'

'Yes,' Dee confirmed.

It was obvious to her that Ward was waiting for a more detailed explanation, but why should she give him one? After what he had done to Anna he didn't deserve an explanation—he didn't deserve anything.

'Have you *any* idea just what you've done to Anna, just how much you've hurt her? You let her think...' Dee stopped, pressing her lips together. 'Do you really think there's any way she'd want to see or speak with you ever again? You've had your pound of flesh and your money.'

'Is that her decision or yours?' Ward demanded bitingly, but Dee refused to be intimidated.

'Anna's my friend and it's my right as her friend to protect her. I blame myself in part for what you've done to her. The only reason she ever got involved with Julian Cox in the first place was to help me.'

'To help you? Why? What is Cox to you? An ex-lover...?'

'No,' Dee denied sharply.

'You're accusing *me* of behaving unfairly towards Anna, but it seems to me that you've scarcely treated her very kindly yourself,' Ward accused Dee angrily. 'By exposing her to Cox's malice and—'

'*I* didn't tell Anna that I loved her. *I* didn't allow her to believe we were lovers. *I* didn't take her to bed and—' Abruptly Dee stopped, suddenly conscious that she had said too much, trespassed too far into private and intimate territory.

It was useless trying to talk to this aggressive and angry young woman, Ward decided, and if he continued to stand here and argue with her he was going to be in danger of losing his own temper. He was still trying to come to terms with the bombshell Dee had dropped with her revelations regarding the truth about Anna's relationship with Julian Cox.

Strangely, despite his resentment at the way Dee was speaking to him, Ward knew instinctively that what she was telling him *was* the truth. Suddenly everything clicked into place. No wonder he had been so confused about the apparent dichotomy in his misjudgement of Anna's character and the way he had seen her behave. It made him feel as if someone was twisting a knife in his heart to know how badly he had misjudged Anna, how despicably he had treated her. No wonder she didn't want to see or hear from him again. He couldn't blame her.

It had been one thing to tell himself that his love for her was so strong that he could overlook her involvement with Julian Cox, it was quite another to have to acknowledge how totally their roles had just been reversed.

And, besides, even if Anna allowed him to talk to her for long enough for him to tell her that he had known how much he loved her *before* he had discovered the truth about her, Ward was afraid that he simply wouldn't be able to convince her. After all, in her shoes, he would not have been easy to convince.

He had treated her in the most cruel and unjustifiable way and it served him right that she now no longer wanted anything to do with him.

Without another word he turned round and walked back to his car.

Dee watched him get in and drive away before climbing back into her own car and driving up to Anna's house.

'Anna, what are you doing out of bed?' she asked as she opened the kitchen door and found Anna humming as she filled the kettle.

'I feel so much better that I didn't want to stay in bed any longer. After all, I'm not an invalid, you know,' Anna responded dryly. '*You* don't look very happy,' she added perceptively. 'Something's wrong. What is it?'

Dee, who had had no intention of telling Anna anything whatsoever about her run-in with Ward, suddenly discovered to her own chagrin that she was actually flushing a little as she tried to mumble a protective fib.

'Oh, it's no good,' she finally admitted. 'I shall have to tell you. Anna, just… I was just turning into your drive when…when Ward Hunter turned in after me.'

'Ward's here? Where?' Anna demanded, immediately flying to the kitchen window to peer out into the garden.

'No, he's not here,' Dee told her. 'I…I told him that you wouldn't want to see him and, in fact, I actually told him that you weren't even here.'

'He's gone? When? Just now? Oh, heavens, that means… Dee, I have to go after him. He'll have gone home; I know the way.'

'Go after him? What? After what he's done…?' Dee looked stunned.

'No, it isn't like you think,' Anna assured her, quickly explaining to Dee what Ward's mother had told her during their telephone call.

'And you believe her, do you?' Dee asked Anna.

'Yes, I do,' Anna confirmed quietly.

Dee was both startled and impressed by Anna's unfamiliar decisiveness and determination.

'It seems I've done the wrong thing, then, in sending him away,' she commented ruefully. 'I'm sorry, Anna, but I...'

'It's not your fault. After all, you didn't know about Ward's mother's phone call. I know you just wanted to protect me, Dee, and I'm truly grateful to you for that,' Anna told her friend, hugging her. 'Can I ask you a favour, by the way?' When Dee nodded Anna asked her, 'Could you look after Missie and Whittaker for me? I don't know when I shall be back—later this evening, if Ward refuses to listen to me.'

'Yes, I'll look after them,' Dee agreed. 'It's the least I can do.'

CHAPTER TWELVE

WARD hadn't eaten anything since breakfast but as he forced himself to go through the motions of preparing a meal he acknowledged that he didn't really have any appetite for it.

What was Anna doing now? Where was she? He only hoped that wherever she was she was being treated with tenderness and the love she so much deserved, the tenderness and love *he* should have given her, he should *be* giving her, he *so* longed to give her.

As he had driven north he had kept picturing her in the hospital when she had looked up at him, her eyes shining with relief and love; at her house when she had turned her head and smiled at him; in his bed when she had told him, shown him…

Ward could almost taste the bitterness of his own pain. His eyes felt gritty and sore. He pulled open the fridge door and then closed it again, blinking fiercely. He had switched on the radio when he had come in, hoping that the sound would blot out the agony of his thoughts, but the voice of the woman talking jarred on him. The only voice he longed to hear was Anna's quiet, soft one, the one she used after they had made love, all warm and tender with the emotion of what they had shared.

'Oh, God, Anna!'

'Yes, Ward?'

He swung round in disbelief, opening his eyes, which

he had closed as he had cried out her name in helpless longing and despair.

'Anna… What are you doing here…?'

Anna smiled tremulously at him.

It had been such a relief to drive into the courtyard and discover that his car was here, but now the courage and determination which had brought her in hot pursuit of him had been overwhelmed by her awareness of the risk she was taking, the way she was exposing herself to further hurt and rejection. Only Ward wasn't looking at her as though he was going to reject her. He was looking at her as though…

Anna took a tentative step towards him and then stopped as he abruptly turned his back on her and re-opened the fridge door.

There was so much they both needed to say, so many potential dangers and hazards in doing so that she was afraid they might still lose one another in a morass of explanations and apologies.

There had to be a way she could reach out to him, tell him…show him…

And suddenly, as she studied his back, remembering achingly how it had felt beneath her fingertips, the skin so smooth and taut over his muscles, the breadth of his shoulders so thrillingly masculine and powerful, she knew what it was.

Taking a deep breath, she asked him gently, 'You might want to turn your back on me, Ward, but do you want to turn your back on your son or daughter as well?'

The speed with which he moved surprised her. One minute he was opening the fridge, the next he was jerking her forward against his body into his arms, demanding thickly, 'What are you saying, Anna? My God, woman, are you really…? Have we…?'

Behind her back Anna crossed her fingers, hoping that Mother Nature wasn't going to make a liar out of her as she told him shakily, 'It's early days yet, but yes, Ward, I…I think we have…'

'A child—you're having my child…'

'Our child,' Anna corrected him firmly.

Ward shook his head, groaning.

'My mother warned me that this could have happened, but I thought she was exaggerating the risk…'

'I think maybe we were the ones who did that,' Anna told him demurely.

'You're pregnant…with my child…' Ward repeated. He was running his hands tenderly over her body, his eyes dark with emotion. Anna could feel his fingers trembling slightly as he cupped her face.

'Oh, God, Anna, I've missed you so much,' he told her rawly, adding, 'Can you ever forgive me?'

He was a very proud man and Anna knew how much it must be costing him to ask for her forgiveness and understanding. Another woman might have been tempted to punish him a little more, to remind him of just what he had done and how much he had hurt her, but Anna's gentle nature did not incline her that way.

'We both made mistakes and got things wrong,' she told him softly, adding truthfully, 'We've been very lucky, Ward, because we've been given the chance to start again.'

'I loved you before your friend told me the truth about Cox,' Ward told her huskily.

'I know; you told me so—after we made love…'

'You heard that? I…' He smiled painfully.

'I heard it,' Anna confirmed. 'And even if I hadn't,'

she added in a more light-hearted voice, 'I would have to believe that you love me because your mother told me so.'

'My mother? She's spoken to you? But…'

'But what?' Anna demanded provocatively, lifting her mouth towards his.

'But nothing,' Ward responded thickly, accepting the soft invitation of her half-parted lips with the hungry pressure of his own. 'Hell, Anna, you shouldn't be allowing me to do this,' he groaned as he kissed her. 'There are things we ought to talk about, explanations I ought to make; apologies…I need…

'What is it?' he demanded as she tried to silence him by placing her fingertips against his mouth.

'Later,' Anna told him simply. 'Take me to bed, Ward. I want that so much. I want *you* so much,' she breathed ecstatically as he started to kiss gently and then nibble the fingers she had touched to his lips.

'If we go to bed now, I'm not sure I dare trust myself,' Ward confessed as he held Anna's face and looked deep into her eyes.

'*I* trust you,' Anna told him steadily—and meant it.

'Oh, Anna…'

Anna could see the emotion in his eyes darkening their colour and sparkling on his lashes.

'We both…misinterpreted the facts,' Anna told him gently. 'But, Ward, if *you* hadn't thought I was Julian's partner and if *I* hadn't thought we were lovers, then we would never have had…this…'

'How could I ever, ever have misjudged you so badly?' Ward groaned as he reached for her.

'Ward…? I've been thinking,' Anna murmured happily over an hour later as she lay nestled at Ward's side in bed.

'Hmm…' he responded. 'I don't want to think; I just want to hold you and touch you, kiss you and—'

'Ward,' Anna protested half-heartedly, snuggling blissfully and murmuring her appreciation of the way he was lovingly nibbling at the delicate flesh of her throat. However, as his hand reached out to cup her breast, she caught hold of it and told him severely, 'It's about the baby…'

Immediately she had his attention.

'I'd like Dee to be his or her godmother,' Anna told him quietly.

'Dee?' Ward demanded suspiciously, knowing the answer to his question even before he had asked it. 'She wouldn't be that man-hating virago who refused to allow me to see you this afternoon, would she?'

Anna shook her head chidingly.

'Dee isn't a man-hater, Ward, and as for her being a virago… Underneath she's really very kind—and I think very vulnerable. I promise you, once you get to know her you'll like her,' Anna coaxed him lovingly.

'I'll try to believe you,' Ward offered ruefully. 'But right now,' he added in a softer voice, 'I've got far more important things on my mind…'

'Oh? What things?' Anna teased him.

'Come here and let me show you,' Ward said tenderly.

EPILOGUE

THE telephone was ringing as Beth hurried back into the shop. She had just nipped out to buy some sandwiches for her own and Kelly's lunch and Kelly was reaching for the receiver as Beth walked in.

'It's for you,' she told Beth, holding out the receiver. 'Someone from Customs and Excise about that stuff you ordered from the Czech Republic.'

Handing Kelly the sandwiches, Beth hurried to pick up the phone, relief washing over her. She had begun to think that her order would never arrive. She had begun to think, she admitted to herself, that Alex might just have been right after all when he had warned her against buying the pretty reproduction antique glassware she had fallen in love with.

'I'm paying you to be an interpreter, that's all,' she had railed furiously at him. 'If I'd wanted your advice on anything else I'd have asked for it.'

She had fallen in love with the richly coloured glass stemware the moment she had seen it on the market stall, and she had been determined to order some for the shop, but Alex had done just about everything he could to dissuade her from doing so.

She knew why, of course. He had wanted her to give her order to his precious cousins. Talk about nepotism. Well, *she* had shown him that she had a mind of her own.

Beth could feel her face starting to grow hot with a

mixture of guilt and anger. She had been so determined to order the glassware that perhaps she had behaved in a way that was out of character for her. Perhaps? a cynical little inner voice demanded. There was no *perhaps* about it.

Hurriedly Beth concentrated on what the Customs and Excise official was telling her—namely that her long-awaited stemware had finally arrived and that they would be sending her the documentation which would enable her to collect it.

'You'll have to call for it in person since there are certain handling charges to be paid,' he told her.

'That's no problem,' Beth assured him happily, too thankful that her order had finally arrived to worry about the fact that she would probably have to spend half a day away from the shop in order to go through the formalities of collecting it.

'Good news?' Kelly asked her once she had finished her call.

'Very good news,' Beth confirmed. 'The stemware I ordered has finally arrived—thank goodness.'

'I'm looking forward to seeing it,' Kelly told her. 'We can use some of the glasses to celebrate Anna's new-found happiness. It *is* good to see her so happy,' Kelly added warmly.

'Mmm… It is. Dee and Ward are still circling one another a little bit warily, though, aren't they?'

'Just a little,' Kelly agreed. She had seen Dee the previous day and had raised with her the subject of Julian Cox.

'Doesn't Anna have any idea of where he is?' she had asked Dee.

'Apparently not,' Dee had confirmed. 'He's been

seen in Hong Kong, and then later in Singapore. He had investments in both places at one time, but it seems, in Singapore at least, that he was spending his time gambling.'

'Well, I'm just glad that he's gone out of our lives,' Kelly had told her truthfully.

Dee hadn't said anything.

'I'm going to need to drive over to Manchester Airport,' Beth told Kelly now, breaking into her thoughts. 'Can you hold the fort here for me when I do?'

'No problem,' Kelly assured her.

All in all their first year or so in business in Rye had been unexpectedly turbulent, but now, thank goodness, they had sailed into much smoother waters, both in their private lives and professionally.

'Mmm… I must say this order of yours is arriving just at the right time,' she praised Beth as she unwrapped her sandwich. 'We're getting pretty low on stock and I was beginning to think we might have to rush out and buy in.'

'Yes, we are getting pretty low,' Beth agreed. Her throat had gone uncomfortably tight. She still hadn't admitted to Kelly just how much of their partnership funds she had invested in her Czech purchases. On her return from Prague, rather than cast a shadow on Kelly's happiness with Brough, Beth had kept the exact details of what had happened and how much she had purchased to herself, but now, thankfully, she could stop worrying quite so much. At last, at last the order had arrived, and Beth knew that once it was displayed it would simply walk off their shelves.

Oh, yes, everything was quite definitely going to be

alright now, proving that she had been right to ignore all of Alex's dire warnings.

Yes, everything was going to work out fine now!

* * *

Beth and Dee have their own stories in
SWEET SEDUCTION
by Penny Jordan
On sale next month!
0 263 84531 1

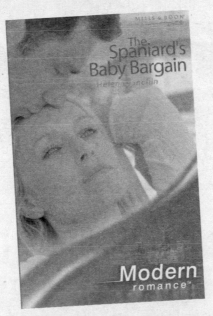

MILLS & BOON

Volume 10
on sale from
2nd April
2005

Lynne
Graham

International Playboys

Bond of
Hatred

Carly Phillips is Simply irresistible!

And when she was bad she was...

SIMPLY SENSUAL

the final book in this exciting trilogy

"This is sexuality at its finest."
—*The Romance Reader*

"Alluring sexual, seductive power at its best."
—*Wordweaving*

On sale 18th March 2005

CP/SENSUAL

Published 18th March 2005

New York Times Bestselling Author

Jennifer Crusie

Charlie All Night

"Crusie has a gift for concocting nutty scenarios and witty one-liners…" —*People* magazine

MIRA®

M404

SILHOUETTE®

Desire 2 in 1

Passionate, dramatic love stories

BEAUTY AND THE BABY
Marie Ferrarella

SOCIAL GRACES
Dixie Browning